The Jeweller's Wife

JUDITH
LENNOX
The Jeweller's Wife

headline
review

First published in 2015
by HEADLINE REVIEW
An imprint of HEADLINE PUBLISHING GROUP

1

Cataloguing in Publication Data is available from the British Library

ISBN 978 1 4722 2365 4 (Hardback)
ISBN 978 1 4722 2366 1 (Trade Paperback)

Typeset in Joanna MT Std by Palimpsest Book Production Limited,
Falkirk, Stirlingshire

Printed and bound in Great Britain by
CPI Group (UK) Ltd, Croydon, CR0 4YY

HEADLINE PUBLISHING GROUP
An Hachette UK Company
Carmelite House
50 Victoria Embankment
London EC4Y 0DZ

www.headline.co.uk
www.hachette.co.uk

To Carwyn George Bethencourt-Smith

Acknowledgements

Heartfelt thanks to my agent, Maggie Hanbury, for her suggestions and invaluable support, and to my editor at Headline, Clare Foss, for her incisive and sensitive comments on the text. Much appreciation is also due to Clare's assistant, Emma Holtz, and to my editor at Piper, Bettina Feldweg.

Grateful thanks to my brother, David Stretch, for his advice about photography in the 1960s, and to my husband, Iain, for explaining to me about tide tables and currents. Any errors are mine.

I have taken some liberties with the geography of the Maldon area. Thorney Island does not exist, though it was inspired by the islands of the Blackwater estuary.

THE WINTERTON AND SINCLAIR FAMILIES
AND THEIR FRIENDS

At Marsh Court:
> Henry Winterton
> Juliet Winterton, his wife
> Piers, their son
> Charlotte (Charley), their daughter

In Maldon:
> Jonathan Winterton (Jonny), Henry's younger brother
> Helen Winterton, Jonny's wife
> Aidan, their son
> Louise, their daughter

In St Albans:
> Jane Hazelhurst (née Winterton), Henry's sister
> Peter Hazelhurst, Jane's husband
> Eliot and Jake, twins, their sons
> Gabrielle (Gabe), their daughter

In London:
> Gillis Sinclair, Henry Winterton's friend

Blanche, Gillis's wife
Flavia and Claudia, their daughters
Nathan (Nate) and Rory, their sons

At Greensea:

Joe Brandon, a farmer
Christine Brandon, his aunt
Neville Stone, Joe's godson

And:

Freya Catherwood, a photographer
Anne Carlisle, an American visitor

Part One

The Pearl Necklace

1938–1946

Chapter One

October–December 1938

At breakfast, the housemaid dropped a kipper in Henry's lap and he called her stupid and sacked her. She was stupid, Juliet Winterton conceded, a poor, uneducated little thing, the youngest of a large family living in a cramped cottage in Maylandsea. But she felt sorry for her, and after the girl had fled the room, wailing, she pleaded for her.

The mean look she had become accustomed to during the three months of their marriage came into Henry's eye. Ripping the backbone from the unfortunate fish, he said, 'You can be so weak, Juliet.'

She stood her ground. 'Ethel can't help it. You frighten her, Henry, you make her nervous. My father always said you should be kind to servants because they are less fortunate than us.'

'Your father was a fool.' He slit open an envelope with the paper knife. 'He threw away his money and left you penniless, I recall. God knows what would have happened to you if I hadn't rescued you.'

She hated to hear her father, who had been dead not six months, talked of in this way. But she had learned to be

3

wary of Henry's tongue, so she occupied herself with scraping butter on the toast that Ethel had burned. She had lost her appetite, and the oily smell of the kippers turned her stomach.

When his plate was clean, Henry put down his knife and fork. 'We are to have a guest for dinner tonight,' he said. 'I've received a letter from Sinclair.'

Gillis Sinclair was a Member of Parliament and lived in London. Henry was the godfather of Gillis's younger daughter Claudia and had often spoken of him, but Juliet had not yet met him, or his wife, Blanche.

'I'll have a room made up,' she said. 'Will Mr Sinclair be coming alone?'

'Yes. Blanche is indisposed. You must make up a room in the cottage. When the Sinclairs are at Marsh Court, they always sleep in the cottage.'

Henry blotted his mouth with his napkin and stood up. Henry, his brother Jonathan and sister Jane were all cut from the same cloth, sharing the Winterton fair good looks, but Henry was the tallest of the three and the most imposing. 'You had better send over an invitation to Jonny and Helen,' he added. 'And the Barbours. Make up a party.'

Charles and Marie Barbour were neighbours of the Wintertons, owners of a substantial farm that lay to the south of Marsh Court. 'Let me speak to Ethel,' Juliet coaxed. 'I'll make sure she promises to do better. We'll need her tonight, and you know how hard it will be to find another girl.'

'No.' He bared his teeth. 'I said that she's to go.'

There was far too much to do that morning, with only the help of the cook, Mrs Godbold, and a maid so long in the tooth Juliet feared for her life each time she tottered up the stairs. She herself made up the bedroom in the smart little cottage in Marsh Court's grounds that they used for

4

guests, consoling herself with the thought that she would see Helen and Jonathan that evening. Jonathan's character was milder than Henry's, and as for Helen, her sister-in-law, she was fast becoming a friend.

After lunch, she went outdoors. The leaves had fallen from the trees early that year, torn from the branches by a sharp October storm, and the Japanese maples had painted their blood-red swirls on the lawn. Had it not been for her quarrel with Henry, Juliet would have taken out her sketchbook and tried to capture the mingled colours of the fallen leaves, but she felt too unsettled to paint. *Your father was a fool. He threw away his money and left you penniless. God knows what would have happened to you if I hadn't rescued you.*

Rescued me, she thought. The wet grass brushed against her ankles as she walked. Was that what you did, Henry?

The rain had exhausted itself, leaving in its wake pale blue skies and a peaceful stillness. Marsh Court stood on a peninsula that jutted out into the North Sea and was bordered by the Blackwater estuary to the north and the River Crouch to the south. The low-lying countryside that surrounded the house was made up of soft shades of green and grey and brown, restful to the eye. Juliet watched as a flock of gulls wheeled above the water, sunlight catching on their white breasts, so that they seemed from a distance a single bright organism.

The garden melded into first field and then salt marsh with no fence or hedge to mark the border of the property. The only other house in sight was the red-brick cottage, built in the previous century for a Winterton maiden aunt, that would be used that night by Henry's friend Gillis Sinclair.

Juliet looked back at Marsh Court. Decades of sun and

rain had softened the walls and roof to tawny pinks and gold, so that the building seemed to melt into its surroundings. The three broad gables faced out to the marsh and mudflats of the estuary, where water was sewn into the creeks and saltings like strands of metal thread. Inside the house, French doors opened on to terraces cluttered with pots of geraniums, and bees buzzed in the chipped dustiness of a coloured glass window. The drawing room chimneypiece was decorated with rustic carvings of Adam and Eve, Eve fat-bellied and perky, Adam straggle-haired, going to seed. In the boot room there were worn pins and bats intended for games Juliet did not know how to play; in the library was an album filled with snapshots of Winterton dogs. They all looked the same to her, but when Henry's sister Jane turned the pages, she sighed and said, 'There's Lucky, and oh, look! My darling old Sally.' And her brothers smiled and nodded their heads.

Juliet had loved Marsh Court from the first moment she had seen it, emerging from a sea mist at the end of her long journey from Egypt to the east of England. And yet three months of marriage had not rid her of the feeling that she was acting the role of mistress of the house, that it did not yet belong to her, that she was an intruder, an imposter. She would run a hand along a polished banister or press her face into a faded velvet curtain as if by doing so she would become part of the house, and part of the Winterton family.

As the land sloped down, the grass became roughened and tussocky, blurring seamlessly into the field beyond. She reached the spot where the Wintertons lit bonfires in celebration of important family events. All that now remained in the fire pit was a circle of ash.

Juliet began to gather up fallen leaves, sweeping them into a heap: golden oak leaves, scarlet and coral tongues of cherry, and palmate horse chestnuts, like brown, crinkled outstretched hands. In her pocket she found an old shopping list – *stockings, stamps, Beecham's Powders*. She crumpled it into a ball and stuffed it into the leaves. Her elegant gold cigarette lighter was from Winterton's, a present from Henry. She held the flame to the paper until it caught, and then she stepped back. A column of smoke found a way through, and she breathed in the acrid autumnal smell.

A movement caught her eye. A man was walking along the path that ran by the foot of the field. Although the land bordering the estuary did not belong to Marsh Court, few people went there, and the Wintertons liked to think of it as their own. She had been enjoying her solitude, burning her unhappiness along with the dead leaves, and she felt . . . not embarrassed, exactly, but exposed, as if she had been glimpsed in some private activity such as cleaning her teeth or putting up her hair.

The man on the path was tall and moved with a spring in his step. Juliet watched as he left the footpath and made his way inland, towards the bonfire. She anticipated a request for directions, or perhaps a glass of water.

But as the stranger drew within earshot, he called out, 'You must be Juliet. When I heard that Henry had brought a wife home from Egypt, I was intrigued. I've been longing to meet you.' Approaching her, he held out his hand. 'Forgive me for startling you. I'm Gillis Sinclair. Henry warned you I was coming, I hope.'

His forehead was high and his expressive blue-grey eyes were framed by straight brows. His light hair had a curl to it; his nose was long and straight and narrow and his mouth wide and well-shaped. Juliet thought him quite startlingly handsome. She shook his hand, murmuring a greeting.

His features were alive with laughter. 'Am I not what you were expecting, Mrs Winterton? Perhaps you had envisaged some middle-aged politico, prematurely worn down by affairs of state?'

It was true, she had expected an older man. Henry was seventeen years older than her, and Juliet had assumed his friend to be a similar age.

'Not at all,' she said. 'I'm delighted to meet you, Mr Sinclair.'

'Gillis. I hope we need not be formal.'

'Then you must call me Juliet. Gillis is an unusual name.'

'It's Danish. My mother came from Copenhagen.'

'Do you speak Danish?'

'Some. You must forgive me, turning up in your garden like this. My motor car's in Maldon, having its exhaust repaired. The wretched thing was billowing out black smoke all the way from Chelmsford. A fellow at the garage offered me a lift, but I decided to make my way here on foot. I love to walk along the estuary.'

As he spoke, his gaze rested on her. What was it, she wondered, in a smile, a glance, that could so discomfort you, and at the same time make you feel suddenly alive, as if you had been living in shadows and now, gloriously, had stepped into the sun?

She said, 'I'm sorry to hear your wife is unwell.'

'Poor old Blanche. She thinks she caught it from the children. I keep away from them as much as I can.'

This said with a twinkle in his eye. She still struggled with the English habit of saying one thing and meaning another. She feared it made her rather plodding company.

The fire had burned down to ruby-red, white-fringed embers. As they set off for the house, she asked Gillis how old his daughters were.

'Flavia is four and Claudia is . . . let me see . . . two.'

'How delightful.'

'The next time I come here, I shall bring them. You would think them dear little things.'

'I'd like that.'

'Henry told me you met in Cairo. Were you born there?'

Juliet shook her head. 'No, I was born in England, but my father and I travelled a great deal. I met Henry a fortnight after Father died.'

'Difficult for you.' And as they headed up the wet lawn, he gave her a slanting glance. 'It's always hard to lose a parent. And Henry, though I love him dearly, isn't the easiest of men.'

Juliet's father, Alexander Capel, had been fluent in half a dozen languages and could learn a new one with remarkable rapidity. An Egyptologist and an Hellenic scholar, he had quarrelled with his parents at the age of twenty-one, and, quitting England, had spent the rest of his life roaming the countries of the eastern Mediterranean. Her mother had died when Juliet was twelve, worn out by ill-health and wandering. The bereavement had left Juliet heartbroken. She had not minded the absence of a settled home until then. Her mother had made every house a home, and after her death Juliet felt dislocated and rootless.

She and her father moved to Cairo when she was seventeen. At first, they rented an apartment in Zamalek, a district of leafy streets and airy villas. They kept a servant and ate out in restaurants. Juliet took drawing lessons while her father worked as a translator for the British Embassy. Their friends were the sort of friends they had always had, a mixture of nationalities: writers, intellectuals and vagabonds. She loved the long, leisurely dinners and the conversations that never faded before midnight, and the cool early mornings and the inky shadows that pooled in ancient streets.

When his health deteriorated, her father could no longer work and so they moved from the apartment to rooms in the southern part of Gezira Island. They no longer had a servant and Juliet herself kept house and cooked. She earned a small amount of money as a companion and letter-writer to an old Frenchwoman (she had for several years acted as her father's amanuensis), and taught drawing to three spoiled English schoolgirls. Her father drank cheap spirits to dull the pain. Always outspoken in his admiration of Arab culture, he took to wearing a grubby galabiya and fez and quarrelled with his British acquaintances, who called less often. Juliet expected they thought he had gone native.

Six months before he died, her father's editor, a Frenchman – Alexander Capel's historical monographs were modestly popular in the French-speaking world – took her out to dinner. Jean-Christophe warned her that war was coming and that she and her father should leave Cairo. The Italian victory in Abyssinia, to the south of Egypt, had been one of the first moves in the coming conflict, which would, he calmly explained to her, be unimaginably terrible. He had tried to speak to her father but he had not listened. She must persuade him.

They then turned to lighter matters. They had a pleasant evening, and afterwards Jean-Christophe took her back to his villa on Abou el Feda Street and made love to her. She let herself be seduced because she needed the comfort of human touch. He was a kind and sensitive lover and made her believe that she was beautiful. She fell in love with him and felt very low when, a month later, he returned to his chateau in the Loire, and his wife and children.

As her father's illness worsened, Juliet sold off their valuables to pay for morphine. His suffering was long drawn out and terrible to watch, and during his last weeks she was unable to comfort him, which left her after his death with a sense of failure she never quite managed to throw off.

After she paid off the most pressing of her father's debts, she had no money left at all. It was summer, and the weather was already unbearably hot. She had never liked Cairo, which was a noisy, clamorous and secretive city, but she did not know where else to go and could not have afforded the fare if she had. She took to running her hand through coat pockets in search of coins and hiding in the dim interior of the shuttered rooms, pretending she was out, when the landlord knocked on the door for the rent.

She was alone and poor and afraid that she might fall through the cracks. Plenty of people more deserving than she slept on Cairo's pavements. At night, she was kept awake not only by the heat and by grief, but by fear of loneliness, abandonment and penury. She had lost the capacity to feel much more than a horror of the past and a dread of the future. She was nineteen years old and her heart felt desiccated. Her yearning for love was more powerful than her hunger for the sugary sweetmeats they sold at the roadside stalls.

She decided to sell her last remaining item of value, a pearl necklace, which had been a gift to her father from a wealthy trader in Aleppo. Alexander Capel had taught the man's six sons to speak English and had translated texts for him from Aramaic into modern Arabic and English. Her father had given her the necklace on her fifteenth birthday. At first she hadn't cared for it, thinking it old-fashioned and heavy, but she had since come to love it and to appreciate the magic of the three strands of lustrous, large, round greenish-gold pearls. They were salt-water pearls, formed in a volcanic atoll in the Pacific Ocean, set in yellow gold, and between each gem was a diamond.

Henry Winterton came into the shop as the jeweller, no doubt sensing her desperation, was trying to fleece her. To Juliet's surprise, he immediately countered the offer with a better one. While the shopkeeper protested, Henry introduced himself to her.

'I have a jewellery business in London,' he said. 'Winterton's of Bond Street. Do you know it, Miss . . .?'

'Capel,' she said. 'No, I'm afraid not.'

'Well then, do you accept my offer?'

Because it pleased her to thwart the shopkeeper, and because the offer was generous, she shook hands on the bargain and thanked him. It felt shady, though, as if she was agreeing to something other than the exchange of money for a pearl necklace.

As they left the shop, Henry Winterton's cheque in her handbag, he held out to her the green leather case containing the pearls. 'Look after them for me,' he said. 'I'll be in Cairo for a fortnight. You can return them to me before I leave.' When she demurred, he added, 'If they aren't worn, they'll lose their lustre. I'm staying at Shepheard's Hotel. I'll buy you dinner tonight and we can make arrangements for the necklace's return. I don't make a habit of seducing innocent schoolgirls, if that's what you're worried about. Tell me where you're lodged and I'll send for you at eight. And wear your necklace. It's a remarkable piece.'

Henry bought her dinner that first evening, and then each evening for a fortnight. Juliet did not cash his cheque, but put it in a cedarwood box in her bedroom and looked at it now and then.

The shabbiness of her days contrasted with her evenings at Shepheard's Hotel. At eight o'clock a car would arrive and drive her there. Henry would be waiting for her at a table in the Moorish dining room. The first evening she was ill at ease and dumbstruck, so he filled in the silences. His great-great-grandfather, he told her, had established the first Winterton shop in Colchester in the 1850s. Thirty years later, the family had bought a second premises in Bond Street. There was a special Winterton cut, he explained, his large, elegant hands sketching the shape, that made a diamond glow with exceptional brilliance. He travelled abroad several times a year to buy raw gemstones but only purchased made-up items of the most exceptional quality. His gaze lingered on her pearl necklace as he spoke.

Then he told her about his family. His sister Jane was married to Peter Hazelhurst, a surgeon, and they had twin sons, Jake and Eliot, and a baby daughter, Gabrielle. Henry's younger brother Jonathan was his partner in the family firm. Henry oversaw the finances and sourced gemstones while Jonathan dealt with the staff and the day-to-day running of the shops. Both men were involved in the creation of new pieces because both understood the characteristic Winterton combination of flamboyance and elegance. Jonathan and his wife Helen lived in Maldon in Essex, in the east of England, just four miles from Henry's home, Marsh Court.

Juliet imagined Marsh Court to be a damp, gloomy place. In the heat of a Cairo summer, that appealed. She noticed that though Henry spoke of his family with affection, he took pleasure also in describing their failings and weaknesses – Jonathan's indecisiveness, Jane's adherence to fashionable methods of child-rearing.

Three evenings before Henry was due to leave Cairo, he proposed to her.

'Well?' he barked when, taken by surprise, she did not immediately respond. 'Have you nothing to say?'

Panicked, she took her cue from the nineteenth-century novels she liked to read. 'I am most honoured—'

'I don't seek to honour. Or flatter. I never do.'

Then he pointed out to her the advantages of marriage to Henry Winterton. He was thirty-six years old, seventeen years older than she, and so would comfortably be able to support her and any children they might have. He enjoyed society and kept a flat in London, so she need fear neither boredom nor insecurity. She would be part of his family. She would have a home.

Juliet, who was already half in love with him, longed for all these things. Henry Winterton was good-looking, confi-dent and intelligent, and he had been generous to her. In so many ways, marriage would resolve all her problems. But he had not told her that he loved her.

He reached across the table and took her hand. 'I'm afraid you don't have time to shilly-shally. I have urgent business in London that I need to return to as soon as possible.' His voice lowered. 'Juliet, I want you.'

Not 'I love you' or 'I adore you', but I want you. She discov-ered that it was a powerful thing to be wanted, to be the focus of someone else's desire. It captivated, it subjugated. Many Englishmen found it hard to talk of love, she told herself, and she was certain that the heat in Henry Winterton's eyes conveyed everything she needed to know.

A week later, they were married at the Ministry of Justice. They spent their honeymoon night at Shepheard's Hotel. Before she emerged from the bathroom in her nightdress, she faltered, afraid to turn the door handle. The thought occurred to her that she was about to go to bed with a stranger. But the ordeal was soon over, and really, it was not so bad as she had feared. Henry was a vigorous lover whose pride demanded that he give her equal pleasure to his own. Jean-Christophe had ensured that she was not a complete novice, and if Henry noticed that, he did not remark on it.

They set sail for England the following day. After overnight calls at Valletta and Gibraltar, they left the boat at Dieppe and took a train to Paris. There, Juliet purchased her trousseau at the House of Worth. Henry had instructed her to order four evening gowns. Assistants spread out bales of fabric on the counter, and after an hour of pleasant deliberation, she settled for a black, a rose-pink and a red.

She couldn't decide on the fourth. The assistant, a tiny, elegant woman in her sixties, suggested a simple ecru gown threaded round the hem and neckline with a narrow black ribbon. Juliet voiced her reservation that the shade was too close to her sallow skin and wavy dark-gold hair, but the assistant gave a scornful hiss. Cowed, Juliet gave in. Six weeks later, the box containing the four gowns, wrapped in tissue paper and tied with satin ribbon, arrived at Marsh Court.

She wore the pearl necklace with the ecru gown to dinner that night. The necklace needed a simple gown to set it off. When she looked in the mirror, she saw that the gleam of the pearls brought out the warm tones in her complexion. Her cheeks were still flushed from her afternoon in the garden. She pressed her face into her palms and breathed in

15

the bonfire smoke that had drenched into her skin, and in her mind's eye she saw Gillis Sinclair walking towards her, out of the marshes.

Henry must still have been angry with her, because when she went into the drawing room, he said, 'There you are. I was beginning to think we'd lost you. I thought you must have gone to the river to rescue more lame ducks.' Then he addressed Jonathan and Helen and Charles and Marie Barbour, who were sitting on sofas arranged round the fire. 'Juliet has a soft heart. If she had her way, she'd fill my house with spongers and fools.'

'You would hardly have sought out a hard-hearted wife, Henry.' Gillis Sinclair was standing in the shadows by the bookcase. He inclined his head to Juliet. 'Mrs Winterton, may I compliment you on your appearance. Henry, I congratulate you on unearthing such a treasure.'

'Pff,' said Henry, with a curl of the lip. 'I despise credulousness. It's a quality that's sometimes passed off as kindness when in fact it's closer to stupidity.'

'A capacity for sympathy is hardly a bad thing.'

'I don't doubt you're good at pretending sympathy, Sinclair, when it suits you.'

Thankful to be out of the spotlight, Juliet sat down with Helen and Jonathan. She hated it when Henry was in such a bitter mood, seeking out low motives even in those dearest to him, and she guessed that the Barbours felt the same, because they were looking down, taking great interest in their drinks. Jonathan and Helen appeared unperturbed. They must have seen such displays countless times before. Besides, Juliet had discovered that even the most amiable Winterton took pleasure in a fight.

She was afraid that Gillis might take offence, but instead

he gave Henry a sweet smile. 'You're right, I'm perfectly capable of a little hypocrisy, when it suits me.'

'Gillis has a heart, you see,' proclaimed Jonathan. 'I've always suspected that whatever pumps the blood round my brother's veins is made of some dense, non-porous stone.'

Henry raised a thin smile. 'But then you're not the ambitious sort, are you, Jonny?'

Henry had something in him of the jealous four-year-old who teases his little brother with sly prods and pokes. There was more than a dart of unkindness in his last remark. Henry was the money-maker in the family, and it had been he rather than Jonathan who had taken Winterton's from an old-fashioned, traditional jeweller's to a successful, up-to-date company.

Jonathan acknowledged the barb by raising his glass. Having made his point, Henry returned to Gillis.

'So you'll admit you're ambitious.'

'It's a necessary ingredient of success.'

'Ambition and hypocrisy go hand in hand, wouldn't you say?'

'If you're implying that politics requires a particular skill at dissimulation, then I won't disagree with you.'

'Honest of you,' said Henry sarcastically.

'And if I pointed out to you some modest, humble parliamentary men . . .'

'I'd say they were the biggest liars of the lot.'

Gillis looked down at the fire, but Juliet saw the smile that curved the corners of his mouth. 'So if I were to tell you that beneath this admittedly attractive exterior, I am modest and humble . . .'

Henry gave a roar of laughter and clapped Gillis on the back. 'Arrogance suits you, dear fellow, you mustn't be ashamed of it.' And everyone laughed.

Shortly afterwards, the maid announced that dinner was served. Juliet continued to observe at the dinner table how clever Gillis was at coaxing Henry into a more pleasant frame of mind. She studied him, trying to learn how he did it. Henry tolerated good-humoured teasing from his friend that he would have reacted to with sarcasm or ill-temper from anyone else. As the dinner progressed, he showed his most attractive side and became charming and amusing, an excellent host. As for Gillis, he was urbane, cheerful and unruffled, a wonderful conversationalist who could make an entertaining tale from any subject. Juliet thought Blanche Sinclair fortunate to have married a man who was such good company.

She wondered whether the two men's friendship had been forged by what they had in common – their quick wit and informed intelligence, their steel-trap minds and sharp memories – but as the evening wore on, she came to the conclusion that it was their differences that they enjoyed. She suspected that Henry appreciated that Gillis ignored his ill-humour, and that this allowed him to take pleasure in the cut and thrust of unbridled argument. Whatever the basis of their affection, Gillis brought out the best in Henry and she was grateful to him for that.

Marsh Court's dining room had a warm and comfortable dignity. Candlelight gleamed on the fragile old porcelain, Bohemian crystal glasses and Georgian silver, and the crimson damask curtains shut out the night. The conversation was at first of shooting and yachting and Henry's recent purchase of half a dozen cases of French wine. Ignorant of these subjects, Juliet said little, and it was only when the talk moved on to a discussion about a series of concerts at the Wigmore Hall that she began to join in. She had always taken great pleasure in listening to music, which had the power to intensify her happiness and console her in sadness. Both Jonny and Jane Winterton were fine pianists and she loved to hear them play.

Throughout the meal, she had to measure out the direction of her gaze, to prevent it always coming to rest on Gillis Sinclair. She was drawn to him, and it was all too easy to find herself studying the curve of his mouth or the angle of his jawline. She saw how fluidly his expression moved between laughter and melancholy, and how his blue eyes sparkled at a witticism or became gloomy when the talk turned more sombre. Once, his gaze met hers and he gave her a smile that was inviting, almost conspiratorial. After that, she tried not to look at him again.

The political events of the last two months hung so heavily over them that it was inevitable that they would discuss the recent events at Munich. Because Gillis Sinclair was a Member of Parliament – and, at the age of thirty-one, a parliamentary undersecretary – he was viewed by them all as a man with access to inside information. Charles Barbour asked him whether he thought Hitler would keep the promises he had made in Munich the previous month. The relief and gratitude that had greeted the return from Germany of the Prime Minister, Neville Chamberlain, with what had appeared to be a guarantee of peace in exchange for Czechoslovakia's loss of the Sudetenland, had quickly soured and been replaced by a mixture of guilt and apprehension. Juliet had not forgotten that her French lover had told her that the coming war would be a terrible one. She hoped that at Marsh Court she had found a place of safety.

'Naturally he'll renege on it,' said Gillis. 'Every thinking man knows he will.'

'So all that scuttling off to Munich, umbrella in hand, was futile.'

'Not completely. It's given us time, and we need that very badly to build up our military strength.' Gillis looked angry. 'We've nothing like enough aircraft. Good God, we haven't even enough spares to repair our ships.'

'Perhaps we'll have time to find a lasting peace,' murmured Helen.

Gillis shook his head. 'No, Helen, I'm afraid not.'

'We were talking earlier of the arrogance of politicians,' said Jonny savagely. 'What greater show of arrogance could Chamberlain have displayed than to believe he could change Hitler's mind?'

Soon afterwards the women rose from the table, leaving the men to their brandy and cigarettes. While Marie Barbour powdered her nose, Helen clutched Juliet's hand.

'I've been longing to tell you. I'm expecting a baby!'

'Helen, how wonderful! I'm so happy for you!' Juliet hugged her. She knew that Helen and Jonny had been trying for a child for several years.

The infant was due in March, Helen told her. She let out a sigh of happiness. 'I can't wait to be lumbering around like an elephant, knowing that soon I'll be holding my own dear little baby in my arms.'

Helen was tall and slim and had no interest in the latest fashions or hairstyles. That evening she was wearing a plain olive-green wool gown, and her thick chestnut hair was trying to escape from the chignon in which she had attempted to confine it. Juliet thought how beautiful she looked, with her bright hazel eyes and her face lit up with joy.

Marie came back into the room and the subject of pregnancy was dropped. Though the three women tried to talk of other things, the conversation soon drifted back to the political situation. Helen voiced her fear that Jonathan might be called up. Marie's husband Charles had been badly injured during the Great War and so would not be liable for conscription. For the first time it occurred to Juliet to wonder what, if there were to be a war, might happen to Henry – and to the family business and Marsh Court.

The sound of men's voices interrupted the three women's intimacy. 'It's a clear night,' Jonathan said as he flung open the door. 'We're going to look at the stars. Are you girls coming?'

Henry had built himself a small observatory in the grounds to house his telescope. Juliet switched off the electric lights and they all donned their overcoats and trooped outside. The grass had crisped with frost and stars scattered the sky like grains of sand on a black-tiled floor.

They put up their coat collars and shivered, letting out puffs of cold, cloudy air while they took turns to peer through the telescope. After a while, Juliet found herself apart from the others. She heard footsteps behind her; turning, she saw Gillis Sinclair.

He smiled at her. 'Juliet, it's been such a wonderful evening.'

'I'm glad you came. Henry looks forward to your company so much.'

They fell silent, looking up at the stars. Then, suddenly, he said, 'You should stand up to him. Forgive me, but that's what Henry wants, someone who stands up to him.'

She shrank from the pity she heard in his voice. She felt that it degraded her. And though he meant it kindly, she knew he was wrong. Henry respected men who stood up to him – yes, that was true. But Juliet had discovered already that he did not care for defiance in a wife.

Side by side, they walked back to the house. There was the smell of autumn leaves and the organic scent of the river, but there was something else in the air that night, she thought: a taste of the coming of winter.

For her twentieth birthday, Henry offered to have a bracelet made for her. Inside the dim, refined opulence of Winterton's Bond Street shop, jewels winked at Juliet from their glass cabinets. Necklaces coiled in blue velvet beds and gemstones the size of grapes nestled in the gold embrace of rings.

The premises reflected Henry's perfectionism. The contents of the vitrines were arranged with precision; every half-hour, a member of staff checked that there were no fingerprints on the plate-glass windows and not a speck of dust on the royal-blue carpet. An assistant showed Juliet to a seat. Another brought glasses of champagne and a bowl of salted nuts.

Henry asked Juliet which gemstones she liked best.

'Emeralds,' she said. She loved their vivid green light.

He studied her sitting on the chair, trying not to fidget. 'No,' he said. 'The bracelet will be made of aquamarines.'

She tried to damp down the flush that rose to her cheeks. She knew that Henry's manager and assistants were listening to their exchange. Tears pricked at her eyes. Carefully, she directed her gaze to the tray of gems placed on the counter.

Henry expected her to travel to London with him two or three times a month. They stayed in the flat above the Bond Street shop where Henry kept his London staff, a cook, maid and butler. He preferred to entertain in London, only inviting his closest friends to Marsh Court.

At the end of every evening, he meticulously examined their guests' characters, holding up their foolishness and conceits to the light. Juliet hated his dissection of their acquaintances' smallest flaws. No human folly, no vanity, escaped his mockery. She found his need to discover the self-aggrandising or shameful in everyone wearying and demoralising. She preferred to see the best in people.

She came to understand that one of Henry's chief pleasures was in searching out the faults of others. He seized upon a moral failing or an error of judgement or a display of ignorance about those things most important to the Wintertons – music and art and the countryside – with delight, holding it up for ridicule. He had chosen to interpret her desire for an emerald bracelet as a display of greed, and had punished her for it by humiliating her in front of his staff. She had not known then that the finest emeralds were worth more than diamonds. She had simply named a jewel that had taken her fancy.

She learned. She didn't make the same mistake twice. She educated herself, so that Henry would not have the opportunity for criticism. When they were in London, she visited museums and exhibitions. She had always had a hungry mind. During long walks round the capital, she discovered that, in spite of the different languages and climate, London had much in common with Cairo. Poverty existed cheek by jowl with great wealth. On West End streets where couples dined in glittering restaurants and cabs disgorged laughing young people into glamorous nightclubs, you could, if you cared to look, find another London. She took to keeping coins in her coat pocket to give to those men in shabby, inadequate clothing who crouched in shop doorways, cardboard signs beside them explaining that they were out-of-work war veterans. Her problems seemed small compared with theirs, and as she dropped the coins into the tin cup she felt herself to be both patronising and spoiled.

During the Munich Crisis, trenches had been dug in the parks and sandbags piled outside government buildings. These remained, giving the streets of London an air of expectancy and dread. One night, dining with Gillis and Blanche Sinclair, Juliet was jarred by the realisation that even Henry – the pessimist, the realist – had hoped that Gillis would have better news of the international situation. But he did not, and spoke only of murderous attacks on Jews in Germany and the failure of diplomacy, until his wife caught his eye. Blanche, who was petite, black-haired, pale-skinned and lovely, reminded her husband that they were supposed to be having an enjoyable night out, and then the subject of politics was dropped.

Juliet was happiest at Marsh Court. She tried to be a better wife to Henry, to carry out the roles of housekeeper and hostess with grace and competence. She learned from Helen, copying the way in which her sister-in-law drew up a menu and arranged the flowers and welcomed the guests who came to her house.

In the afternoons, she took her watercolours and easel and rambled along the Blackwater, trying to capture the river's moods in her sketchbook. When the tide turned, it rushed out of the estuary, revealing sheeny grey-brown mudflats. Small boats bobbed and whirled, and seabirds and fallen branches were hurried on by the current.

Like shallow-bottomed boats, the islands in the estuary seemed to float on the water. Thorney Island, downriver from Marsh Court, was linked to the mainland by a tidal causeway, a fragile strand that was sometimes there and sometimes not. Crossing the causeway to the island, Juliet felt as if she was walking inside the river. Glistening brown weed clung to the stones; she breathed in rich smells of mud and decay while low winter sunlight stabbed the sodden, unstable ground to either side of her.

On the island she found a stand of trees, a narrow road, a few fields and a house, beyond which the land fragmented, criss-crossed by creeks and gullies, hardly solid at all. The house was of modest size and looked well cared for. Asters browned in the flower beds and the lawn was neatly clipped.

Who, she wondered, would choose to live in such a desolate, evanescent place? Standing in the gateway, she imagined the waters rising, flooding the fields and obliterating the garden, drowning flower beds and lawn and pouring through doors and windows.

Turning, she hurried back to the causeway before the tide came in. And when she reached the mainland, she let out a sigh of relief.

When they quarrelled, she found herself wondering what Henry had thought when he had first encountered her in the jeweller's in Cairo. She would hate to think that he had rescued her, as he had claimed. To be the object of pity would demean her. But Henry wasn't capable of pity. So it couldn't have been that.

Her mirror, and the way men looked at her, told her that her looks must be striking in some way. All the Wintertons admired beautiful things and would not have allowed anything ugly or ordinary into their tight circle. Henry had seen her and her pearl necklace, and from their conversations in Shepheard's Hotel he had concluded that she was not uncultured. Perhaps it had pleased him to know that his return from England with a new young bride would be greeted with shock and envy. Or perhaps he had thought her compliant, a woman he could mould into whatever shape he desired.

But he had not loved her. This she had come to understand. She had only to see Jonathan and Helen together to discover how different a marriage could be. When they danced, Jonny's hands rested lightly on Helen's shoulders, and now and then his thumb stroked her neck in an endearment so obviously comfortable and practised that Juliet felt a rush of pain. It was not that she was jealous of their relationship – she loved them far too much for that – but she wished that she and Henry had a fraction of their closeness.

She wondered whether, for a certain type of man – a man like Henry – wanting someone, desiring them sexually, was the closest they came to love. But it was not enough for her. It appalled her that she might live the rest of her life without love, and at night she wept silent tears into her pillow.

Sometimes she pictured herself packing a suitcase and taking the train from Maldon to London. Selling her pearls – though by rights they belonged to Henry – and renting a room in a boarding house. She would find work to pay for her food and rent. She would be poor, but she would be free. And in time Henry would agree to divorce her.

Then, one morning at breakfast, after the maid had brought in Henry's fried herrings, she didn't make it to the bathroom in time. She was sick over her frock and the piece of toast she had been trying to eat. The maid looked as if she was going to be unwell too, but Henry, who to do him credit wasn't squeamish, muttered something about having got the day off to a good start and sent her back to bed.

Later that morning, Dr Vincent called. After he had examined her, he told her that she was pregnant, and that her baby would be born the following spring. When he had gone and she was alone again, she lay on the bed, her palms resting on her stomach, her gaze on the window.

She knew by then that if she left Marsh Court, she would ache for it. She would ache for the neighbours who had been kind to her and for the family she loved and had come to feel a part of. She would ache for the mist that veiled the salt marshes in the early mornings and for the cries of the seabirds and for the water that rushed over the causeways to the islands. Exiled, she would close her eyes on a hot August day and imagine herself in Marsh Court's garden. She would dream of the silky flicker of the river and remember the languorous, rose-scented air.

After many years of wandering, she had found a home.

So she wouldn't be packing her suitcase and heading off to the city. She wasn't going to leave Henry after all. Instead, she would stay at Marsh Court and have his child.

Someone to love.

Chapter Two

April 1939–May 1945

'I hope Harper remembered to pack Flavia's tonic,' said Blanche.

They were driving out of London. The nanny, Harper, was taking the children to Maldon by train, to Gillis's relief. The girls were awful in the car, sick whenever he turned a corner.

Gillis suspected Blanche would have preferred to travel by train too, with the children. She found his beloved Crossley sports saloon frightening, and was apt to cling on to the dashboard, white-knuckled.

'I'm sure she will have,' he said soothingly.

'I'm afraid she'll let the girls look out of the window.'

Blanche had a tendency to fret. Gillis knew that in her mind's eye she was envisaging a frightful accident – a child toppling out of the railway carriage, a beautiful daughter hideously disfigured after striking her head in a tunnel.

'Darling, they'll be fine. They'll have great fun.' He reached across and squeezed her hand. She did not respond, and after a few moments he took hold of the steering wheel again.

He had been twenty-five years old and working for a law firm in the Inns of Court when he had met Blanche Carteret at a dance in a house in Belgravia. Her delicate prettiness and small, perfect figure had captivated him, and he had proposed to her just six weeks after their first meeting. Blanche was the only daughter of a wealthy Jersey financier and had brought much-needed money to the marriage. Though he had been very much in love with her, Gillis was honest enough to acknowledge to himself that had she been penniless, he would not have married her. He had ambitions. He had to be practical.

Their union had allowed him to put aside the law and go into politics. His spectacular rise – Member of Parliament at the age of twenty-seven, parliamentary private secretary at twenty-nine, and parliamentary undersecretary of state at thirty-one – had been remarked on in the press. 'Golden boy' was a term he had become accustomed to. Because he was young and good-looking, his photograph often adorned the front pages of newspapers. His fellow MPs sometimes teased him about it.

Though the Carterets, with their influence and contacts, had been useful to him, Gillis knew himself to possess the necessary ingredients for political success. He was confident, talented, hard-working and charismatic. All he had lacked was money, his father having frittered away the family fortune on drink, mistresses and grandiose architectural projects before dying at the age of fifty and leaving his son only debts. Gillis nurtured an ambition to have a cabinet post by the age of thirty-five. He saw no reason why that should not be within his grasp.

He supported and admired Eden and Churchill for their opposition to Chamberlain's policy of appeasement. Earlier in the year, he had considered resigning at the same time as Anthony Eden, in protest at the government's foreign policy. He had not in the end done so, telling himself that

29

he would have more influence where he was than if he retreated to the ranks. As the months had passed, he had concluded that he had made the right decision. It didn't matter a damn how he or Eden or any of the rest of them shuffled themselves around the parliamentary chessboard: war was inevitable. In March 1939, Hitler's occupation of the savaged remnant of Czechoslovakia had extinguished the last spark of hope of avoiding it.

They had left London behind and were driving through open countryside. The trees and fields were coming into leaf, spreading a haze of spring green. Pale yellow primroses dotted the verges. His spirits rose.

'How are you doing, darling?' he asked Blanche. 'There's a roadhouse not far ahead. Shall we stop there, have some lunch?'

Blanche looked at her watch. 'I'm afraid we'll be late for the girls' train.'

'They can always take a taxi.'

'A stranger driving them, Gillis!'

'Jolly good, then, we'll head on.' He took a corner. 'A double christening!' he added jovially. 'You'll enjoy that, won't you?'

'Oh yes. You know how I adore little babies.'

He did not respond. He hoped she might drop the subject. But she said, 'I wish you would change your mind!'

'We talked about it,' he said shortly. 'We agreed. You know it's not a good time. As soon as Hitler makes his move I'll have to join up.'

'But you'd like a son, wouldn't you, Gillis?'

'Yes, of course I would.'

'*Please*, darling . . .' She turned to him, her eyes brimming with tears.

Though in most respects Blanche was the perfect wife,

running their house in St James's Place with sophistication and competence and charming the great and the good when they entertained, she had one flaw. She was only enthusiastic about lovemaking when they were trying for a baby. The rest of the time she appeared to regard it as a chore. In the early days of their marriage he had tried romantic weekends away, champagne and roses and gentle seduction, but she had continued to view sex with reluctance, even distaste. With a feeling of disappointment and resentment he had come to accept that though she loved him in her way, what passion she had would always be focused on her children. Blanche adored children, would have filled the house with them, and was active in promoting various children's charities. Agree to go along with her longing for another baby and she would welcome his lovemaking. He was tempted.

But no. The future was too unpredictable. He felt it wrong to bring a vulnerable infant into the world at such a time.

'When war breaks out,' he said, 'I shall have to send you and the girls away somewhere. You won't be able to remain in London. You'll be safer in the constituency house.'

Blanche disliked the constituency house, which was in Wiltshire and was damp, gloomy and over-large. It had been a poor purchase; they had intended to smarten it up, make something of it, but neither of them had had the heart and they had never got round to it.

She said bravely, 'I'm not going to cut and run, Gillis. I want your home to be there for you, to welcome you, whatever happens.'

'Darling.' A rabbit ran across the road ahead; he braked, and the creature scuttled into the undergrowth. 'Listen, please. I am not nobody, and I have not tried to hide where my sympathies lie. The Nazis make short work of their political

31

opponents, and as my wife and children you would all be at risk if there were to be an invasion. If you were pregnant – or if there was a newborn baby – it would make everything so much more difficult.'

'Invasion?' she murmured, her eyes wide and alarmed.

'Hitler will no doubt soon turn his attentions to Poland. And then, next . . . who can tell? France for sure. And maybe us.'

'Daddy said that Germany might settle for Czechoslovakia.'

'He's wrong.' Again he had to suppress his annoyance. Blanche's father, Gerald Carteret, was prone to making ignorant political pronouncements. 'Blanche, you have to trust me on this, he's wrong.'

Then, seeing her turn away, biting her lip, he felt ashamed of himself for frightening her.

'I may be worrying unduly,' he said, softening his voice. 'Perhaps things won't be as bad as I fear. No one can see into the future.' He changed the subject. 'I'm frightfully flattered that Henry and Juliet have asked me to be little Piers's godfather. Good of them, wasn't it?' He would do his best to be a suitable godfather to Piers Winterton; when the boy was old enough, he would take him to tea at Gunter's and to see the cricket at Lord's.

The christening, in the church of All Saints in Maldon, went smoothly. The Winterton babies – Henry and Juliet's son Piers, and Jonny and Helen's son Aidan – did not yowl too much, and their parents and godparents looked suitably proud.

Afterwards, the christening party drove to Marsh Court for lunch. Seated between Helen Winterton and the doctor's wife, Gillis watched Juliet Winterton beckon to the maid to tell her to clear the table. Juliet was a lovely creature, long-limbed and slender, her golden colouring made out of the ordinary by her long, slightly slanting greenish-hazel eyes.

He wondered whether she was happy, and what she really thought of her marriage.

Though Gillis was fond of Henry, he knew him to be capable of spitefulness. Their friendship had blossomed because Henry answered that part of Gillis's character he usually tried to hide, the cold, calculated, self-interest he had adopted during his teenage years in order to survive his disordered home life. Juliet was good-natured, affectionate, kind and anxious to please, none of which were traits Henry Winterton was likely to admire. Gillis assumed he had married her for her beauty, for her ability to set off a necklace of Winterton diamonds or a pair of flashing emerald earrings. And who could blame him?

After lunch, the nannies took their smallest charges off for afternoon naps and the adults and older children trooped outside. To celebrate the birth of the two cousins, the Wintertons planned to light a bonfire. Henry had had his gardener dismantle an old, rotting shed and pile the slats into a heap. Fallen branches, newspapers, cardboard and corrugated paper had been added for kindling.

It amused Gillis to watch the family on such occasions. They all – sardonic Henry, cheerful Jonathan and their sparkling sister Jane – became seized by a spirit that he could only think of as primeval. They dashed around, fetching fuel to feed the fire, shrieking with pleasure as the wind caught the flames and lashed them into the sky. They peered recklessly into the pyre whenever the inferno threatened to die down, regardless of the red sparks spat out by damp wood. Family squabbles were forgotten and they became unified in their pagan pleasures.

Gillis loved the Wintertons with a straightforward, generous affection. They were an exclusive, clannish lot, and he felt a very genuine gratitude towards them for welcoming him into their tight circle. His own family had always been a

33

disappointment to him, and he disliked his in-laws, the Carterets. His friendship with Henry Winterton and subsequent acceptance by the wider family had filled a gap in his life. He and Henry had met in 1934, at the dinner table of a mutual acquaintance. They had argued much of the evening about the usefulness, or otherwise, of the League of Nations, and had remained firm friends ever since.

There was Henry, in tweed coat and shooting cap, using a stick to bat a burning spar back on to the heap. Beside him stood Jane Hazelhurst, Henry's sister. Her long hair was the same honey blonde as her mink coat, and her face, with its typical Winterton features of high forehead, good bones and rather chilly blue eyes, was burnished by the fire. Jane was a good sport and Gillis was very fond of her. She had great energy and a thirst for life, like all the Wintertons, and would share a bottle of whisky with you at the end of an evening or walk beside you for miles through the countryside.

Jonny Winterton and Peter Hazelhurst were standing on the far side of the circle. Jonny's dry sense of humour lacked the cruel edge that informed his elder brother's wit. Like his sister, he was a talented pianist. Gillis wondered whether, given the choice, Jonny might have pursued a musical career instead of going into business. But he had not had the choice: he was a Winterton, and so he worked for the family firm. Jane's husband Peter was tall and dark. He was a consultant surgeon at a London hospital, a calm, unruffled man – qualities that must come in useful, Gillis thought, when rearranging a person's insides. And when married to Jane.

Jonny's wife, Helen, was talking to Marie Barbour. Catching Gillis's eye, she gave him a wave and beckoned to him. He smiled back, but did not yet go to join her. Blanche was carrying little Claudia, who was wailing, back to the cottage.

34

Gillis's gaze moved once more to where Juliet Winterton stood. It was hard not to look at her. Something drew you to her. She looked wild and radiant, her dark gold hair taking orange and copper tints from the flames, her expression one of joyful expectancy. Yes, Henry was a lucky bastard.

Gillis had always been subject to sudden changes of mood, dark humours that would come upon him without warning. One did so now. It occurred to him that in six months' time, every man now standing round this bonfire might be in uniform. If the war was as savage as he feared it would be, they might not all be alive. And what of the women and children? Would Stanley Baldwin's warning, that the bomber would always get through, be proved horrifically true?

To dispel these melancholy thoughts, he seized his daughter Flavia's hand and began to dance round the fire, emitting a Red Indian war whoop as he beat his palm against his mouth. Jane and her twins joined in, leaping and whirling, and then Jonny too. And then even Henry, seized by an untypical bonhomie, forgot his dignity and cavorted with the rest of them.

Gillis had always loved the sea. One of his earliest memories was of paddling on a Cornish beach, watching the turquoise water lap over the milky-white sand. He had screamed with delight as the retreating waves had scooped the sand out from beneath his soles, threatening to topple him.

He had been given his first boat at the age of seven, a squat, curmudgeonly craft that took in water in any sea more lively than a millpond. Later, he had sailed his father's yacht, until that had been sold along with the family home, the motor car and the Cornish cottage. After that, he had crewed friends' yachts, sailing across the North Sea to Holland or up to the far north of Scotland, Orkney and Shetland.

So it was inevitable that when war broke out in September 1939 he should join the navy. As a very green ex-amateur yachtsman granted a commission by the Admiralty selection board, his first posting was as a sub lieutenant to a destroyer. The Phoney War extended into the early months of 1940. One of the other subs, a car salesman called Thompson, expounded his theory one evening in the wardroom when rather the worse for wear. Hitler wasn't going to bother with western Europe, Thompson bet his bottom dollar on it. He'd wait a while and then have a go at Russia. The British Expeditionary Force, freezing their arses off in one of the worst winters for decades in their bivouacs in northern France, were wasting their time.

In April, Hitler invaded Denmark and Norway. Then, in early May, all hell broke loose as western Europe burst into flames. Norway surrendered and German forces attacked the Netherlands, Belgium and Luxembourg. German armoured units stormed south, trampling through the Ardennes into France, where they encircled the British and French armies, trapping them against the coast in a narrowing pocket at the seaport of Dunkirk.

Gillis's destroyer had returned to Liverpool after a bruising, freezing-cold encounter in Norwegian waters had given him his first taste of action. Though he had sent Blanche and the girls to Wiltshire the previous September, they had returned to London at Christmas, and, using the excuse of the inaction of the early months of the war, remained there, something he now bitterly regretted consenting to. He was hoping for a few days' leave so that he could help them get back safely to the constituency house.

But instead of being given leave, he was handed a message from the Admiralty telling him to report without delay to Chatham Naval Barracks in Kent. Others were heading in the same direction. No one knew why. No one had a clue what was going on. He and Thompson travelled south together, along with half a dozen of the destroyer's ratings.

A few days later, he found himself on a Thames Dutch barge at Dunkirk, aiding the evacuation of the shattered, defeated BEF across the Channel, back to the south coast of England. Clouds of smoke hung over the French port and billowed from the burning oil of the wrecks. Soldiers queued eight abreast, column after column extending from the beach waist-deep into the sea, at the mercy of dive-bombing Me 109s. Hundreds more men waited for rescue on the moles that jutted out into the water. Destroyers took off the troops who waited on the mole, or stood out to sea, their hulls too deep to come in closer to the beaches, while smaller shallow-bottomed vessels – pleasure craft and motor launches and lifeboats – ferried the soldiers back to the bigger ships.

Because of her shallow draught, the Dutch barge *Rosa* was able to nudge in close to shore. The soldiers waiting in the water clamoured round the boat, reaching out for the ladders that were thrown down to them. But they were too cold and exhausted to climb, and the tide was rising, and they began to slip and slide back into the sea. Gillis and the rest of the crew of the *Rosa* had to seize the men bodily and haul them over the rail, where they collapsed, drenched and limp, on the deck.

Gillis and Thompson worked together, hauling one man after another out of the water and on to the barge, grappling with wet straps and sodden clothing to drag the inert bundles on to the boat. However many they hauled out, the sea still seethed with men waiting for rescue. Thousands of others remained on the beaches, trapped between the conquering Wehrmacht and the Channel.

A whine and a roar: a Messerschmitt burst through the

covering of smoke. Instinctively, Gillis ducked. When he straightened, the plane had gone, and Thompson, a few feet away from him, had flopped over the guardrail. Gillis called out to him. He reached out a hand, then saw that a bullet had lodged in the back of Thompson's skull.

'You can't do anything for him, sir.' A short, sturdy, Welsh-accented petty officer was addressing him.

Gillis stared at the Welshman. 'He's dead,' he said stupidly.

'Yes, sir, very dead.'

Together they moved Thompson's body away from the rail. 'You all right, sir?'

Gillis gave himself a mental shake. 'Yes, of course.'

'Have a nip of this, sir.' The Welshman handed him a flask. He drank. Rum scorched his throat.

Around the Dutch barge, corpses of soldiers bobbed in the water, casualties of the same Messerschmitt attack that had killed Thompson. The sky was black and the sea was bloody, and there came into Gillis's mind a long-forgotten image from a hot childhood summer, when a pond at his Hertfordshire home had dried up, trapping the fish. Some of the creatures had leaped and writhed in their fight to survive, but others had floated on the shrinking surface of the pond, bloated and rotting.

Gillis and the petty officer started to haul men out of the sea again. The Welshman worked like an automaton, sifting the living from the dead. He never seemed to flag. He had the powerful upper body of a blacksmith, or a coal miner, and showed no fear when the Me 109s returned.

When they had taken around one hundred troops on board, they ferried them to a destroyer anchored further out to sea. Then they went back to the beach. The tide was going out and the Rosa sat on the sand in shallow water, so it was easier for the soldiers to board her. When the tide swung back in, refloating them, they took the troops out to the destroyer.

Before they turned back to the beach, the Welshman offered Gillis his flask again. 'What's your name?' Gillis asked him.

'Morgan, sir. David Morgan.'

'You're doing a good job, Morgan.'

'Thank you, sir.' Morgan gave him a slightly mocking salute. 'You too, sir.'

October 1940. Gillis was standing on the platform at Salisbury railway station, waiting for the London train. It was Sunday evening, a rotten time to be travelling at the best of times, and this was certainly not the best of times. In the capital, the Blitz was raging. Gillis doubted if a single train in the country was running on time. His train was already very late. The blacked-out platforms smelled of soot and frost, and the only light came from the moon and a dusting of stars.

Growing chilly, he went into the waiting room. There were two people sitting there already, an older woman in a sealskin coat, and a red-headed girl, who was reading a book. The redhead was wearing the blue-grey uniform of the WAAF. Gillis wished them both good evening, then sat down.

The passing of time was marked by the tick of the clock and a series of comically loud, disapproving grunts from the older woman. The WAAF went on turning the pages of her book, slipping outside now and then to check whether there was any sign of the train. Gillis registered her nice legs and neat ankles. After half an hour, the woman in the sealskin coat picked up her basket with a last resounding sigh, and walked out. There was an odd, suppressed noise and Gillis saw that the WAAF had clamped her hands over her mouth.

As soon as the waiting room door closed, she let out a peal of laughter.

'Oh God . . . I'm so sorry . . . I thought I would burst!' She mimicked the woman's displeased exhalations, and then howled with laughter again.

He smiled. 'It was quite something.'

Her cap had rolled off the bench; she picked it up, patted her unruly coppery curls, gave the cap a quick dust with her sleeve and put it back on her head.

'Do you think this train's ever going to come?'

'I'll go and see if I can find someone.'

He went back out into the chilly darkness of the station. When he returned to the waiting room, she said, 'Anything?'

'Not a dicky bird. I had a word with the stationmaster. Apparently it's stuck at Andover.'

'Oh Lord.'

'Cigarette?' He offered her his packet.

'Thanks.'

'Don't let me keep you from your book.'

'This?' She gave the paperback a disparaging glance. 'I've read it before. It's the most awful piffle anyway.'

She put the cigarette between her lips and inhaled as he held his lighter to it. Her hair was a rich red, her eyes a soft, warm brown, her mouth full. There was a powdering of freckles across her pretty snub nose and she had a redhead's fine, pale complexion. He wondered how old she was. Mid-twenties, something like that.

She offered her hand to him. 'My name's Frances Hart.'

'Gillis Sinclair.'

'Pleased to meet you, Gillis Sinclair.'

He caught in her eyes a mixture of amusement and interest, and his heart speeded a little. He said, 'Miserable place.'

'Isn't it? They might have lit us a fire.'

'How long have you been waiting?'

'Five hours.'

'You poor thing. You must be frozen.'

She touched her face. 'My hands are like blocks of ice. Feel that!'

Her fingertips brushed against the back of his hand. He forgot his boredom and fatigue. He wondered whether to ask her for a drink. He probably shouldn't. But he knew he would anyway.

He glanced at his watch. 'The stationmaster said there wasn't much hope of anything turning up for another couple of hours. There's a hotel a few hundred yards away. Perhaps we should go there and warm up a bit.'

They left the station and walked down the road. In the private bar of the Station Hotel, there was a fire lit and some tired armchairs and enough customers to make the room cheerful.

He bought the drinks; she told him about herself. She was from Broad Chalke in Wiltshire. Her father owned a dairy and she had a younger sister. She had been working as secretary to the undermanager of a bank when the events at Dunkirk had prompted her to volunteer for the WAAF. She had just completed her basic training. 'I made a frightful hash of it,' she said, with a snort of laughter. 'I was afraid they wouldn't let me through.' She would have hated that, she told him, because the other girls were such good sports and it was such an adventure. Her mother had recently been taken ill and Frances had been granted three days' compassionate leave to visit her in hospital. She was on the mend now, thank goodness.

They had another drink and Gillis managed to persuade the barman to rustle them up some food. The sandwiches contained a scrap of fatty meat and a blob of luminous piccalilli. 'Lord, it looks like something the cat sicked up,' Frances said, but they were both ravenous and devoured every crumb.

It was late; they were closing up the bar. All the other customers had gone. He thought of Blanche, who was pregnant again, and jarringly of Thompson, flopped over the guardrail.

He said, 'Shall I see whether I can get us a room?'

She looked at him. Then she nodded. 'All right.'

When he came back from the reception, he handed her the key. 'You go on up. I'll come along in fifteen minutes or so.'

'Okay.' She stood up. Her mouth twisted to one side and she looked momentarily uneasy. 'I don't normally do this sort of thing.'

'I know. You're a beautiful girl, Frances. And if you change your mind, then I'll sleep on the floor.'

She left the room. He had another drink, then he went upstairs and tapped softly on the bedroom door.

And that was how it began.

After Dunkirk, Henry had joined up and was now living in an army camp on Salisbury Plain. Jonathan was called up in 1941, but was excused active service after he was found to have a weak heart. He spent much of his time in London, staying in the Bond Street flat, where he looked after the shop in his brother's absence, supervising the orders for the chronographs and watches for naval officers that Winterton's manufactured in the war.

Juliet made only one long journey during that time, in the late spring of 1941, to visit Henry, who had been taken ill with a grumbling appendix and was in a military hospital outside Salisbury. The Blitz had been going on since September.

She would be away for several nights and planned to break her journey at the London flat. Helen would look after Piers, and the Land Girls billeted at Marsh Court had promised to keep an eye on the house and water the vegetable garden during her absence.

Henry requested that she bring certain legal documents with her. To the despair of his solicitor, a Mr Kendrick of Maldon, he frequently made alterations to his will. She suspected that, though he would never have admitted it, he was afraid he might not survive the operation.

Though she left Maldon first thing in the morning, trains had been cancelled after an air raid the previous night, and it was four o'clock by the time she arrived at Liverpool Street station. As the Underground train travelled west, more and more passengers squeezed into the packed carriages, so that they were crushed up against each other, jabbed by bags and gas masks. Juliet had never liked confined spaces, and had grown accustomed to the openness and isolation of Marsh Court. Panic rose inside her, making her heart race. She abandoned her plan of making for Bond Street station, and when the train stopped at Tottenham Court Road, she left the carriage.

The moment of blessed relief as she emerged out of the dark labyrinth of escalator and ticket hall to blue spring skies was quickly followed by shock and dismay at the desolation she discovered. As she walked westwards, she found it hard to recognise the great stores in which, on pre-war visits to London, she had passed the time shopping or lunching. Their dignified facades had been blasted to pieces by bombing or covered over with sandbags and hoardings, and their walls had been scorched by the fires that had raged inside them. These were buildings that had seemed to her as much emblems of London – and Britain – as St Paul's or Buckingham

Palace. Now they were ruins and shadows. Peter Robinson's Oxford Circus storefront had been boarded up, and John Lewis was a mere shell, its scarred columns and empty window arches reminding her of Greek ruins she had visited in her childhood. Selfridge's smoke-blackened upper storeys and bricked-up ground-floor windows stared sightlessly after her as she turned down New Bond Street.

Jonathan welcomed her to the flat. They dined that evening in a small restaurant in Conduit Street. Over dinner, he broke the news that the German army was now in Athens. The thought came to her then that the civilisation of which she had once been a part was coming to an end, like so many that had flourished and crumbled before it.

Jonny was fire-watching that night; after he had left the flat, Juliet went to bed early. But she slept poorly, the ruined roads through which she had walked that day unreeling endlessly in her mind, the recent Axis victories too terrible to take in.

The next day, she rose at six. Jonny saw her off from Waterloo station, and her journey westwards was calm and speedy. But the darkness of the previous night haunted her, and when she arrived at the hospital, she was almost glad of the distraction of a vile-tempered Henry, recovering from the emergency appendectomy he had undergone the previous night.

One by one, Marsh Court's servants left to join the forces or to earn better wages in factories. After the cook, Mrs Godbold, went to care for her sick mother in Colchester, Juliet alone was responsible for her son and the house and its grounds.

Though she knew how to cook because she had done so for her father, she had to learn to use different ingredients. Sometimes on those wartime mornings she woke dreaming of the tangy black olives of Greece, the sharpness of lemon and garlic and the sweetness of pistachio and date, all unobtainable in England during those years. She and Helen worked together in the kitchen garden as Piers and Aidan grew strong and brown playing between the rows of beans and carrots.

She had been an ignorant little thing, she reflected, when she had first arrived in England. She had known so little. Wartime forced her to acquire new skills and experience and to trust in her own decisions. She wondered whether her incompetence had contributed to her difficulties in her marriage. Henry was an impatient man, not the sort to suffer fools gladly. Juliet imagined how pleased he would be when the war ended and he came home and saw how well she had cared for Marsh Court. They would make a new start, founded on mutual respect. And perhaps, at last, respect would transform into love.

Cold was her greatest enemy. The damp of the marshes penetrated the old building, and on the frostiest days her chilblains turned red and itchy. The house was heated by open fires and the kitchen stove, and as coal was rationed and the rooms were large and draughty, she took to cycling round the surrounding lanes, collecting branches brought down by the wind.

One morning, cycling in the countryside to the east of Mayland, she came across a copse. Seeing inside it some sizeable fallen branches, she propped her bike against a fence post and ducked beneath the trees. A brisk wind was whisking the last of the leaves from their hold. She began to gather up kindling.

The snap of a broken twig, a whirr of pheasant's wings, and she looked up. A man wearing a khaki army coat and muddy boots was standing on the far side of the copse. The wind ripped at his straight black hair. His dark eyes, set beneath level brows, glared at her.

'What are you doing here?'

'Gathering firewood,' she faltered. Understanding dawned. 'Is this land yours?'

'Yes.'

'I'm so sorry, I'll put it back.'

'Take it,' he said sharply. There was no kindness in his voice, only the desire to be rid of her as soon as possible, and an expression on his stern features that said, *go away and don't come back*. As she hurried off, she felt his gaze following her.

That evening, Juliet described the man in the copse to one of the Land Girls billeted at Marsh Court, a Liverpudlian called Meg.

'That'll be Mr Brandon,' she said. 'He farms Greensea.'

'Greensea?'

'Muddy-brown sea, more like. His land runs alongside Mayland Creek.'

Juliet pushed a plate of cake across the table. 'Help yourself.'

Meg took a slice. 'His wife's very ill. My friend Sarah used to work there, but she moved on when Joe Brandon came home on compassionate leave. She didn't like being there with Mrs Brandon so ill and him so miserable.'

'What's wrong with her?'

'TB.'

'How awful. He looked so young!'

Meg licked her forefinger, pressed it into the crumbs on the plate and stuck it in her mouth. 'Mrs Brandon's going to die, everyone says so. It's only *him* won't believe it.'

The next day, Juliet packed up a basket – a jar of plum jelly, made from the small wild fruit that grew in the garden, a cake sweetened using marrow because sugar was severely rationed, a punnet of late raspberries and a posy of Madame Alfred Carrière roses, which flowered into October. She took it with her when she cycled to Greensea Farm.

Geese hooted and cackled, their V-shaped formations inscribed on a dishcloth-grey sky. The narrow road plunged in a series of ninety-degree turns into a deep, quiet landscape of copse and field. She glimpsed the spire of a church between the grey trunks of sycamores, and a still black pond, mallards floating on its surface. The war seemed far away, the upheavals of recent years to belong to some distant land.

Coming across a signpost that pointed her along a rutted track, Juliet dismounted and pushed the bike for fear of being thrown into the puddles. To one side of her were ploughed fields, to the other a hedgerow that gave way to a mere surrounded by trees.

The farmhouse ahead of her stood on a raised green and was almost masked by a stand of silver poplars that seemed to bob and float like the pale masts of a boat. She thought the place suited its name, Greensea. The house itself was tall and solid, with a steeply pitched slate roof. High Georgian windows stood to either side of a square central porch. Juliet propped her bicycle against it and knocked on the front door.

It was opened by a woman in her middle years. Her features were tanned and weathered, as if by exposure to wind and sun, and her greying hair was scraped back into a tight bun.

'Yes?' she said, frowning.

'Forgive me for disturbing you.' Juliet held out the basket. 'I've brought a small gift for Mrs Brandon.'

The woman looked at the basket suspiciously. 'Who are you?'

'Mrs Winterton, of Marsh Court.'

A sinewy hand reached out and grabbed the basket. Then

the door slammed. For a moment Juliet stared at it, and then made her way home.

The following morning, one of the Land Girls, opening Marsh Court's front door, discovered the basket, which someone had left on the front step. Everything was still inside it, including the roses, which were wilting.

There was a note tucked into it. Juliet opened it and read: *Mrs Winterton, thank you for your kindness but we have plenty of food at the farm.*

Well there you are, Juliet thought. Mr Brandon had made his feelings perfectly clear: *keep your nose out of my business.* A few weeks later, catching sight of him on Maldon High Street, she pretended she had not seen him and walked on.

In his cousin Aidan, Piers had a constant companion, yet by the age of five the two boys were already very different in character and appearance. Aidan had inherited Helen's chestnut hair and hazel eyes, whereas Piers was a true Winterton, fair and blue-eyed. Aidan was quieter than Piers, and had a greater capacity for concentration, could amuse himself for hours if supplied with crayons and scissors and paper, whereas Piers needed company and attention. Piers had a temper and was given to tantrums, but Aidan had an obstinate streak, and when he dug his heels in, it infuriated Piers. The two of them squabbled over ridiculous things, but Juliet and Helen told each other that they were boys, that boys were like that and they would grow out of it.

The two cousins started on the same day at the same small kindergarten in Maldon. After taking Piers to school that first morning, Juliet returned to a house that seemed echoing and empty. The discovery of a lone small sock at the bottom of the ironing basket made tears spring to her eyes, so she went out to the garden and searched for snails to drown until it was time to take the bus to town to fetch him.

In April 1944, the military vehicles rumbled out of Essex, taking the men south-west to prepare for the embarkation to France. Henry was finally granted his wish of seeing active service, and during late 1944 and the spring of 1945 was part of a regiment fighting its way through Europe to Germany. The war dragged on; first Paris and then Brussels was liberated, but then the Allied campaign was slowed by the surprise German offensive in the Ardennes. Like everyone else, Juliet longed for the war to be over, but after more than five years, she could hardly believe it possible. She pitied Henry, who must be enduring danger and deprivation. She wanted him to come home safely, for his own sake – hateful to think that he might be lost so far away from the country he loved – but for Piers's sake too, and for hers, that they might make a new start, and do better.

On 8 May 1945, VE Day, Piers was sick with chickenpox. That evening, after checking he was asleep, Juliet went downstairs and poured herself a measure from a bottle of brandy she had put aside earlier in the war. She took her glass outside and crossed the lawn, heading for the patch of ground at the foot of the garden where the Wintertons made their bonfires. None had been lit during the war. Kindling was too precious, and a fire would have been a beacon for enemy aircraft navigating up the Blackwater.

She gathered up sticks and leaves and struck a match, and watched the flames gather and dart. It was a half-hearted bonfire that soon died, but it was her celebration, her way of marking that the war in Europe had ended, and that all the slaughter and vileness was over.

Chapter Three

September 1945–June 1946

J uliet was in the vegetable garden, cutting down the brown stalks of peas and beans for compost. She was looking after Aidan so that Helen, who was in the latter stages of pregnancy, could have a rest. The new puppy, an excitable springer spaniel that Piers had christened Biscuit, worried at the heaps of dead vegetation.

Piers hurtled down the lawn. 'Mummy, there's a man in the house,' he said importantly.

The handyman, she thought, come to fix the stove. She straightened, brushing her hands on her trousers, and looked up.

Henry was standing by the French doors. He stepped on to the terrace.

'Good God,' he said, looking round. 'The state of the place.'

She gathered her wits. 'Henry,' she said, 'how wonderful.'

She went to him, intending to embrace him. But Piers, unnerved by this stranger who had appeared in the garden, clung to her leg, impeding her progress. Henry eyed his son and said, 'His hair needs cutting.' Then he turned on his heel and went back into the house.

Nothing pleased him. Though she washed her hair and exchanged her trousers for a dress, he remarked on the calluses on her fingers and the muscles in her arms — 'like a washerwoman's'. Though she dusted the dining room so that they could eat there once more, he disapproved of the fact that they had only cheap household candles — before the war, they had always dined by the light of beeswax candles. Instead of showing pleasure in his homecoming, Henry saw only decline and dilapidation, in the country at large, and at Marsh Court, for which he held her responsible.

Most painful to her was his treatment of Piers. She suspected he had heard the boy's remark — *Mummy, there's a man in the house* — and that it hurt, though being Henry, he never said so. Having seen his son only intermittently over the last five years, and having been out of the country for eighteen months, he did not know how to talk to children. Piers was a handsome, bright and lively little boy and would have adored his father, given the chance. His appeal might have broken through the reserve of a different man, but with Henry there was always the old suspicion, even with his own child, of hidden motives and hypocrisy. 'I daresay he wants something,' he would say, brushing the boy from his lap. 'What are you after, Piers? A bag of sweets? A new toy?' And Piers would look bewildered and Juliet's heart would bleed for him.

He found fault with Piers's behaviour. The boy must learn to sit still at the table. He should be able to tie his own shoelaces. And why did Juliet still allow him a nightlight, like a milksop, or a girl? Why did he fuss about fetching a toy from the dark, spidery games room? He should be able to read by now – what was wrong with him? Aidan was able to read fluently. And look at Aidan's drawings – they were infinitely superior to Piers's.

This was true, Juliet conceded. Even at four or five years old, it had been obvious that Aidan had a particular talent for art. He loved to draw, and did so each day – it seemed as natural to him as speaking. His sketches were colourful and full of life. Henry, who believed that one could encourage a child to greater efforts through unfavourable comparisons, did not hold back from pointing this out to Piers.

Juliet had longed for more children and was delighted when she discovered that she was pregnant again. Her daughter Charlotte was born at the end of June 1946. After a ten-hour labour, she slipped out into the world with a cry. Bald and blue-eyed, she lay awake for an hour after she was born, surveying the world with a curious eye.

Juliet recovered quickly and was back on her feet after a few days. Charlotte was a hungry baby, and after gulping down her milk, she would flop limply in her mother's arms, blissfully satiated. Cradling her daughter, Juliet forgot her dissatisfactions and disappointments. Unexpectedly, Henry too adored the new baby. Charley, as she soon became, brought out a tenderness in him that Juliet had not known existed, and he was never as hard on her as he was on Piers.

The bonfire the Wintertons and Sinclairs lit to mark Charley's safe arrival was a monstrous construction that towered over the landscape. As he lighted a bundle of reeds and thrust it into the fire, Henry told Gillis and Peter about the man who had come into the Bond Street shop carrying a large carpet bag, which he had flung on to the counter and unzipped, revealing uncut gemstones. 'Bought the lot,' declared Henry as he flapped a piece of cardboard at the flames. 'Hundreds of the damn things at a knockdown price. Rubies, sapphires, diamonds, imperial topaz. God only knows where they came from, filched from some rich Jew, no doubt, but they'll keep us going for the next few years.'

Blanche had stayed home with little Nathan, who had been born during the war, but Gillis and his daughters were at Marsh Court that day, and would stay in the cottage overnight. As the brilliant scarlet flames unfurled, Juliet saw him wander away from the inferno, down the slope towards the estuary.

Looking back, he called out to her, 'I'm just going to take a stroll. Would you keep an eye on the girls, Juliet?' And as he made his way to the salt marsh, the sunlight turned his fair head to gold.

The previous evening, Blanche had almost changed her mind and come with him to Marsh Court, but then Nathan had developed a snuffle overnight and she had stayed at home, thank God. When he reached the estuary, Gillis headed downriver. A band of pearly white light showed beneath the layer of cloud cover. Waders picked at the mud.

After half a mile, Thorney Island came in sight. Soon he saw the children, waiting at the far end of the causeway. The boy, Edmund, gave him a wave and dashed across the narrow path, but the girl, Thea, remained where she was, clinging to the safety of the bank.

Gillis had a quick check round. A column of white smoke rose in the distance, evidence of the Wintertons' bonfire, but the fields and river were empty of people.

Edmund reached the end of the causeway at much the same time as Gillis.

'Hello, Dad!'

'Hello, old chap.' Gillis hugged Edmund and ruffled his hair. The boy was fair, tall and sturdy, and always seemed to have scuffed knees. The girl was a redhead, like her mother. They were twins, born at the end of 1941.

'How's things?'

'Mummy made me a kite.'

'Lucky you. How splendid.'

They walked over the causeway to the island. Gillis took Thea's hand, and the three of them made their way up the sloping bank together. Thea was a slight little thing; Frances had been warned when she was born that she might not survive, but she had pulled through. She seemed to take a while to get to know him after an absence, and today she left most of the talking to her brother.

They walked along the narrow lane that led to the house. The boy chattered and the girl trotted ahead, stopping now and again to pick flowers. The hedgerows were clouded with white butterflies. Thea paused to watch them, her little head darting as she tried to follow their flight.

'Come on, sweetheart,' he said. 'Shall I carry you?'

She allowed him to lift her up in his arms. As the path curved behind him, making them invisible from the mainland, he felt relieved. It was funny, when you thought of everything he had done during the last five years – Dunkirk, a six-month stretch on the Atlantic crossings, and then undercover work in occupied Denmark, where he had helped supply the Resistance with radio equipment and weapons – and yet he felt as much on edge now as he had ever done, walking along this sunlit lane with his two illegitimate children.

Frances was in the back garden, pegging out washing. He called to her. 'Hello, darling!'

She ran to him and they kissed. Then she rested her head in the crook of his neck. 'God, am I glad to see you, Gill. It's been so long. I thought you'd be here *weeks* ago. They both had summer colds. I was afraid we were going to *starve*, stuck out here.'

'But they're better now?'

'Oh yes. Though it went to Thea's chest.' She scooped back her wild red hair with her hands. 'I had to take her to the doctor.'

A gust of wind whipped a badly pinned child's frock from the line; she shrieked and ran off to retrieve it from a hedgerow. When she came back, he said, 'Do you think you ought to let them play on the causeway on their own? Isn't it rather dangerous?'

'I can't watch them all the time.' Her voice was sharp. 'I do have other things to do. They look after each other.'

'Still, it might be better if they played in the garden.'

He followed her into the house. There were muddy boots in the hallway and the kitchen was a mess, dirty dishes piled in the sink and the remains of lunch littering the table. Linen overflowed from a wicker basket.

'I'd meant to clear up,' she said vaguely. 'Isn't it funny how time just slips away? Do you want something? A cup of tea?'

'No thanks.'

When she turned to him, he saw the discontent in her eyes. 'We won't have to stay here long, will we, Gill?'

'I'll find somewhere better soon, I promise.'

'Only I couldn't stand it. It's so lonely. I'm afraid the water will come over the island and we'll all be washed away.'

'Nonsense,' he said briskly. 'The house is perfectly safe.'

'If only you could find us a nice little cottage in a village somewhere, then I'd be so happy!'

She spoke, he thought irritably, as if England was full of nice little cottages, there for the taking, when in fact thousands of people were living in army camps and bombed-out slums, and couples were starting off married life in their parents' spare bedrooms.

'You know how difficult it is at the moment,' he said. 'Plenty of people have nowhere to live at all.' But then, hearing himself pompously lecturing her, he thought of the well in the garden and the dreadful outside lavatory and the terrible tiring dinginess and inconvenience of living on an island miles away from anywhere.

She was scraping the plates into the bin, putting pickle jars and the butter dish into the larder. He could tell by the set of her mouth that she was upset. These days, when he was with her, his principal emotions were impatience and guilt. The wild excitement and desire of the early months of their love affair had died a long time ago. He knew, rationally, that he had experienced those things, but he found it hard to remember them.

'Look, it won't be for long.' He took her in his arms. 'I know it must be hard on you. But I need you to be patient for a while longer, Fran.'

Her mouth searched for his and they kissed. 'So lovely to have you all to myself,' she murmured. 'You'll stay the night, won't you, darling?'

'I can't, the girls are at Marsh Court. It would look odd if I was away overnight.'

There was a flash of anger in her eyes. Was she going to remind him that Edmund and Thea were his children too? But she seemed to pull back.

'I'd meant to cook us a nice dinner,' she said, with a laugh. 'But I didn't get to the shops in time. That bloody causeway! Whenever I want to go out, the tide always seems to be in.'

How difficult was it, he wondered, to check the tide tables and plan accordingly? And perhaps she sensed his exasperation, because she pressed herself against him, her thumb rubbing against the back of his neck. Her breasts, fuller and less taut since the babies, were soft against his chest. He felt ashamed that he didn't want her more.

'Come upstairs,' she whispered. 'I've missed you. It seems ages.'

'Sweetheart, the children . . .'

'But I want you . . .' She sighed and went back to clearing up the kitchen.

'I thought I'd look into buying a yacht,' he said. 'It would mean I'd be up here a lot, going round the marinas.'

'A yacht!' She laughed. 'I should so love to go sailing!'

A picture came into his mind of Frances and the twins, sitting on the deck as he scudded along the Blackwater, watched by Winterton friends and yacht club friends and anyone else who might recognise him. Sometimes she was so infuriatingly clueless.

The twins clattered into the room, talking about a dog.

'A dog?' he said, smiling at them.

'A big dog,' said Edmund. 'I'll throw sticks for it in the river.'

'I said you'd buy them a dog, Gill,' said Frances. 'I'd like one too. It would be company at night.'

She struggled to look after two children, he thought; how was she going to manage a dog as well? She must have caught his expression, because she pushed her hair back from her face again and said, 'I know it looks jolly hopeless, but I am going to get on top of things. We haven't been here long, and then the kids were ill, but I'm going to sort myself out, you'll see, Gill. You mustn't worry about us. A dog would be nice for them, that's all.'

'Okay. A dog it is.'

Edmund hooted with pleasure. Thea ran round the kitchen on all fours, pretending to be a dog.

'Haven't you got a lovely daddy, darlings?' cried Frances. 'Shall we tell Daddy what we're going to do this afternoon?'

'A picnic!' yelled Edmund. And Thea stopped being a dog and jumped up and down instead. 'A picnic! A picnic!'

His affair with Frances Hart, so compelling and passionate from that first night at the Station Hotel in Salisbury, had been made hideously complicated by the birth of the twins. Back in the early days, she had told him she was taking care of contraception, and he, like a fool, had believed her. She hadn't realised she was pregnant until she was five months gone, by which time it had been too late to do anything about it. When she had told him that she was expecting twins, the thought had crossed his mind that it was so typical of her to produce two babies rather than the usual one, thus making everything so much more difficult.

Her carefree, impulsive nature had at first been part of the attraction. Frances had been a refreshing change from Blanche, who fussed and worried about everything. Looking back, he realised that he had equated impulsiveness and forgetfulness with passion and warmth. It had taken him a while, and a series of assignations when she had turned up at the wrong time or in the wrong place, to stop finding any charm in it.

And by then it was too late. The twins were on the way,

and whatever sort of shit he was – and he knew that he was – he wasn't the sort who could abandon a woman and two babies. He had installed Frances and the children in a cottage near a village in Hampshire, and then, when the place had proved unsuitable, a small house near Hungerford in Berkshire. During the war, they had got by. He had been abroad much of the time, and because his work had been very hush-hush, it had been easy to supply excuses to Blanche for his absences.

By then, the heady delight of the first few months of the affair had dissipated. He had imagined that the relationship would gradually fizzle out and that Frances would find someone else. Naturally, he would pay for the upkeep of the children. He would send the boy to a decent boarding school to make up for his rough start in life and find the girl, an affectionate little thing, somewhere nearer to home.

But Frances hadn't found anyone else. She declared herself still in love with him. She had tried to persuade him to leave Blanche, and he had prevaricated, despising himself. The affair had made him appreciate how deeply he valued the order and calm that Blanche brought to his life.

With the end of the war, his problems had multiplied. At the 1945 election he had clung on to his parliamentary seat by the skin of his teeth. His majority of six thousand had been slashed to less than three hundred. He found it hard to forgive his constituents for that. His reward for the years he had spent fighting for his country had been a narrow escape from humiliation.

Labour's victory in 1945 had been formidable, winning a large share of the vote. He had briefly considered defecting to Labour – some of their policies were not so bad – but had not in the end done so. No one trusted a turncoat, and

Gillis believed at heart that the elite, with their superior education and experience, were best prepared for running the country.

He had been unable to shake off his sense of bitterness. After he had been demobilised, he had come home to find his London house wrecked by the army types who had requisitioned it, and few resources available for its repair. Food rationing was more severe, if anything, than during the war, and there was no end of it in sight. He was not a parliamentary undersecretary any more, but a mere MP, and in opposition at that. The golden boy now had more than a few grey hairs. Though he tried to comfort himself with the knowledge that Attlee's victory was a poisoned chalice, that the country had been left bankrupt by the war and the economy was unsalvageable, such consolation felt hollow.

And then, Frances. Earlier in the year, Edmund, who was an adventurous little fellow, had fallen out of a tree and broken his arm. She had phoned him at the office – the *office* – and, because he had been out, had left a message. Someone must have gossiped to someone, because a few days later, there had been a newspaper reporter nosing round the village in which Frances and the children were then living. He had known himself to be on the verge of losing everything. Blanche would divorce him if she found out about Frances. His career, too, hung by a thread. If his liaison became public, it would be only a matter of time. The tap on the shoulder, the quiet word one evening at his club, murmurings about resignation . . . for the sake of the party.

He had had to move them, and quickly. He had thanked God for David Morgan, the Welsh petty officer he had met at Dunkirk. He had kept in touch with Morgan, had asked for him when putting together a unit for Denmark, when he had needed a man who would do whatever he was asked without asking questions. After the war ended, he had continued to employ the Welshman on a private basis, sometimes as a driver, at other times to act for him in the sorts of arrangements he preferred no one else to know about.

It had been Morgan who had found Frances and the children rooms in a hotel in Eastbourne while Gillis had searched for a house. It had been an impossible task. There was hardly a house, flat or room to rent in the country. Too much housing stock, much of which had been in poor condition anyway, had been destroyed during the war.

Then, on a visit to Marsh Court, he had thought of Thorney Island. Miles from anywhere, hardly a soul went there, and the house had been uninhabited for years. Everyone seemed to have forgotten about it. No one would notice them there. It would be easy for him to see Frances and the children whenever he was visiting the Wintertons.

It had seemed the perfect solution. He had Morgan call on the owner, a farmer in Bradwell-on-Sea, and everything was arranged. Frances had moved there in April.

He hadn't realised how much she would hate it. Foolish of him, really: of course she would. Frances liked company – drinks, dancing, chatter, life. She missed her sister in Wiltshire and for the first six weeks or so had nagged him constantly to find them somewhere else to live.

Slowly, she had seemed to accept it. He wondered whether she sensed his loss of interest in her. She had stopped asking him when he was going to leave Blanche. Perhaps their narrow squeak, earlier in the year, had made her realise that he would never do so. He was steeling himself to tell her that it was over. He'd do it as soon as he found them a decent place to live. It would be hard, and Frances would be upset, but it had to be done. She needed and deserved a man who could give her his undivided love and attention. The children should have a father who was there all the time. He would see that she was all right financially.

They picnicked that afternoon on the grassy sea wall behind the house, looking out over the marshland that lay to the north of the island. Afterwards, Frances and the children walked back with him to the causeway. The tide was coming in; he had almost left it too late. He bade them goodbye and then made the crossing. The water was lapping over his feet by the time he reached the mainland, and he felt the force of the current tugging at him. He made a pantomime of squeezing out his trouser turn-ups, and gave them a last wave before walking away.

He felt his burdens slip from him as he headed back to Marsh Court. He had for a long time lived two lives – but then the war, and his undercover work, had given him plenty of practice at that. Tonight he would argue with Henry and make conversation with Juliet, while taking pleasure in her beauty, and he would be able to put aside, for a while at least, his worries about his little family on the island.

Chapter Four

July–September 1946

Some mornings that summer, when she was able to leave baby Charlotte with Mrs Barrett, her daily woman, Juliet walked the dog along the footpath to Marsh Court after taking Piers to school, rather than using the slow and infrequent bus home. She passed the harbour at Maldon, where the wind jangled in the rigging of the Thames barges and fishing boats, an accompaniment to the conversation of the fishermen and the calls of the seabirds. East of the town, once the harbour wall had run out, the footpath followed the estuary to where abandoned boats, reduced to black skeletons, were sunk into the mudflats. She kept an eye on Biscuit, an inquisitive creature, making sure he did not become entangled in the barbed wire that, left over from the war, scrambled over the lowest fields and ditches.

Nearing Thorney Island one day, she heard voices and a peal of laughter. A cry was caught on the wind and tossed over the river to her. Two small children, a boy and a girl in a red frock, were playing on the far side of the causeway. Juliet watched them as they darted shrieking up to the wavelets and then ran back to the bank, the girl's red dress flaring in the breeze, the boy daring her to step deeper into the water. And then perhaps someone unseen called out to them, because they turned and ran up the slope and were gone.

Sometimes she walked for the pleasure of it, and sometimes, when Henry was at Marsh Court during the week, she walked to put off the moment when they would take up again the power struggle that had come to characterise their married life. They fought over how much they should pay the housekeeper and whether Juliet should continue to invite the Land Girls to tea (Henry thought them uncouth). Some of these things were more important to her than others, but she dug her heels in with equal tenacity on each occasion. They were skirmishes in a wider battle that had raged since Henry had come home. And she wasn't going to let him win. Not any more.

Gillis was buying a yacht, which he planned to moor at Burnham-on-Crouch, so he came to Marsh Court frequently that summer. Sometimes Blanche accompanied him. Juliet noticed that except where her children were concerned, she was not a demonstrative woman. She rarely used endearments to Gillis; it was he who, crossing the drawing room to take a book from a shelf, would press a kiss on the top of his wife's head, rather than the other way round; he who would take her hand as the two families walked on the foggy coast near St Peter's Chapel. There was something cold about Blanche Sinclair, Juliet decided. Her ice-queen looks – white skin, black hair, pale blue eyes – betrayed a chilly heart. She thought that Blanche did not appreciate him enough.

One evening, there was an unpleasant scene at dinner, when Henry prodded something brown and shapeless in his stew and declared it inedible. Juliet felt tired and on edge.

She opened the kitchen door so that Gillis could help her in with the tray.

He said, 'Henry's worried about the business.'

'Yes, I realise that.' She ran hot water into the sink. 'But then Jonny's worried about the business too, and he doesn't throw a tantrum at the dinner table.'

'I don't think Jonny feels so responsible for the financial side of it.'

She plunged dishes in to soak. 'Gillis, Mrs Barrett isn't much of a cook and the food was pretty disgusting. And I completely understand that no one has the money to buy jewellery any more and that's hurting Winterton's. But nothing excuses Henry's behaviour, not in my opinion, anyway. You wouldn't talk to Blanche the way Henry talks to me.'

'Maybe I do worse, in my own way.'

'What do you mean?'

'Simply that things aren't always how they appear on the surface.' He squeezed her shoulder. 'Henry's like a child, he's incapable of disguising his ill-humour. Just now he resents the fact that his home is in disrepair and his business is struggling – and yes, his food is plain and unpalatable. And being Henry, he says so. I'm not so transparent. I let things fester.'

'What sort of things?'

'Sometimes I feel I've lost my way. That I'm going through the motions – husband, father, politician – but none of it means anything any more.'

'Gillis, what's wrong?'

'Oh, nothing much.'

'I hate to see you unhappy.' She took his hands in hers. 'We've been friends for a long time, haven't we? You can tell me anything.'

He frowned; his eyes seemed to darken, but then, gently, he pulled away from her. 'I promise you, Juliet, if I had anything to tell, you'd be the first to know. But honestly, it's nothing. I'm just feeling a little blue. A touch of self-loathing.' He gave a light laugh. 'My colleagues would find that hard to credit.'

She didn't. Gillis might give the appearance of utter self-confidence, even arrogance, but she had known for a long time that there was a darker side to his character.

'Look at the work you do for your constituents,' she said, trying to cheer him up. 'And you're so good with the children.'

'Blanche might not say the same. She'd tell you I forget their birthdays and hardly ever make it to speech days and sports days.'

Juliet looked down at the china, stewing in the sink. 'Sometimes I question myself as well,' she said quietly. 'I stay with Henry because of Marsh Court. Because of the children, too, of course, but Marsh Court came first. I loved it even before I had Piers. I'll never leave it, and Henry won't either. So I suppose that means we're rather shackled to one other.'

'Well, lucky Henry,' he said, with a wry half-smile. 'I can think of worse fates than being shackled to such a beautiful woman.'

'Flatterer.'

He shook his head. 'No, I mean it.' Then he picked up her hand, which was wet and soapy with dishwater, and pressed a kiss on it.

Their conversation – and his kiss – remained with her. It comforted her when she felt unhappy, and whenever she recalled it, a fizz of excitement rose in her heart.

*   *   *

They had reached the cheese and port stage of the meal when Helen said, 'I hear poor Molly Brandon has died.'

'How sad,' said Juliet. 'Perhaps I should call.'

'We've never known the Brandons socially.' Henry glared at his crumb of mousetrap cheese. 'I don't plan to start sharing my dinner table with yeoman farmers.'

'Maybe we should.' Jonny looked amused. 'I'd enjoy hearing you make conversation about sheep and pigs, Henry.'

'Farmers and shopkeepers,' Juliet said. 'I can't see much difference.'

'Ha!' cried Jonathan. 'That puts us in our place. You and I, Henry, we're *shopkeepers*.'

'It's ages since I've been to the shop,' mused Jane. 'Perhaps I should come and see my brothers in their green baize aprons.'

Juliet buttered a biscuit. 'I meant, Mr Brandon sells wheat and barley and Winterton's sells emeralds and sapphires. You could say wheat and barley were more useful.'

'But less lucrative.'

'So all that separates us from the Brandons is money.'

'You must forgive my wife's vulgarity.' Henry's contemptuous gaze rested on her. 'Much of her childhood was spent tramping across the desert on a camel. She struggles with polite society.'

Juliet said angrily, 'How can you accuse me of vulgarity, Henry, simply because I mention money? How else do you spend your days other than by making money?'

'Of course, we all need money to live,' said Helen.

'And you like to wear it, my dear,' said Henry silkily.

This was a pointed remark. That night Juliet was wearing round her neck Winterton sapphires, lovely things, a limpid blue, from Kashmir.

'Charles and Marie Barbour dine with us,' she said stiffly. 'And they are farmers. The only difference between the Barbours and the Brandons is that the Barbours have a thousand acres and Mr Brandon' – she had no idea how much land Joe Brandon farmed, so petered out lamely – 'not so much.'

'Juliet dear.' Jonny touched her hand. 'The thing is, Brandon isn't really our sort. He's a bit of a leftie. Perfectly decent fellow, and it's a nice little farm, but there you are.'

The subject of Mr Brandon was dropped. They had finished the bottle of port a grateful patient had given Peter. Alcohol, like cheese, was still in short supply. Jane asked whether there was anything more to drink.

As Jonathan rummaged through the sideboard, Henry said, 'You always could knock it back, Janey.'

Jane looked riled. 'Of course, you're so abstemious.'

'I hold it better.'

'Rot. You drink like a fish, Henry, and then you lose your temper and shout at poor Juliet.'

'Whereas you remain sweetness and light at all times, darling sister.'

'At least I keep a civil tongue in my head.'

'You can screech like a vixen, when it suits you. Especially when you've had a few.'

The way in which Jane straightened, drawing back her head, reminded Juliet of a cobra about to strike. 'How puritanical you've become, Henry,' she hissed. 'At least at Marsh Court.'

Jane's words sank into Juliet's thoughts as Henry gave his sister a thunderous glare. They niggled and hurt, like a stone in a shoe. What did Jane know that Henry had been hiding from her? How humiliating to discover that Jane knew something about Henry of which she was ignorant.

'Shut up, Jane,' said Henry.

'Why should I?'

Peter said, 'Janey.'

Juliet glanced from sister to brother. There was a warning look in Henry's eye.

Helen interrupted. 'We have a bottle of liqueur, don't we, Jonny? We've never opened it, it's probably the most frightful stuff, but it would be fun to try, wouldn't it?'

The liqueur was unearthed, glasses were filled, but the tension remained in the room. Helen made another valiant effort to defuse it. 'How is that new designer of yours, Henry? Jonny tells me he's a marvellous character.'

'Esteban?' muttered Henry. 'He's an awkward bugger.'

'But talented,' said Jonathan. 'Devilish temperamental, even for a foreigner, but by God he knows his stuff. I've put him to work on some of those stones we bought off that chap. Unusual pieces. I might try them out in Colchester first.'

Jane's words were intensifying like a slow poison in Juliet's heart. She wanted to hurt Henry, and she saw her opportunity.

'I thought you were planning to sell the Colchester shop,' she said.

'Henry?' Jonathan, frowning, stared at his brother.

Henry gave her a filthy look. 'Nothing's been decided yet.'

'I should bloody hope not.'

'You can't sell the Colchester shop,' said Jane. 'We've had it for centuries.'

'I can't believe you're even considering it.'

'Henry,' said Helen. 'We've always assumed Colchester would be for Aidan.'

'You can be so tyrannical.'

Henry's fist slammed the table, making the china and silver-ware jump. 'For God's sake, the three of you, stop looking

69

at me as if I'd suggested selling your firstborn sons! Jane, it's nothing to do with you. You sold off your share fifteen years ago.'

'I'm still family,' muttered Jane. 'I still *care* about the business.'

'You're a typical bloody Winterton, shooting your mouth off over something you know nothing about, that's what you are. And *you*.' Henry's furious gaze turned towards Jonathan. 'Have you *looked* at the figures recently? Have you taken the trouble to go to Colchester to see what they're actually selling – or *not* selling? Or have you hidden your head in the sand as usual, leaving the difficult decisions to me?'

Jonathan leaned towards Henry. His voice was quiet and hard. 'You can't sell the shop.'

'I can, Jonny.'

'No. We agreed.'

'That was before the war. Times have changed. Your trouble, Jonny, is that you hate change. You like to pretend that everything is sweet and lovely, just as it always was.'

'Don't treat me like a child.' The warmth and good humour had drained from Jonny's voice.

'Then don't behave like one. I'll find a place for Aidan in Bond Street, I promise.'

'I don't want Aidan to be *found a place*. I want him to have Colchester.'

'No. That's not possible.'

Jane said, 'And what about the twins?' She was always fiercely protective where her children were concerned, especially her eldest, Eliot and Jake, now in their early teens.

Henry's gaze swivelled round to his sister. 'They won't be jewellers, Janey. Neither of them has a creative bone in their body. They'll work in the City, or they'll be sawbones, like Peter.'

Juliet wondered whether Jane would lash out at her brother, but instead her scowl relaxed into a smile and she giggled. 'Oh dear, I'm afraid that's true. Thank goodness for Gabe.' Gabe — short for Gabrielle — was Jane and Peter's daughter. 'Now *she* might do for the business, Henry.'

The party moved into the drawing room. Helen put a record on the gramophone and Jane talked about Gabe's aptitude for ballet. Peter and Juliet sat on the sofa discussing an exhibition they had seen at the National Gallery. The quarrel between the two brothers continued on the other side of the room, Henry raising his voice, Jonathan quietly furious.

Their disagreement lasted until the evening broke up at midnight. As they drove out of town, Henry said softly, 'You bitch.'

Juliet felt a measure of triumph. It was satisfying to have got a reaction from him. But she said with assumed inno-cence, 'What do you mean?'

'You know perfectly well. The shop.'

'How was I to know you hadn't discussed it with Jonny?'

He took a corner too fast, forcing her to grab the dash-board. 'How was I to know you'd see fit to broadcast my private business at the dinner table?'

'I didn't think you'd keep something like that from Jonny.'

'*Liar.* You know I don't tell him everything. If I did, the business would still be mouldering in its Victorian past.'

Another tight corner, taken at speed. 'Stop it,' she said angrily. 'Slow down. You'll kill us both if you go on like this. You'd have had to tell him some day.'

'But not *tonight*.' Henry rammed his foot on the accelerator. 'And not in front of my blasted *sister*.'

They reached Marsh Court and he swung the Jaguar

through the gates. When they climbed out of the car, the cold air stung Juliet's face.

Indoors, she paid Meg for babysitting and waved her off on her bicycle. When she closed the front door behind her, she felt as if she was shutting herself in with the violence of Henry's rage. She did not go to the drawing room for a post-dinner drink, as was their habit after a night out. She wasn't prepared to be conciliating or to ask his forgiveness. Instead, she went upstairs to check that the children slept soundly, and then to her own bedroom.

She had changed into her nightgown and was struggling to unfasten the sapphire necklace when Henry came upstairs. She felt his strong hands brush against her neck as he undid the clasp.

He said, 'Don't ever try to show me up in front of my family again, Juliet.'

'Why not?' She swung round to face him. 'You do it to me.'

He laid the necklace in its white velvet box. 'Ah, but we made a bargain, you and I.'

'A bargain?'

'Marsh Court and a comfortable, easy life for you. All you have to do in return is put up with me.'

'You mean, let you behave like a tyrant. Jane was right, you are tyrannical.'

'And you are a fool.' His tone was biting. 'I don't care what you do so long as it doesn't affect the family. The only thing that matters is to keep the family together. I won't allow you to get in the way of that, Juliet.'

She said bitterly, 'There are other ways of keeping families together.'

'And what's that?'

'Love. You do it with love. Not by pitting people against each other. Nor by keeping secrets from them.'

Henry unknotted his tie. His lip curled. 'I don't want your love, your sugary, sentimental love. It blurs the vision and rots the judgement. Analyse it and you'll find it's made up of egotism and delusion and self-interest and lust. Nothing else.'

She climbed into bed. She was sick of their quarrel by then and regretted having provoked it. But she would have hated to let him have the last word.

'At least I'm capable of loving.'

'Oh, you're hardly an expert. It's not as though you married me for love.'

'I have tried to love you.'

'But you don't, do you?'

'It's you, Henry, you who make it so impossible!'

'Hypocrite.' He bared his teeth. 'You married me because you needed a meal ticket and a way out of Cairo.'

The scorn in his voice made her hate him all over again. 'You're right,' she said coldly. 'How could I love you? How could anyone love you? You're impossible to love.'

'And you're the same. Beneath that sweetly pretty exterior, you're as hard as nails.'

It infuriated her that he should label her as cynical and unfeeling as himself. 'I have nothing in common with you!' she cried.

He was standing at the end of the bed, watching her. He gave a sardonic smile. 'You've got a brain, Juliet, though you don't choose to use it very often. That day we met in the jeweller's shop in Cairo, I saw something in you that I recognised. There you were, bargaining over your pearls, refusing to let that crook get the better of you. You were coarse and

73

uneducated, but I knew there was something there, something we had in common, that I could use. In your own way, you're as calculating and greedy as I am.'

'Dear God!' she cried. 'Piers and I were so much happier when you were away!'

His face went the colour of putty and she knew that she had wounded him. But after a moment he responded coolly, 'I can sympathise with that. A week or two in your company, my dear, and I find it a relief to return to London.'

How puritanical you've become, Henry. At least at Marsh Court. She had not forgotten Jane's jibe, and in her hurt and fury she screamed at him.

'And who do you see there, Henry? Who is she?'

'Control yourself,' he said sharply. 'You're becoming hysterical.'

'What did Jane mean? What does she *know*?'

'Jane was making trouble.' He flung his cufflinks into a dish on the chest of drawers. 'She was drunk and she was bored – that's Jane.'

Juliet knelt up in bed. 'I don't believe you. Tell me. I insist that you tell me!'

Henry frowned. 'Are you sure? Are you quite sure? I had you down as a woman who prefers to turn a blind eye to certain things. But if you insist, I'm afraid Jane saw me with Teddie.'

'Teddie?' she repeated blankly.

'Yes, that's her name.'

And such a ridiculous name, she found herself thinking. To be pushed aside by a woman called *Teddie*. 'This woman . . .' Her voice faltered. 'She's your mistress?'

'Yes, you could call her that.'

'How . . .' It was hard to get the words out. 'How long?'

74

'A few months. It's not important.'

'It's important to *me*!'

Immediately, she regretted saying that. It only added to her humiliation. He was looking at her as if she was a curious, pitiable object he had found washed up on a beach.

'Teddie's a sweet girl,' he said. 'She doesn't make a fuss, never asks for too much, but she's beginning to bore me, so I doubt if I'll see her again. You may make a scene if you wish, Juliet, but I don't choose to witness it, so I shall sleep in my dressing room tonight.'

He left the room.

Juliet lay awake, longing for the oblivion of sleep but unable to find it. Eventually she went downstairs and prepared a cup of cocoa, hoping it would make her drowsy. It was cold in the kitchen, so she put on an old duffel coat over her nightgown and dressing gown. Then she went to sit in the morning room, her favourite room in the house. She pulled back the curtains from the French doors; outside, a wash of silver moonlight sketched out the shapes of the trees and the sheds and the gardener's cottage that lay to one side of the garden.

She could open the doors, she thought, cross the terrace and the lawn, and walk across the fields to the estuary. She could keep on walking until she was far, far away from Henry, so that she never had to see him again.

But she couldn't, of course. There were the children, sleeping upstairs. There was Marsh Court, her home. There was Helen and Jonny and Jane and Peter and the Sinclairs, her family and friends.

She wondered whether she had the right to feel such shock and grief. She had known for a long time that she and

75

Henry did not love each other. And yet her world had turned upside-down that night, and her future seemed strange and unfamiliar and tinged with menace. Perhaps Henry had been right in describing her as someone who chose to avert her gaze from the truth. Perhaps she was like Jonathan and preferred to bury her head in the sand.

She had been under no illusion that theirs was a good marriage. If pressed, she would have said that it was kept together by Henry's desire for her and his need for a wife to run Marsh Court, and by her own need for security and a home. And by the children, of course. That Henry was bedding another woman made her realise how fragile her self-assurance was, and how greatly it rested on her belief that she was, at least, young and desirable. Now she felt unsure even of that. A new torment occurred to her: that Teddie had not been the first one. That there had been others before her, sweet, unfussy girls whom Henry had dropped as soon as they bored him.

They had married on a whim; they had both thought they had seen something in each other that had turned out not to be true. Since then, they had endured disappointment and dissent, and they had not been kind to each other. They knew each other too well now, she thought. They had learned how to wound. *You're as calculating and greedy as I am . . . We were so much happier when you were away.* Such thoughts should not be voiced. They would never go away, and would lurk in dark corners like spiders, creeping out now and then to stab in their poison.

Another discovery: that until now, she had held on to a grain of hope that their marriage would right itself, that Henry would mellow or she herself would settle for something less than love. Her gaze on the moon-grey garden, she accepted that would never happen, and that they would always be at war, and that she must spend the rest of her life longing for something she could never have. She was not a contentious person, she did not thrive on quarrels as Henry did, and had only to look at Jonny and Helen to know that marriage could offer something that was both comforting and delightful.

Nor would Henry change. He would always be contemptuous of her and would never be capable of offering her solace or affection. Perhaps, at heart, he didn't think much of women. He might share the Winterton love of the arts, but in his other tastes he was a man's man, and the company of men suited him well. Whatever she did, however hard she tried, she would not win his approval. If she was to survive this marriage, then she must take responsibility for assuaging her own loneliness.

And it was that which was so hard to bear, the knowledge that she must be denied for ever the support and comfort that other wives took for granted. Henry thought her calculating and greedy, but he was mistaken. He did not know her as well as he thought he did. She was capable of loving a man with all her heart. She could have given herself to him with adoration and passion, had he only loved her in return. Why was it that the only Winterton she had not come to love was her husband?

She finished her cocoa and went upstairs. She must have dozed off, because at five o'clock she was woken by Charlotte's cry. She made up a bottle and took the baby with her to bed. Charley was still feeding when Juliet heard Henry rise and go downstairs. A short while later, the throaty rumble of the Jaguar burst into life and then faded as the car headed out of the drive.

When Charley had finished, Juliet changed her nappy and then snuggled back under the blankets with the baby in her arms. Charlotte cried a little, warm and heavy on her mother's breast, and Juliet cried too, her hand caressing her daughter's velvety head. She was crying because she had married the wrong man and because the decision she had made years ago in Cairo had denied her that most beautiful and precious thing: love.

That afternoon, in a small act of rebellion, she wrote a letter of condolence to Mr Brandon at Greensea Farm. She didn't care that he was only a yeoman farmer – and a leftie to boot. She felt sorry for him, widowed so young. Perhaps his marriage had been a good one. Perhaps he and his Molly had loved each other.

Chapter Five

October–November 1946

The storm that came into life at the end of October rocked the bus in which Juliet and Piers travelled home from Maldon after school. The treetops flung themselves back and forth and fallen branches leaped and thwacked across the road, causing the driver to brake sharply. When they reached Marsh Court, they dashed through sheeting rain into the house. Henry was in London; after their return, Mrs Barrett, who had been minding Charley, put on a mackintosh and went home. While Piers was eating his tea, Juliet walked round the house making sure the windows were closed and the doors to the outside bolted. Pulling a skylight shut on the top floor, she saw a bolt of lightning split the sky in two.

While she fed Charley, Piers stood at the kitchen window until the sky darkened, mesmerised by the sheeting rain. The spaniel whined, cowering under the table, and Piers flinched at the rumble of the thunder. Once the baby was bathed and in bed, Juliet helped Piers with his homework and then played a game of Ludo with him. Then it was bedtime.

Twenty minutes later, she went upstairs to check that both children were asleep. As she left Piers's room, the electricity cut out, plunging the corridor into darkness. Using the banister to guide her, she made her way downstairs, and took a torch out of a drawer in the hall. Power failures were not an uncommon occurrence at Marsh Court, so they kept plenty of torches and candles. In the storeroom, she changed the wire in the fuse box, but to no avail. The darkness seemed to have sunk into the fabric of the house and her torch made only a feeble disc of light. She wondered whether the gale had brought down a power line.

She lit the drawing room fire and arranged half a dozen candles on the mantelpiece and side table. Then she took out her mending box and settled down by the fire. She wished she had the radio to distract her from the howl of the wind and the lashing rain. Now and then a branch, torn from a tree by the violence of the gale, would strike the roof, sending a mad clattering through the house. She listened out for the sound of falling tiles. Lightning illuminated the room with its weird, eldritch light.

Squinting, she threaded her needle and began to sew.

The previous day, Frances had phoned him at the office; he hated her to do that. She was lonely, she had told him, she was going mad in that bloody place. He had soothed her by promising to come to the island the next day.

He had been late setting off from London, detained by some last-minute business in Parliament. Then the storm had slowed his journey, washing puddles across the road and forcing him to skirt round fallen branches. The weather grew more violent as he drove closer to Maldon. The gale had blown in from the North Sea; it had that icy greyness.

Parking the car, Gillis had to hold on to his hat to prevent it being torn from his head by the wind. When he reached the river, he discovered that the tide was in. He had asked Frances to check the tide tables – but, typical of her, she had got it wrong. She had been living on the island for six months now – how hard was it to remember that there was a tide every twelve hours?

He caught sight of a huddle of men on the mudflats. He headed towards them and spoke to one. A woman had drowned, the man told him. A birdwatcher, walking back to the town, had found her.

A terrible foreboding: a shard of ice pierced his heart. As they cleared aside to permit access to the men with stretchers, he saw her lying in the mud. Her white skin, that he had once loved to caress, was already turning blue, and her long red hair was dirtied by the river weed caught up in it.

Somehow he stopped himself crying out. He took a step towards her, but his neighbour grabbed his arm. *Don't look. If you're not used to it . . .*

He was used to it, of course. Yet the bodies that had bobbed in the sea at Dunkirk had been unfamiliar to him. There had been a time when he had loved every inch of Frances's body, and in that desolate place he recalled all the desire and affection he had ever felt for her. Awash with guilt and regret, he swayed as if buffeted by the wind, then pressed his knuckles against his teeth as he swallowed back the bile that scorched his throat. *He* had brought her to this accursed place. *He* had abandoned her there – careless, incompetent Frances, who couldn't understand a tide table. *He* was to blame.

The man beside him was still talking. The woman was a Mrs Hart, he said, and she had lived on Thorney Island. They were searching for her two children. They had looked in the house but they were not there.

The children . . . As they loaded Frances's body on to the stretcher and carried it away, Gillis took off his hat, as did the other men on the bank. Then he moved back, retching violently as he reached the long grass, shock and horror turning him inside out. The children – where were the children? In his mind's eye he saw them bobbing in the river, borne out by the Blackwater to the North Sea. God forgive him: he knew that he would never be able to forgive himself.

When the last paroxysm was over, he turned up his face to the rain to cool it, letting it wash the tears away. He took a swig from the hip flask in his pocket and strode off from the group on the shore. All along the Blackwater, men were tramping across salt marsh and islets, swinging their torches, calling out for Edmund and Thea. Gillis, too, swept his torch frantically over the drenched landscape, desperately searching for a flash of the boy's blonde hair, or the red of the girl's favourite dress. The storm whipped at him. He had lost his hat and his coat was sodden. The gale blew back at him the names that screamed from his throat, mocking him.

Juliet was reaching for another sock to darn when she heard a loud hammering, making her start and drop her needle. At first she wondered whether it was a new trick of the wind, but then she rose, grabbed the torch and dashed to the front door. Who would call at such a time on so dreadful a night? She pulled back the bolt.

Gillis Sinclair was standing on the step. The wind lashed at his uncovered head. His face was uplit by the torch he held in one hand, and his expression was agonised.

'Juliet,' he said. Then he half fell against her.

As she helped him to the drawing room and into the chair

by the fire, she felt him trembling. Rain peeled from his mackintosh to the floor.

Quickly she poured out a measure of whisky and pressed it into his hands. His eyes were wide and staring and he was shaking visibly.

'Gillis,' she said gently. 'You're soaked. Let me help you out of your wet things.'

She pulled off his gloves and put them on the fireguard. She was frightened for him. As well as being drenched through, he seemed absent in spirit. She wondered whether he was ill.

'Something terrible has happened,' he said.

She took his hand. 'Tell me.'

'A woman's been drowned in the Blackwater. And her children . . .' He pressed his fingers against his mouth as a shudder ran through his body. 'At Thorney Island. They found her on the mudflats.'

'Oh Gillis, how dreadful.' She could hardly bear to think of it.

He made a violent, convulsive movement and covered his face with his hands. 'I saw her lying there. So white. If it hadn't been for that, you'd have thought she was sleeping.'

'And the children?'

'Half the town's out, trying to find them. I've been helping to search for them.' Quickly, he rose from the chair.

She would have feared for his health had he insisted on going out into the storm again. 'The police and the coast-guard will find them,' she said firmly. 'You've done enough, Gillis.'

For a moment his eyes focused erratically on her, then they jerked towards the door. 'Henry isn't here, is he?'

'No, he's in London.'

'Your housekeeper?'

'She's gone home.'

'May I use your phone? I drove here because I wanted to call in briefly at the boatyard, but the storm's blocked the road.'

He went into the hall. Juliet assumed he was calling Blanche, to tell her that he had been delayed by the storm, but then she heard his raised voice. 'For God's sake, man, whichever way you can!' The words became inaudible again.

When he came back into the room, she said, 'Gillis, you must stay here tonight.'

'Yes . . . thank you, Juliet.'

A sudden flash illuminated the room, so that it was for a moment as bright as day. A deafening roll of thunder was accompanied by a dreadful rending, crashing sound that made the old house tremble. 'Oh God, Gillis!' she cried, and then she was in his arms, and he was holding her, comforting her in her terror.

And then they kissed. Her tremors had a different cause – desperation, yearning and delight, these were the emotions that shuddered through her, and she knew that he felt the same, because his fingertips dug into her hair, making pinpoints of pain as he crushed her against him, and his mouth moved over hers, searching and urgent, as he kissed her again and again. She was drowning in the rainwater that the storm had soaked into his skin: she tasted it on his lips and on his tongue. It soaked into her clothing, her hair and skin. And she was drowning in the heat and strength and power of him, and she forgot that they were both married to other people, and forgot, to her shame, the poor dead woman and her lost children, and would have kissed him for ever.

A voice from behind her cried, 'Mummy!' and she gasped and Gillis let her go.

Piers was standing in the doorway. 'Mummy, I'm frightened!'

'Darling . . .' She went to him and took him in her arms, trembling as she brushed back his hair from his face. 'Darling, it's all right. It's only the silly old thunder. You mustn't worry.'

She heard Gillis speak. 'Is the key to the cottage in the usual place?'

'Yes.' She struggled to make her voice sound normal. 'I think the grate's made up. You must help yourself to food and candles, take whatever you want, Gillis.'

As he left the room, their eyes met and she thought she saw the ghost of a smile reach his lips. She carried Piers upstairs. She was settling him back in bed when she heard Gillis start up his car to drive the short distance to the cottage.

That night, awake and listening to the scream of the wind, she thought of their kiss, but also of the drowned woman, and prayed that her children might be found safe and well. She remembered the little boy, whose voice had carried across the river to her, and the girl in her red dress.

The tempest did not ease until three in the morning. She went to check on Piers and Charley a couple of times, but they slept soundly. Before going back to her room, she peered out of one of the upstairs windows, trying to see the cottage, but the rain and the darkness hid everything from her.

She must have eventually fallen asleep, because when she woke, the room had lightened. In place of the clamour of the gale, the silence seemed to resound, to pulse like waves lapping a shore. She warmed Charley's bottle and then went back to the nursery to give her her early-morning feed. Then she settled her in her cot, dressed and went downstairs to the kitchen, where she made toast and a flask of cocoa, wrapping them in a tea towel to keep them warm.

She put on a mackintosh and wellingtons and went outside. The pale blue sky shimmered, as luminous as a star sapphire. She saw that the great willow tree that had stood to one side of the house had been felled during the night, by the same thunderclap that had sent her into Gillis's arms, she guessed. Its trunk had been splintered to matchwood and the branches cast over the lawn like the spars of a beached ship. Twigs and fallen leaves were strewn across the path to the cottage, and beads of rain glistened on the wet grass, winking and refracting like jewels. Light-headed from happiness and from lack of sleep, she drifted through Marsh Court's garden as if in a dream. The fresh, cool air was sharp in her lungs and her feet seemed hardly to touch the ground as she floated like thistledown towards the cottage.

But he had gone. She knew it before she opened the door, and disappointment washed over her. His car was no longer there; he must have driven home during the night, while she was asleep. He must have had to head back in the early hours, she thought, because of his work.

Inside the cottage, she closed her eyes for a moment, imagining that Gillis was with her. She pictured him refreshed by sleep, taking her in his arms and kissing her. She hungered for him – had done so, she discovered, for a long time. She wondered how long she had loved him, and at the blindness that had prevented her from seeing it. When she examined her heart, it seemed to her that love had sparked the first time they had met, when she had seen him through the smoke of her bonfire, walking towards her from the marshes.

Her fear was that the drama of the storm had acted as a

86

spark to a passion that he might have chosen in more ordinary circumstances to hide. And if that was so, what would she do? Would she wait by the phone, her hopes slowly crushed by the passing of time?

No. She knew that she would not. She could not regret what had taken place between them, could not regret that she had glimpsed love at last.

They found the body of the boy later that day, carried out by the tide to Bradwell Creek. The drowned woman had been a Mrs Frances Hart, Meg told her, and she had been renting the house on Thorney Island since the spring. The children, Edmund and Thea, had been twins, not quite five years old. It was assumed that they had been playing on the causeway and that perhaps they had been swept out by the tide and the mother had waded out to try to save them. These things happened. Only the previous year, a man had drowned trying to rescue his dog, which had fallen into the river from the harbour wall.

The search for Thea Hart continued, though with each passing day the hope that she might be found alive became more frail. When Juliet walked beside the Blackwater, she scanned the creeks and mudflats, looking for a child's shoe or the rags of a red dress. It haunted her that the girl had been lost without a trace. A few times she dreamed of her, swept out of the estuary and bobbing in the North Sea, a flicker of red becoming smaller and smaller in the tall grey waves until it could no longer be seen at all.

A chilly afternoon. A soft drizzle darkened the paths and greyed the lawns of Hyde Park. A sound, and Juliet looked up, but it was only two youths, running through the rain, splashing in the puddles. Hooting at each other, they disappeared behind the trees.

Gillis had arranged to meet her beside Jacob Epstein's sculpture of 'Rima'. She knew why he had chosen this out-of-the-way place, of course. Gillis Sinclair had a public face. He was young, attractive, and had always been notable. He was not a man you would look at and forget.

Perhaps she should walk away now. Her hands fisted and nerves made her belly ache. If she were to stay here – if they were to meet – it would spark off a series of betrayals. Gillis was Henry's friend. Blanche Sinclair was a family friend of the Wintertons. Gillis was godfather to Piers, as Henry was to Claudia Sinclair. The two families were bound together by affection and years of friendship.

She should go, she thought, before it was too late.

And yet she stayed. She understood then that she had made her choice, and that she had chosen love. There was no pleasure in the realisation; instead, it exhausted her, and she sank into the shadows of the dark, dripping trees, her fingers working at the knot of her scarf. She had taken no particular care with her appearance that day and was wearing an old bottle-green coat, a Hermès scarf from her trousseau, and a plain black hat. A dash of lipstick, a spray of perfume.

Looking up, she caught sight of him, and in that instant all her doubts and reservations slipped away. Love flared inside her like a flame and she felt a trembling joy. He came towards her out of the wet green grass and the fine silvery rain, wrapping his arms round her. A quick glance over his shoulder, and then they kissed. His mouth was cool and dry and his tongue flickered along the inner rim of her lower lip. When, at last, they broke apart, he cupped her face in his hands.

'You're so beautiful. And so adorable.'

'And so are you. I love you, Gillis.' She took such delight in saying it out loud.

'Do you?' He laughed. 'Then that's good, because I love you too.'

They held hands as they walked across the park to the gate. 'A friend of mine has a flat in Pimlico,' he told her. 'Shall we go there?' And as they made their way out of the park, his thumb pressed against her palm, as if he was already trying to reach inside her.

Outside the Pimlico flat, the dead brown stems of the Michaelmas daisies in the window box were crushed up against a low, barred basement window. When Gillis unlocked the door to the flat, the smell of dustbins wafted in with them.

Juliet looked round. The prints on the walls were second-rate, the objects on the shelves ill-matched and dusty. She recognised the place for what it was: someone's faded love nest.

'It's rather chilly, isn't it?' he said.

'Rather.'

'Shall I put the fire on?'

'That would be nice.'

This was a mistake, she thought. Here they were, cardboard characters in a poorly scripted film. She should go home.

The gas fire gave a muffled puff and burst into life. She stooped, warming her fingers.

'Shall I see if I can find us a drink?' he said.

'No, I'm fine.'

'Have you warmed up now?' He took her hands, pressing them against his cheeks. Then he turned her palm towards him and kissed it.

She drew in a breath. The stroke of a fingertip, a fleeting pressure, a caress: all these were better than words. He led her into the bedroom, where he hung his jacket on the back of a chair and took off his shirt. She saw his long, lean white limbs and the muscular triangle of his torso. A jagged scar snaked around his right shoulder.

She tried to work out what it was that made her want him so much, whether it was the angle of his smile or the cloudy blue of his eyes, or something else that she couldn't quite identify. As he unbuttoned her dress, pulling it over her head, and then unpeeled her slip, his lips parted and he knelt to kiss the strip of skin between her stocking tops and her knickers. She shuddered, needing him. He pulled back the sheet and they climbed into bed. His body was hard against hers as his fingers explored the heaviness of her breast and the hollow beneath her hipbone. And when his palm moved down her belly to the soft, secret place between her thighs, she was hardly able to breathe.

Part Two

An Occasional Lover

1957

Chapter Six

Aidan was painting the harbour at Maldon. The tide was in and a Thames barge was sailing downriver, a huge beast eighty feet in length, flat-bottomed, rust-red sails belling as it tacked. The sun drew darts of light from the umber water of the estuary. His brush moved over the paper.

He became aware that someone was watching him. A girl – tallish, slim – was looking over his shoulder at his easel. She was pale-skinned, and her long, straight hair was a silvery blonde.

'It's wonderful,' she said. She pronounced the word 'wunnerful'.

'The masts aren't right.'

'You've gotten the light, though.' She came closer and pointed. 'This section . . . the movement of the water . . . is real good. Are you a professional artist?'

'No.' He laughed. 'Not likely.'

'You should be,' she said seriously. 'Are you going to art school?'

'No.' This was a sore point, and he added, 'I wish I was.'

'Why don't you?'

'Because I'm about to be called up for National Service.'
He grimaced. 'Two years doing drill, being yelled at by
some angry bloke who can't stand middle-class arty types
like me.'

'But afterwards.'

She was persistent, he thought, as if she was personally
responsible for his future. 'Afterwards,' he said, 'I'll work
for the family firm.'

'That's awful.'

That was what he thought too, privately. He wondered
whether she was an artist herself – she was wearing what
he thought of as a beatnik get-up: a tartan skirt of some
hairy fabric, and a black jersey and black stockings, though
it was July.

He said, 'Do you paint?'

'I sketch a little, but I have no gift for it. My father, John
Carlisle, is an artist. He's a constructivist. He's worked with
wood and glass in the past and he's looking at plastics right
now. Charles Biederman is one of his influences. Though Dad
says if you look back far enough, you always get to Mondrian.'

'You're American, aren't you?'

'I was born in San Francisco. We lived there till I was
eleven, when my parents were divorced. Then Dad and I
moved to London.'

There had been a bloke at school whose parents were
divorced, who had been regarded by the other boys with a
mixture of distaste and envy at the aura of scandal that had
clung to him. But this girl spoke matter-of-factly, as if it was
normal, rather than shameful, to have divorced parents.

He offered his hand to her. 'I'm Aidan Winterton.'

'Anne Carlisle.' Her fingers were small and slender, her
skin cool, and as she shook his hand, she gave a gentle

smile. Close to, he saw that her eyes were an extraordinary colour, grey with flecks of a lighter shade, like chips of glass.

'Do you live round here, Aidan?'

'In the high street. You?'

'I'm staying with friends in Heybridge. My father had to go back to the US to sort things out with my mom. I'm to fly over to join him sometime.'

'Have you any brothers and sisters?'

'No, there's only me. Have you?'

'A sister, Louise. And I've dozens of cousins. There's Piers and Charley at Marsh Court, a few miles away. And Jake and Eliot and Gabe in St Albans. And the Sinclairs – Flavia and Claudia and Nate and Rory – they're not officially cousins, but they might as well be.' With Piers away, life seemed quiet. Aunt Juliet had taken Louise and Charley for a seaside holiday in Cornwall, so there weren't many Wintertons around, an unusual state of affairs. The place was usually crawling with them.

'Jeez,' she said. 'What a list. I have cousins on my mother's side, but I hardly even know their names.'

He said in a world-weary tone, 'Actually, it gets a bit much. Sometimes you get sick of the sight of them.'

'You say that because you don't know what it's like not to have much of a family. Mostly, it's only Dad and me. You must have such wonderful times.'

Faced with her earnestness and sincerity, he felt rather cheap. 'Piers is the same age as me,' he said. 'We went to the same school.'

'What's he like?'

'Piers?' Aidan grinned. 'He's clever, I suppose. And funny, when he's in the mood. Likes a quarrel – even if he doesn't think something is true, he pretends he does, so as not to agree with you.'

'Cussed, you mean.'

'Yeah.' The word suited Piers, Aidan thought. 'Cussed. His sister Charley is on holiday in Cornwall right now with my sister Louise. Piers is in New York, with my Uncle Henry.'

'New York? They'll have such a great time.'

'I could have gone with them.' He wasn't sure why he had told her that: perhaps to prevent her from thinking him countrified and clod-hopping.

Her strange grey eyes widened. 'But Aidan, why didn't you?'

He shrugged. 'Other things to do. Have you been there?'

'Plenty of times. It's such fun.'

Now she thought him stupid and unadventurous. He tried to explain.

'I finished school a fortnight ago. I mean, completely finished, for ever. I'm waiting for my call-up papers, so this is my last summer of freedom.'

'And you wanted to get some painting done, go where you want to go. Yes, I see that.' She took a couple of steps back. 'Look, I've taken up too much of your time already. I'll leave you in peace.'

'No.' He reddened, then cleared his throat. 'Have you been to St Peter's Chapel? It's near Bradwell-on-Sea. It's one of my favourite places.' He was gabbling now; he sounded ridiculous.

But she said, 'Are you thinking of going there?'

'Yes. Do some painting. Birdwatching . . .' Oh God, shut up. *Birdwatching.*

'Aidan, I'd simply adore to see it.'

His self-consciousness disappeared, and the heat drained from his face. 'There's a bus from Maldon at nine fifteen,' he said. 'Then you have to walk a bit.'

'I've a car.'

Of course she had a car: she was American. He let out a breath. 'You'll drive?'

'Sure.'

'Then that's great,' he said.

Though it was true that part of his reason for turning down the trip to New York had been because he had wanted some time to himself, he had also been unable to face ten days listening to Piers and Uncle Henry stabbing each other with words, trying to draw blood. Piers might enjoy picking an argument with Aidan, but on the whole their fallings-out were not ill-natured – partly, Aidan acknowledged, because he rarely cared as much as Piers did, and so often let him have his own way. With Uncle Henry, Piers could be mean-spirited. Piers resented his father, and it showed.

Aidan's disagreements with his own father had so far been limited to occasional protests about being required to stay in with Louise when his parents had gone out for the evening. He loved his father, but could quite see that Uncle Henry must be a lot harder to love. He and Dad hadn't even argued about art school – there had been a conversation, and then Aidan had accepted what he had known was inevitable. He had said yes, it would be fine working for Winterton's, even though inside he had felt as if he was dying.

Only to Louise had he expressed how he really felt. She was barely twelve, but a good listener.

'Poor Aidan,' she had said. 'But you can come to my house at the weekend. You'll be able to paint and I'll look after the donkeys.'

Louise had been planning the house in which she intended to live when she was grown-up since she was about three.

It would be in the countryside, near the river. She felt sorry for the donkeys she saw in farmers' fields, and planned to rescue the thin, mangy creatures and keep them in comfort.

The following morning, Anne Carlisle picked him up from the high street. She was driving a little British car, and instead of the hairy tartan skirt and black jersey she had on pale blue cotton slacks, cut off at the knee, and a white blouse. Her feet, in their leather sandals, were bare. As they headed along the Bradwell road, she told him about her plans for the future. She was going to start a secretarial course in September. Once she had good shorthand and typing, she would be able to work anywhere. She intended to find a job in an art gallery. She knew a lot about modern art, had lived with artists all her life.

She wasn't a chatterer and neither was Aidan, and there were times when he found their silences awkward. Her smiles were rare and lovely, and he couldn't resist cracking jokes to court them. She gave his flippant remarks the same consideration she gave to their more serious conversation, and after a while, feeling foolish, he stopped trying to be funny.

Reaching Bradwell-on-Sea, they drove through the village and then along the Roman road that led out of it. Where the road petered into a rutted track, Anne parked the car and they got out. The verges sparkled with ox-eye daisies, sky-blue chicory and scarlet poppies. Aidan had always loved this outpost of the far east of England, with its vast sea and sky and land that dissolved into saltings and mudflats, as if it couldn't decide whether it was solid or liquid. The chapel, which must have seen so much, incorporated into its structure parts of the walls of the old Roman fort of Othona.

'Where I come from,' Anne said, as they walked round

the building, 'we think a house is old if it's stood for more than fifty years. When we first moved to England, I thought it was kind of dingy and old-fashioned. Now I like it.'

They cut away from the chapel, walking along the sea wall beside the salt marsh. Anne had tied her hair back in a pony-tail, which bounced as she walked. It was of so light a shade that the Winterton blonde seemed tarnished in comparison, and Aidan was aware of a fierce desire to touch its smooth silkiness. Her hips swayed as she walked the uneven ground. Beneath the cut-off slacks, her calves and ankles were slim and tanned.

Piers claimed to have had half a dozen girlfriends. He also claimed to have done it with two of them, though Aidan didn't know whether to believe him. Aidan himself had been out with groups of friends that included girls – and once on a spectacularly awful and embarrassing double date arranged by Piers with two local girls, who had giggled and whispered to each other all the time – but he had not yet had an actual girlfriend. Boarding school, and his own lack of confidence, hadn't helped, and he had realised, on the awful double date, that he didn't want to kiss just anyone. Piers said he had done it with a girl he had known for only a couple of hours. The thought of such sudden intimacy repelled Aidan, though he would never have admitted that to Piers, who would have made fun of him.

They stopped and took out their sketchpads. The sunlight was a fierce glare on the narrow strip of sea beyond marsh-land and mudflat. Half a mile out, men scoured the shell beach for cockles. Aidan noticed Anne's silence and the depth of her concentration. After a few conversational forays, he did not feel obliged to talk either and focused on his work instead.

After half an hour she put away her pencils. He said, 'May I?' and she passed him her sketchbook.

'It's good,' he said.

'You don't have to be polite. That's good.' She nodded towards his watercolour, all blurry browns and greys. 'I don't mind.' She put her sketchbook in her knapsack. 'I'm good at other things.'

'What sort of things?'

She gave him one of her rare smiles. 'I've organised my father's last few shows. And whenever he has to travel, I book his plane and train tickets and find him a hotel. When his friends come to stay, I make sure they have somewhere comfortable to sleep. Sometimes ten of them turn up at once.'

'That must be difficult.'

'No, not at all. We all go out to eat and have such wonderful times. And they're artists, so they're used to having nothing much, and they're not picky.'

He thought how exciting and sophisticated her life sounded, artists appearing on her doorstep and having to be found a place to sleep in some presumably bohemian house in Chelsea or Fitzrovia. His own existence seemed stuffy and dull in comparison.

She said, 'Isn't there some way you can persuade your parents to let you go to art college, Aidan?'

'No,' he said shortly, and lay back on the grass, his head cushioned in his hands.

'I'm sorry, I don't mean to intrude. It's just . . . a waste.'

'My family haven't got much money. My father made some bad investments, so things are rather tight.'

He had never told anyone this before. Wintertons thought discussing money vulgar. Even Piers didn't know, but then

Piers could be remarkably incurious about anyone other than himself.

'My dad's been ill,' he said. 'Something to do with his heart. He's had to cut down his hours at work. Louise is still at school and my mother doesn't go out to work or anything, so I need to help out as soon as I can. And artists don't make any money, do they?'

'No, not really. Or not for years and years. Dad has to pay a lot of alimony to my mom, and until a few years ago, he didn't sell many pieces. Then a gallery in London offered to represent him, and since then it's been easier. But we were always okay. We've never starved.'

Aidan knew the sort of things his parents worried about, had overheard them talking late at night. Cars that needed replacing, and Louise's school fees, and repairs to the roof of their Georgian house.

He said, 'Not starving won't do for my family. They think it's awful that they don't have a housemaid any more. Every stick of furniture in our house has been inherited from someone or other. When Rory set fire to the sofa – he's just a kid, he didn't mean to, he was fooling about with matches – and they had to buy another one, it was the first time they'd been inside a furniture shop in their entire lives.'

Rolling up on to an elbow, she considered him with her serious grey gaze.

'You try to protect them, don't you, Aidan?'

'Yes,' he said. 'I suppose I do.'

In Mevagissey, Charley had spent all her holiday money on a figurine of a ballerina with a white plaster leotard and net tutu. On the day they returned to Marsh Court, she dropped it on her bedroom floor and one of the ballerina's legs broke off. Charley wept buckets, and Louise, who had neat fingers (Charley was afraid she herself had very messy fingers), glued it back on. It didn't look quite the same, which made Charley feel mournful, but she thanked her cousin and let her talk about the donkey sanctuary.

Aunt Helen came to collect Louise. 'Darling, you look so brown!' she said, and kissed her. 'And you too, Charley. Did you have a wonderful time?'

Charley's mother said, 'Louise, why don't you go and check you have all your belongings together? Charley, give Louise a hand.' Just before the door closed, Charley heard her mother say in a low voice to Aunt Helen, 'And Jonny? How is he?' Soon afterwards, Aunt Helen drove Louise home.

Charley went out into the garden. Biscuit, their very old springer spaniel, trotted along behind her. She felt at rather a loose end, and though she visited all her favourite places – the orchard, the fire pit and the creek where Piers kept his boat – the melancholy remained with her. She thought there should be a special word for the sadness you felt after a holiday had ended, and she lay on the grass on top of the sea wall, with Biscuit lying on top of her and panting noisily into her face, and tried to think what it should be.

She wished Piers and Dad were home. It was so unfair that Piers should go to New York when she had only been to boring old Cornwall. And he hadn't even sent a postcard. She hadn't expected one: Piers was hopeless at things like postcards. She was looking forward to telling him about her new play. He never looked bored when she read out her plays, never had that distracted look her mother sometimes had, which made Charley suspect she was thinking of something else. Charley had written the first two scenes when she was in Mevagissey. The heroine, Lady Anthea, was deliciously

102

wicked. Charley had thought up lots of exploits for her, but Piers might be able to think of better ones. Louise had been useless at thinking of evil deeds for Lady Anthea, because Louise hadn't a wicked or jealous bone in her body.

She gave Biscuit a shove and skulked along the inside of the sea wall, pretending that she was in the Resistance. She wished it was the end of August, because then Nate and Rory would be at Marsh Court. Nate had curly black hair and greenish-blue eyes and looked like a gypsy. He was terribly good at everything, and because of that, terribly conceited. He had taught her how to bowl overarm and had showed her how to do a very complicated knot called an anchor hitch.

Charley went back to the house. Her mother was at her desk in the morning room, frowning over a piece of paper pencilled with a diagram made up of circles.

'What are you doing, Mum?'

Her mother let out a sigh. 'My seating plan for the concert. It's always such a nightmare.'

'Can't they just sit anywhere?'

'No, I'm afraid not.' Her mother put down her pencil. 'The most important people always arrive at the last minute, so they would end up sitting in the back and then they'd be terribly offended. And then they wouldn't come next summer and the children's home wouldn't have any money.' She pushed her hair back from her face and smiled at Charley. 'Tell you what, darling, you couldn't write all the names on little squares of paper for me, could you? Then I could just shuffle them round.'

Charley knew she was being palmed off with a Useful Task – her mother was a great believer in Useful Tasks – but she said:

''Course.'

'That's marvellous, darling. Such a help.'

Winterton summer holidays had for the last eight years or so followed the same pattern. The children finished school in July, after which Juliet and Helen took them on holiday to Devon or Cornwall. Jonny sometimes came with them, but Henry always worked through the summer months. August was dominated by the concerts; each year, Juliet vowed afterwards never to put herself through it all again – the work, the worry that this time it just wouldn't gel – but she always did.

This year was different. Piers and Aidan had not come with them to Cornwall. Henry was in New York on a buying trip and had taken Piers with him. He had offered to take Aidan too, but Aidan had politely declined and had turned down Cornwall as well, choosing to stay at home instead. In the end, after Jonny had been taken ill, Helen had remained at home too and Juliet had taken the girls to Mevagissey by herself. It had been fun, but not so much fun as usual. Sitting on a deckchair on the beach, she had wondered how long it would be before they dropped the West Country holiday altogether.

The August bank holiday weekend was another Winterton tradition. The entire extended family, Wintertons and Sinclairs, met up at Marsh Court during the final weekend of the summer. The children ran wild while the grown-ups ate and drank and played silly games and lazed around. Everyone was expected to join in the long walks, and they always lit a bonfire to celebrate their reunion. By then the concerts were over for another year and Juliet could relax.

Another reason for looking forward to the August weekend

was that it meant she would see Gillis – though equally, that was a reason for dreading it. He was so good at pretending there was nothing between them that sometimes she found herself wondering whether, distracted by the Wintertons, he had actually forgotten. Over the course of their affair, which had lasted for more than a decade, there had been summers when he had stayed away from Marsh Court because of his work, and when it had crossed her mind that he was avoiding her. Both thoughts were equally miserable. Of course, it was jolly sensible of him to be discreet, and of course his work was important. It should be enough, she tried to tell herself, that he was *there*, enough simply to be with him.

Only it wasn't. When she looked back to the start of their affair in the grey years after the war, she remembered only the bliss. Love and desire and the heat of his body against hers. It had been bliss to be with him and bliss to be away from him and to think about him. Love had transformed her; it had even made it easier for her to put up with Henry. She hadn't known that it was possible to want someone so much, and had discovered in herself a sort of recklessness. One spring afternoon they had made love in an old boathouse by the creek. It had been freezing cold and she had had bruises afterwards from the hard earth floor. Walking back to Marsh Court, they had encountered a fisherman by the river, and she had had to fold her arms over her chest to hide the smear of dust on her silk shirt.

Bliss was scarcer now. She ran her eyes once more over the seating plan. Bliss diminished, whereas guilt multiplied. Once, she had tried to rationalise her guilt. They would be careful, and Blanche and Henry would never know. What a person didn't know couldn't hurt them. Et cetera, et cetera. She had told herself that Blanche did not love Gillis as she,

Juliet, loved him; that Blanche was not a passionate woman, and Gillis needed to express that side of his nature that his marriage could not satisfy.

But Blanche Sinclair was a family friend. She was a good, kind woman, a loving mother and a staunch supporter of various charities. Blanche was no Henry, and Juliet had no right to make judgements about another woman's marriage. In darker moments she hated herself for her hypocrisy and self-serving deceit. She was Gillis's lover because she wanted him. Just that.

Gillis had a terror of the smallest whiff of indiscretion coming to the public eye. She sometimes thought he would have preferred them to be invisible. A near thing – an acquaintance glimpsed in the street, an unexpected telephone call from Blanche – sent him white-faced with panic. Juliet was not permitted to phone him or write to him; he must always contact her. Humiliation and guilt, these had become her daily bread. The inequalities within their love affair, along with the lies she told Helen or her daily woman when asking them to look after the children, inventing dentist's or dress-maker's appointments to cover her absences, shamed her.

After the owner of the Pimlico pied-à-terre had divorced his wife and sold the flat, she and Gillis had taken to meeting in hotels – Hampstead, Highgate, Hendon – a pushing-away from the geographical heart of London in a way that seemed to reflect the widening length of time between their assigna-tions. Insecurity had boiled up into suspicion. One evening, in a dreary little hotel on the outskirts of London, she had confronted him. Am I slipping down your list of priorities, Gillis? she had asked him. Let me guess their order – career, children, marriage, Juliet. Or am I overestimating my impor-tance? Perhaps I come after the club and the yacht?

For the first time, they had quarrelled. *I thought you understood*, he had said, coldly furious. *I thought you were capable of being* adult *about it*. It had been three months before she had seen him again, and by then, worn down by loneliness, jealousy and misery, she had begged for his forgiveness. Love had peeled layers from her, leaving her raw and exposed. The affair had started up again, but something had been lost. Their meetings, always subject to a great deal of planning and always liable to be cancelled by Gillis at the last minute, had become less frequent. Yet they remained for her islands of happiness and consolation for Henry's lack of love. Her children, her home, and Gillis, her occasional lover: these her heart sang for.

Though she had come to see him for what he was – a man who was charming and self-aware, who knew the power he had over women and had little conscience about using it, and whose greatest energies would always be for his career – none of that stopped her loving him. She recognised that he was self-centred but forgave it. She believed that he loved her in his way, that there was a part of his heart that was just for her. She was, she hoped, a sanctuary for him – loving, uncritical and appreciative. He still had the power to make her forget everything and to conjure in her a pleasure that robbed her of breath. Sometimes she wondered at herself – the compromises she made, the lies she told, her bargain in exchange for a few moments of delight.

The Sinclairs' fourth child, a boy, Rory, had been born in 1949. Perhaps she should have resented him, the unequivocal evidence that Gillis and Blanche still lived as man and wife, but she did not, and of Gillis's four children it was Rory whom Juliet loved most. He was a sweet-natured scamp, who did not appear to have inherited one iota of the Sinclair good looks, being brown-haired, snub-nosed and ordinary. Nate and Rory often came to stay at Marsh Court. Charley, between the two of them in age, adored them.

By the time Rory had been born, instinct had told Juliet that it was dangerous to focus all her passion and energy on her love affair, that she must find something else to occupy herself – anything. The first summer concert had been given at Marsh Court in 1949. In time, one concert had grown into a series, which took place on the first three Saturdays of August. Most of the concert-goers bought a subscription, though there were always a few seats, the cheaper ones in the back rows, available through the post office in Maldon. The money earned went to children's charities. Over the years, Juliet had raised a substantial sum.

She was not a natural organiser, and the courting of the great and the good exhausted her. She could not pay the musicians their usual rates and so had to use her charm to persuade them to perform. Marsh Court itself must be a draw, so the buffet she provided for musicians and guests had to be delicious, the house comfortable and inviting and the garden ravishing. She sometimes wondered whether she had set up the concerts as a sort of penance. One of the charities she supported had been established by Blanche Sinclair.

A year after the first summer concert, the headmistress of Piers's prep school had collared her one afternoon while she was collecting him at home time. An art teacher had suddenly quit, leaving them in the lurch – she had some art training, did she not? Might she be so obliging as to consider filling in until someone else could be found? It was a good school, tolerant of Piers's occasional outbursts of bad behaviour, so Juliet had felt bound to say yes. She had been sick with

108

nerves before the first lesson, afraid that the little boys would riot, but she had prepared well and the two hours seemed to speed by, and afterwards she had felt relieved and elated.

For the past seven years she had taught at the school two afternoons a week, continuing even after Piers and Aidan had moved on to boarding school at the age of thirteen. She helped Henry entertain in London, and at the weekends the house was full of Wintertons and their friends. She was always busy, sometimes frantically so, and that suited her. She could not have managed without Meg, who had stayed on as Marsh Court's housekeeper after the Land Army had been disbanded. Meg rented a bungalow in Mundon, which she shared with her friend Sarah.

In 1951, the Conservatives had been returned to power under the leadership of the then seventy-six-year-old Winston Churchill. Gillis's jubilation had been undisguised. He had continued to be a loyal supporter of Sir Anthony Eden, Churchill's second in command, and Juliet had sensed that he thought his luck was changing at last. He had confided in her his belief that he would claw his way back to the heights he had achieved before the war. He was in his mid-forties and his ambition was undiminished, and yet the war had left its mark on him, as it had on all that generation, and from time to time he drank heavily, as Henry did, as did other Winterton friends who had seen things, done things they could not bear to think about.

After Churchill's health failed, Sir Anthony Eden had replaced him as prime minister in 1955. Juliet had witnessed the slow decline of Gillis's optimism as the months passed and he remained on the back bench, Eden having failed to give him the position in government that he craved. A year later, the Suez crisis destroyed Eden's health and reputation and Gillis found himself permanently tarnished by their association. Life sometimes disappointed: it had been a hard lesson for him to learn.

As for her, she had learned to live like a Winterton, to put on a good face, even when she was tearing apart inside. She knew that Gillis did not need her as much as she needed him, and that degraded her. Countless times she resolved to put an end to the affair, a resolution that crumbled as soon as she saw him again.

If she and Henry quarrelled less frequently, it was because they saw less of each other. She must be content with her two children; she and Henry did not share a bed often enough to make any more. He stayed Mondays to Fridays in the Bond Street flat, and Juliet suspected that over the years he had found replacements for Teddie. There was sometimes a waft of perfume on his shirts, and once a so-called friend had gleefully confided to her that she had seen him with a woman in the Strand. Juliet had wanted to slap her.

Their marriage had settled into a series of stand-offs and skirmishes, interspersed, like steam escaping from a whistling kettle, by the occasional pitched battle. In the prime of life, Henry was the watchful and powerful head of the Winterton family. Throughout the 1950s, the business had recovered from the lean post-war years. People had more money now, and some of them spent it in Winterton's on pearls and diamonds and brooches of textured gold. Gems were still hard to obtain, though, and taxes remained high.

Most of the time, Juliet would have said that she was happy. At thirty-eight, she loved her children and her home and had many interests. It was only sometimes that she found herself questioning her own complacency, niggling at the veneer of contentment and shying away from what lay beneath it.

Now she stared at the sheet of paper in front of her, and sighed. A quick adjustment – Mrs Westmorecott suffered from hay fever, so perhaps not place her at the window end of a row of chairs – and then she concluded that the placement was as good as it would ever be, and began to dab glue on to the squares of paper that Charley had cut out.

Piers, Aidan and Anne were in a café on Maldon High Street. Piers and Uncle Henry had returned home that morning, their eyes red-rimmed from the transatlantic flight.

'The Plaza's simply adorable,' said Anne. 'My mom and I stayed there for a weekend.'

Piers said, 'God, I needed that coffee. That bloody flight. So what's been happening?'

'Nothing much,' Aidan muttered.

'Now there's a change. You must be finding it as dull as ditchwater after London, Anne.'

'Oh no, it's been fun. Aidan's showed me some wonderful places.'

'Has he now?' Piers turned his gaze to Aidan. The silky blueness of his cousin's eyes mocked him. 'Tell us where you've been, then, Aidan.'

'St Peter's Chapel . . . Thorney Island . . . Mersea . . .'

'How exciting,' murmured Piers. 'I'm sure Anne's been thrilled. Where are you staying?'

'With some family friends, on a boat at Heybridge.'

'A boat.' Piers gave a theatrical shudder. 'Awfully damp and cold.'

'No, it's fine. Lachlan and Sue have made it real cosy. Lachlan's a constructivist, like my father. Sue paints seascapes.'

'Must suit them, living on a boat, then. Boozy evenings and long conversations into the night about cubism and abstract expressionism.'

'In winter, when it's real cold, they stay with us in London. Sue's such a sweet person, she'd do anything for you. When my father broke his leg a couple of years ago, she helped us out.'

Aidan was amazed by how forthcoming Anne was being. A shot of jealousy ran through him. He knew that Piers, when he put his mind to it, could bewitch. His cousin's gentle mocking witticisms might annoy him, but they charmed others.

Piers said, 'Has Aidan introduced you to the teeming masses of Wintertons, Anne?'

'Not yet,' said Aidan sulkily. If he were to take Anne home to meet his mother and father, they would pick her over later at the dinner table. Not meanly or unkindly, but there would be questions, as well as comments and assumptions.

'I've met Louise,' said Anne. 'She's such a sweetie. Now, let me get us all another coffee.'

'I'll go,' said Piers.

'No, I insist.'

While Anne was at the counter, Piers gave a low whistle. 'Clever old you.'

Aidan frowned. 'What do you mean?'

'She's a doll.'

He hated Piers's phoney Americanism, hated the veneer of knowingness he put on.

'She's a friend,' he said coldly. 'I like her, that's all.'

Most mornings, Piers left the house after breakfast. When Charley asked him where he was going, he said, 'Out,' and smiled in an annoying way.

112

Louise said to her, 'I expect they're with Anne Carlisle.'

'Who's Anne Carlisle?'

Louise explained. They were in the studio at the back of Louise's house, which was full of Helen's paintings, enormous bright pictures of flowers, sometimes just a single petal or anther.

Charley said, 'Have you met her?'

'Yes. She's awfully pretty.'

Louise was herself awfully pretty. She and Charley went to the same school, and Louise was generally acknowledged to be the prettiest girl there.

'Aidan's in love with her,' she added.

'How do you know?'

'He never talks about her.'

'I would have thought if you were in love with someone you would talk about them all the time.'

'Not Aidan,' said Louise, very definitely.

Charley had told her mother and Aunt Helen that she would catch the bus back to Marsh Court, but she headed for the harbour instead. She was not supposed to walk home along the estuary path by herself, but often did.

She minded that Louise had known about Anne Carlisle while she had had no idea. She hated to feel left out. When she thought of Louise's family, it was as a single solid lump. Her own family divided into separate fragments, sometimes talking to or confiding in each other, at other times barely communicating. Charley hated it when her parents quarrelled, it made her feel sick inside. Her father said mean things to her mother; less often, her mother said equally mean things back. She felt herself responsible for cheering her parents up after their quarrels.

She was afraid that they would get divorced, which would

be awful, because what would she do then? Her mother would undoubtedly be the easier parent to live with, but Piers would certainly stay with her, which would mean that Charley would feel obliged to go and live with their father so that he wasn't on his own. And he would be in a bad temper all the time and would make horrible remarks about her mother, which she would hate.

Distracted by these gloomy thoughts, Charley realised too late that she had walked past the turn-off to home. She was about to head back when she glimpsed a flash of blue sail against the brown of the river. Rounding the bend on the bank, she saw Piers, Aidan and a girl with light-coloured hair. Piers's dinghy was moored a short distance away.

Behind them lay the grey-green bulk of Thorney Island. The tide was coming in, slopping over the causeway. Piers and Aidan were standing side by side on the island, and the girl, Anne, was across the water, facing out to them. Her arm was raised and she was holding a white handkerchief. Charley realised that the boys were about to race each other across the causeway.

Anne's arm dropped and the handkerchief fluttered. Piers and Aidan ran through the rising water, their feet kicking up wet sand, their rolled-up trouser legs darkened and soaked. Their faces were red and contorted with effort.

As they neared the shore, Piers pulled ahead. He gave a triumphant howl and clenched his fist in the air. Then he swept Anne up in his arms, lifting her off her feet and spinning her round. Water lapped over Aidan's ankles as he bent over, his hands on his knees, gulping in air.

It was Anne who saw her first. 'You must be Charley,' she said, coming over to meet her. 'You're so cute! You look just like Piers.'

Cute, thought Charley, nauseated.

'Charley, what the hell are you doing here?' Piers looked annoyed.

'Going for a walk. You're not supposed to cross the cause-way when the tide's coming in. Mum said.'

'Mum doesn't need to know.'

'It's teatime.' Charley began to plod back along the path.

Piers caught up with her. 'Don't you dare say anything to Mum.'

Charley gave him a cool look. 'What about? You showing off in front of that girl?'

'Shut up, you silly little nitwit.'

As she walked away from him, tears spilled from her eyes. Because she could never hate Piers for long, her resentment transferred itself to Anne Carlisle. Anne must have made them race to her, she decided. The boys were idiots and would have done it to impress her. Charley had seen the expression on Anne's face as Piers had scooped her up and whirled her round. Joy, along with a soppy sort of devotion that would be completely wasted on someone like Piers.

By late August, the concerts were over for another year and Juliet was able to let out a sigh of relief and turn to thinking about the family weekend.

Jane, Peter, the twins and Gabe arrived on Friday evening. Rising early on Saturday morning, Juliet prepared a Greek salad and ful medames. It was now possible, if one knew where to go, to buy good-quality olives, yoghurt and garlic, and she had enjoyed herself re-creating the dishes of her childhood. Jonny, Helen, Aidan and Louise were due to turn up at any moment, and Peter had been put in charge of drinks. Jane had nipped out to see her old nanny in Maylandsea, and Jake and Eliot, who were both nearing the end of their medical training, had not yet got up. Gillis and Blanche and their four children were expected in time for the Saturday picnic, a Winterton tradition.

Juliet set about blanching almonds for devilled sandwiches, dropping the nuts into a pot of boiling water so that they swirled and rolled. She chopped pickle and chutney and then fished the almonds out of the pot before plunging them into a bowl of ice-cold water and slipping off the skins. She was without Meg, had given her the weekend off because it was Sarah's fortieth birthday, so the two of them could go to the coast. Though she had risen early, she was behind, the sausage rolls pale and uncooked, the lobsters to be disassembled, the mayonnaise still to be made.

She felt a flutter of excitement – in an hour or so, she would see Gillis. She had dressed with care in a summer frock of rose-printed silk shantung, which was now covered with an apron. Her hair was swept to one side, curling softly round her face. It was more than two months since she had last seen him – holidays, the concerts, their obligations to work and family, all had got in the way.

Losing her concentration, she scalded her fingers trying to skin almonds straight out of the boiling water. Her hand under the cold tap, she peered out of the window. Piers, Aidan and a girl were sitting on the lawn. Juliet did not recognise the girl, who was wearing pale blue cut-offs and a white blouse. Her platinum-blonde hair was styled with little concession to the current fashion for curls, lying straight and flat on her shoulders.

Charley wandered into the kitchen. 'Where's Dad?'

'Looking out the croquet things.' Juliet nodded to the window. 'Who's that girl? Do you know her?'

Charley made a face. 'Yuck. *Anne*. She's American. Aidan *loves* . . .' Charley drawled out the word, 'her.'

'Don't be silly, darling.'

'It's true.'

'Even if it were, which I don't suppose it is, it's not something you should repeat.'

The doorbell pealed. Was it Gillis? Her heart contracted.

She passed Charley a bowl of halved lemons and the squeezer. 'See what you can do with those, sweetheart.'

She whipped off her apron and checked her face and hair in the hall mirror before opening the front door. Jonny, Helen and Louise were standing on the front step.

Jonny had brought a bottle of claret and Helen a bunch of roses from her garden. There were hugs and kisses as they came into the house, and Helen said, 'What can I do to help? The lobsters? You know I'm rather marvellous at doing lobsters.'

It had been Piers's idea to bring Anne to Marsh Court. Today, he had pointed out, she could meet all the Wintertons at once. Get it over and done with. Anne had murmured that she didn't want to intrude, but Piers had said, 'Rot. You must stay to lunch. Mum won't mind.'

Aidan suspected that Aunt Juliet did mind, confronted at the last minute by an extra guest. When Piers asked if Anne could stay, Juliet said in a hearty, unconvincing tone, 'You're very welcome, Anne, so long as you don't mind a bit of a squeeze.'

The heat had been intensifying since daybreak. Beneath a hard blue sky, the grass was as pale and dry as raffia. Aidan and Piers put up trestle tables on the terrace and carried out the chairs. Charley and Louise laid the tables. The twins, yawning and tousle-haired, emerged from the house, blinking in the sunlight. Then the Sinclairs arrived and they all trooped out to admire Uncle Gillis's new car.

Claudia Sinclair put her hand to her stomach and said to Aidan, 'I was sick six times. Dad gave up stopping for me and I just heaved in the back of the car.'

'One of our more enjoyable journeys,' said Gillis drily.

At lunch, Aidan ended up sitting between Claudia and Flavia; opposite him, on the other side of the table, Piers was next to Anne until Aunt Juliet decided that Anne should sit between Eliot and Nate. Charley looked cross, because she had been sitting beside Nate and now had to move next to Rory. There was a shuffling round, and then Mum and Aunt Juliet served the meal.

Aidan was supposed to be enjoying himself but wasn't. It was too hot, for one thing; the butter was melting in the dish and the salads and sandwiches looked oily. Claudia kept flapping at the wasps and Piers was showing off, talking loudly about New York to Aunt Blanche. And there was something going on at the far end of the table between his father and Uncle Henry, some disagreement, because Uncle Henry had raised his voice and Dad was looking fixedly at his plate.

Aidan wondered what Anne thought of them, whether she found the Wintertons bourgeois and dull. Although they called the meal a picnic, it was not a proper picnic. There was a tablecloth and napkins and silver cutlery and crystal, and the dishes Aunt Juliet cooked were elaborate. He imagined that when Anne and her father picnicked with their artist friends, they sprawled in a grassy field, eating bread and French cheese and swigging wine from a bottle in a straw carafe. The Wintertons were stuck in the past. They didn't seem to see that times had changed.

118

Mentally he sketched Anne's profile and the fall of her silky fair hair. He could have drawn her from memory – had done so a number of times. That morning, she had told them that her father had written to her asking her to join him in San Francisco. He had booked a plane ticket for her to fly to the States on Wednesday, just five days away.

A trickle of sweat ran down the back of Aidan's neck, and he prodded his lobster as he sank into an overheated, irritable gloom. Anne was the most beautiful girl he had ever met, but he had not yet told her so. Instead, he had dithered, never plucking up the courage to ask her on a date. Since Piers had come home, the easy, comfortable quiet he had thought existed between them had been filled by his cousin's yattering. The sketching trips had been forgotten; in their place, they had taken Piers's dinghy on to the estuary. Anne was a competent sailor, something else he hadn't known about her until Piers had found it out.

Over the last couple of weeks, a terrible jealousy had seeded in him, an inner voice that whispered that she preferred Piers. Why shouldn't she? the nagging voice murmured – Piers was better-looking, a better conversationalist. There was something wrong with Aidan; he lacked whatever it was that girls wanted. Roll on, National Service, he thought bitterly, he couldn't wait to get away.

A wasp whined into Claudia's coronation chicken and she shrieked and flapped her hands at it. 'It'll go away if you leave it alone,' he said for the fifth time, thinking, poor bloody wasp, but she went on waving her hands and fussing. When he looked along the table, Anne caught his eye and smiled at him.

It was then that he realised he had nothing to lose. Better to try and fail than continue with this agony of self-pity and indecision. As soon as he was able to get a moment alone with her, he would ask her for a date. And if she said yes, and if she felt the same way about him, then no matter how long they were separated, by America and by the army, he would wait for her.

The croquet tournament was after lunch. Juliet excused herself to do the dishes. She ran the hot water, plunged her hands into the sink and began to scrub. Her hand stung where she had scalded it that morning, and she could hear the shrieks and cheers of the croquet players on the lawn.

This would probably be the last August bank holiday they all spent together at Marsh Court. This time next year, Piers and Aidan would be in the army. And then they would grow up and move away and marry and have children of their own. Time was short, and this handful of idyllic days was precious. Her heart swelled with love for them all. Through the kitchen window, she watched Gillis, in cream-coloured linen trousers and a white open-necked shirt, the sunlight bright on a head that was still more gold than silver, stride across the lawn.

'May I dry, Juliet?'

She turned. Blanche had come into the kitchen and was picking up a tea towel.

'Don't you want to play croquet?' said Juliet.

'Hate it. So pointless. And such a mountain of dishes.'

'And when we've finished, they'll want their tea. More cups and saucers.' They exchanged smiles of sympathy and female solidarity.

Blanche polished a glass. 'What are Henry and Jonny arguing about?'

'Oh.' Juliet sighed. 'Henry thinks Winterton's should open

120

another London shop and Jonny doesn't think they can afford it. Henry will get his way, of course. It might,' she added, passing a wet plate to Blanche, 'be better for his character if he didn't, but he will, I'm afraid, he always does.'

Charley and Nate were sitting on the shed roof. Charley was watching Piers, Aidan and Anne Carlisle, who were heading down the lawn to the bonfire.

'Louise thinks she's pretty, but I don't think she's pretty at all,' she said.

'Who?' Nate was lying on his back, his curly dark head cushioned by an arm, his eyes closed.

'Her. Anne.'

'Don't you like her?'

'I just *said*, I don't think she's pretty. She has weird eyes.'

'Why don't you like her?' He squinted at the sun. 'Is it because of Piers?'

He had an annoying way of seeing through her. All her hurt at Piers's desertion spilled out.

'He's hardly *spoken* to me all summer! He's always with her and Aidan. I should have thought she would understand that wasn't fair. I think she must be a very selfish sort of person.'

'Maybe Piers wants a change.'

'Not from us. Not from his *family*.'

He swung up on to one elbow, looking at her. The sunlight made sparks of emerald in his eyes. 'It's not impossible, you know,' he said, quite kindly.

'Don't say that, Nate,' she said fiercely.

He shrugged. 'God, it's bloody hot.'

'It is bloody hot, isn't it?' She had learned most of her swear words from Nate. He had learned them at his school.

He stood on the edge of the shed roof and then jumped

121

off, rolling neatly to his feet on the lawn. Charley jumped after him, landing in an undignified heap. She had grass stains on her yellow cotton dress and a stabbing pain in her ankle, and she limped after him as he ran back to the house.

'I simply don't think we can afford it,' Jonathan said. 'We're only just out of the frightful mess we were in after the war.'

'That's why we need to invest, Jonny. You don't make money if you don't invest. We need another outlet.'

'We *had* another outlet. You sold it.'

'I meant in *London*.' Henry folded his newspaper with an angry twitch. 'That's where the money is, and you know that perfectly well.'

'If we had the cash. But to *borrow* . . . I don't know why you're in such a hurry.'

The croquet tournament was over and the adults had taken newspapers, magazines and knitting out to where deckchairs were arranged on a shady part of the terrace. Bees buzzed in the jasmine and roses. The spaniel, Biscuit, lay among pots of geraniums, panting.

Juliet put aside her knitting. 'I'll make some tea.'

'I'll give you a hand,' Helen offered.

'Tricky crossword,' said Gillis. He read out a clue.

'I've spoken to the bank. They're in agreement, in principle.'

'Jesus, Henry—'

Peter said loudly, 'Where's your copy of Wisden?'

'I'll get it.' Jonny pulled at his collar and hauled himself out of his deckchair. 'Need to cool down a bit.' He went inside the house.

In the kitchen, Juliet filled the kettle and put it on the hob. Helen said, 'Which cups shall I use? The lovely little porcelain ones?' and went to fetch them from the cupboard.

As Juliet searched for the sugar tongs, she became aware of a commotion several rooms away. Voices, someone calling out. Probably one of the children, she thought. Rory would have collided with something, smashed something. She hoped whatever it was wasn't too old or precious.

'I'll go and check.' Helen left the room.

Juliet found the tongs and put them on the tray. Biscuits arranged on a plate, a pitcher of lemonade. Afterwards, she thought of it as the last perfect moment: the sun filtering through the window, the tray with its lovely things, the anticipation of the remainder of the weekend, the beloved ordinariness.

Jane's voice, high-pitched and frightened, broke through the stillness.

'Juliet! Juliet, where are you?'

She ran to the door. 'What is it? What's happened?'

'It's Jonny! He's collapsed! Henry's phoning for the ambulance.' Jane's face crumpled and she began to cry.

They went together, hand in hand, to the library. Jonny was lying on the floor and Peter was bending over him, forcing his own breath into his brother-in-law's lungs. Helen was kneeling beside Jonny, stroking his hand and murmuring to him. Louise was sobbing.

Henry turned to Juliet, his expression agonised. 'Was it me?' he whispered. 'Was it because we disagreed? Was it too much for him?'

And for the first time in years she put her arm round him, trying to comfort him. 'No, Henry. No, Jonny was ill, you know that.'

'*Aidan.*' Helen looked up, her eyes wide and fearful. 'I need him. Where is he? Where's Aidan?'

*   *   *

They were at the fire pit. Aidan was trying to stop Piers lighting the bonfire.

'Uncle Henry always does it,' he pointed out.

Piers kicked at some branches spilling out of the side of the heap. He didn't say anything, just smiled.

'Dad said perhaps we should leave it this year because it's so dry,' Aidan went on.

Piers was patting his pockets, looking for his lighter. 'Must have left it in my room.' He turned back to the house.

Aidan thought of going after him, but decided not to. You could never stop Piers doing what he wanted to, and anyway, he didn't care.

Anne was sitting on a tree stump, her arms wrapped round her knees. 'Sorry for dragging you into this,' he said to her. 'My family, I mean.'

'It's been so good to meet you all. You have a wonderful family.' But she looked hot and tired.

Aidan cleared his throat and was about to suggest they head off to Maldon, just the two of them, have a drink, a meal, maybe, but then he saw Aunt Juliet, hurrying down the garden towards them.

He thought at first that it was something to do with Piers. Aunt Juliet was cross about the bonfire, something like that. But she was crying. Why was she crying?

'Aidan, it's your father,' she gasped, as soon as she was in earshot. 'I'm so sorry, but he's been taken ill. You have to come at once.'

And every other thought drained out of his head as, spurred by fear, he ran up the slope, his lungs straining as he built up speed.

* * *

124

At eleven o'clock at night, Juliet was in Helen's kitchen, clearing up the remains of a supper no one had wanted to eat. She dried the dishes and ran over the surfaces with the damp tea towel. Then she hung the tea towel on a hook and stacked the plates and bowls in the cupboard. A sweep of the dishcloth over the sink before she opened the door and went outside.

Helen's garden was walled and full of bright flowers that in the moonlight had become colourless and crepuscular. A moth swooped blindly round her head; she brushed it away.

Jonny had died in the ambulance. He had never made it to the hospital. This fact she must absorb, but it seemed to her now an outrage. She thought of the three siblings, Henry, Jonny and Jane, and how they had hardly needed to finish their sentences because each had known what the other was thinking. How would they manage, the two that had been left behind?

An hour ago, Henry, Peter and Jane had driven back to Marsh Court and the children. Juliet would remain at Helen's house for as long as she was needed. She had coaxed Helen, trembling with shock, to take a pill, and had stayed with her, stroking her hair, until she had fallen asleep. Though Juliet had heaped blankets and an eiderdown on her, and though it was still unbearably warm, Helen had gone on shivering in her sleep.

Then she had returned downstairs and made supper for the children. Poor little Louise had cried without ceasing, breaking off forkfuls of food and pushing them round her plate. Aidan had been stony-eyed and tearless. Juliet supposed that, like herself, he found it impossible to believe that Jonny was gone. Eventually he had given Louise's plait a little tug, and said, 'Come on, I'll run you a bath,' and the two of them had gone upstairs. When he had reappeared, he had poured whisky for them both. Aidan was growing up, Juliet thought sadly. He had little choice now but to grow up.

A fat orange moon hung impossibly low in the sky above the estuary. The most awful thing was trying to imagine Helen without Jonny. It couldn't be done. She had never once even heard them snap at each other. They had been two halves of one whole, and it occurred to her for the first time that great love came at a terrible price, and that Helen, who was only in her late forties and so would have to endure many years without Jonny, must begin to pay it.

Chapter Seven

December 1957

The sky's grey density sucked the light from the surface of the estuary. Redshank explored the salt marsh, heads bobbing, orange beaks probing the mud.

Juliet was walking along the Blackwater, away from Marsh Court. At breakfast, Henry had been rude to Meg, and Meg, not a woman to mince her words, had been rude back. Henry had fired her at much the same time as Meg had given in her notice. As Henry had driven off to London, Meg had cycled home to her bungalow in Mundon. Nothing ever changes, Juliet thought bitterly, remembering the breakfast during the early months of their marriage when Henry had sacked a housemaid just as summarily. Wars might be fought, love and grief endured, but Henry would always have his own way.

Three months had passed since Jonny had died. Though he had been the quietest and gentlest of the three Winterton siblings, they were all, Juliet often thought, much the less without him. They had lost their spark. They would turn, looking for affirmation and reassurance, and find that there was no one there.

For the first six weeks of her widowhood, Helen had retreated into herself, living on coffee and cigarettes, hunched in an old cardigan in the studio at the back of her house. Then, slowly, she had begun to take an interest in family life again. The family had rallied round, of course, cooking meals, driving Louise back to the school she attended with Charley. When Helen had taken up the reins again, Juliet had sensed how hard this was for her, as if it was a role she had forgotten how to play.

After the initial shock had subsided, Henry had reacted to the death of his brother with a furious burst of energy. He had bought a second premises, in Sloane Street, which he had refurbished in the traditional Winterton style – mahogany, brass vitrines and a plush royal-blue carpet – and had hired new staff. Gabe, Jane's daughter, was now working at the Sloane Street branch. Juliet suspected that Henry's dynamism was his way of avoiding thinking about what he had lost.

He was angry at any delay to his plans for the restructuring of the family firm, angry with anyone who tried to sympathise with him, and, Juliet suspected, furious with Jonny for leaving him. As always, he took out his resentment on those nearest to him. He quarrelled with Jane and tried to quarrel with Gillis, who laughed it off. Henry and Piers had been at loggerheads for months, and so it had in the end been a relief when Piers had been called up for National Service in October. Aidan had followed his cousin into the army a fortnight later.

Juliet wondered whether Henry regretted the vulnerability he had shown on the day Jonny had died. Much of the time his vindictiveness was directed at her. She had not even tried to intervene in his quarrel with Meg. She had known it would only make things worse.

She had needed to take a walk that afternoon to escape the atmosphere of turmoil and tension that swirled through the rooms of Marsh Court. She reached the Thorney Island causeway. The tide was out; as she made the crossing, she experienced once again the odd sensation that she was stepping beneath the surface of the river, allowing herself to be consumed by it. White crabs the size of a half-crown were caught in the weed and were desiccating, exposed to the light. Around her, the mud and water had a grey, pearly gleam.

From the shore of the island, she looked back to the mainland. She realised that she was standing at the same spot where, all those years ago, she had seen those poor children playing. She shivered, feeling a momentary urge to run back to the safety and security of the mainland. But after a mental shake, she set off up the road into the heart of the island.

To the left of her, the mud and salt marsh fractured into the estuary. Trees fringed the other side of the narrow lane, their branches frilled with pale green lichen. Beyond, the fields were bordered by low, windswept hedges. Someone must once have kept sheep or cattle here, because an iron trough, rusted and brimming with brackish water, stood beside a gate.

The road curved round, narrowing as it approached the house on Thorney Island. The lawn and flower beds were overgrown with weeds, blackened and rotted by the December frosts. No light showed from the windows that stared unblinkingly out at her. As she neared the building, Juliet noticed faded, peeling paint and gaps where tiles had fallen from the roof.

It was drizzling, so she put up her hood and fastened the top button of her khaki mackintosh. In the back garden, sludgy nuggets of coal smeared the mouth of the bunker and a frayed clothes line dangled from a post, dancing now and then in the wind. Beyond the sea wall a mass of islets, some sizeable, others as small as a dinner plate, were cut up by the waters of the estuary.

Something made her lift the latch on the back door and give it a tug. It opened, revealing a dark corridor that led into the house. Standing on the threshold, she breathed in the damp smells of the island. It was as if the marsh was trying to reclaim its own, absorbing the house, slowly swallowing it up. Stepping inside, she placed her palm against the wall, half expecting it to sink into a surface that was not quite solid.

She walked down the corridor. A set of pegs, high up, suggested that this part of the house had once been used to store coats, and a speckled mirror threw back her own face at her, startling her. She stopped, conscious of a reluctance to go any further. The Harts had been the last people to live in the house, which had been uninhabited for more than a decade. Juliet had her own strange bond with the place. The events of that stormy night in 1946 had brought her and Gillis together, changing the course of her life.

Curiosity impelled her into rooms suffused with a sullen wintry light. The kitchen housed a rusty iron stove, set into the chimney alcove. Beneath the tap, a green mark in the shape of a teardrop stained the white china sink. Set off from the kitchen was a larder, lined with shelves, its small, square window covered with wire mesh. Another small room contained a wooden washtub.

Dining room, hallway, parlour, all empty except for dust, dead leaves and a couple of empty beer bottles, presumably left by intruders. The organic scent of wet and decay followed her as she explored the rooms. She would not have been surprised to see salt tears oozing from the walls and the floor shimmering wet, the river rising up through the boards, shells and shiny brown weed dripping in a corner.

Narrow stairs took her to the first floor. Three doors led off from the small square of landing at the top, two of which gave into bedrooms whose cobwebbed windows looked out over the island. The third door, which faced the stairs, was set into the eaves. Blood pulsed in her ears as she reached out to the handle.

And then she was running down the staircase, stumbling on the treads in her desperation to be out of the house. Emerging from the back door, she would have liked to have laughed at her sudden irrational terror, but she could not, and as she latched the door, the thought crossed her mind that she was trying to shut something *inside* the house.

She headed back through the garden to the road. She was tired and upset by the morning's scene with Henry and still grieving for Jonny, she reminded herself, and her mind was playing tricks on her. It was inevitable that on Thorney Island she would think of the children who had been taken by the river, the boy and the little girl in the red dress. Lost children . . . deserted houses . . . shadows and closed doors: these were the well-worn tropes of many a ghost story.

Though she did not believe in ghosts, she had always thought that old houses possessed their own spirit, made up of the griefs and desires of those who had lived inside them. Henry would have been scornful of such a theory; she suspected Helen and Jane would not. And Gillis? She was unsure. Gillis liked to think he was rational and analytical, but she had seen him spooked by a phrase of music or a line of poetry. He tried to hide his periods of depression but she knew when they came upon him, heard the flatness in his voice, saw how he reached for the bottle to disguise the effort that social interaction demanded of him.

She was thankful when the bend in the road hid the house from her. She knew she would never go there again. The rain was falling more heavily now and the light was fading. She pulled back the cuff of her mackintosh to check her watch and saw to her horror that more than an hour had passed since she had crossed the causeway to the island. She began to run, dodging potholes in the muddy surface, retracing the way she had come.

But she was too late. The river was pouring over the higher side of the causeway, rain pitting its surface, and though she ventured out a few paces, the water was soon churning round her ankles. She felt the tug of the undertow and knew that if she waded out another yard, the estuary would pluck her from safety and hurl her into the river.

Cursing herself for her stupidity, she retreated to dry land. She watched through the curtain of rain as the water tore along the channel, cutting her off from the mainland and bringing with it seabirds and fallen branches and a tea chest that bobbed and whirled in the current. Panic washed over her; she could not work out how long she would be stranded on the island. Four hours? Eight? Piers and Henry were the sailors, not she. Darkness would fall while she was marooned in this watery Essex wilderness.

She had no torch, only the feeble illumination of her cigarette lighter. In spite of her mackintosh hood, her hair was slick with rain. Now the river was swallowing up the markers on the shore – a tree root, a concrete block, a rusty chain, all were gobbled up by the tide, its progress a quick, dark consumption of everything in its path. Scrambling up the incline to the safety

132

of the bank, she groaned aloud as it came to her that no one would look for her – Henry was in London, Charley weekly-boarding at school and Meg sulking in Mundon.

Though the house would have offered her some shelter from the rain, she shuddered to think of returning there. And yet the causeway itself was equally uninviting. Huddled in the failing light, she was aware of the wet chill and the sounds of the estuary, the splash of water, the creaking of branches, the whisper of grass.

Then a voice, calling out, made her gasp and look up.

'Mrs Winterton!'

It took her a moment to make out the direction of the cry and spot the rowing boat that was setting off from the mainland. Another shout, and the man's voice carried towards her across the channel. She looked out, shading her eyes from the rain with her hand.

As the small craft headed out from the shore, it seemed to steer away from her, but she quickly realised that this was to compensate for the fast incoming tide. The vessel swept round in a wide arc and was then flung towards the island. As it drew closer, she recognised the rower as Joe Brandon of Greensea Farm. She had seen him occasionally over the years – Greensea was not such a great distance from Marsh Court, which meant that they were bound to run into each other now and then – but had not spoken to him since their wartime encounter in the copse.

A few yards from the shore, he swung out of the boat and waded through the shallows towards her.

'Mr Brandon!' Laughing with relief, she wanted to hug him but instead seized and shook his hand. 'I'm so thankful to see you! I thought I was going to be stranded here all night. Such a foolish mistake!'

133

'Did you not take notice of the tide times?'

'I forgot – I was thinking of something else, I suppose.'

'We should go. Do you mind getting your feet wet?'

'They are already.'

Inside the rowing boat, she perched beside a canvas knapsack and a pair of binoculars. Joe grimaced as he set the oars against the tide, and his black hair tumbled over his forehead as he strained to pull them. Raindrops beaded his skin and the veins stood out in his throat.

'Tough going,' she said, and he nodded.

She was shivering, though whether through cold or fear, she was unsure. There was a time when she was afraid that the fragile craft might be blown out to the mouth of the estuary. The grey-blue bank receded, hidden behind her.

'I know these waters,' he said. 'I've sailed here since I was a boy. You've nothing to be afraid of, Mrs Winterton.'

His kindness made her garrulous. 'I'm so relieved you saw me. I'd have hated to have to stay there. So cold and dark.'

'It's a strange place. I've never felt at ease on Thorney Island.'

'You too?'

'There are places like that.'

'Did you know that poor family who lived there?'

'Only by sight.'

'I wonder why they chose to live somewhere so lonely and isolated.'

Joe Brandon was looking over his shoulder, guiding the boat to shore. 'Your friend knew Mrs Hart, didn't he?'

She stared at him, bewildered. 'My friend?'

'The politician, Sinclair. I saw him here once, at the causeway, talking to her. The children were with them, the poor little things.'

'I think you must be mistaken.' She spoke more sharply than she had intended; she saw him frown.

They had reached the shallows; he leaped out of the boat and gave her his hand to follow him. Confusion washed over her. *I saw him here once, at the causeway.* If Joe was right, it seemed strange that, in the aftermath of the tragedy, Gillis had not mentioned that he had spoken to Mrs Hart, if only briefly.

'I expect,' she said, as he dragged the skiff up the bank, 'that Gillis and Mrs Hart were just passing the time of day.'

Questions sprang into her head. She tried to envisage it, Gillis and the drowned woman, encountering each other on the footpath and exchanging comments about the weather, perhaps. Something was wrong; she felt uneasy.

'Do you mean you saw them here?' She indicated the mud and scrub on which they stood. 'Here, at this end of the causeway?'

'No, they were on the island.' Joe wrinkled his brow. 'I thought, at the time, that they were saying goodbye.'

Her heart juddered. She put a smile on her face and held out her hand to him. 'I can't thank you enough. You've been so kind.'

'It was nothing,' he said brusquely. 'Can you find your way home from here?'

'Oh yes, I know this path like the back of my hand. Goodnight, Mr Brandon.'

He gave her a nod of acknowledgement and then walked away from her.

The next morning, Juliet drove to Mundon. Inside her bungalow, Meg made them coffee.

Meg had given in her notice before. Juliet had always been

able to coax her into changing her mind. They had a history, had been friends since the war.

'I'm so sorry about yesterday,' she said. 'What Henry said to you was unforgivable. But you know how he is.'

Meg did not respond. She was quick to take offence and slow to forgive, and today her demeanour was frosty.

She handed Juliet a mug. 'What I've never understood is why you stay with him.'

'Because of the children. Henry's their father.'

Meg studied her without sympathy. 'Is that a good enough reason?' Then she said, 'Sarah and me, we're going abroad. We've been talking about it for ages. We've saved up some money and we're going to buy a car and travel round France and Italy. I'm forty, Juliet. I've only ever been abroad once, that weekend we had in Le Touquet. I want sun and blue seas. I want to sit in a vineyard and drink wine. And if we don't go now, we'll never do it.'

And that was that. Meg would not change her mind. Leaving Mundon, Juliet drove a short distance before pulling into a field opening, where she switched off the engine and lit a cigarette. The leafless heads of the trees soughed in the wind; in the field, gulls followed a tractor.

Meg's words lingered – *what I've never understood is why you stay with him* – judging her, finding her wanting. To survive her marriage, she had trained herself to look away from what she did not want to see. She had not defended Meg against Henry's anger the previous morning because she had never once, during all the years of her marriage, persuaded him to change his mind. Instead, she had hoped to re-engage her behind his back, and subtly demonstrate to him that Meg was invaluable to Marsh Court. But Meg herself did not think her subtle; she thought her weak. And perhaps she

136

was. There had been a time, long ago, when she would have fought for what she believed in.

Idly she wiped away condensation from the driver's window. This morning, she had lost a friend. Talking to Joe Brandon by the causeway yesterday, had she lost something more? Though she tried to dismiss his assertion that he had seen Gillis saying goodbye to Frances Hart on the island – he must be mistaken, there must be some simple explanation – she could not. Anxious, frightened thoughts buzzed into her head like wasps through a crack in the glass, and could not be brushed away.

She put the car into gear and drove to Maldon. In the library, an assistant obtained for her copies of the *Essex Chronicle* from October 1946. The incident at Thorney Island and the subsequent search for the missing children had made the headlines several days running. Frances Hart had been thirty-one years old at the time of her death. Edmund and Thea had been twins, four years old. Mrs Hart had been renting the Thorney Island house since the beginning of the summer.

Carefully she read through the columns a second time. Though she had assumed Mrs Hart to have been a war widow, there was no reference to that in the newspapers. A sister in Wiltshire was mentioned, along with a widowed father. But no husband.

A raw wind buffeted her as she left the library. She ducked into a café and bought coffee and a bun. But the coffee only magnified her jitters and she could not eat the bun. A woman she knew through the school, the mother of one of the boys she taught, engaged her in conversation, but her answers were mechanical.

Joe Brandon had assumed that Gillis and Frances Hart had

known each other. What if he was right? Why would Gillis have kept such a thing from her?

Murmuring a goodbye to her friend, Juliet rose and left the café. Think about something else, she said to herself as she walked to the car. Think about Charley, who would be home from school for the weekend. Think about Christmas, only three weeks away. You always love Christmas. Think of decorating Marsh Court with holly and mistletoe, and of the scent of apple logs burning in the grate, and wrapping presents and baking mince pies.

Coming home from school at the end of the Christmas term, Charley thought the house felt funny without Piers, who was enduring ten weeks of foot drill in an army camp on the Yorkshire moors.

At the weekend, the Sinclairs visited. Flavia had recently become engaged to a solicitor who lived in Holt. The diamond in her ring was the size of a garden pea.

Gillis sent Rory to bed, leaving Charley, Louise and Nate in the games room while the grown-ups had a drink before dinner.

Juliet put her head round the door. 'Bed at nine, Charley. Darling, make sure Nate and Louise have everything they need.'

Nate was lolling on the sofa, reading a John Wyndham novel. After Juliet had gone, the paperback lowered.

'Actually,' he said, 'what I *need* is a beer and a fag.' Catlike, he was on his feet in a single graceful movement. Charley raised her eyebrows at Louise.

Nate came back with a glass of beer from the larder. He took a packet of cigarettes and a lighter from his pocket. The girls watched him light up. His mouth curved as he exhaled a smoke ring.

'Can I try?' said Charley.

'No.'

'*Nate.*'

'You're too young.'

'But Nate—'

'No,' he said repressively. 'It's bad for you. You can have a sip of my beer if you want.'

Louise shook her head, but Charley took a mouthful. It tasted foul, but Nate was smiling in a patronising way, so she swallowed some more.

'Three more years at school,' Nate said. 'Then Oxford, then I can travel. Can't wait.'

Louise said, 'Where will you go?'

'Australia. Maybe New Zealand.'

'They're an awfully long way away.'

'I know.' His green eyes glittered. 'That's the point.'

'Won't you get homesick?' asked Louise.

Charley, who had to share a room with her cousin on summer holidays, knew that Louise wept tears of homesickness in Cornwall.

'Shouldn't think so. Maybe, if I was hiking across a swamp and a mosquito bit me, I might think, I wonder how Charley and Louise are doing?' Nate went to the window and peered out. 'The sky's cleared. We'll be able to see.'

'See what?'

'The Geminids. Are you coming?'

They put on their coats and went outside. Charley breathed in the peppery, frosty smell of the night air. Her father's observatory was a sort of converted shed. You slid back the roof and saw the stars. She tried not to shiver as Nate fiddled with the telescope.

She said, 'Can you see anything?'

'Sputnik, orbiting the earth.'

'Honestly?'

'No, of course not, you clot.' Then, after several more minutes, '*Ah*. Have a dekko.'

Louise looked first. 'Oh Nate,' she said, and Charley was afraid she might be about to cry. Louise had cried a lot since her father had died.

Charley put her own eye to the telescope. At first there was just a blurry blackness, and then, miraculously, a star detached itself from its perch high up in the sky and moved across the heavens. And she gave a little gasp and said, '*Nate*,' and he said, 'Yes, I know.'

It was half past one in the morning. Juliet, Henry and Gillis were in the drawing room, having a nightcap. Their other guests had long gone to bed.

Henry yawned and stood up. 'I thought a walk tomorrow morning before breakfast. Take the dogs. Sevenish?'

'Look forward to it,' said Gillis.

'Goodnight, then.'

'Goodnight, Henry.'

'Just a moment, Gillis,' said Juliet. 'I need to speak to you about Flavia's wedding present.'

'Let the poor fellow have some rest, Juliet.'

Henry left the room. Gillis closed the drawing room door behind him. Then he took her in his arms and kissed her. At first, she felt herself melting into him, as she always did, as she tasted his lips and breathed in the scent of his skin: salt and grass and the sea. But then the question inveigled itself into her head again – *what if . . .?* – and desire ebbed away, like the river rushing out of the estuary.

She took a step back. He raised his brows, a reproachful smile touching the corners of his mouth.

'Didn't you miss me?'

'Always.'

'Then what is it?'

'Nothing.' She replaced the top on the whisky decanter. 'Do you remember the family who used to live on Thorney Island?'

A beat. 'What family?'

What family? She watched him go to the fireplace and take out a cigarette.

'The Harts. Frances Hart.'

'Frances Hart . . .' He put the cigarette to his lips and lit it, his forehead puzzled. 'I don't think I know anyone of that name.'

And she knew then. She knew that he was lying. You didn't forget the name of the woman you once saw lifeless on the mud. Not if you were Gillis Sinclair, with a razor-sharp memory for names, facts and figures.

She said, 'Someone told me he'd seen you with her.'

'Then he was mistaken.'

'That's what I told him.'

'Good.' He balanced the cigarette in an ashtray on the mantelpiece and opened his arms to her. 'Come here.'

She didn't move. Her gaze rested on him. 'I thought he'd made a mistake, that he must have mixed you up with someone else, but now I'm not so sure.'

'Juliet, for God's sake . . .' He laughed.

'He was very certain, you see.'

'Someone tells you he's seen me with a woman who drowned ten years ago, and you believe him rather than me?'

'So you *do* remember her.'

A quick frown. 'Yes. Now that I think about it.'

She looked down at her hands. There was an emptiness

opening up inside her, a pit into which she might, if she was not careful, tumble. 'The thing is,' she said carefully, 'what I would mind most is if you lied to me, Gillis.'

His voice was cold. 'I can't think why you're raking this up.'

'I suppose I could go and ask him what exactly he saw. Maybe I should show him some photos of you, just to be certain.'

'No.' His voice, louder now, resounded in the silent house. Then he said more softly, 'No, don't do that.'

She sat down, leaning forward, her elbows resting on her thighs, her feet planted flat on the floor to stop her legs shaking, and waited.

He let out a breath. Then he gave a lopsided smile and shook his head. 'Do you know, I'd almost forgotten about her.'

'You knew her.'

'Yes, she was my lover.' He had sat down beside her and was looking at her, a touch of amusement around his mouth. 'Was that what you wanted to hear, Juliet?'

She balled her fists, driving her nails into her palms. 'And the children?' The words caught in her throat.

'They were mine.' He unstoppered the whisky decanter, poured out two measures and pushed one of the glasses down the table to her. 'It was one of those wartime flings. You remember what it was like: you didn't know whether you'd be alive the next day. I bet you half the men in the navy had someone. Frances understood. She knew we had to keep it quiet. You mustn't think I didn't care about them, about the children. Edmund was a fine little chap, bright as a button and never afraid of anything.'

Abruptly, he paused, his glass halfway to his mouth. Then he opened his mouth as if in a silent scream.

After a moment he said softly, 'They liked to play on the causeway. I told Frances not to let them, but she found it hard, keeping them in the garden.'

Poor little souls, Juliet thought, and in her mind's eye she pictured the Blackwater rushing over the narrow channel between the island and the mainland. From somewhere in the upper storey of the house, a scurry of tiny feet. She must borrow Helen's mouser again. Charley's fat old tabby was hopeless at catching mice.

When she looked at Gillis, she found herself examining him as she examined the plum trees in the garden, checking for disease. He *looked* the same beautiful Gillis, but had there always been something rotten there?

'And Blanche?' she said.

'She never knew. Blanche is pretty hard on infidelity. In her eyes it's unforgivable.'

Juliet dropped her head. For what was she judging him? For his betrayal of Blanche, when she too had betrayed her for more than a decade? Or for keeping his secret from *her*?

He took her hand and squeezed it. 'I hated having to lie to you,' he said.

'Why did you, Gillis?'

'Because I knew that you thought me a good man. I didn't want to disillusion you. I was afraid you might hate me if you knew about Frances and the children.'

'Yes, I might have.'

Yet her hand was still enfolded in his, warm and strong. He pressed a kiss on it. 'It was . . . oh, a sort of madness. I was in a pretty bad way after Dunkirk, you know. And Blanche was expecting Nate, and I hadn't wanted another child, not then, not with all the horrors that were going on, but she hated having to go to the constituency house and I

143

suppose it was a sort of consolation prize. Something to comfort her when she was stuck in Wiltshire and I was away. Obviously, I adore Nathan now, but then . . .' He took a breath. 'It seemed so simple at first, with Frances. She was a jolly sort of girl and I thought, no strings, and I needed that. And then the twins. I was horrified. You can imagine. And after that it was so bloody hard to keep things quiet. I was always afraid someone would find out. I didn't want to hurt Blanche. I was afraid I'd ruin everything.'

She disentangled her fingers from his. 'I keep thinking of that time you kissed me.' Her words choked her. 'That night, in the storm. It was the first time . . . I thought it was because you loved me, but now I wonder whether you kissed me to keep me quiet.'

'No!' His expression became wounded. 'How can you say that? Juliet, please.'

'I mean, you must have been distraught. Such a terrible thing to happen. You must have been afraid of breaking down in front of me.'

'Yes.' He pressed the heels of his hands against his eye sockets. 'Yes, that was it. I had to be alone.' His hands lowered, he gave her a tortured glance. 'That night – can you imagine what it was like for me? To drive up here, thinking I was going to see them, and then . . . Poor Frances . . . and poor little Edmund and Thea. Not much more than *babies*. Such a terrible waste. And I wondered whether I should tell everyone the truth. But then I thought, what good would it do? They were beyond help by then and it would have hurt Blanche terribly.' His eyes burned, pleading for her to understand. 'I longed to tell you, Juliet. That was why I came to you. I've always hated to see the way Henry treats you. I thought you'd understand how hard it is to go on with a marriage

144

that isn't right. I thought you'd understand, you more than anyone.'

'Yes,' she murmured.

'I wanted to tell you, you know that, don't you? But when I saw you, I knew I had no right to burden you with my troubles. I was afraid that if I stayed with you, I'd break down and tell you everything. I was only thinking of you.'

'Yes, I see that.'

She did not stop him taking her in his arms again. His breath against her ear and the rasp of his chin on her cheek. Her thumb, brushing against the short, clipped hairs at the nape of his neck. For a long time he said nothing, but then, suddenly, he spoke again.

'I always tell myself that it wasn't my fault. So why can I never seem to believe that?'

Rolling out pastry for mince pies, she remembered the summer of 1946: Gillis walking away from the bonfire, smiling, raising a hand to her, handsome and golden in the sunlight. *Keep an eye on the girls for me, won't you, Juliet?* He had told her that he was going for a walk. But he had been visiting his lover, Frances Hart, on Thorney Island.

Shopping in town, picking out crackers and stocking fillers in Woolworths, she recalled the pattern of their love affair, the meetings, the phone calls, the half-hours in cold parks, kissing beneath the dripping trees. She wondered whether, when they had lain together in the Pimlico flat, he had been thinking of Frances Hart. Whether he had grieved for the scent of her skin and the soft fall of her hair.

Wrapping up presents on Christmas Eve, listening to carols on the radio, she thought: *this was what happened.* On the night of the storm, Gillis hadn't kissed her because he loved her. He

145

had been attracted to her, yes, but there had never been *love*. She knew that now.

Knotting a ribbon, she thought that they had been made for each other, she and Gillis. Both of them secretive, careless and greedy. She had extra qualities, she thought, of passivity and evasiveness. She shut away the things she did not want to see in a dark corner of her mind, but recently the door would not stay closed and a sullen, sulphurous light leaked out whenever she let down her guard. Whatever he had felt for her had died years ago, a part of her had known that for a long time. She supposed she had been afraid to accept the truth, that her marriage was over and so was her love affair and she had left it too late to start again. The affair had allowed her to survive her marriage; neither had been worth preserving.

She had no talent for love. She had had three lovers: the first the Frenchman in Cairo, with his wife and children, the second Henry, who had married her because of the way her pearl necklace had looked against her skin. And then Gillis Sinclair, who had made an art of betrayal. She was thirty-eight years old and could not imagine ever loving a man again.

Part Three

The Girl in the Red Dress

1964–1966

Chapter Eight

January 1964

'So,' said Esteban. 'What do you think?'

Esteban Galea was Winterton's chief designer. Born in Malta to a Spanish mother, he had lived in first Rome and then Paris before arriving in England in 1946. His designs had been instrumental in enabling Winterton's to recover its creative and financial success after the war.

For the past month Esteban had been working on a necklace commissioned by a Texas oil millionaire, a regular Winterton client. The necklace was to be a fiftieth birthday present for his wife. The design was a glorious rococo swirl of overlapping feather shapes, in which diamonds and sapphires clustered round teardrop rubies.

'It's stunning,' said Aidan. 'Genius.'

Esteban shrugged. 'It's what Winterton's wants,' he said rather disparagingly.

'Have you showed it to my uncle?'

'Not yet. He is busy, I think, quarrelling with your cousin.' Esteban's cool grey-brown eyes studied Aidan. 'I assumed that was why you had come here.'

Aidan gave a wry smile, acknowledging the designer's

percipience. The day had started badly, with a flaming row between Piers and Uncle Henry on the shop floor, witnessed by the staff. Aidan, who hated conflict and found his uncle terrifying when he was angry, had escaped as soon as he was able.

The workshops were on the first floor of the building, above the shop and the offices and below the Wintertons' private flat, which was reached by a separate entrance to the side of the building. In the seventy years since the Bond Street premises had first been established, these rooms had changed little. Traffic might roar through the surrounding streets, Italian coffee machines might hiss and the Beatles and Gerry and the Pacemakers play on the jukeboxes in the nearby cafés, but a dignified Victorian quiet persisted in the workshops. High, wide windows looked down on to wooden tables at which the designers and goldsmiths perched on tall stools. Easels, pinned with coloured sketches, stood beside the tables. One wall was covered floor to ceiling with drawers containing designs for pieces going back to the early years of the shop; on another hung an oil painting of Aidan's great-great-great-grandfather, Hayden Winterton, a handsome man with a mercenary gleam in his eye.

There were now four Wintertons working for the family business. Henry was their somewhat tyrannical boss; until this morning, no one had dared challenge his authority. Aidan's cousin Gabe, Jane and Peter's daughter, managed the Sloane Street store, while he and Piers remained in New Bond Street. The two cousins had begun to work at Winterton's after completing their National Service, and had spent their first three years learning all aspects of the business. For Aidan, design was at the heart of it all, and he had enjoyed the six months he had spent in the workshops. Henry had seemed to recognise this, because he had suggested that Aidan act as liaison between the workshop and Winterton's most favoured clients. Piers, meanwhile, had been promoted to become his father's second in command.

One of Aidan's responsibilities was to see through the creation of special commissions, keeping them on schedule and the client informed of progress. The feather necklace was one such commission. He would call the client that morning and let him know that it was almost ready.

His uncle had recently reminded him of the need to exert his authority over the staff, so Aidan said crisply, 'Thank you, Esteban. I'll speak to Mr Winterton today. He'll want to see the finished design.'

He left the room. On the landing, he paused, looking out of the window. From this high vantage point, he could see down to the roofs of the taxis and into the upper decks of the buses on Bond Street. It was a grey, rainy January day, and in his mind's eye he automatically sketched the umbrellas jostling on the pavements below, their pattern of black and crimson and navy. There wasn't a scrap of green grass or a tree in sight. He felt a sharp yearning for the emptiness of the river and the marshes.

He went downstairs. Outside the door to his uncle's office, he paused, listening. The shouting seemed to have stopped.

For the last two weeks, Henry Winterton had been in Bahrain, buying pearls. Piers had taken advantage of his father's absence by making changes to the shop floor. He had put away in the safe bracelets and necklaces he considered old-fashioned, and had instructed Esteban to design some more contemporary pieces. He had also reorganised the responsibilities of the staff, giving one assistant, whom he did not believe to be pulling his weight, his notice.

Returning to work that morning, Henry had been incandescent with rage. At one point in the argument, Piers had turned to his cousin. 'Back me up, Aidan,' he had barked at him. But Aidan had been tongue-tied, as he always was when confronted by his uncle's fury. No one could turn him to jelly quite like Henry Winterton, not even the permanently angry sergeant majors he had served under in the army. And so he had said nothing.

He felt bad about that now. It wouldn't have made any difference if he had supported Piers; Uncle Henry would have simply been furious with him as well. But that wasn't the point.

Wanting to see how Piers was, and needing to explain things to him, he tapped on the door to his office. When there was no response, he opened it. The room was empty.

In the shop, an assistant was placing a bracelet on a velvet bed to display it to a customer. An uneasy quiet hung over the room. Aidan suspected that if it had not been for the presence of the customer, the assistants would have been discussing the warfare that had broken out between father and son. Now, they were busily tidying, avoiding his eye.

Aidan spoke to Miss Burstein, Winterton's manageress, who had worked for the company since before the war.

'Have you seen Mr Piers?'

'He's gone out.'

'Do you know when he'll be back?'

'I'm afraid not, Mr Aidan. Mr Henry has asked not to be disturbed. By anyone.' She lowered her voice. 'Everyone's to stay late tonight. We're to put everything back how it was.'

Aidan thanked her and returned to his office. As he attacked a stack of paperwork, he listened out for the sound of Piers coming back to the building. By the end of the afternoon, he had dictated more than thirty letters to Miss Rolfe, his secretary, and Piers still hadn't returned.

Aidan glanced at his watch and yawned, stretching out his arms. The phone rang. He picked it up.

'Aidan Winterton.'

'Aidan?' A girl's voice. 'Is that you? It's Anne. Do you remember? Anne Carlisle.'

Juliet heard about it from Helen. 'Aidan told me Piers and Henry had the most frightful argument,' Helen said.

They were sitting in the light-filled studio at the back of Helen's Maldon home. Outside, stillness and cold and a low winter sun burning the horizon.

Juliet said, 'What about?'

Helen made a vague gesture. 'Something to do with the way they run the firm. Piers wanted to make it more *modern*.'

'Good God. He *told* Henry that?'

'Yes, I believe so.'

'I wish . . .'

'What?'

I wish he would learn to *manage* Henry better, she had been about to say. But that was unrealistic: Piers was twenty-four years old and impatient to make his way in the world. And he and his father had always rubbed each other up the wrong way.

She sighed. 'I wish he would learn not to be so confrontational.'

'Piers or Henry?'

'Oh, Piers, of course. Henry will never change.'

'Henry's made him go back to work on the shop floor. And he's promoted Aidan in his place. He's told Aidan to move into Piers's office.'

153

Juliet stared at her sister-in-law. 'Henry's made Aidan his deputy?'

'Yes, I'm afraid so.' Helen looked unhappy.

Juliet had given up smoking three weeks earlier, in the new year. It hadn't been as difficult as she had feared, but she found that she missed having something to distract her in moments of tension, such as this.

'Wretched, wretched man,' she said bitterly. 'So like Henry to punish poor Piers by humiliating him.'

Helen opened her mouth as if to speak. 'What?' said Juliet. 'Tell me.'

'I was going to say, poor Aidan too.' Helen stirred her coffee. 'He hates it just as much, you know.'

For his twenty-first birthday, Henry had bought Piers a small flat in Kensington. That evening, Juliet phoned the flat. She rang half a dozen times before her call was answered, and then Piers claimed to be in a hurry, on his way out. But she managed to persuade him to have lunch in town with her that Friday.

She arrived at Peter Jones's restaurant with five minutes to spare, but had to wait twenty minutes before Piers turned up. A quick greeting and then he slid into his seat, beckoned to the waiter and ordered a steak and kidney pudding. She thought he looked dreadful, baggy-eyed and sallow. His tie was sloppily knotted and she suspected he had worn his shirt for more than a day. But it was the good fortune of the young that even when crumpled and unwashed, they still look attractive, and she noticed a young woman at an adjacent table steal a glance at him.

'It's good of you to spare the time, Piers,' she said. 'Helen told me what happened.'

'Did she?' He glowered. 'Just like Aidan to go crowing to Mummy.'

'Darling, I'm sure it wasn't like that at all.'

'I'm supposed to be working for *Aidan*. The staff all kowtow to *young Mr Aidan*.' His voice dripped with contempt.

Her heart bled for him. It had pleased her that Piers, who was sharp-witted and easily bored, had, after being discharged from the army, taken quickly to working for the family firm. So infuriating, and so typical of Henry, to choose to do the one thing that would hurt his son most.

She touched his hand. 'It was wrong of your father. But darling, I'm sure this is only temporary. He's cross with you and you know he likes to make his point.'

Piers jabbed his fork at the suet crust on his plate. 'He needs to listen to me, because I'm right. The place is stuck in the past, Mum. The figures look good now, but they won't in a couple of years' time if Dad doesn't hurry up and make some changes.'

'Is that what you told him?'

'Yes.'

Dear God, she thought.

Piers was still talking. 'We make too many hideous necklaces for people with more money than taste, and too many mums' brooches. You know, a lumping great sapphire or ruby in the middle of some diamonds.'

She tried to imagine Piers lecturing Henry on how to run the firm he had headed for the last forty years. The thought chilled her.

'The business has to make money, darling,' she said. 'It has to sell what people want to buy.'

'People want *new* things, *modern* things. *Young* people do. They're not going to bother looking at Dad's old junk.'

155

'I'm sure you're right, Piers. But darling, slowly and tact-fully. Not overnight, when your father's out of the country!'

'Some of the staff agree with me.'

She gave him a sharp look. 'I hope you haven't told your father that. Piers, you mustn't involve the staff. If Henry was to hear, they might lose their jobs.'

He scowled. 'Aidan didn't say a thing, of course, just stood there like a dummy.'

'What did you expect him to say?'

Piers shook his head. 'Nothing,' he said bitterly. 'Just like he did. Nothing.' He added sullenly, 'He won't be any good at it anyway. He thinks he can do it, but he can't. He hasn't the fire.'

'He's your cousin,' she reminded him. 'He's family. None of this is Aidan's fault.'

'Isn't it?' His eyes were cold. 'It suits him, though, doesn't it, Dad and me falling out. It's got him what he wants.'

'Piers, I'm sure that's not the case.'

'Mum, you don't know, you weren't there.'

'I know Aidan,' she said firmly. 'And I know he would never try to hurt you.'

He drank a glass of water. 'I'm better than him,' he said softly. 'And Dad knows that. So why won't he listen?'

Because he never has, she thought. He doesn't know how to and would think it a deplorable weakness if he did.

She said crisply, 'Piers, it's your father's business. In the end, these decisions are up to him.'

'Then maybe I'll leave, go somewhere else.'

She stared at him, shocked. 'You can't leave Winterton's.'

'Why not?'

'For one thing, if you did, you'd be handing it to Aidan on a plate.'

'Yes.' The corners of his mouth turned down. 'That's the trouble.'

The conversation was not going the way she had intended. She tried to rein it in. 'Piers, please, no more talk of leaving Winterton's. No one wants you to do that.'

For a moment his face twisted and she glimpsed the hurt that lay beneath his bravado. He let out a breath. 'I won't leave, Mum. The business is *mine*.'

'One day it will be, darling. But you must be patient. I'll speak to your father later.'

'No,' he said sharply. 'I don't want you to do that. I can handle this myself.'

The waiter cleared away their empty plates. When they were alone again, Juliet said, 'I can't think it's going to make Dad any more pleased with you, turning up to work looking as if you've just fallen out of bed.'

'I haven't been in to work today.' Sulkily.

He was still capable of behaving, she thought, like a thwarted two-year-old. He had inherited his father's fierce will and temper, though Piers was less inclined than Henry to storm and rage. His anger was colder, more calculated, and he nursed his resentment for a long time. It was hard to decide who she felt more exasperated with just now – Piers, for reacting in the way most likely to intensify his father's displeasure, or Aidan, for allowing himself to be used by Henry. Or Henry himself, for choosing to humiliate his own son.

Henry, she thought angrily. *Obviously*.

She suggested, 'Wouldn't it be better to prove to your father that you're indispensable? Work really hard, do your best?'

'Suck up to him, you mean?'

'I meant, show him he's made a mistake.'

157

Piers chewed his lip, thinking. 'Show him I'm better than Aidan?'

She felt uncomfortable when he put it like that, but she nodded.

'Good old Mum,' he drawled. 'I never thought you'd tell me to give Aidan a poke in the eye.'

'That's not what I said.' But perhaps it was not so different. Uncomfortably, she felt disloyal to Helen. 'Please, Piers, try to sort things out. For my sake, if nothing else.'

Slowly, he nodded. 'Okay.'

'Good.' She felt relieved. 'Now, why don't we forget about pudding and go to the men's department and I'll buy you a new shirt. And then you can go to work.'

Ten minutes later, they parted at the door of the store. Juliet watched Piers cross Sloane Square, then she ducked back into Peter Jones to buy stockings for herself and Charley before heading to her dressmaker's in Pimlico.

As she walked, she found herself noticing the transformations that had taken place in the city. The London of the 1930s, with its murky glamour, seemed to have vanished utterly. The battered wartime London, bombed and bankrupt: that too had become a thing of the past. In its place was a new city with bright shops and modern galleries. A customer opened the door of a café and 'I Want To Hold Your Hand' spilled on to the pavement. Her fingertips drummed against her palm in rhythm with the song.

She had been visiting the little shop since before the war, and she and her dressmaker, Emmeline, were old friends. In the shop, Emmeline offered her a glass of sherry, which Juliet drank while she described the disagreement between Piers and Henry. Emmeline, who was divorced and on perennially bad terms with her ex-husband, was sympathetic.

Rattled by her conversation with Piers, Juliet bought three dresses and a spring coat. She wouldn't put it past Piers to carry out his threat to leave Winterton's, she thought, as she said goodbye to Emmeline and then made for the Underground station, laden with carrier bags. He was unpredictable when he was angry. In trying to impose his own vision on the family firm, Piers had fired the first warning shot across his father's bows.

She would speak to Henry that evening. Piers had told her not to, but she had made no undertaking to him. Tactfully, she would try to manoeuvre Henry into softening his attitude to his son.

She went back to the flat and made herself first tea, and then a gin and tonic. She and Henry were to dine with clients that night. She bathed, then put on one of the evening frocks she had bought that afternoon. In the shop she had thought the heavy satin a deep violet, but her own looking glass showed her that it was purple, and did not suit her. She exchanged it for an emerald-green knee-length moiré silk with a ribbon tied round its high waist. Was it any better? She studied her reflection but wasn't sure. It would have to do. She pinned a diamond brooch to the bow. Would Piers have dismissed it as a 'mums' brooch'? She looked at it doubtfully.

At seven o'clock Henry came up to the flat. She greeted him and made him a drink.

'I had lunch with Piers,' she told him.

They were in the bedroom. Henry was knotting a silk tie. Now in his early sixties, he had put on a little weight and his hair had thinned on top, but he remained a forceful figure, until Piers's challenge the indisputable head of the Winterton empire. She wondered whether what Piers had done had shaken him, and whether it had reminded him that he was growing older.

'He told me what happened,' she said.

'It's nothing to do with you, Juliet.' His tone held a warning.

'He's my son. I want him to be happy.'

'Don't meddle with things you know nothing about.'

She had listened to the family talk about Winterton's for decades. Sometimes she felt she could have run the business herself. 'Henry, Piers is young,' she said. 'He's ambitious, and he wants to make his mark. Surely you were the same at his age.'

'I respected my father. I respected his authority.'

'He needs to feel you're listening to him.'

He bared his teeth. 'Piers believes the business will just fall into his lap. But it won't. He's not the only Winterton. He has to earn it. What would you like me to do? Pat him on the head and tell him to be a good boy?'

'Of course not. Only . . . go easy on him.'

'Easy . . .' He gave her a critical look. It was hard not to shrink before his gaze, hard not to feel that the green dress did not suit her either and that the brooch was old-fashioned and her hairstyle ugly.

A smile touched the corners of his mouth. 'That's always been your motto, hasn't it? Take the easy way out, avoid making difficult decisions. Refuse to face up to what needs to be done. It doesn't seem to occur to you that this weak, simpering pose you like to adopt is hardly suitable for a woman of your age.'

She flushed. 'I can't see what my age has to do with it.'

'Perhaps you thought you could persuade me into giving in to Piers by fluttering your eyelashes.'

'No, Henry,' she said steadily. 'I'm not such a fool as that. I'm only suggesting you give him a second chance.'

He put on his jacket. 'You might have been able to use that sort of currency when you were nineteen, but it won't work now. You're too old a dog for those tricks, Juliet.'

She turned away, automatically glancing in the mirror to check that her nose was not shiny, her lipstick not smudged. Now, when she saw her reflection, she noticed the fine lines around the corners of her eyes, the slight sag to her neck.

Henry said, 'I suppose Piers asked you to plead his case with me.'

'Actually, he told me not to.'

'*He* has some sense then.'

He left the room. She was trembling. She sat for a while before putting on her coat. She was forty-four years old, no longer a young woman. Henry had always had the knack of exposing her insecurities.

They did not speak in the taxi to the restaurant. She felt his contempt for her along with her own hatred. Yet *did* she hate him? Tonight she felt too tired for hatred. The evening stretched out in front of her, in which she must play the part of elegant, charming Juliet Winterton. She knew she would perform well, she always did. Was that what she had become – a performer, a puppet made of paint and shadows that jerked and darted in front of a glittering backdrop?

And yet, as they greeted Henry's clients and went into the restaurant, it surprised her that she did not feel more upset. As the evening wore on, her earlier distress was replaced, if not by serenity, then by acceptance. Anyone who gave her history a superficial glance, she thought, might assume there was some justice in Henry's accusations. Her decision to marry him after finding herself alone and penniless in Cairo, her later resolve to continue with a relationship that would always be a battleground, all these things could be construed as weakness or passivity. As could her decision to keep secret Gillis's affair with Frances Hart.

But she was not weak. She knew that. She had survived. More than that, she had made for her family a comfortable and elegant home and had brought up two intelligent, delightful children. She had friends – Helen in particular. The music festival and her teaching: these had helped her cope with the deficiencies in her life.

After an unstable, impoverished upbringing, she had grasped at the security that Marsh Court had offered her. For a quarter of a century now she had tried to hold together the separate strands. Though she had attempted to keep from Piers and Charley the worst of her differences with Henry, she did not doubt that they had been affected by their parents' warring relationship. Piers had learned to confront rather than conciliate. Charley longed for love but at the same time found it hard to trust. Perhaps her children had paid a price for her love of Marsh Court.

But now she no longer needed to try so hard. Now she need not attempt to keep together a relationship that had long ago disintegrated. If Henry had lost the power to hurt her, what then did that say about her? What had her long marriage to him done to her? It had made her hard, she thought. And unhappy. Though, through pride and for the sake of her family, she had tried to hide it, a seam of sadness ran through her and had become a part of her. Perhaps her unhappiness had made her fall too easily for Gillis's charm. Perhaps it had been in response to her loveless marriage that she had loved him so passionately.

Their affair had ended six years ago. After the night he had admitted to her that he had been Frances Hart's lover, they had met just once, in a hotel near Epping Forest. They had tried to make love but it had been as if they had both forgotten how to. The rhythms that had once been so natural and easy had become clumsy and disjointed, and neither of them had taken any pleasure in it. They had made half-hearted references to some vague future and then had parted. Driving back to Marsh Court, she had had to pull into a lay-by, where she had wept, not for the loss of him, but for the loss of an illusion. He had not been the man she had wanted him to be. For months afterwards the baseline of her emotions had been grief and a dull disappointment.

Piers was now living in London and Charley would leave school in the summer or at Christmas, depending on whether she decided to take the Oxbridge entrance exams. The time was fast approaching when she need no longer stay with Henry for the sake of the children. That evening, sitting at the table in the restaurant, talking of skiing holidays and the Riviera, Juliet decided that as soon as both of them were settled, she would find a way of leaving him.

It wouldn't be easy. If she left him, then she must also leave Marsh Court. Could she do it? It would break her heart. And divorce would not be possible. Either Henry would have to agree to admit that he was guilty of adultery, which he would never do, or she would have to find evidence of his adultery, which would be distasteful and difficult. She would not force her children to witness the sordid spectacle of their parents flinging accusations at each other in court. The Winterton family must not see its name dragged in the mud; she loved them too much, owed them too much for that. The most she could hope for would be a legal separation. She would never be able to marry again – but then, she could not imagine ever wanting to. She had had her fill of marriage.

*   *   *

Katherine Rose's gallery was in Blantyre Street, in the tangle of streets behind the King's Road. The large front window was topped with a matt-black sign with the name 'World's End Gallery' picked out in silver lower-case lettering. In the window was a painting by Gene Davis, a series of precisely spaced pastel-coloured candy stripes on a pink background. Other works by the artist were on display in the gallery. Anne liked them. They were restful, and they made her think of the English seaside, deckchairs and sticks of rock.

Katherine, a thin, elegant woman in her sixties, who invariably wore a black Chanel jacket over a white blouse and black pants, had been a friend of Anne and her father for many years. After Anne's engagement had ended, it had been Katherine who had suggested she come back to London for a year or two, rent the spare bedroom in her house and work at the gallery. Anne had left America with a feeling of relief at having escaped the messiness of her life. Katherine's Hampstead home, all concrete, glass and unfussy decor, felt like a haven. Anne loved the cool interior of the gallery, enjoyed working with the clients and got on well with Katherine's other assistant, a thin, intense boy called Paul.

In the autumn of 1957, Anne's father had been offered a professorship at the School of the Art Institute of Chicago. Anne had decided to remain in the States as well but had returned to San Francisco, where she had spent her child-hood. There, she had studied for a secretarial qualification. Her days had been spent learning shorthand and typing in a classroom with fifty other girls, her evenings walking along Ocean Beach. The Pacific's never-ending murmur had been a background to her thoughts, and the North Sea, with its uncompromising chilly greyness, had seemed a very long way away. When she had looked back to that summer – the

Maldon summer – it had been with a degree of disbelief. What had happened to her had been so out of character. Falling in love with Piers Winterton had been so hopelessly out of character.

It would have been easy in retrospect to dismiss it as a crush, but she was far too honest to do so. There she had been, enjoying her summer staying on Lachlan and Sue's boat and having a good time walking and talking with Aidan, and then one day, Piers had appeared.

Piers Winterton. Heartbreak in blue jeans and an open-necked white shirt. Tall, fair-haired, eyes the colour of a clear evening sky. Handsome – and didn't he know it. He had strutted into her life with a charming smile and an air of self-possession. Her fall, her plummeting away from the common sense and caution she had believed integral to her, had happened in seconds. She had looked and she had loved. She had looked and she had longed for him.

Piers had flirted with her. She had retained just enough sanity to know that he would have flirted with any passable-looking female. He was that sort of man. Sometimes, she wasn't even sure that she liked him. Sometimes, she thought Aidan the nicer of the two Winterton cousins. She felt safe with Aidan. She didn't feel remotely safe with Piers. Being with him was like peering over the lip of a volcano.

Brought up before the divorce by a mother who liked to inflict on those around her her slightest nuance of feeling, Anne had learned young to hide her own emotions. Afterwards, it had been some small consolation that she felt certain Piers had never guessed how she felt about him.

It had been he who had invited her to his home on that awful day. A picnic, he had said, we're having a family picnic in the garden. She had imagined sandwiches and lemonade, a chequered tablecloth on the lawn. Her first mortification had been to discover that Piers hadn't forewarned his mother. That she had no invitation, had been inflicted on the family unexpectedly, the only non-Winterton present (the Sinclairs seemed to be regarded as adopted family). The 'picnic' had been a formal lunch on the patio at the back of the Wintertons' house. Anne, who had lived for the last eight years in rented apartments, many no more than a handful of rooms, had found Marsh Court oppressive. It seemed to glower down at her, heavy with its weight of history and Britishness.

And then, the Wintertons. Fair-haired, blue-eyed, conscious of their exclusivity, beauty and cleverness, they had, very politely, grilled her. Where was she staying? What did her father do? *An artist . . . how exciting.* Where had she been to school, and on which continent were her parents now living? *Divorced?* They had been too well-bred to raise their eyebrows, but Anne had sensed that they wanted to. Mrs Winterton had moved her away from Piers to sit between two other cousins. *You don't mind, do you, Anne?* She had felt chewed up, spat out. She had felt as if she had failed a test.

She hated formality, recognising it as a ploy to keep out those who did not belong. Well, she didn't; defiantly, she had acknowledged that to herself. The conversation had been of people she didn't know, in jokes she couldn't understand, and some sort of family quarrel had been going on, which had made her feel uncomfortable. The Wintertons were perfectly kind and welcoming and she had felt that it was she who was failing, not them. They were offering her the chance to become, for an afternoon, part of the family. Though she longed to, she couldn't. She couldn't work out how.

As the day had worn on, she had become aware of a deepening unhappiness. It had been too hot, a clammy warmth far more unpleasant than the dry heat of San Francisco, and seeing Piers with his family had brought home to her how different she was to him, and how unimportant. She had been mistaken in reading significance into this invitation. He felt for her nothing more than friendship, and Piers's friendship, she suspected, would be less lasting than Aidan's. He would probably forget her as soon as she went back to America.

And then the terrible thing had happened. Poor Aidan's father had collapsed suddenly from a heart attack. After ascertaining that there was nothing she could do, no help or comfort she could offer, she had melted away and walked back along the estuary. She had wept the whole way home.

She had been working for Katherine's gallery for two months now. During that time, she had alternated between a conviction that it would be unwise to dig up feelings best left buried and despising herself for her cowardice. Aidan and his family had offered her friendship that summer: she owed them courtesy, at least.

When she phoned Aidan at the jewellery shop, his obvious pleasure in hearing from her had proved to her that she had done the right thing. As for Piers, all that was long ago. If she had moved on, then so, surely, had he. She pictured him married to some English rose, a Caroline or a Serena, living in a grand house in bosky English countryside. She'd see Aidan, she resolved, have a friendly chat, and then that would be that, duty done.

Paul held open the door to allow the last client to leave the gallery. Then the three of them began to pull down blinds and lock away valuables in the safe.

Katherine, peering at her over half-moon glasses, said, 'You've a date, haven't you, Anne?'

'Not a *date*. Just a drink with an old friend.'

'Off you run, then. Paul and I will finish here.'

Anne put on her coat, knotted her scarf round her neck, peered at herself in the mirror of her powder compact and left the gallery.

He saw her, coming through the door of the Lord Nelson in the King's Road, and stood up and waved. The pub was packed; he had been lucky to find a table.

'Aidan,' she said, and kissed his cheek. 'How lovely to see you. I won't say you haven't changed, because we both have. We were such kids then, weren't we?'

He asked her what she wanted to drink. 'I'll have a beer,' she said. 'I've missed English beer.'

Queuing at the bar, he found himself glad to have a few moments away from her. He'd take a breath, get the drinks, and when he came back to the table he'd have got used to the fact that she was here with him, Anne Carlisle, the girl he'd never forgotten.

He put the drinks on the table and split open a packet of crisps. 'How long have you been back?'

'A couple of months.'

Aidan absorbed this fact. There had been a tiny and very unreasonable part of him that had hoped she was going to say *a week ago*. Something like that. And then, even more unreasonably, *I've been longing to see you, Aidan.*

'Where are you staying?'

'With Katherine, my friend with the gallery. I'm going to start looking for a place of my own soon. What about you?'

'I've a flat quite near the shop. I live there during the week. I go home most weekends.'

'To Maldon?'

'Yes.'

She asked after his mother, then said, 'So awful, what happened. I felt bad about leaving you.'

He pushed the crisp packet across the table to her. 'When I look back, it feels like my life was cut in two then. But I'm okay now and so is Mum. She wasn't for a long time but she is now.'

'How long have you been working for the family business?'

'Since I finished National Service.' He remembered their afternoons sketching at the harbour. 'Art college was always impossible,' he said, 'but Dad dying made it even more so. I probably wasn't good enough anyway.'

'Aidan, you were.'

He had forgotten the little silvery light-filled chips in her grey eyes, and her seriousness, conviction and honesty.

'I still draw at the weekends,' he said. Though it was no good drawing at the weekends. He knew that and so did she. To get better, you had to draw every day.

He asked after her parents. After she had finished telling him about her dad in Chicago and her mother, who had opened a beauty salon in Palm Springs, she paused and then said:

'I was engaged to be married but I broke it off. I'd made such a mess of things, so when the opportunity arose to come back here, I jumped at it. What about you, Aidan? Is there anyone?'

'There's a girl,' he said vaguely.

'What's she called?'

'Lynette.'

Lynette was small, brunette and bouncy. A drama student, she phoned him now and then to tell him she had theatre tickets. The tickets were always dirt cheap, in the gods, from

169

where you looked down and watched the actors scurrying like ants on the stage.

'It's not serious,' he said. He should break it off, he thought. He had sort of known that anyway but hadn't done anything about it. Often, Lynette's hand crept into his as they were sitting in the chilly heights of the upper circle. They kissed when they parted. It wasn't serious to him, but it might be to her. She might feel the same sort of hunger for him that he felt for Anne.

'I'm sorry about your engagement,' he said.

She gave a regretful smile. 'I'm not. He wasn't the right man for me, poor guy. How's the rest of your family? All those cousins.'

'Fine.'

She took a crisp. 'And Piers?'

Piers was furious with him. Piers had studiously avoided speaking to him since Uncle Henry had taken it into his head to punish him by promoting Aidan in his place. Piers blamed him for what had happened, which was completely unreasonable but typical bloody Piers. Aidan assumed that Uncle Henry would eventually calm down and they'd switch places again and things would go back to normal.

'Oh, Piers is fine,' he said.

They had a dinner engagement in Maldon with the Stanmores, staunch supporters of the summer concerts. In her bedroom at Marsh Court, Juliet made up her face and clasped on a gold necklace and earrings. Then she went downstairs. Drinking a gin and tonic, waiting for Henry, who was driving home from London, she looked through her notes for the next concert series. When she had finished, she glanced at the clock. It was ten past seven. The Stanmores' invitation had stipulated half past seven for eight. Henry was cutting it fine.

Quarter past . . . twenty-five past. She dialled the Bond Street flat, then both shops. Each time the phone rang out unanswered. Exasperated, she called the Stanmores to apologise. Henry must have been delayed, she explained, politely turning down Margaret Stanmore's suggestion that she herself drive over and Henry come straight to their house when he arrived home. Something must be wrong, she knew that. Henry was never late. The car had a puncture, she guessed. He would be fuming at the side of some dark country road, wrestling with tyre levers.

She took notepaper and an envelope from her desk, then sat down and began to write a letter to Charley. The phone rang as she signed her name. She picked up the receiver.

'Henry, is that you?'

'No, it's Gillis.'

A brief exchange of pleasantries. Then he said, 'Actually, I was hoping to speak to Henry.'

'Actually, I was about to call you, to ask you whether you'd seen him.'

'He's not at home, then?'

'Not yet. I'm expecting him. He must have had a flat tyre or something.'

He rang off. Juliet made herself another drink, then went up to her bedroom and changed out of her evening frock. The car must have broken down miles from anywhere, or Henry would have phoned from a box. Restless, she returned downstairs, put on an apron and gave the kitchen sink a good scrub.

The front doorbell rang. She went to answer it. A policeman was standing on the step.

'Mrs Winterton?' he asked, and she said yes. Then he said, 'Do you think I might come inside?'

Henry was dead. His car, his fast little Mercedes, had skidded on an icy patch on a humpbacked bridge near Langford and ploughed into a tree. The steering wheel column had pierced his heart, killing him instantly. So, Juliet thought, as the policeman went through it for a second time, presumably taking her blankness for lack of comprehension, you could say that both Winterton brothers had died of a similar cause. Jonathan was a big-hearted man, but Henry's heart had been small and dry, and she imagined that it had splintered like a seed pod.

The policeman came back from the kitchen and placed a cup of tea on the table next to her. He said, 'Is there anyone you'd like to come and sit with you?' When she did not reply, he began again. 'Mrs Winterton—'

'My sister-in-law, Mrs Helen Winterton, in Maldon.'

He dialled Helen's number. Juliet drank the tea. She heard the distant rumble of a car engine – it must be Henry, she thought. But no, it couldn't be, because Henry was dead. Overhead, a door banged, and for a moment she imagined that he had slipped upstairs while she was talking to the policeman and was cross because he couldn't find his cufflinks, something like that. She simply could not take it in. He was too vital a presence to just – what? Just not be there any more.

The tea was too sweet; she would rather have had whisky. She would not be able to mourn him, she thought, and was for a moment seized by blind panic. She was sorry for his end, for the moment of terror he must have endured as he lost control of the car, but pitied him only as she would have pitied anyone who had died a sudden, violent death.

The doorbell rang. 'I'll get it,' said the policeman.

'No,' she said crisply, rising from her seat. 'I will.'

The phone rang as Piers let himself into his flat. It was three in the morning.

He picked up the receiver. 'Piers Winterton.' It had been a long night, a pub and a restaurant and a nightclub, and he was quite drunk and had to concentrate so as not to slur his words.

'Piers, it's Mum. Darling, I'm so sorry, but I have some very bad news, I'm afraid.'

Then she told him that there had been a motor accident and that his father was dead. At one point he actually took the receiver away from his ear and stared at it, half wondering whether he had fallen asleep and was dreaming.

'Dead?' he had repeated. '*Dead?*'

'Yes, I'm afraid so. I'm so sorry, darling.'

'Are you sure?'

'Yes, Piers. It was a very bad accident.'

He sat down on the floor. He felt sick and was afraid he might have to cut off the call and run to the bathroom.

With an effort he regained control of himself. As the news started to sink in, he ran a hand over his hair and said, dazed, 'But we'd *quarrelled*. Me and Dad. About the firm.'

'Yes, I know. Piers—'

'The last thing I said to him . . .' But he couldn't remember what it had been. Probably a sarcastic acquiescence to a command his father had barked at him. Nothing pleasant. Not a smile or a thank you, certainly not an endearment.

'Christ,' he said softly.

His mother said, 'Darling, your father loved you and you loved him. That's all that matters.'

Was it? Remembering the insults he and his father had recently traded, he doubted that. And had his father loved him? He'd never know now, would he?

'I'll get the car, Mum,' he said. 'I'll drive home now.'

'No,' she said forcefully. 'No, I don't want you to do that. Get some sleep and come home in the morning. Helen's with me, I'm fine.' And then, after telling him she loved him, she rang off.

There wasn't a phone in the building where Aidan rented a room; they used the kiosk down the road or he made calls from his office. So he didn't know until he went into work on Saturday morning. It was a bright, wintry day and he was in a good mood, thinking about Anne, how marvellous it had been to see her, how it had occurred to him that evening as he had walked to the pub before their date that at eighteen his judgement might not have been up to much, and she might be – well, ordinary; and then, seeing her, the relief and delight of discovering that she was even more beautiful and sweet and good to talk to than he remembered.

When he went into the shop, he called out cheerful greetings. Then he realised that all of them – Miss Burstein, the shop assistants, and Miss Rolfe, who should have been working but wasn't – were staring at him. It crossed his mind that Piers had quarrelled with Uncle Henry again, had made a scene or something, but then Miss Burstein went to him, put her hand on his arm and said, 'Aidan. Let's go to your office, shall we?'

*   *   *

174

Her cousin Jake picked Charley up from school. Charley, who had cried since her housemistress had broken the news of her father's death to her, shivered and gulped while he loaded her overnight case into his sports car. The case, which she hadn't done up properly, came open, spilling stockings and navy-blue knickers into the boot of the MG. Jake scooped them up and clicked the lock shut.

He was at least a foot taller than her and had to stoop while he hugged her. Charley sobbed into his sheepskin coat.

'Come on,' he said. 'Let's get you home.'

She got into the car. Her head ached and her eyes hurt from crying.

'Here,' Jake said, and handed her a couple of aspirins and his hip flask.

There was something disgusting in the flask, which burned her throat and made her cough, but she swallowed it down with the aspirins.

'It's my hangover cure,' he said, and she managed a smile. He squeezed her hand. 'I'm so sorry, Charley.'

She bit her lip and stared out of the window as they headed down the drive. 'I'm afraid,' she whispered, 'that no one but me will mind. That no one else will miss him. Poor Dad, hardly anyone missing him.'

'Mum will,' he said. 'She's lost both her brothers now.'

'Where is Auntie Jane?'

'Driving to Marsh Court. And Eliot and I will miss him. We used to joke about what a difficult old bugger he was, but it's hard to imagine Marsh Court without him. We'll all miss him, Charley.'

Mum won't, she thought, as she took a shuddering breath and struggled to turn off the tears. And she wasn't sure

175

whether Piers would. But if Jake didn't already know that, she wasn't going to tell him.

Piers was at Marsh Court before eight. He looked terrible, crumpled and shocked, and there were dark rings round his eyes. Helen made coffee while Juliet cooked bacon, eggs and sausages. Helen offered to cook but Juliet said she knew the oven better.

She wasn't hungry, but Piers ate the lot. He wiped egg yolk from his plate with the last crust of bread.

'Mum, would you like me to look through the financial stuff?'

'I've made a start. Your father's bank accounts are in his name. I was about to phone Tom Kendrick.'

'I'll do it.'

Sensing that he needed to be occupied, she let him take over. He left the room. Juliet ran the hot tap.

Helen said, 'Let me wash up.'

'I need something to do. I feel so *restless*.'

'Did you sleep at all last night?'

She shook her head. 'I was so exhausted I thought I'd go out like a light. But I was thinking about things, I suppose.'

'Anything I can help with?'

'Oh . . . everything that needs to be done. The funeral . . . where to put people . . . whether I've enough sheets laundered. You know.'

'We'll make a list,' said Helen. 'You know that lists are my solution to everything.'

Juliet sat down at the table. 'I keep thinking about how it should have been,' she said. 'I keep thinking about what, if Henry and I had been different people, we would have had. What I'd be grieving for now. Maybe I'd be remembering some wonderful motoring holiday in Italy we'd had when we were young. Or how we'd celebrated when the children passed their exams and comforted each other when they went off to boarding school. Or how, after we'd given a dinner party, Henry would always have washed up while I dried and how we'd have talked and laughed about our guests.' She looked up at Helen. 'But I don't have any of that.'

She was crying now. Outside, snow flurried from a bruised sky.

Piers came into the kitchen. She wiped her eyes with her palm.

'Mum, Kendrick says he'll call in on Monday afternoon, if that's okay.'

'Yes, of course.'

He went away. She blew her nose, tucked her hankie back in her sleeve. The doorbell rang. 'Jane, probably,' said Helen, squeezing her shoulder. 'I'll get it. Juliet, have you told Gillis and Blanche?'

'Not yet.'

'I'll do it. And if you can find me Henry's address book, I'll contact his other friends.'

She had thought him indestructible, Juliet realised as she searched through Henry's desk for his address book. But he was dead at sixty-one years old and their marriage, of which she had sickened a long time ago, was over. The world had taken on a different shape.

The family assembled at Marsh Court. Jane arrived alone, red-eyed from weeping. Peter was to drive up after his Saturday-morning clinic along with Eliot, who was working at St Thomas's Hospital. Charley and Jake reached Marsh Court at eleven. Then, in the afternoon, Louise, who had left

177

school at the end of the previous year and was now studying at a secretarial college in London, travelled to Maldon with Jane's daughter Gabe, with whom she was sharing a flat.

In the early evening, the women gathered in the kitchen. Helen and Juliet chopped and stirred. Jane was dishing out drinks and Gabe was counting out plates. The little girls – though of course neither Louise nor Charley was a little girl any more – were making a trifle. Charley always made her trifles in exactly the same way: Lyons trifle sponges, mandarin segments, Bird's custard and tinned cream.

The funeral was to be on Friday, in six days' time. Helen said, 'Will you stay at home for the week, Louise?'

Louise was sprinkling hundreds and thousands on snowy peaks of cream. 'I can't.'

'I'm sure the college won't mind. I'll phone them.'

Louise and Charley exchanged glances. Louise said, 'I've got a job, Mum.'

Helen scooped up sliced carrots and dropped them into a saucepan. 'What sort of job?'

'Modelling,' said Louise.

'Well,' said Jane. 'How exciting. I'm not surprised. Such a pretty girl, Helen.'

'It's for *Honey* magazine, Mum. I don't know whether anything will come of it, but it's an opportunity.'

'*Modelling*,' said Helen, frowning. 'I thought you'd decided you were going to be a secretary?'

Louise's long, caramel-coloured fringe swept over her face as she scattered hundreds and thousands. She was a tall, skinny, coltish beauty whose blue eyes often held a wistful, dreamy expression. Juliet had never heard her express any ambition other than the setting-up of the donkey sanctuary. She had assumed her to be the sort of girl who would drift seamlessly from school to secretarial work or nursing, and then into marriage.

'If I'm successful,' said Louise, 'modelling will pay much better. And if I'm not, then I'll still have my secretarial qualification.'

'We'll talk later,' said Helen.

'Have we done enough potatoes?' asked Juliet.

'Dozens.' Jane took the peeler out of her hand and put a glass there instead.

Because his father's bank accounts had been frozen following his death, Piers had to have a slightly awkward conversation with his mother about whether she had enough money to live on. He could tell she hated talking about it, considered it vulgar and demeaning, but gently and tactfully he managed to ascertain that she was okay for the time being.

Aidan came up to Marsh Court late on Saturday evening after the shops had closed, and then went back to London on Sunday. With Henry Winterton gone, someone needed to keep an eye on the business. Though Piers hated Aidan being in charge of the firm, he knew that his mother needed him at Marsh Court, and during his cousin's short stay he managed at least to be civil to him. If only Aidan had shown some him loyalty, perhaps it wouldn't have all got so out of hand. Perhaps his father might have seen sense. Though that, he conceded, was unlikely. Although he hadn't forgiven Aidan for failing to back him up in the dispute with his father, he was aware that he himself would soon be taking over the reins of the business so could afford to be magnanimous.

The memory of his quarrel with his father troubled him a lot. Why couldn't Dad have just come into the shop that Monday morning after he had returned from Bahrain, and said, 'Yes, good idea, well done, Piers.' Then maybe slapped him on the back, adding, 'A chip off the old block,' instead of yelling at him. When he'd been a kid, he had always tried to win his father's approval. He'd studied hard for exams and pushed himself to get in the rugby and cricket teams. His father had a way of picking any small failure out of a sea of successes. Eleventh in history, he'd say, glossing over all the firsts. Or, not got your school colours yet, Piers? After a while he had stopped trying, had slid down the form rankings and bunked off games. What was the point?

By the time he'd left school, he'd hated it. He had detested his two years in the army from beginning to end. But he had loved the business from the first day he had started work there. He had always known that this was where he should be, and that he was good at it. That his father had never, ever told him that, and that they had parted on such bad terms, and with such unexpected permanence, tore at him. It occurred to him, lying awake in the early hours of Sunday morning, that he could put right some of what had happened by making Winterton's even more successful than it was already. He could do what his father would have done, if he'd had time. And then he realised he was weeping.

Mr Kendrick, his father's solicitor, called on Monday afternoon. Piers's mother showed him into the morning room, then went off to fetch a tray of tea. Mr Kendrick, who was ancient and cadaverous and had a cold, sniffed and shuffled papers.

His mother poured out the tea. Mr Kendrick said, 'I don't know whether either of you is aware of the fact that Mr Henry Winterton made some alterations to his will ten days ago.'

His mother looked up. 'No, Mr Kendrick, I don't think so. I wasn't – were you, Piers?'

No, he said, he hadn't known.

'Were the alterations significant?'

'Yes, I'm afraid they were.'

Mr Kendrick cleared his throat. He explained that Charley was to have an annuity of fifteen hundred pounds a year. Piers was to inherit Marsh Court and the Bond Street flat along with the residue of Henry Winterton's personal estate. His mother was to have only the cottage and an income of a thousand pounds a year.

And then the solicitor went on to tell them that Aidan was to inherit the business in its entirety. *In its entirety*, Mr Kendrick repeated with another sniff, in case they didn't understand what the word meant. Both shops, Bond Street and Sloane Street, along with the money tied up in the family firm. And that was when Piers discovered that Winterton's would not be his after all. And that instead, Aidan was to have everything.

Chapter Nine

January–February 1964

Though he had loved Henry, he had betrayed him. This thought came into Gillis's mind as the vicar climbed into the pulpit of All Saints' Church in Maldon. It occurred to him that Henry would not have done the same. For all his faults, he had been loyal to his friends.

The church was packed for Henry Winterton's funeral service. Gillis's gaze found Juliet, in the front pew. A black hat covered her bright hair. Piers was sitting to one side of her, Charley to the other. As the vicar began to speak – *a distinguished war record . . . a man of immense drive and determination* – Gillis pondered the nature of betrayal, how you could love someone and yet take what was theirs.

Blanche was sitting beside him. He had betrayed her too, of course. Was that what defined him – not his DSO, nor his political career, but his treachery? Had his foolish affair with Frances Hart, with all its disastrous consequences, been the defining moment of his life? Would the events of that stormy night on the Blackwater haunt him till Judgement Day?

'Hush,' murmured Blanche, touching his sleeve, and he realised that he must have made some sort of sound. Extracting his handkerchief from his pocket, he blew his nose. He felt low today: January, and the death of an old friend. They had risen at six and had driven down from London in the darkness. Even when morning had come, it had seemed half-hearted, the heavy grey sky weighing down on threadbare, snow-sprinkled countryside. After the funeral they would drive on to Marsh Court to lunch with friends and family; they must return to London this evening, as he had an engagement the following day. Just then, he was aware of every one of his fifty-seven years. He felt drained, wearied at the prospect of the long hours before him.

Henry Winterton made an impression on all those who met him, the vicar was telling the congregation, and Gillis gave a mental snort and felt for a moment a little cheered. He certainly bloody had. Frequently an unpleasant impression, but he hadn't been the sort of man you forgot easily. Henry's sarcasm, and the pleasure he had taken in getting a rise out of people, had never bothered Gillis. Blanche told him he was thick-skinned, and perhaps, ordinarily, he was.

But not today. Today he felt scoured, flayed. Henry Winterton's death marked the end of an era. In the years before the war, when they had first met, Henry had been a powerful and entertaining presence. How Gillis had loved coming to Marsh Court, and how he had loved the quick, funny, disputatious conversation of the Wintertons! They had been unstintingly generous to him of their time and company and affection, and a lump formed in his throat and he had to blow his nose again and think about something else: the disarray the government was in following the Profumo scandal, his own plodding efforts to write up his war diaries as a sort of memoir, anything.

* * *

Dear God, let this day be over, Juliet prayed as they lowered the coffin into the earth. Charley was pressing her face into her sleeve. Juliet drew her daughter closer, wrapping her arms round her. She was aware of Piers at her other side, quietly and implacably furious. She had had to use emotional blackmail to persuade him to attend his own father's funeral. Both shops were closed today as a mark of respect, and many of the staff had travelled to Maldon for the service. It would be nice, Juliet thought, if they could get through the day without Piers making some sort of awful scene in front of faithful old Winterton retainers like Miss Burstein and Miss Rolfe. It would be nice if they could maintain at least the appearance of dignity.

She had calculated that around fifty people would be coming back to Marsh Court after the service was over. She hoped they had prepared enough food. She ran through in her head the dishes stowed in larder and fridge, mentally dividing them into portions.

And there, it was done, and the vicar was shaking her hand and murmuring condolences, and all the while her husband was being buried she had been thinking of cold salmon and boiled ham.

They walked down to where Piers had parked the car near the harbour. The tide was out and the water and mudflats were the same pale chilly grey as the sky. Only the buffet lunch and the rest of the afternoon to get through, she told herself, and then she could begin to find out whether there was anything left of her after twenty-six years of marriage to Henry Winterton.

His mother had sent Aidan in search of more chairs. He discovered a couple in the morning room. Pausing, he looked

184

out of the window, down the lawn with its scattering of snow, to the fire pit. He wondered who had built the bonfire. Charley, probably.

A sound, behind him. Piers came into the room.

'You planned this,' he said.

'What?'

'*What?*' mimicked Piers, falsetto, his lip curling. 'You wanted Dad to give it all to you. That was why you didn't back me up when he was laying into me. You were trying to get into his good books.'

This was so ridiculous, so far-fetched, that Aidan almost wanted to laugh.

'I didn't even know that your father had changed his will,' he pointed out. 'I had no idea. How could I?'

Piers shut the door behind him. 'I don't believe you.'

Did Piers seriously imagine that he, Aidan, had been in cahoots with Uncle Henry about the inheritance of the shops? He made an effort to find the right words, the ones that would force his cousin to see sense.

'He never spoke to me about who would inherit the business. Not once, I swear it, Piers. I assumed everything would go to you.' Aidan put down the chair. 'If you must know, I didn't back you up when you quarrelled with Uncle Henry because I couldn't face him being angry with me as well.'

'Liar. You saw your chance and you took it.'

'You can think what you like,' he said angrily. 'I know I was cowardly, but he was bloody terrifying and I always tried to avoid crossing him.' He found himself resenting the derision in Piers's eyes. Wanting to jolt his certainty, he added, 'Anyway, I'm not sure you're right about modernising Winterton's. It seems perfectly fine to me how it is.'

185

The door opened and Louise came in. She looked from one cousin to the other.

'Mum says can you hurry up because some of the great-aunts have nothing to sit on. And if you don't get a move on, all the sausage rolls will have gone.'

The temperature had fallen and they could see their breath against the pale clotted sky. Peter fetched a couple of mouldy old deckchairs from the shed and Jane found some cardboard boxes, and they added them to the pyre. Flavia and Claudia tended their infants while their husbands gathered up fallen branches. Helen dropped handfuls of dead leaves on to the heap and Charley crumpled up old newspapers, stuffing them round the perimeter.

Juliet stood back, watching. She would join in nothing that spoke of honouring Henry. Not a leaf nor a twig would she add to the bonfire. How he must have hated her to have taken Marsh Court from her, leaving her, in its place, the cottage that they used for guests! He had known how much she loved the house, so to punish her for taking Piers's part in their quarrel, he had decided to deny her it. He had known she would not contest the will, because that would mean challenging Piers. Which she would never, ever do.

As Charley put a match to the bonfire, Juliet felt the crushing weight of her anxiety. Marsh Court had been her security, it had been the object of her love. She had kept it alive during the war and had nurtured and cared for it ever since. She had planted its gardens and cooked and cleaned and filled it with music and laughter. She had made it a *home*.

The annuity that Henry had left her had been insultingly meagre, a far smaller sum than he had willed to Charley, and so he had ensured also that she would always struggle for money. The ramifications of his vindictiveness stacked up ahead of her as the fire caught the dry leaves and newspaper and an acrid smoke scented the still air. All the luxuries she had so long taken for granted – the couture clothes, the billing accounts at Harrods and Selfridges, her car, her seats at the Royal Albert Hall and the Royal Ballet – even her scent, which was made for her at a perfumery in Paris – all these were slipping away from her.

But none of that mattered compared to the house. These things were pleasurable, but they were not essential to her. She would have bought her clothing from jumble sales and entertained herself with library books had it meant she could keep Marsh Court.

'Juliet.'

Turning, she saw Gillis. He asked her how she was.

'Oh . . .' She smiled at him. 'Not that much of a grieving widow, I'm afraid. A furious one, in fact. You've heard, I suppose?'

'About the will? Yes.'

'I suppose all Essex has heard.'

'Juliet, it was outrageous of Henry. You must contest it.'

'No, I won't, and neither will Piers. We've spoken about it.' They had, late into the night. She had pleaded with her son, pointing out that a legal dispute would tear the family apart irrevocably. In the end, Piers had agreed to do as she asked.

Gillis frowned. 'As Henry's widow, you have a good case. Let me give you the name of a chap I know.'

'The only people who make money out of that sort of wrangle are the lawyers, you know that, Gillis. And it's so utterly sordid . . . I won't put the family through it – no, never.' Her gaze flew to Piers, standing at the bonfire.

'You must at least get proper legal advice.'

'Gillis, we don't do that sort of thing.' Her voice was crisp and final, suppressing any further discussion. She gave a short laugh. 'Henry always said that family was the most important thing. In that, if in little else, I agree with him.'

He raised his shoulders, acknowledging defeat. 'Will you be all right?'

He meant, *have you enough money to live on?* She supposed other friends and acquaintances were looking at her and wondering the same.

'I'm fine,' she said lightly. 'Honestly, Gillis, absolutely fine.'

'If you should ever have any difficulty, you know I'm always there.' He coughed. The flames leaping into the sky were a violent, angry red. 'You've put on a good show for the old boy,' he said.

'I'm a Winterton,' she said sourly. 'We always put on a good show, don't we?'

He took her hand and squeezed it as his lips brushed against her cheek. She closed her eyes, sharply reminded of old times, different times.

'Blanche and I have to go, I'm afraid,' he said.

'I'll see you out.'

'No need. I'll ring you. Look after yourself, Juliet. And remember, if there's anything we can do . . .'

Gillis and Blanche walked back towards the house. It came to Juliet that she was not without consolation, that she had friends and family, and a feeling of peacefulness crept over her. Her marriage, which had brought her so much and had tormented her so much, was over. She had the chance to start again.

Then Piers emerged from the shed, carrying a can of petrol. Peter called out, 'Hang on, old chap,' but Piers sloshed the petrol on to the blaze. There was a great whump and flames rushed out horizontally across the grass, and everyone leaped back.

'Bloody fool,' shouted Peter. 'Someone could have been badly hurt.'

And as Juliet watched, Aidan turned on his heel and headed away from the bonfire, across the field to the estuary.

Anne Carlisle, who was staying on the boat in Heybridge that weekend, heard of Henry Winterton's death through Lachlan and Sue Macdonald. Poor Piers and Charley, she thought, to lose their father when they were so young, and poor Mrs Winterton too. She wrote a note of condolence and gathered snowdrops from a patch of woodland near the canal, wrapping them in moss and tissue paper.

After a long lunch with Sue and Lachlan and their friends, she drove to Marsh Court. Nearing the house, she saw a plume of smoke curling through the sky and recalled the Wintertons' custom of lighting a bonfire at times of significance. This one must be to mark Henry Winterton's passing.

She parked in the courtyard in front of the house. The smoke was rising into the air behind the roof; you could almost imagine that it came from the house itself. She would give her note and the snowdrops to whomever answered the door. She would not stay; it would not be appropriate at such a time.

She pressed the doorbell. There was a long wait, and then footsteps. The door opened and Anne found herself face to face with Piers Winterton.

Behind Aidan, smoke from the bonfire gathered in ragged white streaks, pressed down low over the fields by the freezing

189

air. The path curled ahead of him, tracking the border of salt marsh and meadow. His footsteps, fast-paced by his anger, pounded on a surface gripped hard by frost, and his breath made puffy little clouds. On distant fields, snow striped the ploughed earth. He dug his hands into his coat pockets and walked on, head down, icy air stinging his face.

Piers's voice rang in his ears. *Liar. You saw your chance and you took it.* Not true: the first inkling he had had that Uncle Henry had left the business to him had been when Mr Kendrick, his uncle's solicitor, had phoned him. After taking the call, he had sat at the desk in his office, dazed with shock. *I don't want it,* he had thought. *I really, really don't want it.*

This day had been every bit as awful as he had anticipated, with Piers looking daggers at him, Aunt Juliet withdrawn and his mother upset by the whole thing. He hated to be the focus of the Winterton relish for a good quarrel and had sensed that afternoon the family dividing into factions, taking sides. Most of all, he resented that Piers had put aside years of friendship so easily, passing judgement on him without even bothering to listen to his side of the story. He felt disconnected and set apart from the people he had known and loved his entire life. He had almost lost his temper after Piers's display of exhibitionism with the petrol can, had wanted to yell at him in front of the entire family to stop being such an idiot. Piers could never just be angry; he had to make sure everyone *knew* he was angry. Unable to stand being in the same place as his cousin a moment longer, Aidan had walked away.

Ahead lay the island, like a grey whale rising out of the water. The trees that crowned it were a thin line of darker grey. Scanning the estuary, he made out redshank and shel-duck, searching for food on the mudflats. Hundreds of gulls

190

rose into the air, squealing. A curlew . . . a black-tailed godwit
. . . and from the scrubby bushes behind him, the loud,
piercing call of a stonechat. Some of the tension slipped
from his shoulders. The further he walked from Marsh Court,
the better he felt.

As he neared the causeway, he saw that a woman was
standing on the shore of the island. She was wearing a navy
duffel coat and wellingtons and had on a scarlet woollen hat
over curly reddish hair. She had set up a camera on a tripod
and was taking a photograph.

Aidan felt a flicker of irritation. He had been enjoying his
solitude and wasn't in the mood for talking to a stranger.
But he called out, 'Hello there!'

She straightened. 'Hello!'

'The tide's coming in! You should head back or you'll get
stranded.'

He saw her glance to where water was lapping across the
lower side of the causeway. 'Thanks!' she called. Slinging a
rucksack over her shoulder, she grabbed the camera and
tripod and hurried back along the narrow path.

Reaching him, she said, 'Thanks so much.'

Close to, he saw that she was tall, only a couple of inches
shorter than him, and much the same age. Her smile was
open and friendly, and in spite of his bad mood he found
himself responding to it. Her blue eyes were set wide apart
in a broad oval face, and the cold had flushed pink her
freckled cheeks.

'I've taken rather a lot of photos of causeways,' she said.
'You'd think I'd know about tides by now.'

'Causeways? Why?'

He was politely passing the time of day, but she seemed
to give his question serious consideration. 'They're like a

191

bridge between two worlds,' she said. 'Between dreams and reality. They seem to be telling me something.'

'What?'

She grinned. 'Hurry up and don't get drowned, probably.'

She scooped back her long hair, stuffing it under her hat. 'This is my third causeway today,' she told him.

'Honestly? Where have you been?'

'Osea and Mersea islands. I should have some nice shots. Do you know how many causeways there are in the British Isles?'

He shook his head. 'Not a clue.'

'More than a hundred.'

'Impressive,' he said obligingly.

'Not all of them go over the sea or across rivers. Some are just paths through marshes.' She laughed. 'Some people take pictures of mountains and lakes, I do causeways. I've a thing about them.'

He thought it an odd obsession. 'Aren't they rather, um, muddy? Rather grey and brown?'

'What's wrong with grey and brown?'

'Nothing,' he acknowledged, adding, 'I paint a bit. You get through a lot of grey and brown living round here.'

'I have this picture in my head of the causeway I'm always searching for.'

'The perfect causeway?'

'Something like that.'

She had an athletic build, and he found it easy to imagine her scrambling across rocks and wading through rivers to get the best shot.

She glanced at her watch. 'I should be heading home.'

'Where's home?'

'London. Holborn.' She offered him her hand. 'I'm Freya Catherwood.'

192

Aidan told her his name and then nodded to the tripod. 'May I help you with that?'

'Thanks. I'm parked just up the road.'

As they walked inland, he said, 'Are you a professional photographer?'

'No . . . I'd like to be, but it's hard to make a living out of it.'

'Nice camera.'

'I practically *starved* to buy a Hasselblad.'

Her car, a red Mini, was parked on the verge. She opened the boot and stowed her bag and the tripod.

'Can I give you a lift anywhere?' she said.

'Thanks, but I'm happy walking.'

She opened the driver's door. 'If you tell me your address, I'll let you know about my next exhibition. Then, if you like, you could see the photos.'

'I'd love to.' He scribbled down his address on a scrap of paper and handed it to her. Then she drove away.

Aidan had intended to walk on, but the sky was the colour of charcoal and it might snow again. He didn't fancy being out on the marshes at night without a torch. What a day, he thought, letting out a breath. His encounter with Freya Catherwood had cheered him up, and from beneath all the shock and dissent of the last week, his delight in Anne's return to England re-emerged.

He knew that he needed to take it carefully. After so recently breaking off an engagement, she would be wary of entering too quickly into another relationship. But he was not, thank God, an awkward, tongue-tied eighteen-year-old any more, and before they had parted at the pub, he had asked her out to dinner.

His resentment dissolved along with the fading light, and

suddenly it seemed important to get back to Marsh Court. He tried to imagine how he would have felt if his father had done to him what Henry Winterton had done to Piers. But he couldn't. It was inconceivable that Dad would have ever hurt him like that, and remembering him, it felt too painful to think about. Let Piers have what he longed for. Aidan didn't want it. He never had.

When the doorbell rang, Piers had in his arms his father's silk dressing gown and his shaving things, along with some books and a writing case.

He opened the door. A fair-haired girl was standing on the porch. She was holding a bunch of flowers.

'Hello, Piers,' she said. 'I'm so sorry for intruding.'

She had an American accent. Something clicked. He said, '*Anne?*'

'Yes.'

'Christ. What are you doing here? You're supposed to be in America.'

'I've been back here for a while. I just dropped by with these for your mother.' She handed him the snowdrops. 'I'm so sorry for your loss.'

'Come in.'

'Thank you, but I won't.'

'You have to. It's been a hellish day and it'll cheer me up. In fact, I insist.'

He dropped his father's belongings on the floor and held open the door for her. She said uncertainly, 'Well, if you're sure . . . I don't want to be in the way. Just five minutes.'

He showed her into the hall. 'It's good to see you. *How many years?*'

'Six,' she said.

194

He let out a breath. 'Feels like a bloody lifetime.'

'I only wish it wasn't in such awful circumstances. Are you having a bonfire? I saw the smoke.'

'Yeah. I was going to put these on it.' With his toe, he nudged the heap of stuff on the floor. 'They're Dad's.'

He saw her trying to hide her puzzlement. 'Your mother asked you to?'

'No, of course not.'

He had forgotten how pretty she was. Or perhaps she had grown prettier since he had last seen her.

She said, 'Is Aidan here?'

'Aidan?'

'Yes. We were going to meet up for dinner next week, but I thought, after what's happened, maybe he won't want to.'

Piers gave her a thoughtful look. 'Maybe not. Let's find something to drink.'

She followed him into the drawing room. Miss Rolfe from Winterton's was dozing in a wing chair by the fire. There was a bottle of sherry on the sideboard; he poured out two glasses.

'Chin-chin.' He chinked his glass against Anne's. 'You got sick of California, then?'

'Kind of.'

'Are you back here for good?'

'For the moment. I'm working at a gallery in Chelsea.'

'Fabulous,' he said absently. He was trying to work something out.

'Piers,' she said gently.

'What?'

'You're drinking awfully quickly.'

He blinked. His glass was nearly empty. 'I can't see how else I'd get through today,' he said honestly.

'I'm so sorry about your father. You must miss him so much.'

He shook his head, turning down the corners of his mouth. 'Not at all, actually. I'm relieved to see the back of the old bastard. I could explain it all but then I'd be even more of a bore than I am already. Sorry, Anne.'

'Piers,' she said seriously, 'you can tell me anything you like.'

What was he glimpsing in those luminous silver-grey eyes? Attraction, yes – and maybe something more. And the idea that had been hovering at the back of his mind since Anne Carlisle's unexpected appearance, the idea that would give him the perfect opportunity to pay back Aidan, crystallised.

'This dinner with Aidan,' he said slowly. 'Is it a *date*?'

She smiled: *silly*. 'No, of course not. We're just friends, Aidan and me.'

She might think that, but Piers had a strong suspicion that Aidan might not feel the same way. Aidan had been soft on Anne that long-ago summer, which was why he, Piers, hadn't made a move.

He gave her his most winning smile, attractively tinged with the sadness and exhaustion of someone who had recently suffered a major bereavement. 'That's a relief,' he said.

'A relief? Why?'

He put a hand on her shoulder and steered her out of the room towards a quieter part of the house.

'Because,' he said, 'I was hoping to take you out to dinner myself.'

'What's *she* doing here?' Charley hissed at Louise.

'Who?'

They were in the games room. Charley had opened the door

a crack and was peering through it. Piers and Anne Carlisle were sitting on the stairs.

Louise came to stand beside her. Charley said, 'She shouldn't be here. She's not a Winterton.'

'Perhaps she's cheering Piers up.'

Charley didn't want Anne Carlisle to cheer Piers up. She wanted her to go away and leave them alone.

But seeing that Louise wasn't at all interested, she gave up and sat down on the sofa. The springs had gone and she pulled at clumps of horsehair stuffing that oozed, like the cream filling of a sponge cake, from between the cushions. Her grief was like an angry fire inside her. It frightened her, and she needed to distract herself from it, so she said to Louise:

'Tell me about the fashion photographer. What does he look like? Is he fabulously sexy and wicked?'

Shadows gathered, making dense patches on the grass. The last of the light was draining from the sky. Juliet's headache flexed its muscles as she retrieved teacups from the terrace.

Movement in the shadows; she looked up and saw Aidan heading back through the garden. She called out to him, 'A good walk?'

'I saw a pair of eider duck. And a girl was taking pictures of the causeway.'

'Goodness. In this cold?'

He came to stand beside her. 'I don't want the business, Aunt Juliet. I never did. Piers has got it all wrong. He should have it, he'll be better at it than me.'

Would he? Juliet wondered. And if their positions had been reversed, would Piers have had the maturity to recognise that? But she felt a wash of relief.

'Go and talk to him,' she said. 'I think he's in the games room with the girls.'

They went into the house. But Piers wasn't in the games room with Louise and Charley. If only, Juliet later found herself thinking, he had been.

Instead, he was sitting on the back stairs with a girl beside him. Juliet heard Aidan murmur, '*Anne?*'

A pool of luminescence fell on them from the overhead light. Piers was speaking in a low, coaxing voice and then leaned towards the girl to pluck something – a leaf, a fleck of ash – from her hair. And the look on her face as he touched her . . . Juliet found herself turning away, pitying her. Adoration. Naked adoration.

Piers looked up. Seeing Aidan, he smiled. 'Anne and I are going to the pub. Are you coming, Aidan?'

'No thanks.'

'Aidan?' prompted Juliet. 'Didn't you want to say something to Piers?'

But the expression in his eyes had solidified, gone hard. 'No, nothing,' he said. 'Nothing at all.' And he walked away.

Six years ago, it had taken a lot of walks along Ocean Beach to get Piers Winterton out of her head, but she had, in the end, managed it. It had been on the beach that Anne had first met Glenn Robertson. She had been sketching a strange blue creature she had found on the sand, and Glenn had crouched beside her, brown-eyed and bespectacled, studying the poor washed-up little thing. It was a velella, he had told her, a hydrozoa. It used its tentacles to swim and the crest on its back to steer. She had liked the fact that he knew such things. It gave them something to talk about.

Glenn had a degree in electrical engineering from Caltech

and was working for a company based in the Market district of San Francisco that made copying machines and typewriters. Anne went to the cinema with him and then for supper in Chinatown. At the weekend, they drove down to Monterey and walked along Cannery Row, where they talked about Steinbeck.

After eighteen months, he had proposed to her. Anne had accepted. She was by then working as a senior secretary at Macy's, and sometimes she felt stuck, as if she had ended up by accident in a life that didn't suit her. She knew that she needed to move on. Glenn drew up a plan by which they would save a third of their salaries each week so that they could put down a deposit on a house before they married. He didn't want them to start off their wedded life in rented accommodation, he said. Two years after the wedding they would have their first child, and another two years later. She had joked, 'A baby every other year?' and he had blinked and said, 'No, Annie, just the two. The world's overpopulated enough, don't you think?'

He liked to visit his parents in Pasadena most weekends. Mom and Pop, as they asked Anne to call them, were kind and quietly religious and Anne and Glenn slept in separate bedrooms. It was not a house in which you would consider creeping along corridors at night for illicit sex.

She might have gone on like this, putting aside a third of her wages for the house, making love to Glenn on Tuesday and Friday nights, sleepwalking into marriage, had not her father intervened.

'He's a nice guy,' he had said to her one evening, 'but he's not right for you.'

He was, she insisted. She was going to marry Glenn Robertson.

'Annie.' He took her hand. 'I know you. And you're not in love with him.'

They were in Sausalito. She was helping her father organise an exhibition of his paintings in a local gallery. She had bowed her head, biting her lip, and he had stroked her hair, as he used to do when she was a small child and afraid of the dark.

A warm Pacific evening: sitting by the harbour, watching the moon rise and the boats move up and down with the swell of the bay, she had gone through the awful process of discovering that her father was right. She didn't love Glenn. She liked him, she respected him, but she didn't love him. They were too alike for love – too introverted, too serious, too quiet. Planners and organisers the pair of them, they would suffocate each other. She had another side to her character, the rackety, bohemian side. If she married Glenn, that part of her would die.

The next day, she ended the engagement. She had thought – or had tried to persuade herself – that Glenn would see it as she did and accept that they weren't right for each other. But he hadn't, and he had broken down, a strong, good man reduced to tears because she hadn't had the sense to realise sooner that she needed something more.

Hating herself, she had given in her notice at Macy's, bought a second-hand Cadillac with her share of the house savings (carefully apportioned by Glenn) and set off inland from San Francisco. As she drove across the vast land mass of the United States of America, from Sacramento to Salt Lake City, and then on to Omaha, Chicago and Cleveland, guilt had gradually mutated into relief. She had been aware of having had a lucky escape. Two weeks after she had left California, she arrived in New York, where she sold the

Cadillac and rented a room in a peeling brownstone where cockroaches glittered behind the kitchen cupboards. She found herself a post as assistant to the editor of a women's fashion magazine. The editor was a loud, complaining woman and the offices were ridden with disputes and factions. She loathed the job but endured it to pay the rent and as a sort of penance. Then Katherine's letter had arrived, telling her about the new gallery. Anne had written back by return of post, asking if there was a job for her. A telegram had followed – 'Hop on a plane, my love' – and so Anne had done just that.

All this she thought about as she walked along the King's Road on the Thursday after the funeral to meet Aidan in a restaurant. She didn't want to get things wrong again. She suspected that there was a limit to the amount of hurt you might recover from.

Aidan was quiet that evening, his conversation now and then tailing off into silence. She put it down to the recent death of his uncle. They were tackling coq au vin when she said, 'Do you know whether Piers is seeing anybody?'

A hunch of the shoulders. 'He doesn't confide in me. Probably.'

'Does he have lots of girlfriends?'

'Yes.'

'Serious ones?'

'No, I don't think so. It depends what you mean by *serious*. I don't think he falls in love with them.' He looked up at her. 'What is it?'

'I made such a mess of things in the States, with Glenn, my fiancé, and I don't think I could face making another mistake. I wondered whether Piers has said anything about me.' Noticing his expression alter, she said quickly, 'I'm not asking you to betray confidences, Aidan. But I've always thought of you as a good friend, and I hope you think of me in the same way. It's just that it's been so sudden, this . . . this thing with Piers. Back when we first met, years ago, I had no inkling he felt anything more than friendship towards me. I'm worried that it might be something to do with his father's death, that he's trying to take his mind off it, something like that.' She smiled. 'I'm being ridiculous, aren't I? You mustn't think I'm not happy about it. Piers is such a special person. And you Britishers, you don't exactly wear your hearts on your sleeves.' She paused, took a mouthful of wine. 'I'm sorry, I'm talking too much. But I guess I'm falling for him.'

Aidan said nothing for such a long time that she began to feel mortified, seeing herself as a caricature of the verbose overly-confiding American that people like the Wintertons probably despised.

But then he said, 'Anne, Piers and I aren't speaking.'

This was news to her. 'Oh. I didn't know. Why not?'

He explained to her that Henry Winterton, Piers's father and Aidan's uncle, had changed his will at the last moment, leaving the family jewellery business to him rather than, as expected, to Piers.

'Gee, Aidan,' said Anne. 'How awful for you both.'

'Not everyone sees it like that. Some of the family blame me.'

She studied him. 'Piers blames you. Is that what you're telling me?'

'Didn't he say?'

'We didn't talk about it, no.'

The pub Piers had taken her to on the evening of his father's funeral had been deep in the countryside near the

202

mouth of the estuary. It hadn't been the sort of place Anne would have thought Piers would like, not glamorous at all, the rooms small and old and dark, and no one had been dressed up. But it had been magical, and everything from the pale wash of snow on the fields to the cold, salty smell of the sea to the slippery silver disc of the moon, bobbing on the water, had enchanted her.

'We mostly talked about America,' she said. 'Piers *adores* the States. He's been to New York more often than I have. And I told him about Glenn. He's such a good listener, isn't he?'

Aidan looked sceptical. Reaching across the table, she put her hand on his. 'It's awful what money can do to people,' she said gently. 'The two of you were such good friends. You mustn't let this get in the way of that, Aidan.' She hesitated, then added, 'I'm sure Piers has his difficult side. He can seem arrogant, can't he? But that's just to cover up what he feels underneath. If his father chose to leave the family business to you rather than to him, it must be so hurtful to him. You do see that, don't you, Aidan?'

Later, heading back to Katherine's place in Hampstead, Anne relived, for the hundredth time, the miraculous moment when she had rung the bell to Marsh Court and Piers had opened the door. She had seen him and something had fallen into place inside her. And then he had insisted she come in and she had allowed herself to be persuaded, even though she had known that the family should be left alone at a time of bereavement.

And though she had suspected that Piers was rather drunk and had known that he was very upset, everything had somehow gone on being miraculous, and when he had said, *I was rather hoping to ask you out to dinner myself,* she had felt her life changing track, the unhappiness that had clung to her for a long time lifting at last and something sparkling and glorious taking its place.

On his way to meet Anne earlier that evening, Aidan had clung on to a shred of optimism that she had gone out with Piers because she had felt sorry for him, and that he had misread the expression he had seen on her face when he had found her with Piers on the stairs at Marsh Court.

It was galling to discover what a fool you could be when you were in love. *I've always thought of you as a good friend, and I hope you think of me in the same way.* With that damning sentence, Anne had demonstrated to him that every scrap of desire had been on his side alone; her words had flexed a knife blade inside his heart.

Aidan let himself into his bedsit. There was just the one room; the kitchen and bathroom were shared. There was a sofa bed that was satisfactory neither as a sofa or a bed, an armchair, and a table with flaps that folded away. Aidan, who rarely noticed his surroundings, thought the room perfectly comfortable. He put on a record – Ella Fitzgerald singing 'Ev'ry Time We Say Goodbye' – and then, because that made him feel even more miserable, took it off again, sat down on the sofa and asked himself why he hadn't told Anne that Piers was only flirting with her to get at him.

Because she wouldn't have believed him. And because it would have hurt her. And because it would have made her hate him. She was at that stage of infatuation that had made it hard for her to talk about anything but blasted Piers. Had he confided in her that his cousin was a gigolo or an axe murderer, she would have found some excuse for him.

Yet he was convinced that was Piers's motive. Piers was saying to him, *If I can't have Winterton's, then I'll have Anne.* He supposed he should punch his cousin in the jaw or something, but it was hard to see how that would help.

But he could play dirty as well. He would keep Winterton's, and if Piers turned up at work – he hadn't since Henry had died – then Aidan would make it clear to him that he was now in charge and that Piers could damn well do what he was told. And if Piers didn't like that, he could go hang. Meanwhile, Aidan would try to take pleasure in his unexpected inheritance instead of feeling guilty about it, and would use the increased income his ownership of Winterton's had given him to help out his mother and buy himself a car.

Sooner or later Piers would get bored with Anne. He had better let her down lightly. He had better not hurt her. It occurred to Aidan – and he disliked himself for thinking this – that he would make sure to be around to pick up the pieces.

He glanced at his watch: half past nine. A heap of papers from Winterton's, assembled by their chief accountant so that Aidan could familiarise himself with the firm's current financial position, were in his briefcase. He pulled them out and opened a file. The thought of what he had taken on – of what Uncle Henry had inflicted on him – horrified him. He had seen doubt in the eyes of Winterton's staff and was afraid that it was merited.

The first time she had seen Marsh Court had been when she had come to it as a new bride. They had been travelling for weeks, she and Henry, and had both felt, Juliet recalled, rather dazed and unreal. The roads had narrowed as they had driven deeper into the Essex countryside, and a mist had descended, so that when they had neared the house, all she had been able to see had been a patch of light grey against an off-white sky. Marsh Court had that day seemed both monumental and impenetrable. She remembered thinking how impossible it would be to paint all those smudged monotones, and how equally impossible it was to imagine being the mistress of such a place.

Twenty-six years later, and as she drove back from an afternoon's teaching in Maldon, the heavy rain of earlier in the day had thinned, and sunlight seeped from between the clouds and flashed on the roof of Marsh Court. The powerful love she felt for her home was now tinged with sadness. Piers had reassured her that she could stay there for as long as she liked, but she knew that though he might feel that now, circumstances could change.

She parked the car and went indoors. Biscuit's successor, a golden retriever that Charley had christened Lulu, padded out to meet her, and she stooped to ruffle the dog's ears. These days, she worried for her children. She worried for Charley, who had been moody and difficult since Henry had died. Charley's housemistress had telephoned earlier in the week with some complaint about her behaviour. Juliet had promised, with a mental sigh, to speak to her daughter.

As for Piers, she both ached for him and felt exasperated with him. He had left Winterton's and was intending to sell the Bond Street flat as soon as probate was granted. He planned to start up his own jewellery business, using the proceeds from the flat as capital. He hadn't attempted to disguise the fact that he meant his business one day to rival Winterton's. Charley had told her that Piers was still seeing that girl, the American, Anne Carlisle, and that Aidan had once been in love with her. Juliet didn't like to think that Piers was capable of dating a girl just to aggravate Aidan, but

206

she couldn't rule it out. Piers was unapproachable these days. Nothing she said to him penetrated the hard, shiny surface of his anger.

Leaving the house by the back door, she and Lulu walked along the path that looped round the side of the house to the cottage. It was the first time she had been there since she had discovered it was where Henry meant her to spend the rest of her days. She hesitated, holding the door handle, and then went inside.

Downstairs, there was a sitting room, dining room, kitchen and a small scullery; upstairs, three bedrooms and a bathroom. The interior had last been renovated in the late twenties, when the old aunt for whom the cottage had been built had died and it had begun to be used as guest accommodation. The decor and furnishings reflected their age: green and white chequered tiles in the bathroom, the paintwork ivory, cream or turquoise, some of it now chipped and cracked. The kitchen, hardly used by Winterton guests, was only sparsely equipped. The building felt tired, forgotten and little loved. Well, if this was all Henry thought she was worth, then so be it. She would make her own way.

And yet she loved Marsh Court and felt in her heart that it should have been hers. She found it hard to believe that it could survive without her: she who had nurtured and cared for it for a quarter of a century. If she were to be exiled, she would become a different person, she realised. She would lose the passion that was at the core of her – and that, presumably, was what Henry had intended.

Chapter Ten

April–October 1964

The premises was on the King's Road, between a green-grocer's shop and a men's outfitter's, whose window display currently included a rowing boat in which sat a mannequin in jumbo cord trousers and a button-down shirt. As he fitted the key to the front door, Piers felt a rush of excitement.

Inside, the shop itself was smallish and littered with old newspapers, cardboard boxes, a battered metal desk and a dozen empty milk bottles. The large front window was so covered with grime that the pedestrians on the pavement and the vehicles on the road moved behind it like ghosts. He would have liked somewhere bigger but hadn't been able to afford it, not in the King's Road, and he needed to be in the King's Road because that was where the money was.

Boutiques were springing up over the most trendy parts of London – Carnaby Street and Soho and, of course, the King's Road. Piers had known that he must not wait, that he needed to catch the crest of the wave as it rose. But the processes of the law were frustratingly slow, and they had not yet been granted probate, and so, though he had a buyer lined up, he could not yet sell the Bond Street flat. To purchase the lease of the shop, he had borrowed from various sources against the promise of his inheritance.

A door at the back of the shop gave into a warren of small rooms, some windowless, all dim with dust and cobwebs. He planned to use them for storage and offices. A sink was set into an alcove; he turned on the tap and rusty water coughed out. He would have to check the plumbing and electrics, he noted. Get a phone put in. And then desks, chairs, a safe, filing cabinets and a till.

He had found a young designer fresh out of art college, who made the most extraordinary brooches in organic shapes, curls of copper or beaten gold with a single pearl or opal, like a dewdrop, half hidden in a fold. Piers imagined them set against black velvet, shimmering, almost alive. He wouldn't lock them away in a vitrine; Bridget Frost's pieces cried out to be touched and held. He'd have to find a better way of displaying them.

The shop itself must shine like a jewel box and beckon people in off the street. He saw it in his mind's eye: no carpets, no hushed voices or ancient, intimidating assistants. He imagined music playing and enthusiastic, pretty girls behind the counter. The shop would re-create the atmosphere of a lively Italian café rather than a funeral parlour, like Winterton's.

He gathered up the milk bottles, rinsing them under the spluttering tap before putting them outside for the milkman to collect. Then he stuffed the newspapers and cardboard boxes into the dustbins in the tiny back area, put on his coat and went to meet Anne at the gallery. He was taking her out to dinner and then they were going on to a party. He and Anne had kissed and held hands – so far, that was it. She gave him the cold shoulder whenever he attempted to take things further. It was difficult enough even to get her into a situation where it might be *possible* to take things further. They met in public spaces, in pubs and cafés and art galleries. She was a beautiful girl, but increasingly he felt like a thwarted sixteen-year-old, and their relationship had become as frustrating to him as the legal process was proving to be. He longed to pick up his life, move it along, get to the next stage. He was sick of waiting; he wanted to be *there*, to be Piers Winterton, successful, enviable and unassailable, someone who *mattered*.

They were having fun, thinking of a name for the shop. 'Winterton's', for obvious reasons, was out.

Anne asked Piers what his designer was called.

'Bridget Frost.'

'Frost . . . that's pretty.'

'I can't call it after her. If her stuff doesn't sell, I'd have to get rid of her.'

They had dined in an Indian restaurant and had a drink in a pub before heading on the party. Now they were in a basement in Islington, where there were cracks in the walls and beer bottles cooling in the sink. The gramophone was playing the Dave Clark Five and people were shouting out the chorus to 'Bits and Pieces'. Outside, a thunderstorm was rumbling; the bare bulb in the centre of the room flickered on and off.

Anne was sitting on Piers's lap in an armchair in the corner of the room. She considered him, admiring the perfection of his profile.

'Could you do that?' she asked him. 'Give someone a wonderful opportunity and then just take it away from them?'

'Yes.' He tipped back his head to swallow the last of his beer. 'Do you want another drink?'

'No thanks.'

'Do you disapprove?'

'I'm not sure I could be so ruthless.'

'It won't work if I'm not. Anyway, I've learned from a master.' Piers gave a sour smile.

'Your father?'

'Yes.'

Though the Wintertons were amusing and good company, and though Anne was attracted to them, she was wary of them as well. Having been through years of analysis to enable her to cope after her parents' divorce, she knew a dysfunctional family when she saw one. Piers still wasn't speaking to Aidan, and therefore – because Piers did not do things by halves – he wasn't speaking to Louise or Helen either, even though he had been close to them since he was a baby. He had a capacity for resentment – for vengeance – that sometimes troubled Anne.

She said, 'Piers, I know this experience has been very painful for you, but aren't you about to make something rather wonderful out of it?'

His fingers ran up and down her spine, tracing the little bones. 'You're not going to suggest that what my father did was a blessing in disguise, are you?'

'No, of course not. But it may not be such a bad thing in the end to have made a new start on your own. Families can be stifling.'

'God, you're so right.' He yawned, stretching out his arms.

Anne considered Piers's family. Henry Winterton, despite being dead, still seemed to wield an awful influence. She thought Piers's mother, Juliet, a little withdrawn, and she sensed that his sister, Charley, didn't like her. She suspected that Charley was overly dependent on Piers because of their parents' troubled marriage, and resented Anne as an interloper. It was possible that Juliet Winterton felt the same way. Women in unhappy marriages often relied too much on their children, especially their sons, for emotional support. Though it was also likely, Anne conceded, that Juliet was cool and distant towards anyone who wasn't a Winterton.

Piers's hand moved down, tracing the shape of her hip before coming to land on her thigh. The heat of his palm sparked a rush of desire. 'What I mean is,' she said, sitting up and tugging down her skirt, 'you're making something of yourself. You're doing it all. You're not dependent on anyone else. Not your father or Aidan or anyone.'

'And I'm supposed to thank Aidan for that?'

'Not thank him, no. But *forgive* him. It wasn't his fault, Piers.'

'You don't know that.'

'I do. I've talked to him about it.'

Angrily, he let out a breath.

'He's my friend,' she said calmly.

A couple were dancing in the middle of the room, swaying, leaning into each other. Anne nestled into Piers's shoulder. Cilla Black was singing 'Anyone Who Had a Heart'. She adored the song and would have liked to close her eyes and surrender to the pleasure of the moment, to the warmth of Piers's arms around her and the aching, passionate lyrics, but she knew she had to make something clear.

'I'd rather you two got on,' she said, 'though if you can't, then so be it. But I've always chosen my own friends and I don't intend to change that.'

It was easier for Piers to blame Aidan for what had happened than it was for him to confront the pain of his father disinheriting him. Anne wondered whether, deep down, Piers doubted he was lovable at all. Amid these complications, she hoped she was a safe haven for him.

'I think you might feel happier if you put all this behind you.' She kissed him. 'Move on. Nurture new friendships instead of making yourself feel bad about old ones.'

'I love it when you're earnest. It's so sweet. And I'm certainly happy to nurture new friendships.' His mouth brushed her upper lip. 'I've had enough of this, haven't you?'

They said goodbye to Paul, dug out their coats from the heap on the bed and went outside. Piers put up his umbrella.

'Come back to my flat for a coffee.'

'It's late, sweetie. I have to work tomorrow.'

Though Piers always asked her, she never went back to his flat, knowing that if she did, he would assume she was going to go to bed with him. It wasn't that she didn't want to; every nerve and skin cell cried out for his touch. What held her back was the voice in her head that reminded her of the mess she had got into with Glenn. It wasn't the going-to-bed part that was difficult: this she had learned. It was after the bed had grown cold that fragments of broken heart littered your path.

Beneath the shelter of the umbrella, he stroked the back of her neck. 'Half an hour. Just a coffee.'

'No, Piers.'

His smile melted her; she felt herself weakening. 'It's miles to Hampstead,' he coaxed. 'You'll get tired, all that travelling. I'm sure I could find room for you at my place.'

'Very generous, but no.'

'I'll sleep on the sofa.'

'Sure you will.'

'Why not?'

'Because.'

He looked sulky. 'I never know where I am with you. Or what you want from me.'

'I just want to be with you. That's all.'

'But not now. You don't want to be with me now. Christ, Anne, it isn't even midnight.' He looked thoughtful, then said, 'You're not religious, are you?'

She laughed. 'No. Why would you think that? Piers, I was born and brought up in San Francisco, not some redneck town in the back of beyond. I'm not refusing to go to bed with you out of puritanism, if that's what you're thinking.'

'Why, then? Are you afraid of getting pregnant?'

'That would be pretty disastrous, but no, it isn't really that.'

'Then you're saving yourself for marriage.'

'No, again. Certainly not that.' She tucked her hand through his arm. 'Come on. Walk me to the Underground station.'

As they headed along the pavement, she felt irritation seeping out of him like the rain that dripped from the edge of the umbrella. Eventually he burst out, 'So you're not sure whether you like me? That's it, isn't it?'

She stopped and turned to him. 'Piers, I'm completely sure that I like you. The problem is that I love you.'

'Oh.' After a short space, he said, 'And I love you too.'

A heartbeat. 'Truly?'

'Yes, of course.'

They walked for a while in silence. She wanted him to say it again, but he did not. She leaned her head against his shoulder, trying to memorise the patter of the rain and the smell of the wet pavements, so that she could keep this moment in her heart for the rest of her life.

Then he said, 'If we got married, we could call the shop "Piers Carlisle". Sounds classy, doesn't it?'

* * *

214

It was past seven when Aidan left the office. The gallery was in Frith Street, in Soho, no distance at all, so he walked briskly, threading through the crowds on the pavement, enjoying the feeling of being on the move again, flexing his shoulders to shake off the stiffness of a day spent sitting at a desk.

A sign in the window announced the title of the exhibition: *Transitions: photographs by Freya Catherwood*. Aidan pushed open the door and went inside. Spotting Freya's bright head in the centre of the room, surrounded by people, he ambled slowly round the perimeter. Someone offered him a glass of wine, which he accepted with a smile.

A few of the photographs were in colour, but mostly they were black and white, the contrast exaggerated to emphasise the composition. The bare stretches of sand and water looked austerely beautiful. A snaking path emerged from rock pools and seaweed at the Brough of Birsay in Orkney, and in an image taken at the island of Lindisfarne, black poles protruding from a sheen of water were all that delineated the disappearing pathway.

'I wasn't sure whether you'd come.'

He turned, and there was Freya. She had on a sleeveless black velvet dress. Her legs were bare and her feet were in flat sandals, as if the dress was a concession and she would have preferred to have been wearing something else. Her curly hair was scooped up in a knot, into which she had stuck long black pins that looked rather like knitting needles, and which were presumably meant to contain it, though tendrils spilled over her shoulders.

'I wouldn't have missed it,' he said. 'I'm sorry I'm rather late. Work, I'm afraid.'

People were starting to leave. 'Thank goodness,' she murmured. 'My jaw's aching, I've talked so much.'

215

'You've been to all these places? Even Orkney?'

'Yes. Orkney was especially wonderful. One day, I'll go back there.'

'Have you sold many?'

'Quite a few, yes. Would you like to see your photos?'

The Thorney Island pictures were on the opposite side of the gallery, in a group of half a dozen. While Freya said goodbye to her guests and thanked them for coming, Aidan admired the simplicity and forcefulness of her work. Her camera had captured the grey opacity of the January sky and the moment when the Blackwater had begun to spill over the side of the causeway. He noticed that she didn't seem to mind areas of emptiness within the frame.

'You told me you weren't a professional photographer,' said Aidan, when Freya came back to him. 'It all looks pretty damn professional to me.'

'Thank you. What I meant is that I don't earn a living from it. It's hard if you do landscapes, like I do. If I wanted to work for a newspaper or if I enjoyed taking photos of weddings or portraits of society girls, maybe I could make a go of it. Or if I was hip and clever – and male – perhaps I could make a living out of fashion photography.'

'But that doesn't interest you?'

'Unfortunately, no.' She broke off to offer kisses and fare-wells to a couple who were leaving the gallery. When they had gone, she said to Aidan, 'I live and work in London but it's not where I want to be. Whenever I'm free, I escape to the countryside.'

He pictured her shouldering her rucksack and hiking over hills and moorland. She would have a long stride and wouldn't mind being on her own, and she wouldn't notice foul weather.

'There's an Italian restaurant just round the corner,' he said. 'Do you fancy a quick supper?'

'That would be lovely. I'll give Charles a hand clearing up, and then I'm free.'

'I'll grab a table.'

At the restaurant, Aidan scanned the wine list and ordered a bottle of Chianti. When Freya arrived, they toasted the success of the exhibition.

She smiled. 'What will I do when I run out of causeways?'

'You'll have to find something else. Bridges . . . ferries . . . What do you do when you're not taking photographs?'

'I'm a medical secretary at University College Hospital.' She wrinkled her nose. 'It's fine. It pays the rent and I don't have to work on Saturdays or Sundays, so I'm free to travel about and do some photography. Patrick, the man I work for, is a friend of my father. He's an orthopaedic consultant. He knows Charles Norton, who owns the gallery. He put in a word for me, which was jolly decent of him.'

'Is your father a doctor?'

'No, he's an academic. A professor at Oxford.'

'What's his subject?'

'He's a linguist. He specialises in Old Norse.'

'Good Lord.'

She grinned. 'Someone has to, that's what I say to him. Only teasing, of course. He writes poetry as well.'

He noticed that she spoke of her father with pride and a warm affection. 'Did he choose your name?'

'Yes.' She struck a heroic pose. 'Freya, the Norse goddess of love, beauty, war and death. Apparently there are lots of Freyas in Shetland. I'd like to go there one day.'

'Hell of a distance.'

'Sleeper train to Aberdeen, then a ferry to Lerwick. Easy.'

217

'Any causeways there?'

'Several.'

'Do you know any Old Norse?'

'Not a word. I'm hopeless at languages.'

'My father was a marvellous pianist, but I can't sing a note in tune.'

'I was adopted. I don't think my father had any great hopes that I'd take after him.'

They talked about their families. Freya's mother had died when she was twelve and she had no brothers or sisters. Aidan told her about Louise, and about how she had modelled clothes in magazines and was going to be featured in the *Sunday Times* colour section. And that his father was dead and his mother still lived in the family home in Maldon.

'My uncle died in January,' he added. 'His house, Marsh Court, is beside the Blackwater. The day I met you was the day of his funeral.' He gave a quick summary of the story of the will and Winterton's, and Piers.

'So now you're in charge,' she said, when he had finished.

'So now I'm in charge.' It still sounded odd, saying it aloud. Fraudulent, almost. 'To tell the truth, it's been hellish.' It was the first time he had admitted that to anyone. He could say it safely to Freya because she was nothing to do with the family. He prodded his pasta with his fork. 'I make mistakes all the time. Thank God for the staff, who actually know what they're doing. Most of the time someone stops me putting my foot in it.'

'I expect you're better than you think you are,' she said kindly. 'I'm always terrified before an exhibition. It's that thing of being in the spotlight.'

He topped up their glasses. And then he found himself

telling her something he would never, ever be able to admit to a Winterton.

'The worst thing is, I don't even *like* jewellery very much. Everyone talks about how beautiful the stones are, but I can't see it. To me, they're just cold and hard and gaudy.' He frowned, looking beyond her, through the window to the darkness of the street. The feeling of dread that he had become accustomed to, and that he associated with Winterton's, was already hovering in the pit of his stomach at the thought of going to work tomorrow morning.

What an idiot, he told himself. So *spineless*.

He produced a smile. 'I don't suppose you're very fond of bones and you work for a consultant in orthopaedics. You don't have to love the things you work with, do you?'

'No,' she said. 'But it helps.'

Piers asked Anne to turn away while he unlocked the door to the shop. Then he made her close her eyes as he led her inside.

'You can open them now,' he said.

'Oh,' she whispered, and a smile spread across her face as she looked round the interior. 'Piers, it's beautiful! So beautiful!'

It had been a hell of a rush getting the place kitted out, and there was still a long list of odds and ends that needed tidying up. He had had to leave some of the pricier alterations to last, but probate had finally been granted, which meant that he could pay off some of his creditors.

'I meant it to look like a treasure box,' he said.

'It does.' She was turning round slowly, taking it in. 'Piers, you're so clever, it does.'

One wall was entirely covered with sheets of beaten copper. He would have liked to have put metal panels on all four walls but hadn't been able to afford to, and had used a sheeny light-coloured wallpaper on the other three instead. The tiles on the floor looked as if they had been glazed with honey, and the wall lamps brought out the red of the copper. He had commissioned from a young sculptor friend of Bridget's stands like bare-branched miniature trees, for displaying necklaces and bracelets. Rings and brooches would be shown in boxes lined with black velvet.

He took Anne round the offices at the back. Here, he had painted the walls white. 'Bridget will have to use her own studio for the time being,' he explained. 'There isn't room for her to work here. This is to be my office, and this' – a corner in a narrow corridor – 'is for my secretary.'

'You've found someone?'

'Kid called Tricia. She's very tiny, which is just as well.'

'It's wonderful. You've worked so hard, Piers. I'm so proud of you.'

They kissed. She was wearing a flimsy white dress and he could feel the warmth of her skin through the fabric. She seemed to melt in his arms, fluid and pliant, as if he was trying to hold river water. When he stepped back, she gasped, and he saw that her eyes were dreamy and dazed. He kissed her again, one hand reaching for the cord of the window blind, the other rubbing her thigh and pulling up the hem of her dress. He knew that this time she wouldn't push him away. A little voice in his head pointed out to him what a great day it was, what a triumph, the shop ready for business and Anne letting him make love to her at last.

Their coupling was quick and almost painfully intense, and afterwards he crushed her to him, stroking her head, while he got his breath back.

Then he realised that she was crying. 'Bloody hell,' he said, horrified. 'What is it? What's wrong? What have I done? I haven't hurt you, have I?'

She shook her head, and then, very muffled, mumbled, 'I didn't mean to do that.'

'Why not?'

A longer pause this time. And then, straightening, she scooped the tears off her face with her fingertips and said in a tired sort of voice, 'You don't love me like I love you, Piers. I can tell that you don't.'

He didn't see why she had to make everything so complicated, but he hated to see her cry – it made him feel horrible and as if there was something lacking in him – and so he said, 'I do. I do, honestly. In fact, I'll prove it to you.'

'You have a good brain, Charlotte, when you choose to use it.'

Charley's English teacher, Miss Stephens – fortyish, dark curly hair, drily sarcastic – had asked her to wait behind after the class. She was packing books into her leather briefcase.

'Have you decided whether you're going to try for Oxford?'

'No, Miss Stephens. I mean, I haven't decided yet.'

'I hope that in the summer holidays you'll find a few moments to spare to consider your future.'

'Yes, Miss Stephens.'

'It's an important decision. Here's a reading list, in case you do decide to go ahead.' A piece of paper was thrust into Charley's hands. 'Think about this carefully, Charlotte. You won't get a second chance.'

It was mid-July, the day before the end of term. The following afternoon, Charley's mother collected her from school. After she had packed Charley and her belongings into the Morris, her mother told her that Piers and Anne were coming for dinner the following evening.

221

'They're driving down after Piers shuts up the shop. So I'll have you both at Marsh Court for the weekend. Just like old times.'

It wouldn't be at all like old times, Charley thought, as she stared out of the car window. Her father wouldn't be there. Before – she always thought of it as *before* – she would have come home from school and given him her report, which he would have read before muttering something like, 'Only forty per cent for chemistry.' And then she would have mimicked her chemistry teacher, Mrs Mackintosh, saying, 'Charlotte needs to approach her work with greater precision,' and her father would have laughed. He would have given her a pound note and told her not to waste it, and she would have kissed the top of his head and said, 'Yes, Father dear.' A little gentle sarcasm had amused him. From her, anyway.

Instead, her father was dead and awful Anne Carlisle was to be at Marsh Court, Charley's favourite place in the whole world, staring at them with her weird fish eyes and making humourless remarks. For the last few weeks, finding school increasingly constricting and pointless, Charley had been longing to go home, but now, driving along the leafy Hertfordshire lanes, the sense of release she had felt in emerging from the school gates dissipated and the old gloom returned.

Then her mother said, 'And Nate and Rory are coming. Did I mention that? Apparently Nate's back from wherever he was. Gillis and Blanche have to be somewhere for the next few days, so Nate said he'd drop in tomorrow and bring Rory with him.'

'Oh,' she said, and immediately felt happier. 'How long will they stay?'

'For Saturday night, at least.' Her mother glanced at her. 'Helen and Louise are coming to dinner as well.'

Well that'll be interesting, thought Charley sarcastically. Piers had hardly spoken to either of them since he had discovered that Aidan was to inherit Winterton's. She suspected her mother of trying to build bridges.

'I thought I'd do duck,' her mother was saying. 'And you could make a trifle, if you like. It would be such a help.'

Once again, she was being palmed off with a Useful Task. But she would see Nate, who had been out of the country for the past nine months, travelling here and there, and that thought cheered her immensely, and she said, 'Of course, Mum.'

'He made me stand in the river. It was freezing. My feet turned white. And then he wanted some shots of me running down the field, and I was so cold I could hardly move, and he shouted at me, "How can I work with a model who looks like a freak and has a limp?"'

They were in Charley's bedroom at Marsh Court. Louise mimed herself trying to run with frozen feet while a furious photographer yelled at her, and they both fell on the bed, snorting with laughter.

Louise said, when they could speak again, 'He tried to make me go to bed with him later.'

Charley was impressed. 'Did you?'

'No. He was revolting. And so *old*. So he was cross with me all over again. Anyway, the photos will be in *Vogue*, in November.' Louise said this offhandedly, in much the same tone as she might inform someone that she was nipping out to the corner shop.

'*Vogue*,' said Charley. 'Gosh.'

'What are you wearing tonight?'

Charley opened her wardrobe. 'This one.' She took out a mustard-coloured Mary Quant dress. It was short and sleeve-less and had a deep pleat in the front of the skirt.

'The hem's down,' said Louise.

'I caught my foot in it.'

'Give me a needle and thread and I'll mend it for you.'

Because Charley didn't have such a thing as a sewing box, she tramped off to her mother's room. Extracting a packet of needles and a cotton reel, she heard the rumble of a car coming down the drive. She wondered whether it was Piers and Anne or Nate and Rory. She hoped it was Nate and Rory.

It was. From above, she caught sight of Rory's brown head and Nate's curly dark one. She stood still, looking down, noting how much Nate had changed since she had last seen him. He looked older and somehow slightly daunting.

She was wearing only her slip, so she called to them from the landing rather than going downstairs. Then she went back to her room.

'Nate's got a tan,' she said to Louise, who set about repairing the hem. 'He's the colour of a conker. And Rory's about a foot taller than he was the last time I saw him. He used to be shorter than me.' Charley studied herself in the mirror. She had been five foot two for the last three years; there did not, she thought regretfully, seem much prospect of her growing any taller. She had recently had her fair hair cut short in a bob, which was a welcome release from years of plaits and ponytails.

Piers and Anne didn't arrive till half past eight, by which time they were all starving and her mother was fretting about the duck. Anne was wearing a short black embroidered jacket over a frock made of a shimmery pale pink fabric. When Juliet complimented her on the jacket, Anne said, 'Gee, this. I found it in Petticoat Lane. It's Schiaparelli.'

They ate celery soup and then roast duck with orange and cherry sauce. Piers talked about the shop. What a triumph the opening weekend had been and how his pieces were going to be featured in a magazine, and how a singer who had had a Top Twenty hit had come in and said how groovy the interior was. Charley thought he was talking too much and being rather boastful, as well as tactless, because Aunt Helen was there, but Piers was often tactless and Aunt Helen said only, when he paused for breath, 'That's wonderful, Piers. I'm sure it will be a great success.' As usual, Anne didn't say very much at all – it was as if, thought Charley, she rationed her conversation, only bothering to bestow it on those she thought worth speaking to.

Eventually Piers shut up and ate his dinner. Charley asked Nate about South America. She thanked him for the half-dozen postcards he had sent, which were arranged on the mantelpiece in her bedroom.

She said, 'Which was your favourite country?'

Against his tanned skin, Nate's eyes gleamed a deep, bright green. 'Patagonia, I think. It had everything. It's beautiful and empty and no one has anything very much but they don't mind.'

Charley had had a liking for seafaring stories when she was younger. 'Did you sail round Cape Horn?'

'Not this time. I'm going to, one day. We hiked up a glacier, though.'

'A *glacier*.'

'It wasn't as white as you'd think. Rather grubby-looking. And I rode the trails in the Torres del Paine.'

225

'On a *horse*?'

'No, a camel.' He lifted his eyebrows at her. 'Naturally a horse. And then I worked on an *estancia*.'

'You were a *gaucho*?'

'More of a farmhand. How's school?'

Charley made a face. 'Despicable. Like some moth-eaten old frock I grew out of years ago.'

Her mother was clearing away the dinner plates. Charley helped her take the serving dishes into the kitchen and then carried the trifle through.

'Yum, trifle,' said Piers.

'It looks so beautiful,' said Anne ingratiatingly. Then she said quietly, 'Piers . . .'

Piers cleared his throat. He said, 'Anne and I have something to tell you all.'

Anne smiled and reached out her hand to him.

'Anne and I got married yesterday,' said Piers.

No one said anything. The atmosphere in the room seemed to vibrate. Charley stared at her brother. He was kidding, she thought. He was causing trouble. When he was in a certain mood, Piers liked to cause trouble.

Her mother peered at him, frowning. 'Married?'

'Yes, Mum.'

'Do you mean . . . engaged?'

'No, Mum, married.'

Auntie Helen said, 'Piers?'

'In Chelsea register office. Yesterday afternoon.'

Anne spoke. 'We wanted a quiet wedding.'

'Congratulations,' said Helen faintly. 'What wonderful news.'

'You can't have.' Charley hadn't planned to say that, it just came out. 'You can't.'

'I can.' Defiance in Piers's eyes as he turned to look at her. 'And I have.'

Charley put down the serving spoon. Her voice shook, and tears spilled from her eyes. 'You have to stop this, Piers,' she hissed. 'You just have to!' And then, addressing Anne, 'Don't you see? Don't you see that he's only married you to spite Aidan?'

Now everyone was looking at her with expressions of shock and disapproval, which was so unfair when it was Piers who was being appalling. Knocking over her chair, she dashed out of the room.

She didn't know where to go and ended up in the kitchen; then, realising she couldn't bear to be in the house any longer, she flung open the door and ran out across the terrace and through the garden. She didn't stop when she reached the fire pit, but hurtled over the circle of ash. Stumbling in the tussocky grass of the field, she kicked off her court shoes and ran on barefoot, wincing at the thistles. When she reached the ridge, she scrambled up the grassy bank, flopped down on its summit and wept.

When eventually she stopped crying, she scrubbed her eyes on her sleeve and lay on her back, looking up at the sky. There was still a scrap of light in the west. She thought how awful everything was, all wrong, and wished she could turn back the clock. She ached from crying.

She became aware of someone coming through the field behind her, footsteps making the long grass rustle. Sitting up and looking over her shoulder, she saw with relief that it was Nate.

He climbed up the bank. Any assumption on her part that he would be understanding or offer her comfort was quickly dispelled by the look in his eyes.

'Christ,' he said furiously. 'What did you think you were doing?'

Nate being angry with her made her feel angry with him. 'I only said what everyone else was thinking,' she said defiantly.

'And that makes it all right?'

'But it's true! That's why he's married her, because he hates Aidan having Winterton's and he knows Aidan likes Anne and he wants to pay him back!'

'Even if it were true,' Nate said stonily, 'and in fact, particularly if it was, you shouldn't have said it. Can't you see? How do you think Anne felt?'

She was about to say that she didn't care, but some instinct that he would find this especially unforgivable stopped her. Instead, she mumbled, 'I know Piers. I know him better than any of you. You don't realise how upset he was about Dad, but he was, awfully. You weren't even here, Nate.'

Nate said nothing, just stood there looking out over the estuary.

'I can't see why you're annoyed with me,' she said resentfully, 'just because I said something that's true.'

'Because it's done and can't be undone. Not if they're really married. And they are, I asked Piers.' His eyes flashed at her. 'And don't you dare say that they can get a divorce. They have to make a go of it now.'

She said bleakly, 'But he doesn't love her.'

'You don't know that.'

'Nate. He talked about his shop for hours. It took him till pudding just to mention her!'

'He was probably,' he said, 'nervous about the reaction.' His expression was severe. 'With reason, as it turned out.'

Then he let out a sigh and sat down beside her. For a long

time they did not speak. The scrap of light between the clouds deepened to dark blue. An owl hooted from the trees in the garden.

'God, what a scene,' said Nate. 'Piers couldn't have found a worse way of telling everyone if he'd tried. I mean, if you're going to do that, if you're going to marry someone without telling anyone beforehand, why not at least break it to your mother in private?' He lit a cigarette.

'None of this would have happened if Dad hadn't died.' Charley tugged at a loose thread in the hem of her skirt; some of Louise's neat stitches had pulled out during her dash from the house, and her stockings had been ripped to shreds by the thistles. 'Everything's gone wrong since then. I know what Dad did was awful, that he lost his temper with Piers and he shouldn't have done, but he would have changed his mind, I'm sure of it. If it hadn't been for the accident, he would have put things right.'

Nate's look, this time, was kinder. 'How are you, Charley?'

'I'm okay.'

'I'm sorry about your father. You miss him, don't you?'

'All the time. Dad was mean sometimes, you know he was. But he loved us, both of us, Piers and me.'

'Your father and Piers weren't a good mix.'

'You can still love someone,' she said meaningfully, 'even if they annoy you.'

'You certainly can.' He ruffled her hair.

She held out her hand and he passed her the cigarette. 'Dad didn't like Piers changing things at Winterton's because he thought that meant Piers was criticising him,' she said. 'And that Piers didn't care about what he thought.'

Nate gave her a sharp glance. 'Do you think so?'

'Yes.' People like her father, who liked to have their own

way and made a lot of noise about it, still had feelings under-neath. Not many people seemed to realise this, but Charley did.

She leaned her head against his shoulder. 'I don't know what to do, Nate.'

'About what?'

'Anything.'

'Tell me.'

'For instance, I don't know whether to go to university.'

'Does Aunt Juliet want you to?'

'She says it's up to me, but I'm sure she does. And so does my English teacher.'

'Do you?'

'I don't think so, no. I don't feel excited when I think about it, and I think I would if it was the right thing, don't you?'

'Yes. So don't go.'

'But then I'll have to do something else, and I can't think what.'

'A career, you mean? You're good with people. You're good at understanding how they feel. Perhaps you should be a psychiatrist.'

She was flattered by this, but said, 'You have to go to medical school first. Jake said.'

'And you don't want to.'

She shook her head. 'I suppose I'll end up doing a secre-tarial course, like Louise.'

'You don't want to work at Winterton's, then?'

She shuddered and handed him back his cigarette. 'God, no. It's awful there now. I feel sorry for Aidan. I overheard the staff muttering about how much better it used to be in Mr Henry and Mr Jonathan's day. Then they saw me and pretended they weren't talking about Aidan. And it's so boring anyway, and so exclusive and snobbish and stuck in the mud. Whenever I go there, I want to tear my clothes off and run round naked and daub communist slogans on the walls.'

'Let me know when you do. I wouldn't miss it for the world.' He picked a blade of grass from his shirtsleeve. 'A secretarial course might be useful. It would give you time to think.'

She began to see a path, faint but distinguishable. 'If I told Mum I was thinking about learning shorthand and typing, she might agree to letting me do the course in London. And then I could live with Gabe and Louise.'

'Would you like that?'

'Yes, I would. I can't stay here,' she added mournfully. 'Not with Piers married to Anne.' Because Piers had so stupidly married Anne Carlisle, that meant that in a way, Marsh Court belonged to Anne as well as Piers, which felt bewildering and wrong.

She said, 'I wish I could just *take off*, like you.'

'You could.' He gave her a sideways glance. 'Come with me.'

She had a brief and glorious vision of herself and Nate sailing round Cape Horn, but then she sighed. 'But Nate, Mum. She'd never let me. Anyway, I couldn't leave her on her own.' She touched his black curls. 'Your hair's too long. You look disreputable.'

He studied her. 'I like the bob. It shows off your fine eyes.'

'*Fine eyes!*' She snorted. 'God, Nate, you do talk utter rot.'

He climbed to his feet and held out his hand to her. 'Come back to the house.'

'I can't.' Vigorously, she shook her head.

'Why not?'

'I'll have to apologise to her!' she wailed.

231

'To Anne? Yes, you will.'

'Nate, I *can't*! It'll be awful!'

He said unsympathetically, 'The longer you leave it, the more awful it'll be.' He gave her hand a little tug. 'And once you've apologised, you can make friends with her.'

'*Friends* . . . Nate, I *couldn't*.'

He frowned. 'Maybe you're right and Piers doesn't really love her. But has it occurred to you that she might love him?'

Into Charley's memory came an uncomfortable recollection of the joy on Anne's face when Piers had scooped her up in his arms after winning the race across the causeway at Thorney Island.

'Anne might need a friend,' said Nate. 'Promise me, Charley.'

At half past one in the morning, unable to sleep, Juliet came down to the kitchen, took the trifle out of the fridge, sat down at the table and began to eat it. She hadn't had much at dinner, hadn't fancied the duck by the time she had prepared, cooked and sliced it, and no one at all had eaten the trifle, which had sat untouched on the table while they had reeled from the shock of Piers's announcement.

Now, Helen and Louise had gone home and everyone else was in bed, thank God, and Juliet had a moment's peace to work out what she felt about her son's marriage. The truth was that she felt horrified. Horrified and disappointed and betrayed. Wretched boy, to spring it on them like that! How could he have gone off and married this girl without even consulting her? She had not had the opportunity to ask the obvious question, whether they had *had* to get married because there was a baby on the way. She wasn't sure whether she would be able to. Piers flew too easily off the handle these days. You had to tread carefully with him.

She felt cheated of all sorts of things, some important, others trivial. She would have liked to have planned a proper wedding for her son. She grieved for the silk dress and big hat she would have worn and the cake she would have made for him, four tiers decorated with pink and cream roses. She would have filled Marsh Court with flowers and music, she would have put her heart and soul into a wonderful wedding that would have cheered up the entire family. She would have liked to have time to get to know Anne and to learn to love her. She hated that Piers had chosen such a hole-in-the-corner affair – a register office, for heaven's sake! Weddings *mattered*, she thought crossly, delving into the trifle for a large spoonful of custard and cream. A wedding should be a public declaration of love, witnessed by two families. This hasty marriage reminded her too much of her own hurried ceremony in Cairo, and that troubled her.

And then there was Anne. Juliet picked off a glacé cherry. Anne was a beautiful girl and she could quite see that men might lose their heads over her. Better, she thought, to marry for looks, for desire, than to wed a woman for spite, as Charley had accused Piers of doing. Was Piers capable of that? No, surely not. She could not believe it of him. Yet their union seemed so quick, so rash.

Was Anne the right woman for Piers? She would have chosen someone with more fire, Juliet thought. She would have chosen a woman who could match his arrogance, who would run him ragged and keep her distance until he begged her to love him.

Piers and Anne were in Piers's old bedroom. Juliet had made up another room for Anne; just before they had gone up to bed, there had been a flurry of realisation, of dismay about the sleeping arrangements, which Anne had quelled by saying firmly that they didn't mind sharing a single bed, not at all, they would be perfectly comfortable. And then they had gone upstairs to this room with its map of the world pinned to the wall and its Airfix models of Spitfires and Hurricanes stuffed on a high shelf. Piers was stripping off his clothes and dropping them on the floor, as, Anne was discovering, he always did, while she sat on the bed.

He made to help her off with her jacket; she pulled away from him. She said, 'Is it true?'

'What?'

'What Charley said about Aidan.'

'No, of course not.' He peeled off a sock.

Somehow she had got through the evening while the words that Charley had shouted over the dinner table – *Don't you see that he's only married you to spite Aidan?* – repeated themselves in her head and induced in her a panicking fear.

She said slowly, 'Charlotte must believe that Aidan has feelings for me.'

'I wouldn't know about that.'

They had not yet drawn the curtains, and moonlight was flooding through the window, outlining his profile. She loved the straight fall of his forehead and the curl of his upper lip, but perhaps these things should not have been hers.

'Piers?' she said.

'I've hardly spoken to Aidan since Dad died in January.' He sounded sulky. 'That was before you came back. How would I know whether or not he likes you?' Naked, he went to the window and stared out at the darkened garden.

This fact comforted her. 'Yes, I see that.' She rose and crossed the room to him, putting her arms round his waist and resting the side of her face against his shoulder. 'It's all been such a whirlwind. I guess Charley finds it difficult too.'

'Charley,' he said, turning round and taking her in his arms, 'likes everything to stay the same. We're not going to quarrel, are we?'

'I'm not sure I've ever quarrelled with a naked man before.'

He undid the buttons of her jacket, then slipped it off her shoulders and over her arms. Reaching round, he unzipped her frock; she wriggled until it lay, a shimmer of pink silk, at her feet.

Kisses skimmed her forehead, his palms cupped her buttocks. 'Here's another first, then. I've never made love to anyone in that bed.'

'I thought you British types liked to tumble the parlourmaid.'

'I thought,' he murmured, as his hands explored her body and he gave her a wicked smile, 'that American women were very prim and proper. You know, baking cakes and going to church, all that.'

By then she couldn't speak at all, so he scooped her up in his arms and carried her to the bed. His lovemaking was quick and thorough and silent – Rory was sleeping in the next room. Afterwards, they curled against each other, glued skin to skin.

Piers fell asleep immediately. Anne thought she would sleep but then realised she had to go to the bathroom. She prised herself out of Piers's arms, careful not to disturb him. Putting on her bathrobe, she made her way down the corridor. There was only one bathroom at Marsh Court, though it was a large house. It was a big, draughty room that even in July felt a little chilly. No shower, of course, just a huge enamelled bathtub that stung you with cold when you sat in it, even after you'd run the hot water. Everything in the bathroom, though very clean, was worn and old and of a style decades out of fashion. The entire house was like that, Anne reflected, as she washed her hands and looked at herself in the old silver mirror, an object that summed it up: perfectly lovely, but so flecked by age it hardly did the job of telling you what you looked like. She wondered whether the Wintertons believed it wasteful to replace things before they fell apart, or whether they couldn't afford it, or whether they didn't notice or didn't care.

She went back to the room. She heard footsteps as someone came up the stairs: she wasn't the only one wakeful tonight. Then there were a couple of clicks as a door opened and closed.

Piers had rolled on to his back. She looked at him fondly and then climbed in beside him. Might Aidan have been in love with her? He had given no indication of it. But then Aidan wasn't like Piers. He considered things deeply and had a quiet, measured side to his character that Piers lacked. Years ago, when she had first stayed on Lachlan and Sue's boat, she had spent the entire summer with Aidan. Piers had only turned up partway through. She had never even considered falling in love with Aidan. She had thought of herself as his friend, but never his lover.

But now she remembered the pleasure in Aidan's voice when she had phoned him after she had returned to England six months ago. He hadn't said *Anne who?* or *sorry, I'm busy*, but had straight away asked her out for a drink. Parting from him that evening in the pub, he had invited her to dinner. Though she had assumed his offer to be a friendly invitation rather than a date, perhaps Aidan had thought otherwise. She wondered whether she had been so absorbed by her craving for Piers that she had failed to notice Aidan's feelings.

But if she hadn't noticed that Aidan was keen on her (if he was), then would Piers have? Though he was capable of being perceptive, he often wasn't. Piers was the sort of person who became carried away by his own projects, and just now he was able to think of little but his new business, which he had, flatteringly, christened 'Piers Carlisle'.

The first time he had asked her to marry him, after they had made love that evening in the shop, she had refused him. He had asked her again the next day, and then the next. Something had made her hold back. After her parents had divorced, she had felt separated from everything around her. She had felt, she had tried to explain to her father, as if she was looking at the world through glass. A therapist had been engaged, who had explained to her that trauma could impair emotional response. This, she thought, was what had happened to Piers. His father's death, along with Henry Winterton's painful rejection of him, had blunted his emotions.

Should you marry someone who wasn't quite in one piece? In the end, she had said that she would. It was what she too had wanted, after all.

She had assumed that Piers had suggested a quick register office ceremony because of the business, because he didn't feel able to spare the time. Anne, who still had to contend with the ghost of her broken marriage to Glenn – all those wedding arrangements she had had to dismantle before leaving San Francisco – had gone along with it.

'If you ask my mother, then we'll have to ask Charley,' Piers had pointed out to her when they were discussing weddings, 'and then Charley will tell Louise and soon all the cousins will know and we'll end up with everyone.' And so she had let herself be persuaded.

But now she saw that they shouldn't have done it, that it

had been a terrible idea, and that she had agreed to it partly through cowardice – her own dislike of being the centre of attention – and, much more shamefully, because of a barely acknowledged fear that Piers's love for her might not be strong enough to survive the public scrutiny of a big family wedding. All those Wintertons, with their questions and opinions.

What they had done had hurt Juliet, Anne had known that tonight. Her father would mind as well, though he would never say.

Piers still hadn't forgiven Aidan for what had happened at Winterton's. It occurred to Anne, lying in bed, that Aidan might not have forgiven Piers either. Well, it was done now, she thought. She and Piers were married, and if Aidan had once felt something for her, he would have to put it behind him. The best she could do would be to try to help heal the rift between the cousins.

Katherine Rose from the gallery and an old school friend of Piers's called Jamie Mortimer had been the only guests at the wedding. Smiling in the dark, she recalled it. She had forgotten about a bouquet, so Katherine had nipped out to a florist and bought an enormous bunch of apricot and cream roses, as well as cream-coloured rosebuds for Piers and Jamie's buttonholes. For the ceremony, they had used an old signet ring that belonged to Piers. Bridget Frost, Piers's designer, was making engagement and wedding rings for her, of textured gold and diamonds, that would cleverly slot together. Afterwards, they had dined at Prunier, where Jamie had bought champagne and Katherine had taken photographs. And then they had gone back to Piers's flat and made love.

Piers had suggested they buy a bigger flat; Anne, who had been brought up to be careful with money, thought they should stay where they were. The day after the dinner at Marsh Court, driving home, they discussed it. They had plenty of room, she pointed out – a kitchen, sitting room, bedroom and bathroom.

'No dining room,' said Piers. 'How will we manage when we entertain?'

When she and her father had had friends to visit, they had gone to Italian cafés or eaten fish and chips out of newspaper. 'We'll go out,' she said. 'It'll be more fun.'

'Less washing-up.' Piers gave the steering wheel a one-fingered flick to take them round a corner.

Now that she was married to him, she began to learn the reality of a life lived with Piers Winterton. He worked a six-day week, often a twelve-hour day, sometimes more. Frequently he took off for a day or two to another part of the country to look at a designer's work or buy a piece of equipment at a bargain price. So it fell to Anne to purchase food and run the flat. Twice a week, after work, she took their washing to a launderette, where she handed over her half a crown, collecting the pile of clothes the following day, washed and folded. On the evenings they didn't go out, she made simple suppers of spaghetti and cheese or sausages, Piers's favourite. She wasn't much of a cook, had little interest in cookery.

She liked a tidy room, though. Piers's coffee cups were left stranded on chair arm and carpet, and the bathroom basin was flecked with little hairs after he shaved. He kept the shop so tidy and yet was a real dust-bug in the home. She supposed his mother had cleaned up after him. Anne didn't like to nag, so she promised herself a cleaner when they had more money, and meanwhile did a quick dash round the flat before she went to work.

In their free time, they went out with Piers's friends, who owned modelling agencies or recording studios or had set up businesses, strings of boutiques or secretarial agencies. These friends drove Austin Healeys or MG Midgets and they lived in flats in Chelsea or were doing up houses in Islington. Some, like Piers, came from comfortably-off families and had been to boarding school; others were self-made men, their accents – Cockney, Glaswegian or Liverpudlian – so thick that in the noise of a fashionable restaurant or night-club, Anne found them hard to decipher.

'London's blossoming,' said Katherine. Though she had been born in the States, she had spent the last thirty years of her life in England. 'You can see it unwrapping itself, shaking off the cobwebs and the soot.'

In September, Anne's father came to stay. Because there wasn't a spare bedroom in the flat, he booked a room in a small hotel round the corner. Anne took some time off work and they went out together. They went to the shop, where John Carlisle admired Piers's jewellery. Juliet came up to London for the day and the four of them lunched together, though Piers had to rush off before dessert.

'You do like him, don't you, Dad?' she said, one afternoon when they were ambling round the National Gallery.

'I do. He works hard. I never could abide an idle man.'

'I knew you would.'

They were standing in front of Turner's *The Fighting Temeraire*. 'Look at that,' said her father. 'How you can make a ship look sad. Piers is a busy fellow, isn't he, though, Annie? I wouldn't want to think you were lonely.'

Was she lonely? She cried, later that week, parting from her father at Heathrow.

In October, she became unwell. She thought she had

recovered, but then had to rush off one morning to the bathroom at the gallery.

When she returned to her desk, Katherine said, 'Are you all right, darling?'

'I'm fine now.' Anne patted her stomach. 'Oysters, I think.'

'Never touch them myself. Not after having a bad lot in Livorno. I thought I was going to die.'

The next morning, she was sick again. By the time she emerged from the bathroom, Katherine had sent Paul out to buy coffee beans.

She said, 'I thought you were on the Pill, Anne.'

'I was, but I gave it up. It made me so wretchedly sick.'

Katherine glanced up from her order book and peered over her glasses at her. 'What?' said Anne. 'What?'

'Might you be pregnant?'

'Pregnant?'

'Presumably,' said Katherine gently, 'it's not impossible.' Then the phone rang and she answered it.

Anne was supposed to be writing copy for a new catalogue. She clicked the end of her biro but the phrases wouldn't come. She had missed her last two periods. She had put it down to getting married, having regular sex, a great deal of sex; she had thought maybe that had upset her system. She had read somewhere that these things might happen.

She wished she had someone to talk to. She wished she had a sister or the sort of mother who listened when you confided in her. There was Juliet Winterton, of course, but she could not possibly have discussed the symptoms of pregnancy with her mother-in-law. Nor any of the other Wintertons. She found it hard to tell what they thought of her.

There was a girl called Ceridwen, whom she had met one

day at the launderette. Ceridwen was the same age as Anne and had a little boy, Owen. Anne had amused Owen while Ceridwen was taking wet washing out of the machine, and then they had got talking and Ceridwen had invited her round for coffee. She was quick, clever and Welsh, and had black hair, a pale, papery skin and shadows of exhaustion like thumbprints beneath her eyes. Ceridwen's parents had thrown her out of the family home in some mountainous Welsh valley after she had fallen pregnant out of wedlock. Now she lived in a shared house in one of the dingier parts of Notting Hill, worked in a café by day and studied English and librarianship at night school. Anne often babysat for her.

Leaving the gallery at five that evening, she caught a Circle Line train to Notting Hill, and from there walked through streets heaped with copper curls of fallen leaves to Ceridwen's house. She thought, a baby, and sometimes wanted to cry for joy. Then she thought, a baby, and felt a flutter of panic. What on earth would she do with a baby?

Chapter Eleven

December 1964–May 1965

The play was a farce called *'Scuse My French!*, and the director of the amateur dramatic society, a man in his forties called Kenneth, who always wore a black roll-collar sweater and mustard corduroy slacks, had written it. Charley was playing the maid, Fifi, and had to run on stage now and then, brandishing a feather duster.

They had been rehearsing for three weeks; the play was due to go on the following month, January. After rehearsal one evening, Kenneth gave them their notes before they left for home.

'People will want a change from pantomimes,' he finished, rather overconfidently, Charley felt. 'I'm sure we'll get a decent audience.'

'Ever the optimist,' muttered the man playing the lead role.

Charley realised he was addressing her. She felt herself flush. He was called Christian Fraser and was breathtakingly handsome, with toffee-coloured hair and long, sleepy grey-blue eyes. Up until now, his remarks to her had been confined to 'Can't you time that entrance better?', or, 'Hand me that script.' He was rumoured to be having a love affair with the ingénue, a dashing dark-haired girl called Lizzie Scott.

The meeting broke up and everyone said goodbye and put on their coats and hats. Charley found herself leaving the hall at the same time as Christian.

'I mean, it is the most frightful load of tosh,' he said.

'It is rather,' she agreed.

The path from the cold, ill-lit church hall in a Kensington back street ran beside a graveyard. Shadows fell from the yew trees, which were beaded with red berries and made Charley think of Christmas.

'It's one of Ken's vanity projects,' Christian went on. 'I do my best with the role but there's a limit, isn't there? I may have to think of going somewhere else.'

'Leaving the society, you mean?'

'I don't want to waste my talents. There are other groups.'

'You are awfully good,' she ventured.

She heard running footsteps. Lizzie Scott drew level with them.

'Bloody Ken. I'll miss my bus. I hate him.'

At the end of the path, they turned in different directions. Charley said goodbye.

'Bye, Charley,' said Christian. 'See you next week.'

She walked back to the Chelsea house she shared with her cousins Louise and Gabe in a haze of happiness and optimism. Christian Fraser had spoken to her. He had *known her name*. He had seen her as the sort of person a man like him could chat with; more, he had thought it worth confiding to her that the play was awful, which it was, and that he might leave to act somewhere else. She imagined him suggesting that she forsake the Kinwell Road am dram society at the same time as him. He would study her with a thoughtful frown and say something like, 'You put a lot into that role, Charley. The play would have been nothing without you. You've got something special. We work well together.'

She crossed the Fulham Road and headed down Sydney Street. She had been living in London for the last three and a half months. During the day, she went to secretarial college, where she studied shorthand, typing and commercial practice. It was all right; not exciting, but all right.

Both Louise and Gabe had boyfriends. Louise's boyfriend was called Josh. He was thin and dark and clever and was studying for a PhD in theoretical physics at Imperial College. He wasn't at all the sort of boyfriend Charley would have thought Louise would have. Louise had given up secretarial work to become a full-time model. She was invited to parties and weekends where she met famous actors, pop singers, photographers and fashion designers. When Charley enquired whether any of them ever asked her for a date, she said carelessly, 'All the time. But I don't find them interesting.' She preferred Josh, she explained. He was interesting.

Gabe's boyfriend was called Adam. He had longish tow-coloured hair and a long, beautiful, mournful face, and was a soloist in a ballet company in Pimlico. He had given Gabe and Charley tickets for a performance. It was a modern dance company, so no tutus; instead, all the dancers wore black leotards and there wasn't much in the way of scenery. The ballet had seemed rather dull and bewildering to Charley until Adam had danced a duet with the company's prima ballerina, and then, confronted by a raw emotion that had touched her to the heart, she had found herself thinking about all sorts of things – her father and Piers, and Nate being on the other side of the world again, so far away – and tears had welled up in her eyes. She had sniffed very loudly, and the person in the seat in front of her had turned and glowered at her.

Louise and Josh had very kindly asked Charley to come out with them when she had first come to live in London, but she had had the sense to refuse. Sometimes she went for a drink with Aidan or Jake and sometimes she went to see her cousin Eliot, who was married and lived in Richmond. Whenever she could, she bought herself a ticket for the theatre. She didn't mind going on her own, preferred it in some ways, because when she didn't have to talk to someone else, she could lose herself properly in the drama. After the performance, emerging into the street, she felt jarred and a little bewildered, as if the world inside the auditorium had been the real one, and what was outside was only a pallid imitation.

Sometimes, goaded by the memory of her promise to Nate, she walked to Piers's flat after she had finished college for the day. Piers was hardly ever in, but Anne almost always was. Charley thought that if being pregnant made you feel as awful as Anne looked, then she'd rather not bother. Anne, always pale, was now translucent. She was often either running off to be sick or trying to eat something dreadful, like liver, because her doctor had told her that she was anaemic. The flat was a mess – even Charley, who was not a tidy person, recognised that Anne had given up on it.

Charley strained to keep the conversation going with amusing anecdotes about her secretarial course or whatever she could scrape up, but it was an effort, and she couldn't help feeling sorry for Piers, married to such a wet fish. Piers, in contrast, was invariably full of energy whenever she went to see him at the shop. Charley adored the small, glittering interior and could see how proud of it Piers was. He was always busy, talking on the phone or calling out instructions to his secretary or unpacking boxes. Though Charley was uninterested in jewellery – a terrible failing for a Winterton – she bought from him a copper brooch in the shape of a fox because it reminded her of the foxes that loped across the lawns on misty mornings at Marsh Court. Having turned eighteen, she had her own money now, the annuity that her father had left her.

Now she unlocked the door of the terraced house in Chelsea she shared with her cousins and went inside. Louise and Josh were in the kitchen. Louise was frying eggs. She looked up when Charley came in.

'Do you want an egg?'

'Two, please.'

'How did it go?'

'Lizzie forgot all her lines. Every single one of them. Kenneth screamed at her. How was your day?'

'Good.' Louise cracked eggs. 'Hector took some lovely shots. It was bridal wear. He made me look like Miss Havisham.'

'What about you, Josh?'

'I had a very exciting day, but it's pointless trying to explain to you because you wouldn't understand.' Josh said this in an uncondescending, matter-of-fact way, and Charley knew that he was right, she wouldn't.

'We were talking about Christmas,' said Louise. 'I told Josh he should come to us, but he says he's going to work.'

'I'll have the place to myself.' Josh buttered toast. 'I'll get masses done.'

'You can't work at Christmas,' said Charley.

'I always do. It's one of the pluses of being Jewish, you see. You're allowed to ignore it.'

There was one more rehearsal before Christmas. Lizzie Scott was off with 'flu, and the understudy took over her role. At the end of the evening, Christian Fraser caught up with Charley as she walked down the path by the graveyard.

He said, 'I'm going to tell Lizzie that Ken said she should have come to the rehearsal even if she was dying.'

Charley looked up at him. He had smiled at her twice that evening, friendly, conspiratorial, why-do-we-put-up-with-this smiles. She said boldly, 'Is Lizzie your girlfriend?'

'We've been out a few times, yes. Why?'

'I just wondered.'

'Are you putting yourself forward as a candidate for the post?'

Her face went hot. 'No . . . I'm sorry . . . I didn't meant to be nosy.'

'You're a very pretty girl, Charley.'

'Oh.' It was the first time any man had ever said that to her. Her mother told her she was pretty, but then she had to, mothers were supposed to say that. Her father never had, perhaps because he had thought it would make her big-headed, or perhaps because he hadn't thought she was, particularly. Piers − obviously not. Piers only ever noticed himself. And as for the aunts and uncles and cousins − why should they pick her out when she was overshadowed by beautiful Louise? Nate had told her that she had fine eyes, but that was just Nate being silly.

Christian said, 'You sound surprised. Don't you think you're pretty?'

'I hadn't thought about it much,' she said honestly.

He laughed. 'How creditably modest. I would ask you out for a drink but I have to dash for a train. After Christmas, perhaps.'

Two days later, she went home to Marsh Court. It was their first Christmas without her father. He had always got in the tree and packed it into a large pot with stones and earth, but this time Charley and her mother did it. The tree kept slipping over sideways in the pot and they both ended up weeping with laughter, and then they puffed and panted, hauling the thing indoors, with Lulu getting under their feet. Then her mother said in a shaky voice, 'Let's have a little rest before we decorate it, shall we?' Charley went upstairs to her bedroom, where she cried for a while. She wondered whether her mother was crying too: it was hard to tell.

Later, strewing tinsel and attaching baubles, she relived her conversation with Christian. She would marry for love, she resolved; she suspected her mother and father hadn't. She went to her bedroom to dress for dinner and studied her reflection in the glass. *You're a very pretty girl.* She rubbed in some eyeshadow, spat in her mascara and brushed it on. *I would ask you out for a drink . . . After Christmas, perhaps.* She pondered on Christian's use of the word 'perhaps'. Did he mean perhaps he would ask her out for a drink – and in that case perhaps not – or did he mean perhaps after Christmas or perhaps later in January? And what about Lizzie Scott? Was she really his girlfriend or not? And if she was, would it be right for Charley to go for a drink with him?

There were no rehearsals between Christmas and New Year. Louise, who had bought a new car, a Mini, gave Charley a lift back to London at the beginning of January. On Thursday, she went to the rehearsal. As she arrived at the hall, she looked out for Christian. Her heart tripped as she caught sight of him. He gave her a friendly hello as she manoeuvred herself closer to him, but then continued his conversation with a couple of other actors. She did not have the nerve to insert herself into their group.

Lizzie was back and had learned her lines, thank goodness,

and she and Christian were rather brilliant that night. At coffee break, the two of them huddled together in a corner. As the evening wore on, Charley's spirits lowered. Christian had forgotten he had ever thought of asking her out for a drink. Or he had never meant it in the first place, or she had misunderstood him.

At the end of the third act everyone clapped and even Kenneth managed to say something pleasant. Leaving the hall, Charley clung to the hope that Christian would catch up with her as she walked down the path by the graveyard. The girl who did props accompanied her to the street, chattering about a mistake she had made in the first act – 'I thought Kenneth would be furious!' – as they passed the gravestones and yew trees.

When they reached the main road, the props girl said, 'You go the same way as me, don't you?' Then a voice called out, 'Charley!' and she looked back and saw Christian running to catch up with them.

'I thought I'd missed you,' he said.

The evening suddenly became quite perfect. The props girl looked at Christian and then at Charley. 'I mustn't miss my bus,' she said. 'See you next week.'

It was a cold, frosty night and Christian was wrapped up in a coat and scarf. He rubbed his hands together and blew on them to warm them.

'Fancy rushing off like that. I thought we were going for a drink.'

'I thought you'd forgotten.'

'Me? I never forget. Come on. I know a smashing little place.'

They walked side by side along streets and alleyways unknown to Charley. Frost glittered on the pavements and gave a sharp smokiness to the air. The lit interiors of the cabs, and the pubs and cafés with their dribs and drabs of custo-mers, looked mysterious and sophisticated.

They talked about the play and Kenneth and Christmas. Christian didn't say any more about leaving the amateur dramatic society. His smashing little pub looked to Charley much like other London pubs – brownish decor, air thick with cigarette smoke. They drank in the public bar rather than the saloon bar. The barman asked her how old she was and she said she was twenty-one, because she was afraid Christian would think eighteen childishly young.

He bought her a gin and lime and a pint of bitter for himself. 'Did you miss me?' he said, as he split open a packet of crisps.

Though she knew she should reply with the same offhand hauteur with which she had lied to the barman, she found herself saying, 'Yes.'

He untwisted the blue paper and scattered salt on the crisps. 'You've rather caught my eye.'

'Have I?'

'Yes. Don't look so surprised, you silly girl. I like you a lot. I've been thinking I might like to date you.'

Charley felt that Christian's phrasing implied some impedi-ment, a hurdle that must be got over. She said, 'I haven't got a boyfriend, if that's what you're worried about.'

'I was thinking about Lizzie, actually.' He ate a crisp. 'She has a very jealous nature.'

'Does she?'

'She hates me even looking at another girl.'

'Have you been going out with her for ages?'

'Oh no, I didn't know her before the play. But I would have to make a choice.'

Was he trying to explain to her that he would need to

251

drop Lizzie gently? Or perhaps that they should wait until after the play, which was to have its run of three performances the following week.

'I wouldn't want to hurt anyone,' she said. 'I don't mind waiting.'

He gave her a penetrating stare and drank some of his beer. 'The thing is, it's more of a question of choosing between you. It's quite tricky, fancying two women. It would be easier to make a decision if I had more of the facts.'

She said, bewildered, 'What facts?'

'I don't know you well enough. Lizzie and I have been to bed a couple of times. I'd have to go to bed with you before I made up my mind.'

Charley couldn't think what to say. Christian couldn't have meant *that*, surely – she must have got the wrong end of the stick.

'Then I'd be able to decide which of you I liked best,' he added, making it clear to her that he had meant exactly that. He took her hand and threaded his fingers through hers, looking into her eyes, smiling warmly. 'I'd know which of you suited me better.'

'You mean,' she said, scrabbling through her brain for the right words, 'a sort of *competition?*'

'I wouldn't put it like that. It sounds rather heartless. You'd like to be my girlfriend, wouldn't you, Charley?'

His thigh nudged against hers. Would she? she wondered. 'I don't think so,' she said. 'No – probably not.'

He looked put out. 'Why not?'

'I don't know.' If she told him how shocked and disappointed she felt, he might laugh at her.

But he laughed anyway. First, his frown deepened. 'You're not a virgin, are you?' A shake of his head and then a short,

252

amused outward breath. 'Oh God, you are, aren't you? Okay, forget it.'

'Christian—'

'I said, forget it.'

'I thought we could be friends,' she whispered, trying to salvage something.

He swallowed the rest of his drink, then stood up and put on his coat. Charley gathered up her things.

Outside, in the cold, she said, 'Christian, I do like you awfully.'

He ruffled her hair with his fingers. 'You need to grow up, do you know that? You can't play at being Daddy's little princess for ever.'

Then he walked away. Charley watched him disappear into the night. She turned off in what she thought was the right direction home but became lost, stumbling around unfamiliar streets, which only added dismayingly to her sense of humiliation. Eventually she came across an old woman, slowly pushing a wicker shopping basket along the pavement. Inside it was clothing, a grubby blanket, a tattered paperback book, a length of greyish-white knitting, as well as a cup and saucer and cutlery – as if, Charley thought, the basket contained her home.

The woman directed her to Sydney Street. After she had thanked her, Charley walked on, wondering whether she should have lied about being a virgin. She imagined Christian telling his friends at the dramatic society. They would laugh at her. She wondered whether he would have judged her for her prowess, or lack of it, in bed. Points out of ten. She wondered whether some girls would have gone along with what he had suggested or perhaps would have had the sexual confidence to laugh at him. She did not regret turning him down, but wished she had done it in a more spirited way.

She found the Chelsea house at last and let herself in. Louise called out, 'Charley, is that you?' and padded in her pyjamas to the top of the stairs.

'It's me.'

'How was it?'

'Fine.' She would never be able to tell anyone, not even Louise, about Christian.

Louise yawned. 'Early start tomorrow. Night-night.'

Charley took off her coat and hat and went upstairs to her bedroom. There was a moment when all she wanted was to be back at Marsh Court, cross-legged on the rug in front of the drawing room fire, reading a favourite book, with her mother sitting in an armchair nearby, knitting or writing a letter. But then she took a deep breath and reminded herself that this was what she had chosen, London and freedom and adventure.

She never went back to the drama society, so missed the performances; someone else, perhaps the props girl, wore Charley's black frock and white apron and waved the feather duster. She joined another drama group in Bayswater, too far away and unfashionable for Christian, which put on plays of a more serious nature instead of French farces. The men wore Arran jumpers and the girls black or olive-coloured turtlenecks, and after rehearsals they went to the pub, where they discussed great issues, exposures of injustice and the nature of socialism, before heading off home.

Juliet was driving along the Maldon road in heavy rain when she caught sight of a jeep parked on the verge. The bonnet was open and a man was bending over it. There was no garage for miles, so she pulled in beside it.

'Can I do anything?'

The man looked up and she recognised Joe Brandon. His khaki jacket was turned up at the collar and his wet black hair fell over his eyes.

He shut the bonnet, then smacked it with his palm. 'Something's up with the electrics. I'll have to tow it back to the farm.'

'Perhaps I could help.'

'Thank you, but it's a hefty beast and I wouldn't ask it of your Morris. I'll take the tractor out first thing tomorrow.'

Rain was hurling itself from a heavy sky and drumming on both their vehicles. She said, 'At least let me give you a lift to Greensea.'

'It's good of you to offer . . .'

'I couldn't let you get wet again, Mr Brandon.' She smiled, remembering the afternoon he had rowed her back from Thorney Island. 'It's the least I can do, considering. And it'll make a change for me to rescue you.'

For a moment she wondered whether he would refuse and obstinately insist on walking all the way to Greensea. But then he said, 'Thank you, Mrs Winterton. It's good of you.'

As she pulled out on to the road, the downpour obliterated the route ahead and her windscreen wipers thrashed. She had to concentrate hard to see her way and did not mind that he made no attempt to engage her in conversation. On the narrow side roads, the surfaces were awash.

'You need to take the next turn to the left,' he said.

'I know the way.' She glanced at him. 'I've been to Greensea before, remember. It was a long time ago, during the war, when your wife was very ill and I sent over a few little gifts for her.'

'I don't remember.'

'You sent them back to me.'

255

'Did I? How impolite.'

'They were only silly little things.'

A fork of lightning, a crackle of silver in a violet sky, revealed to her the salt marsh, not so far away. Her Morris rattled and bounced as she took the narrow road that swerved through drenched countryside. Ahead of her, the poplars that surrounded the farmhouse were masked by sheets of rain.

She parked the car on the courtyard in front of the farmhouse.

'Thank you, Mrs Winterton.' He seemed to hesitate. 'Would you like a cup of tea?'

She accepted, curious to see how Joe Brandon lived, then dashed through the rain after him to the porch.

He opened the door and showed her inside. Their coats dripped water on to the red quarry tiles in the hall. Three dogs of varying sizes and breeds hurtled out to greet them.

He took her coat and hung it on a peg. 'Christine?' he called out. 'I've brought a guest.'

A door opened, footsteps, and a woman appeared. Juliet guessed her to be in her seventies. Her thin, straight grey hair was cut in a bob, and her face was lean and brown and lined. She was tall and wiry, and was wearing grey trousers and a bottle-green hand-knitted jersey.

Joe Brandon introduced them. 'Mrs Winterton, this is my aunt, Miss Christine Brandon.'

They shook hands. 'That telephone's been ringing all afternoon, Joe,' Christine said accusingly.

'Never mind, I'm here now. Do you think we might have some tea?'

Christine Brandon went away. 'She hates me making tea,' Joe explained, as he showed Juliet into a sitting room. 'She says I make a mess of her kitchen.'

256

The dogs followed him; they sat by the fireplace, tongues out, panting, looking at him adoringly. The phone rang.

'I'm so sorry,' he said. 'I really should take this. Forgive me.'

He asked her to make herself comfortable; Juliet murmured thanks but did not immediately sit down. She was distracted by the fact that one of the sofas was taken up by a boy perhaps a few years younger than Piers, who was stretched out full-length along the cushions, and who appeared to be asleep.

As Mr Brandon took the call – 'Roy, how good to hear from you. Yes, it'll be fine for that week, whatever you think best' – she looked round the room.

It was large and airy, square in shape, with a high ceiling. Cream-coloured curtains hung from the tall sash windows. Two sofas, covered in faded chintz, faced each other across a large marble fireplace. A dresser stood to one side of the fireplace, a small upright piano to the other. On the mantelpiece was a nice old casement clock and a couple of Dresden figurines. Elsewhere, a gramophone with a stack of records beside it stood on a low cupboard, and several tall bookcases were filled with books, hefty historical tomes as well as Penguin paperbacks. Copies of the New Statesman, the Guardian and Tribune lay on the table. Today's Guardian was folded open at the crossword, almost complete.

The window faced out over a walled garden, beyond which lay an orchard, grey and dripping in the rain. Joe Brandon mouthed a silent apology at her as the telephone call continued. 'Roy, it's your decision. You know I'm happy to leave that side of it to you. What does Paddy think?' It was hard to ignore the young man on the sofa. Though his features were pleasing, there was, even in sleep, a sulky turn to the corners of his mouth.

Juliet studied the collection of framed photographs on the sideboard. One interested her, a group of young soldiers in desert fatigues. Another was of a pretty young woman with dark curly hair and an infectious smile.

'That's Molly,' Joe Brandon said as he put down the phone.

'She's beautiful.'

'She was. None more so.'

She shot a glance at the phone. 'Problems?'

'Nothing that can't be resolved. I help out with an educational charity based in London. We send city boys to my farm to give them some experience of the countryside. They camp out at Greensea. Not all of my land is suitable for farming, so I like to make use of it. Some of them have been in trouble with the law or have had a spell in Borstal. We're trying to show them there are alternatives.' Then, raising his voice, he said, 'Neville.'

The boy on the sofa opened his eyes and sat up so quickly Juliet wondered whether he had really been asleep or had been feigning it all along.

'Hello, Uncle Joe.' His longish wavy brown hair was tousled, his clothing rumpled.

'Neville, this is Mrs Winterton. Mrs Winterton, this is my godson, Neville Stone.'

They shook hands. Neville gave her a sleepy smile.

Joe said, 'The jeep's packed up, Nev. I'll need you to give me a hand with it tomorrow morning.'

''Course.'

'Have you got the hens in?'

'Not yet.'

'It's getting dark. The fox won't wait for you.'

The door opened and Christine Brandon came into the room carrying a tea tray. She put it on the table, then left.

Neville unpeeled himself from the sofa, grabbed a handful of biscuits from the tray, then went to the door. Something seemed to strike him, because he frowned.

'If the jeep's conked out, how will I get to the pub tonight?'

'You can borrow my bike.' Joe was pouring tea.

'Bike.'

'Yes. It's the thing with two wheels and handlebars in the small barn. You may need to put some air in the tyres.'

Neville gave a sigh as he left the room. Joe called after him, 'I'll knock on your door at six tomorrow morning.' A disgruntled 'Six!' was heard before Neville went out of earshot.

Joe said to Juliet, 'His father was a friend of mine. He's a good lad, but idle as sin.' He handed her a cup of tea, then fetched the photograph of the soldiers in desert fatigues. 'That's his father, Richard Stone.' He indicated a tall, good-looking man at the end of the row. 'He was killed at El Alamein. I've tried to keep an eye on the boy since, do what I can.'

'Is his mother still alive?'

'Virginia's an actress. She's on tour a lot. Neville was sent down from university a couple of weeks ago. He hasn't told me the full story yet, but I'm hoping he'll be able to go back and complete his degree. I said he could come here and help out while he works out what to do next. When he puts his mind to it, he's capable of doing a good job.'

Juliet looked at the photograph more closely. 'That's the Gezira Sporting Club, isn't it?'

'You know it?'

'My father and I lived in Cairo for a while.'

Humour touched the corners of his mouth. 'I imagined you a Home Counties girl,' he said. 'Boarding school, a good marriage, Country Life, some riding to hounds and wearing of pearls.'

She shook her head. 'You're completely wrong.' She looked at the photograph again, at the smiling, darkly good-looking man standing next to Richard Stone. 'Is that you?'

He nodded. 'Cairo was fascinating. I only felt I scratched the surface, though. Were you there long?'

'A couple of years. I was very young when I lived there. Younger than your Neville, perhaps.'

'He's twenty-two.'

'Yes, younger than that. Such a long time ago. It was where Henry and I met.'

'I'm sorry for your loss. I remember how hard it was after Molly died. Christine kept the place together. Without her, it would have fallen to rack and ruin. But you have children, don't you? They must be a comfort to you.'

Were they? Juliet wondered. She worried for Charley, in London. She was too young, she felt, to live on her own, and the knowledge that she herself had lived alone in Cairo at the age of nineteen was of little comfort. She remembered her terrible loneliness and the decisions she had made which she had later regretted. The brightness seemed to have been rubbed out of the house since Charley had left home. Juliet had tried to coax her into finding a secretarial course nearer to Maldon, but Charley had been adamant that she wanted to go to London.

She worried for Piers and Anne, too – of course it would be wonderful to have a grandchild, and of course a baby might draw them together, but what if it did not? Though some women sailed through pregnancy, Anne was not doing so, and she looked ill and tired. If only she would give up working at the gallery and take a rest, Juliet thought. If only Piers would not be so occupied with his new business and notice that Anne was having a miserable time.

But none of that could be explained to Joe Brandon, any more than she could have told him that she was, in truth, quite relieved that Henry was dead.

'Yes, of course,' she said. 'Such a comfort.'

She thought about Joe Brandon as she drove home. Greensea's rooms had been neat and clean, and yet an air of seriousness, an absence, had clung to them. Something had been missing – fresh flowers, perhaps, a bright cushion or two, a light novel, open on the table, ready for the reader to return to it when she had time. Juliet wondered whether he populated the house with lame dogs – the good-for-nothing godson, the tearaways from the slums – to keep loneliness at bay. And yet, to have loved and lost as Joe Brandon had – was even that, painful though it must be, preferable to having failed at love, as she had?

Joe had to hammer on Neville's door three times before he emerged, yawning and with shoes untied and a jersey pulled on over his pyjama top. He put a mug of black coffee into Neville's hands and went to fetch the tractor. He drove, while Neville perched on the footplate. There was nothing much on the roads, and the rain had dried up, leaving coffee-coloured puddles.

Neville helped him hitch up the jeep. He let the boy drive the tractor back to Greensea while he steered the jeep. Christine had breakfast waiting for them when they got back to the farm. Over bacon, eggs and sausages, Joe asked Neville what time he had got in the previous night.

'Dunno.'

And then, whether he had phoned his college to find out whether they would reconsider their decision and allow him to finish his degree.

'Not yet.'

'You need to get on with it. You're asking them a favour.'

Neville stuffed another piece of bread in his mouth, grunted something unintelligible and left the table. Five minutes later, the front door slammed behind him.

Joe knew that he had mishandled the situation. He had intended to strike up a conversation and had ended up inter-rogating the lad. He should phone Virginia and talk to her about Neville, he thought, but Virginia was touring with a play in the north of England. A letter, then. He needed to remind her that she had a son, and that he was becoming a little lost.

Virginia Stone was now in her mid-forties, talented, amusing and beautiful. Years ago, Joe had had an affair with her. At the time, he had put her seduction of him down to the fact that they had both lost their partners very young in life, and that perhaps she had felt they had something in common. With hindsight, he suspected that she had felt sorry for him and had been trying to jolly him up. The affair had lasted on and off for five years. He had been left with a feeling of responsibility towards Neville, whom Virginia had cheerfully neglected, bundling him off to boarding school at the age of five, depositing him with friends or relations when she was away on tour.

Reminding Virginia of her responsibilities was likely to meet with little success, but he had to try. The boys he came across through Roy and Paddy's educational charity showed all too clearly what happened when a family gave up on a child. They played truant or left school at fifteen, and if there wasn't a father around to find them work at the docks or in a car plant, they often ended up failing to hold down a job. Sometimes they became involved with a bad crowd and got into trouble with the law.

Though Neville had the protection of money as well as class, he had never learned to knuckle down. He had, when he chose to use it, charm, which he employed to enable him to get away with, Joe thought, far too much. It was a pity he had not inherited Virginia's acting talent – but then Virginia, whatever her failings as a mother, had always worked unremittingly hard. Single-handedly, she had clothed and fed Neville and paid his school fees, and Joe admired her for that. Whereas Neville moaned and groaned at the thought of working hard at anything.

Joe took the dishes through to the kitchen and thanked Christine for breakfast. Then he went outside. The bulk of Greensea farmhouse had been built in the mid-eighteenth century. Wings and extensions had been added on over the years. It was a good, solid house rather than a beautiful or striking one, but it sat well in the flattish fields, and the salt marsh and estuary were only a short distance away. In the summer, you could taste salt and sea lavender in the air.

Molly had been a keen gardener, and descendants of the daffodils she had planted in the lawns surged round the building, a sea of gold, heads nodding in the wind. Joe added to them each autumn, planting more bulbs in memory of her. Beyond the garden could be traced the remains of a medieval moat. All that was left of it now was two sizeable ponds, on which they taught – tried to teach – the London lads to fish and row before letting them loose on the Blackwater. The rowing was generally more of a success than the fishing. Fishing required patience.

Greensea was a mixed farm of six hundred acres. Half the acreage was planted with winter wheat or barley; a dairy herd grazed the other three hundred. Christine kept poultry, and a few pigs to eat the scraps and make bacon. During the war, they had had to put more acres to the plough, but without any great success; those meadows, too near the salt marsh for anything much to thrive, had since been allowed to go fallow and were now used only on two fortnights a year, when the charity pitched their tents there.

Joe spent the morning repairing the jeep and the afternoon mending hedges and clearing ditches, with the help of his labourer, Ted Blacklock. It was cold, damp work and Ted wasn't a talkative sort, and Joe's mind drifted. Sometimes he worried about Neville and sometimes he thought about Juliet Winterton. He had glimpsed her often enough in the streets of Maldon, but on only two occasions before yesterday had he spoken to her. The first had been during the war, when he had found her trampling round his copse. It had taken their second meeting, when he had rowed her from Thorney Island to the mainland, to make him suspect that he had misjudged her.

He had seen her, stranded on the shore. Her dark gold hair, a bright colour among all the muted shades, had caught his attention. He had felt sorry for her, heading back to Marsh Court, a slim figure in the dusk, walking alone along the path by the estuary. You heard stories. The marriage was not thought to be a happy one.

He was no gossip, yet even he had heard that when Henry Winterton had died, he had left his wife only a pittance and a small cottage. Something like that, the whole county got to know. He had offered her his condolences yesterday because that was what you did, and because he suspected that she would hate him to know of her humiliation.

After she had driven away from Greensea, he had become aware that something had changed. He was sorting through the day's post when Christine said, 'What's that? You, singing? What's got into you, Joe?'

There was a lightness inside him that he hadn't felt for a long time. In spite of his run-in with Neville, in spite of the cold and the wet, it lingered, and he realised that it was something to do with Juliet Winterton.

He and Ted completed their work and locked the tools back in the outhouse. Joe thanked Ted, who headed off for his cottage in Mundon. Then he walked round to the front of the house. The sun was sinking, pasting the land with apricot and violet. He remembered the day Molly had planted the daffodil bulbs, her hair tied up in a red and white chequered scarf, khaki dungarees on, stooping in the soil. And then her memory was superseded by a more recent image of Juliet Winterton, climbing out of her car in the pouring rain, offering him a smile and a lift to Greensea.

Savagely, he said aloud, 'Well, what are you waiting for?' and took out his pocket knife and began to cut daffodils. Stem after stem, golden and orange and frilled white, until his arms were full of them.

The school had offered her more teaching hours, which she had accepted with relief. At Marsh Court, dressing for a morning's teaching in a navy skirt, white blouse and cardigan, she clipped on a suitably modest pair of earrings. She should, she thought, sell some of her jewellery. There were showy pieces from Winterton's that she did not love, that had been Henry's taste rather than hers, and that she, a widow, would have little use for in the future. Over the course of the last year, she suspected she had been struck off certain lists: the inconvenient single person for whom no dinner hostess could find a seat. She wasn't wealthy, enviable Juliet Winterton any more. She was a widow, rather hard-up, who had to work for her living.

A touch of powder, a dash of lipstick, and then she was ready. She checked that her purse and handkerchief were in her bag, gave Lulu a farewell cuddle, picked up her work bag and keys and opened the front door.

Her gaze was caught by a flash of gold. In the shelter of the porch lay a huge bunch of daffodils, wrapped round in brown paper and roughly tied with a length of twine. She picked them up, marvelling at their colour, which spoke of spring and optimism.

A scrap of paper was tucked inside the bouquet. She unfolded it.

It said, *Dear Mrs Winterton, thank you so much for your kindness yesterday.* And it was signed, *Joe.*

Daffodils, she thought. Why had he sent her daffodils?

When she came home from school that afternoon, she put the bunches into vases and dotted them round the house. In the fifteen months that had passed since Henry had died, the place seemed to have become oddly colourless. Or had it been that way for a long time and she had only recently noticed? She had found herself thinking from time to time, *I should paint that room, brighten it up.* But she had done nothing. The effort had seemed beyond her.

Now, the yellow of the flowers caught her eye as she walked from room to room. They were telling her something, but she could not yet make out what it was.

Aidan and Freya were at the causeway. Freya propped up the tripod on a flat piece of ground and took photographs as the tide went out. The water drained away from the causeway and she looked down the viewfinder and adjusted aperture and shutter speed. The snap of the shutter, a whirr as she wound on the film.

Aidan rested his back against the fence. He was drawing Freya, hunched to the camera. A wiggly line where a strand of curly hair escaped from a barrette, soft shading where she had tucked her trousers into her boots. The level of the river was receding visibly, as if someone had pulled out a plug. A sky the colour of forget-me-nots threw planes of blue on the water, and the air smelled of spring, sharp and green and full of promise.

The last six months had been rotten in many ways, but his friendship with Freya had provided some consolation. Though nothing could compensate for the nauseated fury that had washed over him when he had discovered that Piers had married Anne, the long walks he and Freya took at the weekends at least provided a distraction. In his fantasies Anne had wept, regretting her marriage and begging his forgiveness. The intensity of his rage had shaken him and had, in the end, made him dislike himself.

When he had heard that Anne was pregnant, anger had been replaced by a sense of miserable futility. That, and the unremitting grind of his work at Winterton's, had induced in him a feeling of hopelessness.

The causeway emerged from the channel, sheened with water. Freya looked back at him. 'I'd like to go to the island.'

They packed up their belongings and crossed the causeway. The trees on Thorney Island's only road were coming into leaf. Their conversation, as they headed up the slope and the road curved round, was of what they saw, the birds and flowers and hedgerows. Freya had brought with her two cameras, the Hasselblad, which she used with the tripod, and a smaller model, a Leica M2, which she wore slung round her neck. When two hares appeared on the field to one side of them, she pointed the compact and took a dozen

photographs, shooting and winding on the film with practised ease.

'You're quick,' he said.

'You have to be.'

'I hadn't realised you took so many pictures.'

'I take hundreds. I select them at the negative stage.
Sometimes I'll only keep a couple. I'm like you, rubbing
something out over and over again, trying to get it right.'

They ate their picnic, cheese and pickle sandwiches and a
flask of coffee, on the sea wall to the back of the island. Below
the wall lay a large area of salt marsh, the clumps of sea
purslane and sea lavender pale green and grey. The wind that
buffeted them seemed to Aidan to be blowing his problems
away. He'd had a better week at work, he told Freya. Most of
the time, he'd thought he'd known what he was doing.

They looped back round the sea wall to the place where the
causeway joined the island. The mud and water reflected the
sky like a mirror.

Freya said, 'You know that feeling when you have an image
in your head and you're not sure whether it's a memory or
something you've seen in a dream?'

'Or a memory of a dream.'

'That's what this place feels like. Like a dream.'

'A good dream or a bad dream?'

She shook her head. 'Just a dream.'

They went back across the causeway. She walked ahead of
him, balancing the tripod on her shoulder. Her long hair
flailed in the wind as she strode over the wet stones. She
looked wild, he thought. He could picture her running here
five thousand years ago, spearing fish, chasing along the bank
after a wolf or a deer or some other beast.

*   *   *

At least she wasn't being sick any more, Anne thought. She didn't think anyone – except, of course, another pregnant woman – was capable of understanding how wonderful it was not to be sick. She had been sick for the first five months of her pregnancy, far longer than her mother-and-baby book said she was supposed to be. Her doctor had told her to eat a dry cracker before she got out of bed in the morning, but that had made her gag. When she had tried to tell him how miserable it was, feeling sick or being sick most of the time, he had asked her whether her marriage was happy. After that, whenever he enquired, she said that she was fine.

Was her marriage happy? A lot of the time it was. She was happy when Piers came home from work at seven and they went out and ate spaghetti in an Italian café. She had been happy when, on her birthday, he whisked her away to a hotel in the Surrey countryside and gave her one of Bridget Frost's beautiful brooches as she was dressing for dinner. The hotel and the brooch were surprises; Piers was good at surprises.

She visited Aidan at his new apartment in Chelsea, bright top-floor rooms a few streets away from the terraced house where Louise, Gabe and Charley lived. There were high ceilings and big sloping windows. He had painted the walls white and hung pictures and prints.

'I love it,' she said, looking round. 'So light.'

There was a photograph on the wall, criss-crosses of black and grey netting a blurred coastline. 'And this,' she said. 'This is good.'

'A friend of mine, Freya Catherwood, took it.' He flicked open a sketchbook. 'That's her.'

Aidan had coloured in the woman's hair and jacket bright red. The remainder of the drawing was inked in black. Whenever Aidan showed her his work, Anne wanted to ask him what he was doing sitting in an office all day when he should be doing that. She didn't, though. She knew she might not get an answer she wanted to hear. She could tell Aidan didn't love working at Winterton's – he was doing it conscientiously and well, she suspected, because Aidan would do everything conscientiously and well, but he didn't love it. So you had to ask yourself why he didn't just hand the whole wretched business over to Piers. Perhaps it was because he was too angry with Piers, who had behaved badly towards him. Or perhaps Piers had taken from him something – someone – whom Aidan had thought – hoped – might belong to him.

'How's the new flat?' asked Aidan.

'Oh.' She sighed and sat down on the sofa. 'I painted the kitchen cupboards. At least they're not so brown any more. Louise is making curtains for me. Ivory linen instead of that hideous floral chintz.'

Anne found it hard to like the new flat. She reminded herself not to be so spoiled, that plenty of people didn't even have a roof over their heads, and that she would get used to it. But that didn't make her any fonder of it.

The new flat had two bedrooms and a dining room as well as a sitting room and kitchen. It had been very expensive and so she felt she ought to like it, but the sitting room faced north and the windows were small, so it was dark and chilly and not somewhere you wanted to sit for long. Piers was proud of the grand marble fireplace, which Anne, who preferred lightness and modernity, loathed. The kitchen was small and narrow, with only one tiny, high-up window, and the cupboards had been the colour of mud before she had painted them, the lino a similar shade. She would have preferred to have found somewhere they could have restored to their own taste, as Aidan had. Only she couldn't have put it to Piers like that because she never talked to Piers about Aidan.

She had stopped mentioning her visits with Aidan to Piers ages ago, in the early months of pregnancy, when she had been so sick and fatigued that she had been unable to face the arguments and sulks. Piers assumed she no longer saw Aidan, and she hadn't corrected him. She hadn't intended for this to happen. Now, if she told Piers the truth, he would assume she had been deliberately keeping her visits secret. Which she had, in a way. As soon as the baby's born, she promised herself. When the baby was born, and when she felt normal again, she would find a way of talking to Piers about Aidan.

'Slice of cake?' Aidan waved a tin at her.

'Aidan, you have *cake*?'

'I bought it for you.'

'You're a darling. A huge piece, if that's okay.' She was a thin woman with a very large bump. She felt she had ground to make up.

'We gave a dinner party,' she told him.

'Who for?'

'Piers's friends. Bridget – she's very sweet – and her boyfriend. And that fashion designer he hopes will display his jewellery. And Sylvie Duvallier and her husband – she was interesting, she's starting up a magazine. She's looking for writers and photographers. Your friend Freya should contact her.'

'She only does landscapes.'

'Sylvie might be happy with that.' Anne opened her handbag and took out her address book. She scribbled on a page, tore it out and handed it to Aidan. 'Have her phone

that number. Tell her to say that Anne Winterton recom-
mended her. She was a charming woman. I talked to her a
lot at the dinner.'

'How did it go?'

'Oh Aidan, it was awful!' Anne made a face. 'I tried to
make a pie. I bought a copy of *Good Housekeeping* and I really
tried. It took me an entire day and it was inedible!'

Aidan, amused, said, 'What did you do?'

'Phoned Piers. *Wept* down the phone to him. Pathetic, isn't
it? He sent Tricia out to Fortnum's to buy a lobster and
mayonnaise and a coffee and walnut cake. The guests were
perfectly happy. But . . .'

'But what?'

'All Winterton women can cook! Louise can – even Charley!
I should be able to cook, shouldn't I?'

He shrugged. 'You have other talents. It doesn't matter.'

Anne rather thought it did. 'The trouble with you
Wintertons,' she said in a voice that was more than a little
tart, 'is that you do everything so darned well. Your mother
and Piers's mother are wonderful gardeners. They support
charitable causes. They run those enormous, draughty old
houses and don't turn a hair if half a dozen guests come to
stay. *And* they cook delicious meals.' She shook her head. 'I'm
not a proper Winterton wife.'

'You're missing the gallery, aren't you?'

She sighed. 'Enormously. But I was too tired, Aidan. And
no use to poor Katherine, waddling around like an elephant.'

She had given up work a month ago. It had been a relief
because she had been so tired, but it meant she had to spend
more time in the apartment, where she found herself too
uncomfortable to seek out occupations to counteract her
boredom.

272

After she had finished her cake, she said goodbye to Aidan. As he saw her out, she said, 'Tell your friend Freya I'll have a word with Katherine, too, if she'd like, about her photos. We do little shows now and then for up-and-coming artists.'

As she walked home, the sun bathed the streets with a rosy glow. Sometimes, in the evenings, when Piers came home late, Anne went out to see Ceridwen, the Welsh girl she had met at the launderette, at the shabby, ramshackle house in Notting Hill she shared with her friend Maria, who was a nurse. Maria had a little girl called Nancy and had left her husband because he had hit them both. Anne often brought a bottle of wine and the three of them talked for hours.

While she understood that it was easier for Piers to blame Aidan for what had happened than to accept the fact that his father had chosen to hurt him, this was not something Piers was yet able to hear. It was sixteen months since Henry Winterton had died, a long time to bear a grudge. Piers nursed his resentment and was practised at finding ways of keeping the smouldering embers stoked up. Anne had suggested he visit a therapist; he had refused. He preferred to nurture his anger.

There had been a time when she had thought she might act as an intermediary between the two cousins, but that was long past. Only the Wintertons could resolve their quarrels, and perhaps it had been arrogant of her to think she might be able to help. *Don't you see that he's only married you to spite Aidan?* In darker moments, Charley's words haunted her. Unwittingly, she had become caught up in a battleground.

The following afternoon, Louise came to the apartment and they put up the new curtains. After Louise left, Anne tidied up the lunch things and then, wearily, went to lie down on her bed. She rested her palms on her distended abdomen. The baby was moving less now, as if it was short of room. People asked her whether she wanted a boy or a girl, but she truly didn't mind. Earlier on in her pregnancy, she had worried that her months of sickness might have affected the baby, that it would be small and feeble or ailing. Today, running her hands over her bump and feeling a foot, a shoulder, she felt confident that all would be well. What food she had been able to keep down the baby had taken from her, so while she might have got thinner, it had grown. She and Piers hadn't decided on a name yet. She drifted off to sleep thinking about names that became less and less probable. Archie . . . Meg . . . Salome . . . Elvis . . .

She awoke feeling confused, hot and creaky. She looked at her watch. It was a quarter past eight. 'Piers?' she called out, but there was no answer. Needing to go to the bathroom, she heaved herself into an upright position. There was a trickle of fluid from between her legs, then a flood. At first she was afraid she hadn't made the bathroom in time, but then she realised that her waters had broken.

She changed her clothes and phoned the shop. No answer. She hoped desperately that Piers was on his way home and longed to hear his key in the door. A low, sickening ache in her belly, like really bad period pains, came and went. She phoned the hospital and described her symptoms, and they told her that she was in labour and should come in straight away. In labour. Anne closed her eyes and took several deep breaths, as instructed in Childbirth Without Fear. Then she dialled the shop again.

The phone rang out unanswered. She tried to remember the restaurants Piers liked to take his business associates to and phoned them one after the other, but couldn't trace him. She fetched her overnight bag and wrote a note to Piers, which she pinned to the kitchen door where he would be bound to see it. Then she phoned Ceridwen, who said that she would leave Owen with Maria and hop into a cab immediately.

While she waited for Ceridwen, she looked out of the window, willing Piers to turn the corner of the street. But the taxi appeared and she went downstairs. The pains were getting worse; inside the cab, Anne held her friend's hand and concentrated on her breathing.

'I'll wait till Piers gets here,' Ceridwen said, when they were at the hospital. 'How will I know him?'

'Dark. Handsome. Always in a hurry.' The nurse led Anne away.

She was told to change into a gown and then left in a room with a high bed. Eventually a different nurse came and examined her and told her that she was four centimetres dilated, and then gave her a shave and an enema, even though Anne, who had studied Childbirth Without Fear very diligently, protested that it wasn't necessary.

'Is my husband here yet?' she said, when the horrible procedure was over.

'I'll go and find out.' The nurse, a short, thick-ankled woman, plodded off.

Waves of pain swept through her body. Anne breathed deeply and tried to visualise the muscles of her womb pressing her baby into the birth canal, towards the moment when she would see him for the first time. The pain was good because it was bringing her son into the world. She knew it was a boy, impatient to get on with life like Piers.

The nurse came back. 'Your husband's here, Mrs Winterton.'

'May I see him?'

A chuckle. 'No, dear.'

Then she would get through this on her own, she resolved. A doctor came into the room and examined her. Then he tried to press a mask over her face.

'No,' she said, and batted it away. 'No, I don't want that. Leave me alone.' It had occurred to her that though she might not be able to cook or housekeep like a Winterton, this was a task that she and no one else could do. And she was going to do it well.

The phone rang at five in the morning. Juliet hurried downstairs.

She knew it was Piers before she picked up the receiver. 'Hello? Piers? Is everything all right?'

Anne had had the baby, a little boy. 'Both well,' he said. 'He weighs eight pounds and five ounces. He's the biggest baby on the ward. We're calling him Edward, Eddie for short.' He sounded dazed, talking too fast, phrases tripping over each other.

'I'll come,' she said, relieved and full of joy. 'Today.'

She made a cup of tea and took it back to bed. Though it was almost the end of May, in the early morning the house was still chilly. She wrapped herself up in the eiderdown and thought about her grandson. She wondered whether she would love him straight away or whether it would take time. She thought of Anne and felt pity for her, remembering the tearing and bleeding and rawness of childbirth.

They had closed the Maldon line, so she drove to Witham station and from there took a train to London. Piers was going in the hospital entrance as she arrived, so she walked up to the ward with him.

Anne's face was as white as the pillows she was propped up on. Juliet kissed her and gave her a shawl she had knitted for the baby and the parcel she had made up for Anne herself, things that she suspected Piers might not think of – nice soap, a new flannel, Yardley's hand cream.

'Would you like to hold your grandson, Mum?' said Piers.

She had been holding her breath, she discovered, waiting for this moment for the last nine months. She sat on the chair and Piers put the baby in her arms. She felt his weight, his warmth. How neatly he fitted into the crook of her arm! She studied his round pink mouth and the lines on his forehead, which seemed to have been sketched there as if in preparation for when, a long time in the future, he would grow old. His eggshell skull had been elongated by his journey into the world, giving him an elfin appearance, and his wrinkled hands looked disproportionally large on stick-thin arms and made slow movements, like seaweed wafting in deep water.

'Hello, my darling,' she whispered, as love rushed into her heart. 'Hello, Edward. Welcome to the family.'

When the visiting hour was ended, she went with Piers back to his flat. Though she suggested he have a nap – he had been up all night at the hospital – he told her he wasn't tired. From the kitchen she heard him phone friends and tell them about the baby.

She made tea and took it into the sitting room. 'Have you phoned Helen?'

'You can tell her, Mum.'

Though she felt exasperated, she couldn't bring herself to remonstrate with him. He had the glazed, jittery look of someone whose world had changed overnight.

After they had drunk their tea, he said, 'I might just close my eyes for a few minutes,' and stretched out on the sofa. He was asleep in moments.

Piers and Anne were almost out of milk, so after checking the kitchen cupboards and making a list, Juliet left the flat. On her way back from the shop, she went inside a phone box. She dialled Helen's number and gave her the news about the baby.

Then she asked Helen for Aidan's phone number, scribbling it down on her shopping list. Babies were miracles, babies offered a new start. Edward was the first of a new generation of Wintertons. She hoped this wonderful event would bring the warring cousins together.

Aidan answered the phone. 'It's Juliet,' she told him. 'I thought you'd like to know that Anne had her baby last night, a little boy.'

'Is she all right?'

'She's very well. Tired, but very happy.' After she had told Aidan the baby's name and weight, she added, 'She'll be in hospital for a week. Do you know Piers's address?'

He did, Aidan said. Then he thanked her for calling and rang off.

Aidan went to Hamleys, where he bought a pale blue teddy bear. Then to Harrods, where a shop assistant helped him pick out a tiny white outfit.

His long falling-out with Piers sickened him. It seemed foolish and disproportionate. There had been a time when Piers had been his constant companion. He thought of their games in the garden at Marsh Court when they were children, the dens and rafts they had constructed, the cycle rides and boat trips. When they had been older, fifteen or so, they had capsized Piers's dinghy, and he still remembered the shock of the cold water and his panic, unable to see Piers, then his relief when his cousin had emerged from the estuary, coughing and spluttering, shaking his wet head, laughing. He and Piers had shared their first cigarette, which Aidan had stolen from his father's case. They had drunk their first pints together in a dive of a pub in the back streets of Maldon that hadn't cared whether they were of age.

All that, thrown away because of some futile quarrel about money and a girl. He should have found a way to mend the rift long ago.

A week after the baby was born, he walked to Piers and Anne's flat and rang the doorbell. Footsteps on the stairs and then the door opened.

Piers stared at him. 'What the hell are you doing here?'

'I've come to give you this.' He offered his gift. 'They're for the baby.'

'No thanks. We don't want them.'

He kept his temper under control and tried again. 'I know things haven't been good between us lately, but can't we at least be civil to each other?'

'Anne and I don't want you here. You're not welcome.'

'I'm family,' he said softly. 'You and I are family, Piers. For God's sake, man, how long are you going to bear a grudge?'

Piers whitened. 'For as long as it takes. Now push off.'

The door closed. Aidan, strung out with rage and hurt and humiliation, walked away. There was a pram parked at the foot of some steps a dozen houses up the road. He dropped his parcel inside it and headed on.

Chapter Twelve

W hen Juliet had been a child, her father had told her the legend of the golem, a creature in human form but made of clay, moulded out of the riverbank. The boy she discovered on the mudflats made her think of her father's story. Grey and viscous, he slid in the wastes of Marsh Creek.

'Can I help you?' she called out. 'Are you all right?'

Another slither, then the figure in the marshes lost his balance, falling on his back in the mud. He crawled into a sitting position, groaning and clutching his ankle. Ten yards away, a dinghy lay at an angle in the narrow channel of water. A gust of wind toppled the boat further on to the mudflat, staining its white sail a dirty grey.

Another groan. 'They're going to bloody kill me.'

She threaded through the grassy islets towards him. 'Who's going to kill you?'

'Roy and Paddy. And Mr Brandon.'

So this was one of Joe Brandon's Borstal boys. Younger than Piers, just a lad. She said, 'The boat isn't yours, then?'

A shake of the head.

'Does Mr Brandon know you've taken it out?'

Another shake. 'I told you, he'll bloody kill me.'

'Before he does,' she said practically, 'you'll need to get off the mud.'

'Can't. Hurt me foot.'

Her gumboots sank into the ground as she edged down the bank towards him. 'Give me your hand.' She helped him on to the vegetation.

'The boat.' He looked back at it.

'Mr Brandon will sort it out. Come on, you're shivering, let's get you back to my house.'

She gave him her arm and he hobbled slowly back to Marsh Court with her. His name was Gary, he told her, and he was seventeen years old and came from Battersea. Hated the countryside. Mud everywhere, and all those bloody animals giving him funny looks.

When they reached Marsh Court, she ran him a hot bath. She told him to leave his muddy clothes on the floor while she found him something else to put on. After she had given him a towel and some old clothes that belonged to Piers, she went downstairs and dialled Greensea's number.

Joe Brandon answered the phone.

'It's Juliet Winterton,' she said. 'Have you by any chance mislaid a boy called Gary?'

'You've found him?'

'Yes, he's here at my house.'

'Thank goodness.' She heard the relief in his voice. 'I'll come and collect him. He didn't happen to have a boat with him, did he?'

'It's in our creek. I'm afraid it's capsized.'

Joe turned up in the jeep ten minutes later. 'How long had he been missing?' she asked him as she showed him into the house.

'Since this morning.' His brow creased. 'I was about to alert the coastguard. You worry when they do something stupid like this because they don't understand the estuary. We try to get over to them how dangerous the tides are and how easily you can be swept out to sea, but you know what boys are like, they don't always listen.'

Yes, she knew what boys were like. The reconciliation she had tried to engineer between Piers and Aidan had gone disastrously wrong. She had made things worse; she regretted interfering, and her heart seemed to hurt when she thought of it.

'Gary seems a nice lad,' she said.

'He's a troublesome little blighter, but I can't help having a soft spot for him. Don't tell him that, though.'

Before today, she had mostly seen Joe battling the elements, in the wind or driving rain. Now, tidied up, wearing dark trousers and a white shirt, open at the neck beneath his jacket, he looked unexpectedly and disconcertingly hand-some. She remembered the daffodils, that great extravagant bunch he had left in her porch, and wondered, not for the first time, why he had sent them. He seemed a serious, reserved man, not the sort to make a flamboyant gesture.

Gary limped barefoot down the stairs, breaking a silence that had begun to feel awkward.

Joe said, quite kindly, 'You're an idiot. You might have drowned.'

Gary looked surly. 'The stupid bloody thing—'

'Gary.'

'Sorry,' he mumbled to Juliet. 'It wouldn't do what I was trying to get it to do. I think there's something wrong with it.'

'Let me have a look at your foot.' The boy sat down on a stair and stuck out his leg.

'I'll make some cocoa,' said Juliet.

'Thank you, but no, I'll take him home.' Joe gave Juliet a grim smile. 'I don't think his ankle is broken, just badly bruised, but we should get it bound up. And we've caused you enough trouble. Roy and I will come back for the boat later, if that's okay with you. Thank you for all you've done. I appreciate it. We both do.'

He and Roy put on oilskins and waders and drove out to rescue the dinghy. Standing in the creek, hauling the hull upright, Joe thought of Juliet Winterton. He seemed to spend a lot of time thinking about her these days. Her hair had been tangled by the wind and there had been a smear of mud on one cheekbone, but she had looked utterly beautiful. She probably thought he was a damned nuisance, letting his tearaways trespass on her land.

Roy rowed the dinghy back to Mundon Creek while Joe stowed the muddy sail in the jeep and drove back to Greensea. At the house, he changed out of his oilskins and waders and then Christine served supper. Christine was no chatterer, but this was an unusually quiet meal even for them. The house seemed to swallow up their words. He wondered whether Juliet Winterton felt the same, alone in that great empty place. He had not been inside Marsh Court before today. The house had seemed dark and forbidding, with the air of a fortress, built either to keep out the world or to secure the power and wealth of the Wintertons. Though they were near neighbours, he had never had much to do with the Winterton family, and their paths had rarely crossed. He knew them more by repute than acquaintance: affluent, staunch Tories, friendly with only a few families in the locality. He had not until now felt any desire to know them better.

He was drawn to Juliet Winterton in a way he had not been drawn to a woman for a long, long time. The qualities for which he mildly disliked the Wintertons – exclusiveness, snobbery and a sense of their own superiority – he did not see in her. Goodness and honesty shone out of her – kindness, too. She had made no complaint about Gary treading mud through her house and had treated the boy with sympathy and gentleness.

After supper, he checked on the livestock, then let the dogs run around the orchard for a while. It was a fine evening and the air was sweet with the scent of roses. He had never thought cowardice one of his failings, but he did so now. Why was it so hard to formulate the words, to ask a simple question? Molly would not have wanted him to live the rest of his life alone, he knew that. What, then, made him falter? He knew it was fear that held him back. Fear that, having found something he longed for, she would turn him down. Fear of another loss. He was afraid of falling in love again, of getting in too deep, of exposing himself to the risks and pain that love made inevitable.

But he was already in too deep. He had stepped out along the causeway and the waters were flooding across it, cutting off his retreat. He began to cut the pink and white roses that had the finest fragrance. Then he called in the dogs. Do it, he said to himself. Don't think about it, do it.

Juliet cleaned out the bath, swept the mud out of the hall and then ate her supper. Afterwards, though she tried to work on her lesson plan, she found it hard to concentrate. Something was distracting her. There was a fizzing sensation in her stomach, reminding her of how one felt before setting off on a long journey.

The sound of a vehicle coming down the drive made her glance out of the window. Recognising Joe's jeep, she opened the front door.

Twilight sketched dark shadows round his eyes and mouth. 'Forgive me for calling so late,' he said. 'These are for you, to say thank you.'

He handed her a bunch of roses, tied up, like the daffodils, with twine and brown paper. 'Joe, they're beautiful,' she said. She buried her nose in the petals. 'Such gorgeous scent. How's Gary?'

'A bit of a limp, but fine.'

'Did you manage to free the boat?'

'Yes, Roy's taken it back to Greensea.' He cleared his throat. 'I wondered whether you'd like to come to tea on Sunday. My brother and his family are coming to visit. I'd like you to meet them, if you're free, that is.'

'Yes,' she said. 'I'd love to.'

After he drove away, she went back inside the house and arranged the roses in a white china bowl. It came to her, adjusting the blooms, that she was attracted to Joe Brandon. It seemed so long since she had felt as much as a flicker of desire for a man that it had taken her a while to recognise it. What did he think of her? She could not tell. The daffodils, she thought, the roses. She recalled Jonny saying, years ago, that Joe Brandon was not their sort. Might she be Joe Brandon's sort? Might she?

Sunday afternoon. Juliet drove to Greensea. Peeling off from the main road and taking the narrow country lanes, she experienced the same emotion she had felt travelling here before, of immersing herself in a landscape that was ancient and cut off from the passing of time. Sunlight splashed the dark waters of the mere and turned the leaves of the poplars white.

She parked on the forecourt and rang the doorbell. A woman of around her own age opened it. Brown-haired, smiling, jolly-looking.

'You must be Mrs Winterton,' she said. 'I'm Hazel Brandon, Joe's sister-in-law.'

They shook hands. Then Hazel Brandon swept her through the house to where wide-flung French doors gave on to Greensea's back garden.

'Joe!' Hazel called out.

He was sitting in the group of deckchairs set out on the lawn, talking to a thickset, red-faced man. A short distance away, some girls were throwing a ball for the dogs. But it was on Joe that her gaze alighted and settled.

'Juliet, welcome to Greensea.' He rose and crossed the lawn to her. 'Come and meet everyone.'

Joe's brother Fred was a bigger, burlier, noisier version of him. The same dark brown eyes were set in a broad, scarlet, weather-beaten face, so different to Joe's lean, tanned one.

'Joe's been telling me about you,' Fred said. 'Rescued one of his ruffians, didn't you? Slip of a girl like you.' He raised his voice. 'Girls! Come and say hello!'

Four large, brown-haired, pink-cheeked girls in their mid to late teens bounded across the grass to them. 'Susie, Debbie, Heather and Glenys,' said Fred, introducing them.

The adults sat down in the deckchairs and the girls went back to playing with the dogs. Joe's Aunt Christine put a tray on the table and poured out the tea. Juliet's gaze moved back to Joe, only for her to discover that his eyes were focused on her. She looked away quickly, as if stung by one of the bees that buzzed in the lavender.

The lawn led down to a large area of rougher grass, dotted with apple and plum trees. Everything looked as if it had been there for ever: a mulberry tree tucked against a wall blotched grey and gold with lichen, the perennials in the flower beds with their bursting buds. Even the rusty wrought-iron table beneath the trees seemed to grow out of the long grass.

Tea was served, scones distributed. Fred asked Juliet where she lived.

'At Marsh Court,' she said, 'north-east of Mundon.'

'You can see it from the sea wall,' said Joe.

'Three gables?' said Fred. 'Red roof?' He turned to his wife. 'Didn't we once build a boat for a fellow who knew the Wintertons, Hazel?'

'Nice little yacht,' said Hazel, handing Juliet a cup.

'Years ago, not long after the war.'

'Political chap . . . tall, fair-haired . . .'

'Never forget a boat. What did he call her? *Sea Dancer*, that was it. *Sea Dancer*.'

A shadow fell over the bright June afternoon. 'Gillis Sinclair,' she said. 'You're talking about Gillis Sinclair.'

One of the girls threw a stick into the orchard, and then they and the dogs vanished beneath the trees. Juliet's thoughts drifted back nearly twenty years, to the summer of 1946. Gillis had come to Marsh Court frequently that year. He had told her that he was in the area to buy a yacht, but in fact he had been visiting Frances Hart on Thorney Island. He still sailed *Sea Dancer* in the North Sea and the east coast estuaries, but Frances Hart and her children were long dead, drowned in the Blackwater. Once more she stole a look at Joe. Did he remember that he had once told her he had seen Gillis with Frances Hart? He gave no indication that he did.

287

She tried to steer the conversation away from the past. 'Where do you live, Fred?'

'West Mersea. Do you know it?'

'I've visited the island often. We used to take the children there when they were little.'

'Best place in the world. I wouldn't live anywhere else. You can keep your Capris and Monte Carlos, Mersea's the place for me. I started boatbuilding after the war. Your friend Sinclair was one of our first customers. It's a decent little business now. I was going to pass it on to my sons, and look what I got.' A howl of laughter. 'Four daughters!'

'Susie would be perfectly capable of running the business,' said Joe.

'*Susie*,' said Hazel scornfully. 'She's seeing that lad at the tennis club. Thin fellow with spots. It'll be wedding bells before the year's out, Joe.'

The conversation moved on to crop yields and sailing. After they had eaten, Christine carried the tea things back into the house and Fred and Hazel and the girls took their leave.

While Joe saw his visitors out, Juliet went to examine the roses planted against the wall. A bee, its round brown body dusted gold with pollen, buried itself in the heart of a bloom. She felt restless and confused. What was she doing, taking a fancy to a man she had met only a handful of times? She knew hardly anything about Joe Brandon.

Joe came back into the garden. 'I mustn't keep you, Joe,' she said. 'I should go.'

'Must you? I was hoping to show you round the place.'

A flicker of pleasure. 'All right, then. Thank you, that would be lovely.' Perhaps he liked her. It was so hard to tell.

Garden lay to all sides of the house, which stood on a

slight rise. It had been built two hundred years ago, he told her, to replace an earlier, smaller farmhouse. Brandons had always lived at Greensea; there were Brandon graves in Mundon churchyard going back to Stuart times. Which, Juliet thought, made the Wintertons parvenus in comparison.

Runner beans flared their scarlet flowers, and marigolds were planted between the rows of vegetables in the kitchen garden. Their conversation, of seed types and yields, gave her something solid to cling on to. She felt as if the ground was slipping away from beneath her feet, altering a landscape she had become accustomed to. She was Juliet Winterton, who had been unhappily married to Henry, and who had fallen in love, blindly and disastrously, with Gillis Sinclair. She had believed that the end of her story.

Sunlight filtered through the leaves as they walked through the orchard, dappling the rough grass. They grew four different types of plum at Greensea, Joe told her, as well as damsons and greengages. Christine made preserves from the soft fruit. A part of Juliet's mind still functioned, enabling her to talk of jams and jellies, but the rest of it darted like a butterfly, exploring this new world. Her awareness of Joe Brandon, as he walked beside her, was heightened; her gaze was compelled to him and she seemed almost to feel the heat of his body. The swell of muscle beneath his white cotton shirt, the slight sheen of perspiration on his upper lip as they came out of the orchard into the stifling warmth of the open fields: all these she noticed, and they unsettled her. And in the dark depths of his eyes – what did she see there as he turned to speak to her? It was like gazing into a black mirror; she felt herself drawn inside.

She shaded her eyes from the sun. Dust motes floated lazily in the hot air. Pencil-strokes of masts protruded out of the fields, delineating where the creeks of the estuary snaked into the land. The silvery glitter of the water seemed to bob and float above the green grass like a mirage.

Greensea land extended to the salt marsh, Joe told her. 'It's a maze in the creeks,' he said. 'I got lost out there once when I was a kid. I'd taken the dinghy and stayed out too long. Darkness fell and I ended up wandering round in circles. My father belted me when I got home. It taught me to learn my way round there even in the dark.'

'Were you born here?'

'In the farmhouse, yes.'

'I can't imagine what that's like, to have always lived in one place.'

'I missed it, in the war, when I was in North Africa.' He looked out to the marshes. 'I used to think of it when I was in the desert. I'd try to imagine the creeks and the salt marsh. They seemed a lifetime away. Almost as if they belonged to another world.'

As they walked back through the orchard, they fell silent, their strides in step. When he opened the door of her car and she climbed inside, she noticed that his hand lingered on the handle, as if he was reluctant to let her go.

Anne's body, which had once been neat and obliging, seemed now to have a mind of its own. Her stomach sagged and her breasts wept milk at the most embarrassing times: when she was wheeling the baby to the clinic to be weighed, or when she nipped out to the shop for bread. No, that was wrong, she couldn't nip anywhere any more. Any excursion, however minor, required her to check Eddie's nappy, to put on him a jacket and bonnet if it was at all chilly, to haul the heavy pram down a flight of stairs (the downstairs tenant,

290

a Mr Lord, made a fuss when she left the pram in the hallway),
while Eddie screamed upstairs in his cot as if she had abandoned him for ever. Then bump the pram down the flight
of stone steps outside – why on earth had they thought it
a good idea to buy an apartment with steps up to the front
door? – and rush back up the stairs to fetch the baby, who,
like as not, would have got himself into a state and sicked
up over his clothes so she had to feed him to calm him
down and then change him all over again.

She worried that someone, some madwoman who had lost
a baby, would get in the house and steal him while she was
sorting out the pram, and she worried that someone would
steal the expensive Silver Cross, a gift from her father,
while she was dealing with the baby. She had become very
good at worrying since Eddie had been born. She was an
artist at it. She wondered whether that was because she wasn't
getting enough sleep – hardly any at all, really; a good night
was one where the baby managed a stretch of three hours
at a time – or whether it was something to do with becoming
a mother. Whether that was the deal, the deal that no one
told you about before you had a baby, because it was too
outrageous and you wouldn't have believed it anyway, that
pregnancy and childbirth weren't the half of it, that nothing
ever went back to what she had once thought of as normal,
neither her body nor her daily routine, and yet she was
expected to go on doing things, housework and laundry and
shopping and cooking, even though some days her son slept
for no more than half an hour at a time, and when he was
awake, it was impossible to get anything done.

When Eddie was eight weeks old, Piers decided they should
give a dinner party. Just family and close friends, he said,
ease themselves in. Anne went along with it because she

knew Piers felt as she did, that their old life, which they had both enjoyed, seemed to have slipped away without either of them intending it. While she was feeding Eddie, she leafed through cookery books. She would make a cheese soufflé for a starter, she decided. The cookery books claimed that soufflés were not as difficult as their reputation implied. Baked ham and a Waldorf salad for the main course; she could buy a boiled ham from the butcher's, so that would mean no cooking, and anyone could make a salad, couldn't they? And then an orange salad and macaroons, which Piers would fetch from Fortnum's on his way home, for dessert.

They invited three couples: Piers's cousin Gabe and her boyfriend Adam; Claudia, who was Gillis Sinclair's younger daughter, and her husband Toby; and Jamie Mortimer, who had been their best man at the wedding, and his girlfriend, Gloria. On the evening of the dinner party, Piers came home late and Anne discovered that he had forgotten to buy the macaroons. There was a packet of Nice biscuits in the cupboard: they would have to do instead.

The sitting room looked messy; she had meant to tidy it but hadn't got round to it. She asked Piers to sort it out while she was feeding Eddie, but when she went into the room, he was stretched out on the sofa, fast asleep. She felt a rush of fury – that he should sleep when he didn't have to get up to feed a baby at night! – but knew she was being unreasonable. He worked such long hours. The baby was her occupation; making a success of the business was his.

She put Eddie down and quickly changed into a black linen shift dress and pinned on the brooch that Piers had given her. She put an apron over the dress and grated the cheese for the soufflé, hurrying because she was afraid that Eddie would start crying again. She was halfway through making the white sauce when she heard his wail. The cookery book stipulated that it was fatal to leave the sauce at this stage, so she ran to the nursery and picked the baby up and put him in his little chair on the kitchen table, and sang to him while she stirred.

Piers loped into the room. 'God. *Shattered.*'

'Can you keep an eye on him?'

'I need to get changed.'

'Piers, I have to make the soufflé. Did you tidy the sitting room?'

'Not yet.' He picked up Eddie, who stopped crying. Eddie cried a lot less with Piers. Anne wondered whether this was because he looked at her and thought milk, or whether it was because Piers was better at winding him, or whether Piers was just better with babies, full stop, and it would be preferable if he was at home doing the feeding and changing while she went back to the gallery.

The front doorbell rang. 'Christ,' said Piers. 'What time is it?'

'Seven. We said seven for half past.'

'No one comes at seven when it's seven for half past.' Grumbling, he went downstairs and let in Jamie and Gloria. Gloria was short, dark, plump and curly-headed and was wearing a tight sparkly crimson frock. Anne said hello and then went back to the soufflé.

Piers stuck his head round the door. 'She only drinks Babycham,' he hissed.

'I thought you bought a bottle of champagne?'

'She doesn't drink champagne, only Babycham. I'm going to have to go to the off-licence. Can you hold the fort?'

Anne put the soufflé in the oven and went into the sitting room. Piers had settled Eddie in his cot. Anne talked to Jamie and Gloria, and then Gabe and Adam arrived. Piers returned with the Babycham for Gloria. Anne dashed off to the kitchen. The soufflé looked all right, risen and light brown on top. She remembered that she hadn't yet laid the table and began to count out cutlery. The table was small for eight people. If Claudia and Toby turned up – it was already twenty-five to eight.

A long peal of the doorbell: Claudia and Toby had arrived. There was a howl from the nursery.

Gabe cocked her head. 'Is that Eddie?'

'Oh dear.' Anne stood poised, a bundle of serving spoons in her hand.

'I'll get him,' said Gabe.

'No, I'll top him up and then he'll last through dinner. If you'd all excuse me.'

Eddie was a hot, red ball of anger. She murmured to him, cradling him, calming him. He choked taking the nipple, so she patted his back, soothing him. Wild with hunger, he rooted and began to suck.

There was a tap on the nursery door and Claudia came in. 'Anne, darling, I'm so sorry to bother you but I'm afraid the soufflé has burned.'

'Badly?'

'Yes, I'm afraid so. I could put on some eggs, if you like, for eggs mayonnaise? There are a dozen in the fridge.'

'Please.' She squeezed the word out. She wanted to cry. She had completely forgotten about the soufflé, which only fifteen minutes ago had looked so perfect. She suppressed the tears, winded Eddie, then changed him and put him back in his cot. He chewed his hand, making sucking noises.

Claudia and Gabe were in the kitchen. Gabe was washing lettuce, and a pan of eggs simmered on the hob. When Anne saw the soufflé, black and cratered and stranded in the sink, she wanted to cry again.

'The first dinner party I ever gave for Toby's parents, the cat got at the salmon.' Claudia roared with laughter. 'I had to fit the pieces of it together like a jigsaw puzzle. I felt dreadful, giving my in-laws food that had been nibbled by a cat.'

Anne emptied the eggs into a colander and ran them under the cold tap, then they all shelled them, cut them in half and arranged them on nests of lettuce.

'Thank you both,' said Anne. 'You go and sit down.'

'We'll help you dish up,' said Claudia.

'No, please sit down.'

Anne took a moment by herself, spooning mayonnaise over the eggs, trying not to mind everything too much. Then she took the dishes into the dining room.

Piers said, 'I thought it was soufflé.'

'I burned it.'

'I don't know about this wine, with eggs.'

'Oh don't be such a fusspot, Piers,' said Claudia cheerfully. 'Just pour it out.'

'Gorgeous brooch,' said Gloria, looking at Anne.

'It's one of Piers's.'

'You should come to the shop,' said Piers.

There was a cry from the nursery. 'Not again,' said Anne, dismayed. She rose from the table.

Eddie was hungry again. *I've fed you four times in two hours,* she wanted to say to him, but it wouldn't have done any good. She sat down in the low chair and unzipped her dress. He fed a little, then looked round, wide-eyed.

Claudia came into the nursery. 'Tummy ache?'

'Maybe.'

'Do you know, he just looks wide awake.'

'He can't be awake! He's been awake all day!'

'Natasha was always tricky in the evenings. May I?' Claudia took the baby from Anne. 'Gives me a chance to have a cuddle. Gorgeous, gorgeous little boy. Mean old Toby says we can't have any more.'

They went back into the dining room, Claudia cradling the baby against her shoulder.

'Isn't he supposed to be asleep?' said Piers.

'He's supposed to be,' said Anne, in a taut voice. 'But he isn't.'

She cleared away the plates to the kitchen. A headache stabbed at her skull. She poured a large glass of water, then drank it. She put the gammon on a serving plate and found the carving knife. Gabe wandered in and ate the leftovers of egg. Gabe ate a huge amount but was tall and very thin.

Anne looked at the salad, which she had made earlier. 'I forgot the walnuts.' She peered into a cupboard. 'I don't think I bought any.'

'I wouldn't worry,' said Gabe. 'No one even likes walnuts. Like eating chunks of wood.'

They took the food into the dining room. Piers was talking about the business. 'The shop was bursting at the seams this morning. Masses of customers. You must all come and have a look.'

'I suppose you're working all hours,' said Toby.

'Pretty much.'

'I hardly saw the kids when I started up the firm.'

'You hardly see them now, darling,' said Claudia. 'I thought that was how you liked it.' She shuffled the baby into a more comfortable position. Eddie's irises were dark slits beneath drooping lids.

'Are you hoping to go back to the gallery, Anne?' asked Gabe.

'I don't know. I'd like to, but I don't know.'

'You wouldn't want to leave Eddie, would you?' said Piers.

'No, of course not.' Anne thought longingly of the gallery, the cool, quiet interior, the soothing business of choosing and selling pictures. It seemed not only to belong to a different life, but as if that life had belonged to some other person.

'You should find an au pair,' said Claudia. 'I'd go mad without Karen. It gives me the chance to get my hair done and go shopping without the pushchair.'

'That's why I have to work all hours,' said Toby, smirking. 'To pay for the au pair, the hairdos and the shopping.'

'Shut up, Toby. I'll put this little one back in his cot now, shall I, Anne?' Claudia kissed the baby's head. 'He's had great fun sharing our dinner party with us, but he needs his sleep.'

Anne served the dessert. Then she made coffee. It was her only culinary skill, she thought: rich, good coffee instead of thin, tasteless British stuff. Piers put on a record and they drank a bottle of brandy, and then, at half past eleven, their guests began to leave.

Anne cleared away the coffee things and brandy glasses. Piers came into the kitchen. She said, 'I don't think I'll ever be any good at this.'

'What?' He was rifling through the cupboards, looking for something more to drink.

'Cooking. Entertaining.'

'It was great. Everyone had a great time.'

'Piers. The meal was *awful*. Burned soufflé and Waldorf salad without any walnuts. I bought the ham from the butcher's and the biscuits were from a packet. All I did was slice up a few oranges.'

He pressed his lips against the curve of her neck. 'What does it matter?'

She jerked away from him. 'It matters to *me*. There you all are, you Wintertons, so beautiful and clever, with everything you share. Your memories, your childhoods. Even your darned bonfires. And there's me, always on the outside.'

He looked at her, frowning. 'Anne, that's nonsense. Everyone's tried to make you feel part of the family. You're thinking like this because you're tired because of the baby.'

'Oh yes, the baby,' she said bitterly. 'Why doesn't anyone tell you the truth about babies? Because no one would have them any more, I suppose. The human race would grind to a halt.' She plunged her hands into the washing-up water. 'Perhaps we should get an au pair, like Claudia said.'

'Jesus, there's nothing to drink in this house.' Piers ran himself a glass of water.

'Or a cleaning lady. I've been thinking about it, Piers. Just for a few hours a week, to help out while Eddie's still waking up at night.'

He drank the water, then he said, 'We can't afford a cleaning lady. Or an au pair.'

She was hacking burned cheese from the soufflé dish with a knife. 'What do you mean?'

'I mean we can't afford it. We couldn't really afford the champagne. Or the blasted Babycham, for that matter.'

'Piers?'

'I've had to take out some loans.'

'How much?'

'I'm not sure exactly.' He avoided her eye.

'You should have told me.' How could he not have? She felt frightened.

'I'll sort it out. We need to be careful for a while, that's all. Till things get better. Then you can have all the cleaning ladies you want.'

'I thought,' she said, careful not to sound cross or anxious, 'with what you inherited from your father, and the sale of the flat . . .'

'The business eats it up,' he said, picking at the remains of the ham. 'I didn't want to worry you.'

'Piers.' She put down the knife and wrapped her arms round him. She could tell he was worried, though he would never admit to it. 'You should have told me,' she said. 'We need to share things. Bad things as well as good things.'

'It'll turn round soon.' He stroked her back. 'It's always the same, starting up a new business, everyone says so. The first year's always tricky.'

They kissed. They hadn't made love since Eddie had been born; now, for the first time since the birth, she felt a stirring of desire.

Then a cry cut through the quiet. Anne went to the nursery. She took Eddie out of the cot and fed him, thinking about what Piers had just told her. It wasn't the fact that they were short of money that troubled her so much as the fact that he hadn't told her they were indebted. And *how* indebted? And why, if they were short of cash, had they spent all that money on an apartment she didn't even like?

It was half past midnight and she had been awake since five that morning. She kept falling asleep feeding Eddie, drifting off for a few seconds at a time. She dug her fingernails into the ball of her thumb to keep herself awake.

When he was fed and changed, Eddie's dark eyes focused on her and his mouth parted in a smile.

'Hello, trouble,' she whispered lovingly.

She sat with him in her arms, singing very softly. She had learned how, with the baby, to take on a stillness that seemed to send him to sleep. No eye contact, just a quiet presence and a soft, murmuring song. That was another thing they didn't tell you beforehand, she thought as she settled him in his cot: just how deeply you ended up falling in love.

Checking on how the wheat was doing in the big field, Joe remembered Juliet walking beside him through Greensea's orchard. In the evening, writing up his accounts, she intruded, distracting him with a smile and a gesture. After a week of errors and inattention and Christine asking him whether he was feeling unwell, he knew that he needed to do something about it. But what? He had forgotten how to court a woman. It wasn't that he was afraid of making a fool of himself, more that there was something bruised about her, a vulnerability that both touched and warned him. He would never hurt her intentionally, but he could see that he might do so accidentally.

He decided to ask her out to dinner. Obstacles – complications – strewed themselves across his path. If they went to a restaurant in Maldon, then it would be all round the district in a day, Joe Brandon and Henry Winterton's widow dining together. For himself, he wouldn't have cared, but he had no wish to make her the focus of gossip. But then where to go? He rarely dined out. Bread and cheese in a pub when he was visiting an agricultural fair, or a light supper in some modest establishment if he had business in London and was staying overnight. Fred would be full of kindly, curious questions if he asked him for advice. Christine thought a cup of coffee in a café in Maldon was a waste of money.

And then there was the problem of transport. He couldn't drive Juliet Winterton to a restaurant in the jeep. Left behind by the American army in 1944, it was now more than twenty years old, its paintwork battered and scarred. They knew each other, he and the jeep, and he always nursed it back to health, but what if it broke down on the road to the restaurant? And even after it was cleaned, you could smell the farm on it.

He visited a used-car dealer near Colchester that had a good reputation and bought a two-year-old Rover. The salesman seemed pleasant enough, so Joe asked him whether he knew of any decent restaurants in the Colchester area and was given several recommendations. On the way home, he wondered how he had become so cut off from the world that he had to ask such things of strangers.

That evening, he phoned Juliet Winterton. When she accepted his invitation, a rush of excitement and pleasure fired parts of his heart that had been derelict for a long time.

He had a haircut, checked that his best suit was in good order, and shined his shoes. He looked at his shirts, bought a couple of new ones. He thought himself ridiculous, behaving like a teenager. Dressing on the evening of the dinner, he seemed to look at his reflection properly for the first time in years. He had grown old: he noted the wings of silver at his temples and the deep lines to either side of his mouth. Old and shabby and out of touch. What use would a woman like Juliet Winterton have for him?

Their conversation, on the journey to the restaurant, darted and then faded away into silence. Perhaps he should have found somewhere nearer to home: the journey exposed their ignorance of each other. He hoped their exchange might flow better in the restaurant, after a drink. She complimented him on the car; he did not tell her that he had bought it to take her out because it would have sounded irrational, over-eager.

The restaurant was a stiff, formal place on the outskirts

301

of the town. Tables with white napery and silver cutlery in a room with tall windows that looked out over a terrace and a rectangular pond. She slipped away to tidy up. He flicked a speck of dust from his cuff, glanced at the menu.

He stood up as she returned to the table. She had taken off her jacket and was wearing a dress of some sheeny fabric, of a similar dark gold shade to her hair. The waiter helped with her chair; they sat down.

'You look very beautiful,' he said.

She smiled. 'Thank you.'

'I don't know what this place is like. Have you been here before?'

'I'm afraid not. It's ages since I've been out to dinner.' She dipped her head, frowning a little. 'I'm rather rusty at all this.'

'Not as rusty as me, I suspect.'

'We can muddle along together, can't we?'

He liked her, he thought. He was attracted to her, and he liked her a lot. 'Shall we have wine?'

'I'd like that.'

It was the sort of place that described the dishes in French; when she read out the names, he noticed that her accent was perfect. They placed their order, and after much flourishing and performance, the waiter poured out the wine.

Their glasses chinked. 'To muddling along,' she said, and he echoed her toast.

They talked of the countryside, of walks they enjoyed, of books they had read. She told him about the concerts she arranged each summer to raise money for charity. He explained that he went to the Proms every year with Paddy, his friend Roy's wife, Roy being someone who disliked music and couldn't see the point of it. While they conversed, he noticed the fall of her hair on her shoulders and the flecks of green in her eyes and the elegance with which she made every movement – a turn of the hand to illustrate a point she was making, the way she tipped back her head to laugh.

Afterwards, he drove her home to Marsh Court. The windows of the house were in darkness. He disliked thinking of her on her own in that great empty house. He disliked thinking she might be lonely. He knew he was falling in love with her. A strange thing; he had for so long thought love impossible for him.

She kissed his cheek. 'I had a lovely time, Joe. Thank you so much.'

He waited until she had let herself into the house and then he drove back to Greensea. A high crescent moon spilled sparkles of light on the fields, and the new car slipped along the turns and folds of the road that led to the farmhouse.

Indoors, pouring himself a brandy, taking off his tie, his gaze moved to the photograph of Molly on the sideboard. In the days and weeks after she had died, he had taken a piece of her clothing to bed with him each night. But the scent of her had faded, and in the end he had asked Paddy to help him clear out the wardrobes. In the years that had followed, he had continued to lose pieces of her. There had been a day when he had realised he could no longer remember the sound of her footsteps, another when he discovered that he had forgotten which songs she had liked to sing as she did the washing-up.

How memory stole what was most precious to you. Falling in love with Juliet Winterton would be like putting Molly into a box all over again. He had never forgotten *that* sound, the rattle of earth falling on the coffin.

*   *   *

303

On Charley's first day at her new job, working for the Water Board in Finsbury, she knocked over a cup of tea as she was collecting letters for the post room. The tea spread over the surface of the desk in a pale brown deluge.

The young man at the next desk sprang up to help. As she frantically rescued papers and files, he mopped up the puddle with his handkerchief.

'Put them on the radiator,' he said. 'They'll soon dry off. Look, good as new.'

'Thanks.'

'S'all right. New here, are you?'

'It's my first day.' She made a face. 'Probably my last, as well.'

One of her jobs, even after the debacle with the tea, continued to be collecting the post, so she saw him every day. He always gave her a smile, offered her a Spangle.

One morning he said to her, 'I missed you yesterday.'

'I had the day off. I went to the Old Bailey.'

He raised his eyebrows.

'I needed to do some research,' she explained. 'I'm writing a play, a courtroom drama, and I wanted to see what a trial was like.'

'Who's going to put the play on?'

She liked that he assumed it would be performed, that it wasn't some little hobby to keep herself amused. She said, 'My drama group, next year, providing I finish it in time.'

The next week it was his turn to be away, for two days. When he came back, she spoke to him as she gathered up his post.

'Were you on holiday?'

'My wife was ill so I had to look after our little boy.'

A man in a navy-blue pinstripe suit drawled, 'Mr Renfrew,

if you've time to chatter, perhaps you would be so kind as to let me have those figures.'

'Yes, Mr Fielding, they're nearly ready.' He lowered his voice to Charley. 'Do you have lunch in the canteen?'

'Often, yes. One-ish.'

The Metropolitan Water Board was housed in a big red building, rather imposing. The covings and carved ceiling sat a little oddly with the battered metal desks and chairs.

At one o'clock, Charley went down to the canteen. Carrying her tray from the counter, she spotted Mr Renfrew eating sandwiches out of a greaseproof paper wrapping.

'I saved you a seat,' he said.

'Thanks, Mr Renfrew.'

'Daniel.'

'I'm Charlotte. Well, Charley, really. I hope I didn't get you into trouble this morning.'

He shook his head. 'Fielding's having a dig at me because I had to take time off last week, that's all. How's the play going?'

'Slowly.' Until she had visited the Old Bailey, Charley's experience of courtrooms had been limited to episodes of Perry Mason. The Old Bailey hadn't been like that at all. Most of the time it had been boring, but some of the time it had been sad, the people's lives had been sad.

She said, 'Is your wife better?'

'Improving, thanks. My mother-in-law's helping out. She usually takes care of Simon when Jeannette is ill, but last week she was away. I tried to get him some extra days at his kindergarten, but they couldn't help. Fielding's a sarcastic devil and seems to think it's a matter of poor organisation on my part.'

His tone was weary rather than rancorous. Charley wondered

what was wrong with his wife that she should be ill frequently, but didn't feel she knew him well enough to ask.

He said, 'Are you enjoying working here?'

'It's fine.'

He had a nice smile, she thought, that lit up his eyes, which were a birdlike, inquisitive hazel. 'I take it, then,' he said, 'that you're not intending to spend the rest of your life working for the Metropolitan Water Board?'

'Probably not.'

'We're not research, are we, for a play?'

'No, I needed a job. Though you never know.'

'A murder in the stationery cupboard . . . romance over the tea trolley.' He darted a glance at her. 'I'm not taking the mickey, Charley.'

'I know you're not.'

'I used to love English when I was at school.'

'Do you go to the theatre much?'

'Not now.'

'I'm going to get a cup of coffee. Would you like one?'

'I'm okay, thanks. I've got a thermos.'

'Kit Kat?'

'No thanks.'

She bought a Kit Kat anyway and broke off a finger to give to him.

They lunched together often over the next couple of weeks. Daniel was funny and intelligent and perceptive and she liked him a lot. He was slightly built and of average height, and his face, with its broad cheekbones and narrow chin, gave him the look of a cheerful, clever elf. She liked to make him laugh, to see his quick smile. He had fine brown hair that flopped over his forehead; his supervisor, Mr Fielding, drawled in his sarcastic way: *if you were a member of the Beatles,*

306

Mr Renfrew, but it won't do for the office. Though they enjoyed themselves making fun of some of the more tedious characters at the Water Board, Mr Fielding especially, Charley sensed that Daniel took his work seriously and did it well.

After a while it occurred to her – and she felt idiotic for not realising it before – that he was hard up. The sick wife, she supposed, and the little boy. Because he seemed to feel obliged to take turns buying Kit Kats, she told him she was on a diet and didn't want to eat them any more.

Daniel had been working for the Water Board for five years. The Renfrews lived in Islington; Daniel's son, Simon, was four years old. It took her a while to feel they were good enough friends that she could ask him about his wife's illness.

They were walking to the bus stop after work. 'She has a type of rheumatism,' he explained. 'It started after Simon was born. She was perfectly well before that. It comes and goes.'

'How awful,' said Charley. 'It must be so horrible for her.'

'Her joints get very swollen and painful. When it's bad, she can't pick Simon up or do the cooking, anything. The doctors can't seem to do much except tell her to take aspirin.' A quick raise of his eyebrows, which sat like pointed Chinese hats over his slanting eyes. 'The worst thing is that she hasn't really been able to enjoy having a child. She hates not being able to look after Simon herself.'

'Oh Daniel.' She gave him a hug to cheer him up, and then his bus came.

Spurred on by a sense of guilt and an awareness of her own good fortune, Charley decided to make for South Kensington to see Anne. On the train, she wrote some lines of dialogue for her play, but they had the consistency of

307

cardboard and she crumpled the paper up and, leaving the Underground station, dropped it in a litter bin.

Anne let her in to the house. The sound of a baby crying grew louder as they climbed the stairs. The flat was big and ugly and pretentious: trust Piers, Charley thought, to choose something as awful as this. There was dusty plaster moulding on the ceilings, and the sitting room fireplace was made of a pink stone that looked like luncheon meat. It was a cold, foggy autumn day, and Anne had put on the electric fire to warm the room.

Anne picked a red-faced Eddie out of his pram. 'Hey, honey,' she said gently.

'Is he hungry?'

'He can't be, I've just fed him. Would you like coffee?'

'I'll make it, if you like.'

'You won't know how to use the machine.'

Anne sounded resigned rather than critical, which made Charley feel useless, so she offered to hold Eddie instead.

'He's a little cranky today,' Anne said. But she put the baby in Charley's arms.

Eddie screwed up his face, preparing to cry, so Charley propped him against her shoulder and did a jiggling walk round the room. He seemed to like looking out of the window, so she stood with her back to the sill, swaying from side to side, until Anne came back with the coffee.

'Has he gone off?'

'I think so.' Eddie's head lay heavily on her shoulder; Charley brushed her cheek against his downy head.

'Thank God.' Anne sat down, closing her eyes, and pressed her fingertips against her cheeks. She hadn't any make-up on, and the dress she was wearing had dried baby sick over the shoulder. Before getting pregnant, she had always looked annoyingly well turned out, but she didn't look like that any more. Charley's chief emotions when she was with Anne were boredom and guilt. Today she felt sorry for her as well.

'I could babysit,' she offered, 'if you and Piers want to go out.' When Anne did not respond, Charley said, 'I do know what to do with babies, you know. I babysit for Eliot sometimes.'

'It's not that,' said Anne. 'It's not a question of finding a sitter.' She poured coffee. 'Piers is hardly ever home till nine or ten, and by then I'm too tired to do anything. Louise sometimes comes in the early evening so I can get out on my own.'

Charley felt put out that Louise hadn't mentioned that. 'Oh,' she said. 'Well, the offer's there.' She knew she sounded ungracious.

'If he's asleep, he should go in his pram,' said Anne. 'I'm trying to get him out of the habit of only sleeping when he's being cuddled.'

Charley put Eddie in the pram and tucked the blankets around him. 'Is Piers working awfully hard?'

'He won't rest until he's doing better than any other jeweller in London. Winterton's especially, of course.' Anne's tone was drily detached. She spoke without amusement or fondness, and Charley detected an undercurrent of anger in her words. She was scouring her mind for alternative topics of conversation when Anne said:

'Do you remember that meal at Marsh Court, the one where Piers told your family we'd got married?'

All Charley's senses became alert. Of course she remembered it. She could have recited the dialogue of that evening line for line. It was annoying how hard it was to forget awful things, like Nate being angry with her, when nice things seemed to slip out of her head almost as soon as they had happened. She had hoped that Anne had forgotten what she had said, but now she saw how naïve that hope had been, and how constructed on a desire to assuage her own conscience.

'Yes,' she said cautiously.

'You said that Piers only married me to spite Aidan. Why did you say that?'

Charley didn't answer. She wished she hadn't come. She wished Eddie would wake up and start crying again.

'Charley, you only have to say,' said Anne, with a slight laugh. 'I'm not blaming you for anything.'

'I shouldn't have said it. It was horrible of me and I'm sorry. I was in a bad mood and it just came out. I didn't mean it.' Which was pathetic and not even quite true. She sensed that Anne didn't like her very much; unreasonably, she minded that.

'I think you did,' said Anne quietly.

'Well. I thought it was true at the time, but I was wrong.'

'Was Aidan in love with me?'

She shook her head. 'I don't know.'

Anne looked down. 'I keep thinking about it. I keep thinking *would* Piers do that? Surely he wouldn't.'

Say something, Charley told herself angrily. Don't just sit there like a dummy. 'Anne, Piers loves you and Eddie. He does.'

Anne raised her head. Her expression was bleak. 'So why is he never here?'

'Piers has always been like that. He gets obsessed about things and doesn't notice anything else.'

But that didn't help. 'Doesn't notice his *son*?' Anne said. 'Doesn't notice *me*?'

Charley couldn't think of anything more to say, and every-thing she had said had only made things worse. Anne seemed to try to pull herself together. She asked after her job and Charley croaked out an answer. Then the conversation died again. Ten minutes later, she left. Walking home, she wished she was a man and could go into a pub and order a gin, but she hadn't the nerve to drink on her own. She felt deeply ashamed of herself and was relieved to discover, when she arrived home, that Gabe and Louise were out.

She had got up late that morning and, the last one to leave the house, had left the kitchen strewn with cereal bowl and toast crumbs. She would ordinarily have assumed that Louise or Gabe would clear up later – both were tidy people – but now she saw that was pretty obnoxious, too. Really, she wasn't awfully keen on herself just now. Perhaps being untidy and clumsy wasn't as lovable as she had so easily and conveniently assumed. She wished she could forget about her interchange with Anne, especially the last ten minutes of her visit, which had passed in almost complete silence. From that part of her memory where she stowed the things she didn't want to think about, another voice emerged: Christian Fraser's, saying, *You need to grow up, do you know that?* She thought, as she ran the hot tap and began to scrub the dishes in the sink, that he was probably right.

A few days later, she told Daniel what had happened. She had to tell *someone*. She would have exploded with self-loathing and regret had she kept it to herself, and Daniel was an understanding person and not family.

Briefly she explained about her father's death, Piers's quarrel with Aidan and her antipathy towards Anne.

'Why don't you like her?' he asked.

Nate had once asked her the same question. It was lunchtime, and they were in the canteen. Needing the comfort of chocolate, she had bought a Kit Kat. She broke off a finger and passed it to him.

'When she was there, Piers spent all his time with her and just ignored me. And she was always so *perfect*.'

'Why did you mind that?'

'Because I'm not perfect at all!' Tears spilled over her lids.

'I think you are.'

This took her so by surprise that the tears were quelled at source. 'But I'm not,' she said querulously. 'Not at all.'

'You're funny and clever and good company. And beautiful.'

Now he was being ridiculous. 'Daniel, I'm not,' she said firmly. 'I'm short and fat. I shouldn't be eating this.' She pushed the last chocolate finger across the table to him. Then she sighed. 'I need to put it right.'

'You might not be able to.'

'I *have* to.'

'Charley, not everything is repairable.'

Then he told her that he and Jeannette had met at grammar school, in the sixth form. They had been dating for five months when Jeannette had discovered that she was pregnant. They had married six weeks later. They had both been eighteen years old.

'I wanted to go to university,' he said, 'and Jeanette wanted to be a nurse. We never even finished our A levels. Instead, we got married and had Simon. I'm not complaining, he's the best thing that ever happened to me. But I won't ever go to university and maybe I'll work here for the rest of my life. You can't wind the clock back.'

'You could go to night school.'

'One day, maybe. Just now, in the evenings, I give Simon his bath and put him to bed and then I cook our tea and do the housework. Jeannette can't do much, you see. We play a game of Scrabble or watch the telly and then, if Jeannette's bad, I help her get ready for bed. I try and read a book in bed, but I rarely get through more than a few pages without falling asleep.'

While she felt incredibly sorry for Daniel, Charley didn't, at the time, believe that he was right. She was sure she could find a way of mending things. At the weekend, she went home to Marsh Court. Her mother was painting the hall, changing it from the dingy brown that Charley had grown up with, and loved, to a pale yellow. Charley gave her a hand. Perched on stepladders, swooping emulsion over the pale, ghostly rectangles of paintings that had been taken down, she had an idea. She would have a word with Piers.

After a lot of phoning and leaving messages, she found herself heading off on Thursday evening to meet her brother at a pub in the King's Road.

He had ten minutes to spare, Piers told her, as she slid into a seat at the bar beside him. He ordered her a gin and tonic. Was something wrong? Was it Mum?

'Mum's fine. She's decorating the house.'

'Good God.' He raised his eyebrows. 'That should keep her busy for the next decade.'

'Actually, I wanted to talk to you about Anne.'

'Anne?' He took out a packet of Rothman's, slid out a cigarette. 'Want one?'

'No thanks. I don't think she's very happy, Piers.'

'She's tired, that's all. The baby . . .' he said vaguely.

'It's not just the baby.' She couldn't think of a way of saying it tactfully, and anyway he was beginning to annoy her, so she said baldly, 'It's you, actually. Maybe you could come home earlier sometimes.'

'Maybe you could keep your nose out of my business.'

His expression made her nervous. He had always been able to make her feel small and stupid, an insignificant little sister.

'Piers. She's awfully miserable, you know.'

'You go and see her . . . how often?'

She flushed. 'I don't know . . . every three or four weeks, maybe.'

'And that makes you an expert on how my wife is feeling?'

'I didn't mean—'

'You caught her on a bad day, that's all. Anne knows I need to work hard to get the business off the ground. She understands that.'

Charley looked away to the crowds of people in the pub. Her gaze moved from one couple to another – some happy, some bored, and one or two who had come here to fight.

'She's lonely, Piers. And though Eddie is perfectly adorable, he's hard work.'

'Did Anne say that to you?'

'No,' she admitted.

'Keep out of it, Charley. You don't know what you're talking about.' His eyes cold, he stabbed his cigarette into the ashtray. 'You really, really don't.'

Louise and Josh were watching Z-Cars when Charley arrived home. Josh had bought a box of Maltesers. Charley ate some, watching the telly. She thought of Daniel telling her that not everything was repairable. She knew he had been talking about himself. He had told her that his son was the best thing that had ever happened to him, but he hadn't said the same about Jeannette. They had had to marry because there had been a baby on the way, but perhaps he hadn't loved her.

As for Piers, he was probably right. His relationship with Anne was nothing to do with her. And yet she felt horribly responsible. *I keep thinking about it*, Anne had said to her. Charley's own words, shouted out over the dinner table at Marsh Court, now haunted Anne. Charley would have given almost anything to be able to take them back.

She went upstairs and took out the manuscript of her play. That night, she stayed up until the early hours, cutting out portions of text and excising anything that seemed weak or dishonest, digging deep into her heart to convey thought and emotion. Words mattered, she had discovered. They had consequences. You needed to get them right.

Chapter Thirteen

October–December 1965

'Joe told us you were a teacher, Juliet,' said Paddy.

They were at Greensea, in the room with the tall windows and faded chintz sofas. I'd like you to meet my closest friends, Joe had said to her a few days earlier.

Roy and Paddy – Patricia – ran the charity that organised the camping trips for the boys from the slums. Paddy was around Juliet's age, small and dark and vivid. Roy, a Yorkshireman, was thickset, bearded and bespectacled, with greying fair hair. He was looking through Joe's bookshelves.

'I teach art at a boys' school in Maldon,' she explained.

Roy looked up. 'State or private?'

Joe handed Juliet a glass of sherry and she thanked him. 'Private,' she said to Roy. 'But we take several boys each year on scholarships.'

'Scholarships,' repeated Roy dismissively. 'For the bright and the capable, I'd guess. Not the lads who most need a decent education.'

'I don't imagine,' said Joe, passing Roy a beer, 'that Juliet chooses the scholarship boys.'

'I don't have any say at all,' she said. 'I'm only a part-time art teacher. I got the job by accident when one of the teachers had to leave suddenly. The headmistress knew I drew a little because I'd helped with the scenery for the Nativity play when my son was in kindergarten.'

'So your son was privately educated?'

'Both my children were.'

'Very nice for them, too,' said Roy, as if he had proved a point.

'People are entitled to choose what's best for their children, surely?'

'What if that entitlement affects other people's choices?'

'Stop grilling her, Roy,' called Joe over his shoulder, as he opened another beer bottle.

'Sorry.' He gave an apologetic smile. 'One of my hobby horses.'

'The trouble with Roy,' said Paddy, as she accepted a glass of beer from Joe, 'is that he's a hopeless idealist. You've only known poor Juliet for five minutes, my love. It's a bit quick off the mark to be accusing her of a sense of entitlement.'

'Education's the key to the betterment of society. I'd like to see it spread a bit more evenly, that's all. Can I borrow this one, Joe?' Roy brandished an Isaac Asimov paperback.

'Of course.'

Roy settled himself in an armchair. 'Some of the lads we try to help have grown up without having a single book in the house. Try to imagine that, if you can, Juliet. We were falling over them at home when I was a lad.'

'In the war,' said Juliet, 'when I was rather hard up for books, I decided to read every volume in Marsh Court's library. I couldn't do it. The war ended before I'd got to the top shelf. I ploughed my way through *Decline and Fall of the Roman Empire*, though. I was rather proud of that.'

'Good Lord,' said Paddy. 'I couldn't get beyond the first chapter.'

Joe sat down on the sofa beside Juliet. 'I took a volume of Andrew Marvell's poetry with me to North Africa. Tiny print, it had to fit into my kitbag.'

'Joe, you old romantic,' said Paddy. She quoted, '"The luscious clusters of the vine, Upon my mouth do crush their wine."'

Her father and his books had been fixed points in an unstable childhood, thought Juliet. Characters in novels had been her friends, their houses her neighbourhood. A memory came to her from early on in her marriage, of herself, sitting in Marsh Court's drawing room, watching Helen and Jonny dance. Their mutual ease had shown her what she and Henry lacked. She had wondered whether a good marriage was a matter of luck or whether you had to be the right sort of person for a marriage to work. She could not imagine a house without books, but nor could she imagine what it would be to love a man who loved her as much as she loved him.

She wanted this evening to go well. She wanted Joe's friends to like her and she wanted to like them. She was aware of Joe, sitting beside her. How easy it would be to move her fingers an inch or two and let them rest on his arm. She longed for him to turn and take her hand and press it against his cheek.

Two and a half months had passed since he had taken her out to dinner in the restaurant near Colchester. Since then, though they had gone for walks together and had dined out several more times, she remained uncertain of what he thought of her. She was sure that he liked her, but it was possible that he was looking for company rather than love.

She could not tell whether he had buried his capacity to love a woman along with his wife. And if that was so, would friendship be enough for her? She knew it would not.

Joe went to check on the progress of dinner; when he came back into the room, Paddy asked after Neville.

'Sticking out the theatre job. I'm keeping my fingers crossed.'

'Best, with that lad,' said Roy.

'He'll sort himself out,' said Joe. Roy gave an incredulous snort.

'Such a beautiful frock,' Paddy said to Juliet.

'This?' She was wearing a simple black silk Hardy Amies dress. 'It's an old favourite,' she said. 'I've had it for years.'

'And your necklace . . . so pretty.'

Juliet had set off the dress with a diamond pendant and matching earrings. 'My late husband was a jeweller,' she explained, 'so I'm very spoiled. I have a great many lovely things.'

She was, she had realised, rather overdressed. Roy was wearing a checked shirt and corduroy trousers, Paddy a knee-length tartan skirt and hand-knitted jersey. Joe looked handsome in dark trousers and jacket and a white shirt.

Joe came back to tell them that dinner was ready, and they went into the dining room. Over the soup, conversation moved on to the political situation in Rhodesia and South Africa.

'Of course,' said Roy, 'this country is every bit as divided, but by class, not race.'

'I'm not sure you can compare our class system to apartheid.' Joe offered round the bread.

'Plenty of similarities, once you start looking.'

'The class system isn't defined by law.'

'Rot. You're talking rot, Joe.'

319

'Roy,' said Paddy, warningly.

'We do it in a different way, that's all. We're more *subtle*.'

Juliet said, 'People don't end up in prison because of the class system.'

'Are you sure about that?' Roy rattled off a statistic demonstrating the disproportionate prison population among the working classes. 'This country's every bit as divided as South Africa,' he finished.

When Juliet looked across the table, Joe caught her eye. The smile he gave her was one of complicity and understanding. There was affection there, too, and something more, and a thrill jolted her heart. Though the discussion continued to rage around her, she took little part in it. In that moment, something had changed. Her doubts had been rubbed away; hope and optimism took their place.

The remainder of the evening became something to get through; pleasant enough, but a staving-off of a conversation she knew they would later have. Roy's words – *plenty of houses still have servants' entrances . . . this country's all about knowing your place* – sometimes interrupted her glow of happiness, but then she always returned to the true matter of the evening, that spark of rapport and desire that she'd read in Joe's eyes. If he felt something for her, was she ready to love again? She sensed their mutual wariness, their equal fear of getting hurt. Joe Brandon seemed a good sort of man – but hadn't she thought the same of Gillis? She had been waiting, she realised, these past weeks, for Joe to reveal some defect. He would be controlling, like Henry, or faithless, like Gillis.

No, Joe was different; she knew him well enough now to realise that he was by far the better man, that he possessed a blade-sharp integrity that Gillis lacked and a kindness that had been utterly absent in Henry.

'We're not married,' Paddy was telling her. 'We don't believe in marriage, Roy and I. It doesn't mean we disapprove of marriage for other people, but it doesn't suit us.'

'The neighbours disapprove,' said Roy.

'A toast.' Joe raised his glass. 'To shaking up the bourgeoisie.'

And if – that if again – they both broke through the fences with which they had surrounded themselves, what then? Could she bear it, courtship and quarrels and making-up and absences, all the inevitable paraphernalia of love? Wouldn't it be far easier to go on as she had assumed she would do for the rest of her days, having given up on that part of her life, finding satisfaction in her work, her children and baby grandson?

'You should take a holiday,' Joe was saying to Roy. 'Get away for a while.'

'Me? What about you, Joe? When did you last have a holiday?'

'Farmers don't have holidays, you know that.'

As Paddy reached across the table to take Roy's hand and spoke of a planned week in the Peak District, Joe's gaze turned once more to Juliet.

'What would I need with holidays?' he said. 'I've everything I want here.'

A sense of calm and certainty enveloped her, like the mist settling over the marshes. All she had to do was wait, be patient, and the future would work itself out. Some things were worth waiting for.

The evening came to an end at midnight. Roy and Paddy were driving back to London that night; farewells were made and Joe waved them off at the front door.

He had earlier insisted on fetching Juliet from Marsh Court and driving her home after the evening was over. 'These dark autumn nights the country roads can be treacherous,' he had said when she had protested that there was no need, she could drive herself.

As they headed off from Greensea, a blustery wind blew leaves from the trees, ragged black fragments that were illuminated in the car's headlamps.

Joe said, 'Roy's a good bloke, but he can never stay off politics for long. I hope you didn't mind.'

'I liked him. And Paddy, very much. And I was married to Henry for twenty-five years, so I'm used to disagreements.'

Joe waited for a car to pass and then took the junction. She glanced at his profile: firm chin, straight nose, high forehead. 'One day I'll tell you about Henry,' she said. 'But not now. I've had a good evening, Joe, and I don't want to spoil it. Thank you for inviting me.'

A full moon cast its pale light over the fields and hedgerows. A barn owl dipped low, skimming the grass as it mapped out its territory. She would have liked the journey to last longer, and yet at the same time, she yearned for it to come to an end, for the glances and exchanges of the evening to reach their natural conclusion.

Joe took the turning off to Marsh Court. He parked the car in the courtyard and walked round to open the passenger door.

She climbed out and he took her in his arms. His lips touched hers. They were warm and dry and made gentle little questions. She answered his kisses and felt the tips of his fingers pressing into the bones of her spine.

When they drew apart, she said, 'I wasn't sure what you thought of me.'

'I think you're a formidable woman.'

'Formidable sounds awful, like battleaxe.'

322

'I don't kiss battleaxes.'

They kissed again, more deeply this time, their lips parting. Her body was close to his and his mouth explored hers. They should take it slowly, she had made so many mistakes in the past, she should be careful. But these thoughts flitted away, coming to nothing compared to her need of him.

'Come indoors,' she said.

She fitted the key to the lock. They went upstairs. In the room she had once shared with Henry, Joe unzipped her black silk dress. Underskirt, stockings, bra – he took off one after the other. Her fingers fumbled with his shirt buttons and belt. Their clothing was half unpeeled and scattered over the bed when she opened herself for him, and gave a gasp of pleasure as she felt him inside her.

Afterwards, they lay back on the bed. They had not put on the lamp or drawn the curtains, and moonlight spilled in fragments on to their entwined bodies, a patchwork of black and silver. He kissed her, caressing every inch of her, exploring the folds of breast and thigh. The chill of the air and the spilling moonlight and his skin, which tasted of salt and lemons and the cold outdoors. He made love to her again, and she lost herself in him, forgot who she was and where she was and was aware only of the deep delight that burned at the core of her.

Early the next morning, he left to go back to the farm. At the door, they kissed. Neither of them said much; she suspected that he felt as she did, depleted with happiness. After he had gone, she took the dog out for a walk. The world looked beautiful that morning, the sky a bruised violet in the west, the air crisp and scented with fallen leaves and the last of the late roses. A fresh wind sent flurries of leaves across the paving stones, and the asters in the borders nodded their pale purple heads. She had always loved autumn.

When she had been a girl, she had thought love was for young people, that it went with smooth skin and hair without strands of grey in it. She was learning how wrong she was. It would be like walking into a foreign land, falling in love with Joe Brandon. Part of her felt elated and part of her felt afraid. She didn't trust her judgement where love was concerned. She had made such mistakes before. If there had been an exam in love, she would have failed it. She did not think, though, that she was making a mistake this time.

A twist of unease as she reflected on how little she knew about him. What he did when he went to London, and who he met there. Who his friends were, and whether there were old lovers she knew nothing about, that he bumped into from time to time. And how little she had told him about herself. One day she must tell him about Henry. And then, Gillis. What would he think, if she told him the truth?

We just need to be careful for a while, Piers had said to Anne, until things get better. He hadn't told her the half of it.

The truth was, he was in debt up to his eyeballs. Rents were high in the King's Road and fitting out the shop had cost a lot more than he had anticipated. He had to buy stock in, and though Bridget didn't add much of a mark-up, other more established goldsmiths did. Then there were the bills – electricity, telephone, water rates and wages for his staff, Tricia the secretary, and Gareth and Deborah, who worked in the shop.

Of the capital his father had left him, some of it had been swallowed up by the business and the remainder he had added to the sum raised by the sale of his bachelor flat to buy the new place in Kensington. He had still had to take out a sizeable mortgage. Add to that a new cooker, fridge and twin-tub – as Anne had pointed out, she couldn't be expected to cart bags full of dirty nappies to the launderette – as well as pram, cot, carry cot and nursery furniture, and the bills kept tumbling in.

Six months of trading had taught him that he had been naïve in believing that customers would catch sight of his window display of beautiful and unusual jewellery and walk in and buy stuff. It just didn't work that way. Sometimes they came in, oohed and aahed and handled the pieces, and then walked out again without buying anything. Too often, they glanced in the window and then walked on. Entire mornings passed when they had only half a dozen customers. He had had, in the end, to buy vitrines to display the most valuable pieces of jewellery. Although Gareth and Deborah tried to keep an eye out, items had been filched, had found their way into a coat pocket or handbag, further eroding his already slender profits.

He had needed the bigger flat because he needed to entertain. Six months ago, he had imagined giving intimate little dinners to which he would invite this journalist who worked for that fashion magazine, and that photographer who worked with that sought-after model. He would use his personal contacts to build his business. And then the baby had come. Now the flat was always a mess and Eddie was always wailing, and when, the previous Sunday, he had asked Anne how she would like to throw a little party, she had screamed at him. *How would I like it? Do you know what I'd like, Piers? I'd like to be allowed to sleep till I felt like waking up! People do that, don't they?*

Shocked, he had dropped the party idea and offered to

take the baby out in his pram while Anne got some rest. As he trudged round the park on a murky November afternoon, Eddie had stared beadily out at him from between layers of blanket and bonnet. Piers assumed his son would be more interesting when he was older, when he could talk and do things. Just now, Eddie was a ball of white wool, frequently damp and slightly rancid, liable to howl at any moment. His smallness and fragility made Piers feel nervous and incompetent.

After an hour, he went home, estimating that Anne might not be cross with him any more. She was often cross with him these days, and complained about his long hours, which rankled, because what was he supposed to do? The business had to succeed. The thought of failure made him feel physically sick. With Anne no longer working at the gallery, he was solely responsible for feeding, clothing and housing his little family. The business was his responsibility, the baby hers.

Then came an awful, memorable day when they didn't sell a single thing. Nothing. Not an earring, nor a brooch. He couldn't meet the eyes of his staff when they said goodbye to him before going home at night. In his office, he leafed through the sales and purchase books, seeing nothing, his mind numb. The spectre of failure stalked him. What if he'd got it wrong? What if he just didn't have the knack? Maybe he'd bought in the wrong pieces. Maybe his sales staff were no good at their jobs.

There was a bottle of Scotch in the bottom drawer of the filing cabinet. Piers poured himself an inch of whisky. A few mouthfuls, a cigarette, and his belief in himself began slowly to return. First he would cut back, but not on anything that directly affected the image of the business. Get rid of his accountant, do the books himself. Sitting at his desk, he gave a sour smile. One advantage of the years of training his father had given him at Winterton's was that he knew all aspects of the jewellery business. He still had faith in his chief designer and he felt in his bones that the shop was in the right location. But he had to get his name around; he had to be known. Success would come when Piers Carlisle was featured in the right newspapers and magazines, and when the right people wore his designs. Then, customers would flock to the King's Road shop.

He put on his coat and locked up. He thought of phoning Anne to tell her he would be late home, but couldn't face getting a flea in his ear again. And anyway, he resented that he should ask her permission to stay out at night.

He went to the Ad Lib, in Soho. The place was buzzing, a group belting out a number, and girls in short skirts on the dance floor. Piers found a spot to sit down. Find another, less expensive designer, he decided. Maybe Bridget's stuff didn't have a sufficiently universal appeal. The girls on the dance floor might look as fashionable and with it as Jean Shrimpton and Mary Quant, but most of them were probably nurses and shorthand-typists. Sell the sorts of things they could afford, instant fashion, made of cheaper materials, fun, modern and different, to complement Bridget's pieces. He needed to increase his turnover to keep his creditors off his back. If he could only get customers into the shop, they might be tempted by the more expensive pieces.

The waitress, bringing him a drink, whispered to him that George Harrison was in the Ad Lib that night. Piers's gaze slid round the room.

And then he saw him. Aidan, sitting at a corner table. He was with three other men and a couple of girls. One of the girls was Louise Winterton. Piers recognised a couple of the men

327

as Winterton clients. A champagne bottle was upended in a silver bucket; as Piers watched, Aidan gestured to the waitress to fetch another one.

Piers's sudden rage made his heart pound furiously. Why was everything always so damnably easy for Aidan? There was he, working all hours God sent, and there was Aidan, drinking away the profits of the company that should have been his. There was he, trying to scrape up a clientele, and there was Aidan, wining and dining Winterton's favoured customers. There was he, trying to get his business off the ground, while Aidan reaped the rewards offered by an established and successful company.

Louise laughed and flicked back her long, glossy hair. Aidan said something that made the others smile. A fashion photographer that Piers recognised from the newspapers paused at their table to exchange a few words. He, who had once been their closest friend, was excluded from the enchanted circle. He tasted bitterness and defeat.

The band struck up 'The Last Time', and a mass of people surged on to the dance floor. And it occurred to Piers that he was not without assets. Marsh Court was his, both the house and the valuable land that surrounded it. Could he sell it? Not while his mother was still living there – but if she were at some time in the future to move out, then why not? He was not someone who felt much attachment to places. Marsh Court had been his childhood home and his father's fiefdom. His father's ghost still stalked the corridors.

He couldn't fail. If the business went under, it would mean that Aidan had won. He had to make a success of it, whatever the cost. Whatever it takes, he thought as he swung his jacket off the back of his chair and walked out.

As he emerged into the night air, he spotted a familiar

figure crossing the road. 'Hey, Esteban!' he called out, and the designer turned and came to greet him.

'Piers. How are you?' Esteban Galea shook his hand. 'How's the shop?'

'Great. You should come and see it.'

'Find out how the opposition's doing? I might do that. Hey, we miss you, Piers. It isn't the same without you.'

'Isn't it?'

Esteban laughed. 'I'm telling you the truth, the life's gone out of the place.'

'Maybe you should think about a change.'

A thump on his shoulders. 'If I do, I promise you'll be the first person I'll call.'

Juliet heard Joe's Rover coming down the drive and hurried downstairs to open the front door.

She made omelettes, which she and Joe ate sitting at the kitchen table. They talked about this and that, finding out about each other. The opera he loved and the modern jazz, and her favourite chamber music. He told her that he had thought of selling Greensea after Molly had died. The farm-house had been full of reminders of her and he had come to hate it. He had put it up for sale, but no one had been buying back then, and in the end, he had taken it off the market. Sometimes Juliet wondered whether for Joe, Molly's ghost still drifted through the orchard and beside the salt marsh.

That he, in spite of everything that had happened to him – friends lost in battle, young wife to a foul disease – still believed the world could be changed astounded her. She exposed her cynicism to his idealism. The way she saw it, she couldn't be responsible for everyone's well-being. It was hard enough keeping the family together. You'd drive yourself mad worrying about all the problems in the world.

They kissed, standing in the kitchen doorway, the jamb knobbly against her back. He slid his fingertips along her jaw and gave her a long, slow smile. Then they went upstairs to bed.

After he left, she cleared up the lunch things and fetched her sketchbook and pencils and put on her coat. A mist had settled over the landscape, and as she walked down the garden, she saw the beads of water that clung to each stem of grass and rolled from the last leaves on the branches. The boundary between land and water had blurred, so that the marsh seemed to melt into the river and the birds were invisible: you heard a cry, a muffled flap of wings.

She tried to think what it was she loved about Joe, but it was as hard to pin down as the shifting landscape. A gesture, a smile. His generosity, his concern for those less fortunate than himself. She loved his calmness and solidity, and his unexpectedness as well. That he should send her armfuls of daffodils. That he should be a fierce and tender lover. She wondered how her luck could have turned so, that a man she might love should be living only a few miles away from her.

She was heading towards Thorney Island. The path ran along the summit of the high bank. Shallow puddles clotted the mud between mats of straw-coloured grass. The tide was out, the Blackwater reduced to a narrow, sluggish coffee-coloured channel. She could not at first see the island, and then it formed out of the fog, shifting and evanescent.

The path curved round and she caught sight of a man standing on the bank, no more than twenty yards ahead of her, where the causeway joined the mainland. Short and thickset, with cropped grey hair, he was wearing a navy pea coat and had a muffler at his throat. A dog skittered along the bank in a blur of white.

The man turned to look at her. As she drew closer, his gaze stayed on her. No smile, no greeting; instead, an alert, considering expression, as if he was wondering what to do with her.

She felt a flicker of danger: the quiet, the mist, the solitude of this place. Anything could happen. She turned, retracing her path, but seemed to feel his gaze hot on her back as she made her way to Marsh Court. Once or twice she looked over her shoulder, but there was no one there.

When he was five and a half months old, Eddie started to sleep at night. Suddenly, as if a switch had been flicked. People had said to Anne that once the baby slept through the night, she would feel a new person, but in her stew of exhaustion she had not believed them, had not believed he ever would.

Sleeping seemed to make Eddie feel happier too. He chortled at her and tried to grab the spoon when she sat him in his high chair and fed him mushed-up rusk. The birds in the park, the dogs in the street made him chortle as well. She made him a mobile for his cot, cardboard birds suspended from lengths of narrow wire. She put him in his cot to look at the twirling birds while she washed her hair and put on make-up. Dipping her head under the tap, brushing on mascara, she heard him laugh and coo.

She was starting to enjoy him. She took him to the gallery and showed him off to Katherine and Paul; she pushed him in the buggy to Ceridwen's house, where the three women had a game of Scrabble as the babies and children played

331

and fought in the chilly, scruffy sitting room. Anne and Eddie took the train to Witham, where Juliet met them and drove them to Marsh Court. They stayed there for four days. She was getting to like Marsh Court more. She helped Juliet work out new colour schemes for the rooms. The mists reminded her of the fogs of San Francisco.

She felt as if she was coming out of a long tunnel into the light. She bought herself a recipe book, very simple, and learned to make stews and cook fish. She cleaned the apartment while Eddie had his nap and bought pots of paint and redecorated. While she slapped paint on to the walls and Eddie lay on his tummy, trying to haul himself towards a plastic car or brick, she thought about her marriage. It seemed to her that she and Piers were living on different tracks, which ran parallel but rarely converged. Some of their problems came about because conversations had become a rushed exchange of words before Eddie would cry or the phone would ring or Piers would rush off to the shop. Some were more deeply rooted.

Even if it wasn't entirely correct that Piers had married her to spite Aidan, Anne had come to believe that there had been some truth in what Charley had said. Charley, after all, probably knew Piers better than anyone. She wasn't sure that Piers himself knew why he had married her. When she had gone to Marsh Court on the day of Henry Winterton's funeral, what had sprung from that moment had seemed to her miraculous. But for Piers their meeting had represented something else. She hoped that if she thought about this long enough, it would lose the power to hurt, but discovered that was not so.

Helen said, 'What are you doing for vegetables?' She opened the fridge. 'There are some leeks.'

They were in the kitchen at Marsh Court. Helen had come to lunch so that they could start the early planning for the next series of summer concerts. Margaret Stanmore, who had agreed to sponsor one of the concerts, was lunching with them as well.

Juliet peered inside the fridge. 'They're rather tired-looking, aren't they? Do you think Margaret would mind frozen peas?'

'I'm sure she won't. How's the quiche?'

Juliet took it out of the oven. It sizzled, golden-brown and perfect. Margaret was due any moment. After Margaret left, when she and Helen were alone again, Juliet planned to tell Helen about Joe. She was bursting to tell her about Joe.

She hurried upstairs to her bedroom to run a brush through her hair and apply more lipstick. Looking out of the window, she saw that a man was coming down the path to the house. She went downstairs and out into the courtyard.

'Have you come about the drive?' she called out. Someone was supposed to be coming over from Mundon to repair the potholes.

As he approached the house, she recognised the visitor as the stranger she had glimpsed a few days ago on the causeway to Thorney Island. The dog, an English bull terrier, white with a black patch over one eye, pattered along beside him. What was he doing here? Juliet stepped out of the porch.

The man took the cigarette out of his mouth and flicked it into a puddle. 'No, I haven't come about the drive. I wanted to talk to you about Gillis Sinclair.'

His voice had a Welsh lilt. Close to him, she estimated that he was in his fifties, not tall, but powerfully built, with broad, well-muscled shoulders and a weather-beaten, fleshy face. The cuffs of his pea coat were threadbare, and though his shoes were well-shone, they were creased with age. A tattoo of an anchor was visible on his wrist.

'He doesn't live here,' she said. 'He lives in London.'

'That's right, he does. Bryn!' Sharp now, to the dog, a nervy little thing, who had bolted off, after a rabbit, perhaps. 'Heel now, sir. Heel! You've known Gillis for a long time, haven't you, Mrs Winterton?'

That he knew her name unsettled her. She said, 'Is Gillis a friend of yours?' He didn't look like the sort of man who would be a friend of Gillis.

'My name's David Morgan,' he said. 'Perhaps Gillis has mentioned me to you.'

'I'm afraid not,' she said coldly. 'Now, I am very busy . . .'

'I served under him during the war. We were in the navy together.'

In spite of his downtrodden appearance, he had that air of authority that went with service life. She wondered whether, down on his luck, he was hoping to capitalise on his acquaintance with Gillis, maybe touch him for a loan or get some casual work. But why come here? And how did he know her name?

'Are you trying to get in touch with him, Mr Morgan?' she asked briskly. 'You can contact Mr Sinclair through his parliamentary office, you know.'

His blue eyes, set in swollen red lids, drifted to the house. 'Nice place you've got here. I remember it being a nice place. Of course, I only saw it in the dark.'

His smile conveyed an air of being in the know − of knowing her, she realised jarringly. She sensed that for some reason not yet clear to her, he was trying to upset her. He was succeeding: unease coiled round her heart, and the awareness of danger she had felt encountering him on the Blackwater had magnified.

334

'I'm sorry, you must excuse me,' she said. 'I have to get on.'

'I didn't see you that night. Gillis was staying in the cottage, but you were in the house.'

The cottage. That night. Her heart skittered; she stared at him.

Helen's voice, from behind her: 'Darling, shall I make you a G and T? Or will you have sherry?'

Juliet turned; Helen was at the door. Morgan said, 'Aren't you going to introduce us?'

'A gin and tonic, please,' Juliet said quickly. 'I'll be in in a moment.'

When Helen had gone, Juliet pulled the door to. *Gillis was staying in the cottage, but you were in the house.* She knew that Morgan was talking about the night of the storm, the night Frances Hart had drowned and Gillis had come to Marsh Court. Morgan had called here today to tell her something, of this she was now sure. She was afraid of what he might say next.

'Forgive me, but I really must go. I have guests.' Her voice sounded shrill. 'Perhaps you'd leave me a telephone number where Mr Sinclair could contact you.'

'He won't. I've tried that, and he's very good at making himself unavailable.' Morgan slid a cigarette out of a packet of Senior Service. His gaze flicked up to her. 'I wanted to remind him about the little girl, you see. I wanted him to know that I haven't forgotten.'

She must have betrayed her shock, because Morgan smiled. 'You do know about the little girl, don't you, Mrs Winterton?'

Her heart was hammering against her ribs. She kept her voice low. 'Are you talking about Thea Hart? About the little girl who drowned?'

'She didn't drown.'

That was when she began to think that he was mad. Yes, he was mad, and she must get rid of him.

'She did,' she said. 'I know she did.'

'No. If he told you that, he was lying to you.'

'That's impossible.'

'Actually, it was easy.' Morgan was standing too close to her. He gave off the musty, rancid smell of clothing worn too long and not washed enough. 'Gillis phoned me from your house, and then he hid her in the cottage. I should know, it was me who took her away from here. I've been thinking about it a lot. You could say it's been preying on my mind. That little kid, sent away like she was nothing to him.'

Thea Hart had drowned. Gillis's illegitimate daughter had drowned that stormy night on the Blackwater. Somehow Morgan knew about Gillis and Frances Hart; somehow he knew that Gillis had spent the night in the cottage, and had made up this preposterous story to use against him.

'You're lying,' she whispered. Yes, he must be lying – why, she could not be sure. To blackmail Gillis, perhaps.

'I think you know I'm not. I took his kid to an orphanage in Southampton. I handed her over to the woman who ran it. Her name was Mrs Farmer. You're a good actress, Mrs Winterton, but I think you know all this.'

His eyes were shrewd. She recognised an accusation – of what? Of involvement, of complicity. Was it possible that this man knew about their affair? That he knew she had been Gillis's lover? She had to suppress a shudder.

'You have to go,' she whispered.

Morgan shrugged. 'I'm short of cash.' Again he glanced at the house. 'You said you had visitors, didn't you?'

His implication was unmistakable. She heard the sound of a car on the main road a short distance away and ducked back into the house. Her handbag was on the hall table.

Inside it was the money with which she had intended to pay the man who was repairing the drive. With fumbling fingers she extracted the pound notes and ran back outside.

Morgan was sitting on a stone bench beside the turning circle. His large, square hand fondled the bull terrier's neck as he crooned to the beast.

'Go now,' she hissed at him as she pressed the money into his hand. 'And don't ever come here again!'

He shoved the notes into an inside pocket of his pea coat. 'Tell Gillis I'll be getting in touch with him. Tell him he'd better speak to me next time.'

He walked away, Bryn at his heels. There was a moment when she could not catch her breath and was afraid she might faint. Then Margaret Stanmore's car came into view, heading down the driveway. Juliet forced a gulp of air into her lungs and went to greet her.

She didn't, in the end, tell Helen about Joe. She couldn't face it; it was all she could do to carry out a sensible conversation about programmes and guest artists. She knew that Helen was aware that something was wrong, and when Margaret left the room for a few moments, she made herself smile and murmur that she had a frightful headache. And so Helen, dear Helen, hurried on the remainder of the proceedings, and eventually Margaret left for home.

Helen said, 'May I get you anything? A cup of tea? Aspirins?'

'Sweet of you, but no thanks.'

'Have a lie-down and maybe a snooze.' Helen gave her shoulder a little squeeze. 'I always find that helps. I'll ring you tomorrow.'

And then she was alone, and yet she was afraid of being alone. She was afraid that David Morgan might come back

337

to the house. She was afraid of what she might discover, picking over the past.

Helen had washed up; Juliet dried, then put the plates and glasses away. Lulu whined at her feet, pleading to be taken for a walk. Juliet opened the back door to let the dog out into the garden. She found herself looking out to the fire pit and then to the sea wall. She was afraid she might see Morgan standing there, against the grey clouds and sky, watching her.

She cast her mind back nineteen years, struggling to separate memory from the layers of time and supposition that covered it. On the night of the storm, Gillis had made a phone call from Marsh Court. Morgan had told her that it was he whom Gillis had called. Morgan had said that he had driven to the cottage and taken the child, Thea, to an orphanage. Her mind reeled, unable to take it in, unable to make sense of it.

Gillis had slept in the cottage, leaving before dawn the following morning. A decade later, on the night he had admitted to her that he had had an affair with Frances Hart, he had told her that he had stayed in the cottage because he had been afraid that, if he remained with her, he would break down and admit to her the truth about Frances and the children. He hadn't wanted to involve her. *I was only thinking of you.* And there had been Piers, wakeful because of the storm and the tree that had come down in Marsh Court's garden.

Morgan had revealed a colder, starker truth to her. His story made sense of Gillis's departure before dawn without saying goodbye. She was discovering that there were lies beyond lies, and they crowded in on her. She was remembering that they had found the boy's body, but not the girl's.

338

She walked down the terrace until she was able to see the cottage, the small building hidden in the shadow of a cypress tree. The wet cold of the November afternoon slapped against her face. Lulu scampered towards her, across the lawn. They returned to the house.

Though she went to her room and lay down, as Helen had suggested, she could not rest. *Gillis phoned me from your house, and then he hid her in the cottage. I should know, it was me who took her away from here.* How could Morgan have known about Marsh Court and the cottage unless he had been here before? How could he have known about Thea Hart's connection to Gillis unless Gillis had told him? Morgan knew everything. He had known things she was only just beginning to comprehend. He had been telling the truth.

At six o'clock, she phoned Joe and put off the supper they had planned that evening, telling him the same lie she had told Helen, that she had a headache. All the while she was deceiving him, she despised herself.

An hour later, she rang the Sinclairs' London house. Blanche answered the phone. Juliet asked her how she was; fine, said Blanche. Brief exchanges about their children, murmurings about how long it was since they had seen each other. Blanche sounded flat and tired.

Juliet said, 'Is Gillis there? There's something I'd like to ask him about. A little legal problem, nothing important, but rather delicate, and Tom Kendrick's away.' More lies.

'I'll fetch him for you.'

Gillis picked up the phone. Juliet said, 'Can you talk?'

'Not really.'

'I have to see you. Something's happened. I have to speak to you alone.'

'It's difficult at the moment.'

'This is important.' She spoke sharply. 'I'm in town on Thursday. I have the dentist in the morning but I should be free from about twelve.'

'Come to the house,' he said. 'One-ish. I'll be here.'

Thursday: she poked the tip of her tongue at the newly filled tooth as she walked through Green Park. The local anaesthetic was wearing off by the time she reached the Sinclairs' house in St James's Place.

She rang the doorbell. Gillis showed her indoors. 'Blanche is at a charity lunch,' he said. 'Have you eaten?'

She patted her face. 'Filling.'

'Poor old you. Tea? Coffee? Drink, to take your mind off it?'

'Nothing, thanks.'

The Sinclairs' house had been built in the eighteenth century and had a certain grandeur. You could imagine important conversations taking place there. The rooms were spacious and high-ceilinged, but Blanche knew how to make a house feel like a home, and the severity of the drawing room was softened by colourful cushions, bright paintings and house plants. Two huge metal vases of bronze chrysanthemums stood to either side of the fireplace. In her anxious, heightened state, Juliet thought they looked like funeral urns.

Gillis went to the sideboard and poured himself a drink. He had put on weight since the last time she had seen him; there was a thickness at his waist she hadn't noticed before. Beneath his tan – he was still a keen sailor, and the Sinclairs liked to take skiing holidays – his skin looked lax and dull.

She said, 'A man called David Morgan came to see me.'

She saw him flinch, as if the name had struck him with the force of a blow. Then he put down the whisky decanter and replaced the stopper.

340

'Morgan came to Marsh Court?'

'Yes.'

'Damn him.' The words low, muttered.

Was that horror she saw in his eyes? She became aware of a little pulsing pain beating in her jaw near the tooth that had been filled.

He said, 'What did he want?'

'Ostensibly, for me to give you a message. I was to tell you he'll be getting in touch with you and that you're to speak to him. But I think he really came to tell me about your daughter.'

'Daughter?' he repeated.

'Yes, Gillis, your daughter. Thea.'

Her voice dry, touched with derision. Any doubts she had clung on to, any shred of hope that Morgan's story had been false, dispersed like the motes of dust that danced in the squares of sunlight falling from the sash windows.

She said, 'Thea didn't drown, did she? You found her and you pretended she was dead. Then you sent her to an orphanage. Morgan told me he took her there. Please.' She held up a hand, silencing him. 'Don't say anything. Not yet. I can't bear to hear you lie to me again. I'm sure I could, if I tried, check out his story. He didn't remember much about the orphanage, but he told me the name of the woman who ran it.'

Gillis sat down in an armchair. 'I wasn't going to lie to you,' he said.

He looked old, she thought, old and tired. Time had caught up with Gillis Sinclair. Once, he had walked towards her out of the smoke and the marshes and the sunlight had touched him with gold and she had fallen in love with him. Her sorrow and regret seemed to fill the room.

341

He swallowed some whisky, ran a hand over his face.

'Tell me,' she said softly. 'Tell me the truth.'

His mouth worked, then he spoke. 'Morgan served under me during the war. I met him at Dunkirk. I've always thought Dunkirk did something to him – it did to a lot of us. He's a mad dog, Morgan. Useful, but you have to keep an eye on him. No pity, no conscience, and he was always a drinker and it got worse over the years.' He pressed his lips together, then let out a breath. 'We fell out some time ago. He'd worked for me after the war. There was one incident too many and I gave him the sack. I didn't see him for more than a decade. And then a year or so ago he turned up on my doorstep. I don't think things had been going well for him. I told him to push off. He used to call me now and then but I always put the phone down on him.'

She whispered, 'What did he want?' Though she had guessed the answer to that.

'Money, of course.' Gillis's smile was resigned. 'I didn't give him any. I knew once I let it start, it would never stop.'

The tick of the clock; out in the street the jangle of a bell as an ambulance sped by the house. He said softly, 'I hoped he'd drink himself to death. Or pick on the wrong person in a fight. I never thought he'd come to *you*.'

'The child, Gillis.'

He looked up. 'Thea? Yes, it's true, she survived.'

For a moment she dipped her head, closing her eyes. Her tooth hurt, a dull throb that reverberated through her jaw. She made herself look at him. She had loved him once, she thought. All that seemed a lifetime ago.

'How could you?'

'You can judge me if you like, Juliet. I daresay I deserve it.'

Secrets and lies, she thought. There had never been anything of substance between them, only secrets and lies. She whispered, 'Where did you find her?'

'At the house, at that hellish house on Thorney Island.' He gave a bitter smile. 'The search party looked there but I thought I'd have another go. I knew the place better than they did. She was a quiet girl, a home girl, Thea, not like her brother, and I thought she'd go back there if she was frightened. I couldn't find my son but I found her. She was hiding in the cupboard on the landing, under some sheets. It was where she used to go when we played hide-and-seek. Little kids, they always hide in the same place, don't they?'

He looked down at his glass, which was empty again. She found herself rising and taking it out of his hand and refilling it for him. She poured herself a Scotch at the same time, hoping it would help her tooth, hoping it would blur the pain.

'She wouldn't speak to me,' he said, as she put the tumbler in his hand. 'She was in a bad way, bone cold and shivering. Her clothes were soaking wet. I dried her and then I dressed her in warm things and wrapped her up in a blanket. She didn't say a word all that time, not one word. She wasn't crying. You'd think she'd have been crying. I could feel her trembling, like a piano wire that just sings on and on. I was frightened for her. I left her on the bed while I looked for Edmund.' Another mouthful of whisky. 'Anyway, I'd lost him. I knew it. I searched for him but I knew he was gone . . . I *felt* it. He must have paddled into the water after his ball or his boat and been swept away, something like that. Frances must have gone in after him. She was negligent, but she loved those children. She'd have tried to save him. Maybe Thea saw what happened and then the tide took them away, and then . . .'

His words drifted away, like autumn leaves whisked up on a breeze. He was silent for several minutes. Then, with a sigh, he said, 'She must have gone back to the house. I've never been able to bear thinking about that, poor little Thea walking all the way back to the house on her own. Perhaps she thought she'd find them there. Perhaps, when I found her, she was waiting for them to come home.'

He ran a hand across eyes that shone with tears. Then he cleared his throat and his voice became firmer.

'I was going to take her back to the mainland and let the search party know she was all right. I knew that as soon as I told them about her, it'd all be over for me. I thought of handing her over and hoofing it and hoping for the best, but all she'd have to do would be to say "Daddy" and that would be it – my career, my marriage, the lot, down the drain, and I'd never get any of them back. And I'd worked so damned hard. But then, when I was halfway across the causeway, I realised I didn't need to tell anyone. No one knew I was there. No one knew of my connection to them. So I hid her under my coat. I kept away from the men searching the mudflats and took her to my car.' He looked up at her. 'I suppose I panicked. I couldn't face it . . . Blanche . . . my work . . . everything. You make these decisions in a moment, don't you?'

She could not think of any circumstances in which she would have abandoned her own child. She said, 'Why did you take her to the cottage?'

'I thought of going to a hotel, but I was afraid I'd be recognised, and that someone would ask questions. I couldn't take her back to London, obviously. And then I remembered your cottage at Marsh Court. I thought that if I took her there, I'd be able to work out what to do next. I knew she was in shock. She was cold and floppy and she kept drifting off to sleep, so I had to act quickly. I had to warm her up and get some food inside her. Marsh Court was nearby and I knew Henry was in London, I'd seen him just the previous evening. I wondered whether I should go straight to the cottage and hope I'd find enough fuel for a fire, keep you out of it, but then I saw that wouldn't work. You might notice the smoke from the chimney, and anyway, I had to get some food and drink for Thea and phone Morgan. I knew Morgan would be discreet. I trusted him then. He did odd jobs for me, the sort of jobs I didn't want anyone else to know about. I'd used him to arrange the rental of that damned house on the island six months earlier. I hadn't told him about Frances and the children, but he must have worked it out.'

He paused, staring into the depths of his whisky glass. 'I left Thea in the back of my car while I went into Marsh Court and spoke to you. When I got her into the cottage, I lit the fire and warmed up the milk I'd taken from your kitchen. I put sugar in it for the shock. She wouldn't drink from the cup, so I had to spoon it into her mouth. I managed to get half a cup of milk down her and her skin pinked up a bit and I knew she was going to be all right. I held her in my arms all that night. I held her in my arms till the dawn came.'

'And in the morning you gave her away to a stranger.'

'Yes.' His eyes, pink with unshed tears, settled on her. 'Yes, that's what I did. I thought that would be the end of it. When Morgan took her away, I felt relieved. Of course, it wasn't the end of it. Something like that, it never comes to an end.'

'Gillis, she was your *daughter*.' Her voice scratched.

345

'What use was I to her?' His glance was defiant. 'I'd been a rotten enough father. She deserved something better than me. Anyway, I'd met a woman who ran an orphanage in Southampton, when I was campaigning for the '45 election.'

'Mrs Farmer.'

'Yes. It was a little place, half a dozen children. I'd given her a donation, made sure it got in the papers.' He gave a cynical, humourless smile. 'She was a good, kind woman but hopeless with money, you know the sort – motherly, but impractical. Never married, no children of her own. I knew she'd take good care of Thea and I told myself it would be best for her, that I'd be giving her a new start, a new life. Morgan was to take her there as I would have been recognised. And anyway . . .'

'You wanted to see the back of her?' She despised him.

'I wanted,' he spoke softly, 'for it not to be happening. To get back my life. It was a nightmare . . . I wanted it to be *over*.'

His hands twitched at the fabric at the knees of his trousers. 'I told Morgan to tell Mrs Farmer that Thea was a foundling, that she'd been discovered in the street during the Blitz. We gave her a new name, of course. Morgan was to say that the orphanage she'd been living in had shut down and she needed somewhere else to live. Mrs Farmer must have suspected the story was a farrago of lies, but there was the money, you see, she needed the money. Those children were her life. I heard that she died a couple of years after Thea was given up for adoption and that the orphanage closed afterwards. It was a funny, old-fashioned place, a leftover from before the war. You wouldn't get away with it today; there's too much paperwork now – they do these things differently.'

Then he made a sound somewhere between laughter and a cry. 'I had Morgan call the orphanage a couple of weeks later to find out how she was. Do you know, she still hadn't said a word. Not one single word. Shock can do that to kids, it can make them mute. God knows how long it was before she spoke again. So I might have got away with it. I might have handed her over to the search party and walked away. I might not have had to involve Morgan. But I didn't know that at the time.' The emotion had gone from his voice, as if whatever feeling he had once invested in the events of that night had burned out long ago.

'What happened to her, Gillis? Where is she now?'

'I don't know. That's the truth,' he added quickly, staving off her interruption. 'I didn't want to know, I was very clear about that. Morgan was to give Mrs Farmer a sum of money when he took Thea to the orphanage and make another payment when the girl was placed with suitable adoptive parents. It was all done anonymously. There was nothing to link me with her.'

'Except Morgan.'

'Yes,' he said grimly. 'Except Morgan.'

For a while, neither of them spoke. Then, draining his whisky glass and rising, Gillis said, 'They found a family for her pretty quickly. She was a bright, attractive little thing, and girls are easier to place than boys. A decent family, a good home. Morgan won't trouble you again, Juliet, I'll make sure of that. You needn't worry about it.'

Did he really believe that? 'Gillis, it's not just your secret any more,' she said quietly. 'It's mine now, as well. And I don't want it. I'm sorry, but I don't.'

She hated it. She regretted deeply that she had agreed to keep quiet about his affair with Frances Hart. She had been such a fool. She had made him promises because she had been in love with him.

'You have to tell Blanche,' she said.

He shook his head. 'I can't.'

'I can't just let it go, not this time. What if Thea had family?'

'If she did, what does it matter now?' His voice was cold.

'They'll have mourned her all these years. You need to tell them the truth, to put it right.'

'No.'

'Mightn't Blanche forgive you? It's all such a long time ago.'

'No, Juliet, it's impossible.'

Just then she hated him for his weakness, hated that he had ensnared her in his web of deceit.

'Then I'll tell her,' she said coldly. 'I'm sorry, but I can't go along with this. It's too awful. It's one thing to conceal a love affair, Gillis, but hiding the existence of a child, letting people believe she's dead when she's really still alive, that's a different matter altogether.'

'Blanche is sick.'

'What?' She stared at him. She regretted drinking the whisky; it had made her head ache and her mind slow. The tooth still hurt, and she felt tired and gritty-eyed.

'She has cancer.'

For a fraction of a second it crossed her mind that he was lying to her. Trying to obtain her sympathy, dig himself out of a hole. But she saw the ashen tinge to his skin. Defeat had settled over him like a veil.

'Oh God, Gillis.'

'We haven't told anyone.' He lit a cigarette. 'Haven't told the children. Blanche wouldn't let me. Hoped it could be fixed without them knowing. I went along with it, but now she's been told it's terminal, so they're going to have to know.

348

Nate will have to come home. I dread telling Rory, they're so close. She's seeing a chap at the Royal Marsden. Saw him on Monday. He said . . . he said to me while Blanche was off having a blood test that it's only a matter of months now.'

He rose and went to the window, looking down to the passing traffic. She went to stand beside him.

'It's all so bloody unfair,' she heard him say. 'These things shouldn't happen to good people. If it was me, there'd be some sense in it, wouldn't there?'

'You mustn't think like that, Gillis.'

'I can't tell her.' His eyes implored her. 'You see that, don't you? I can't tell Blanche and I can't tell the children. I beg you not to say anything to her, Juliet.'

What else could she do but agree to what he asked? When she nodded, tears trailed from his eyes.

'Poor Gillis,' she said. 'How awful. Poor Blanche.'

'She's in pain a lot of the time. She's trying to think about Christmas. You know how much she loves Christmas. She's thinking of presents for the grandchildren, that sort of thing.' He seized her hands, crushing them between his own. 'You won't hear anything more of Morgan, I promise you, Juliet. You must forget about him.'

But as he spoke, she was aware of a dull weight inside her and wondered whether it would ever go away again.

Gillis gave a sour laugh. 'It's funny,' he said. 'You have a taste of success, of good fortune, and somehow you think it's going to last, and when it slips through your fingers you think you're entitled to it, you think you *deserve* it, and you'd do anything to get it back. It's taken me this long to see that all that ambition, all that *glory*, never really mattered. And I thought I was *clever*. I thought I was *special*.'

*   *   *

349

A quarter of an hour later, she left the house. Earlier that morning, she had thought she might call on Anne and see her grandson, but she knew herself unable to fake the necessary equanimity. Blanche, Thea Hart, it was too much to take in. Anne would know that something was wrong. Besides, her tooth hurt.

In Pall Mall, too wrung out to cope with the Underground, she hailed a taxi to take her to Liverpool Street, reaching the station only minutes before her train was due to depart. It was crowded, and she ran along the platform, peering through windows until she spotted an empty seat in the packed carriages. There was a shuffling of knees as she squeezed into the central seat of a compartment, and then the train hauled itself out of the station.

She felt a rush of nausea. She mustn't make an exhibition of herself, falling sick or faint in a crowded railway carriage. She delved in her handbag and found a tube of Polos, and peeled off a sweet. She hadn't eaten since breakfast at seven. The sugary mint helped, and her stomach calmed and her heart quietened. She made herself concentrate on the view through the mud-spattered window, counting off the stations: Stratford, Manor Park, Ilford, Romford. But the thoughts intruded, rattling through her mind – Blanche, Thea Hart, David Morgan.

At last they reached Witham, where the train came to a halt and she picked up the car. She breathed more easily as she drove along the familiar roads that surrounded her haven, her place of refuge: Marsh Court. She let herself into the house, dropped her bag and coat on the stairs, went to the kitchen, slotted bread in the toaster and boiled water in the kettle. Aspirins from the bathroom. The phone rang and she wondered whether it was Joe. She did not answer it.

She took the tea and toast into the morning room and sat down in her favourite chair by the window. She ate the toast carefully, keeping it to the good side of her mouth. Joe, she thought, what shall I do about Joe? Could she tell him the truth?

No, she could not, and not only because she had promised Gillis not to tell anyone. Joe would find Gillis's story contemptible. He would despise him for abandoning his daughter, and he might despise her, too, for loving a man who could do such a thing. She could not tell him about the Harts without admitting that she had been Gillis's lover. The two things were inextricably bound together. She would be unable to make him understand the choices she had made without explaining to him how deeply she had loved Gillis.

Perhaps she must end the affair. If she could not be honest with Joe, perhaps she should leave him.

But that was too heartbreaking to contemplate, and wearily she closed her eyes. A short nap, she said to herself, ten minutes, no more, and she slipped off into a deep, dreamless sleep.

When she woke, it was dark outside. Her tooth was no longer hurting, and along with her headache, her bleak mood and uncertainty had lifted. She drew the curtains.

She had been lonely for long enough, hopeless for long enough. You didn't get many chances at happiness. Her love affair with Gillis belonged to the distant past. The choices they had made: these, too, were in the past. She had played no part in Gillis's abandonment of Thea Hart and need feel no shame for what she had learned today. Gillis had promised to deal with Morgan. She must learn to let the past take care of itself. She need not pay for Gillis's mistakes.

Besides, wasn't she entitled to some happiness? Wasn't she entitled to live?

*   *   *

351

Blanche Sinclair died three days before Christmas. The funeral was in the bleak, disjointed time between Christmas and New Year. Throughout the service Gillis wept, the awful, choked sound of a man unused to showing deep emotion. His daughters, Flavia and Claudia, sat to one side of him in the church, and his sons, Nathan and Rory, to the other. Somewhere, scattered long ago to the four winds, Gillis's other daughter lived in ignorance of her true parentage. Juliet still remembered the dream she had had, shortly after the drownings, of the little girl in the red dress, tossed about by the waves of the grey North Sea.

She shut away the image and made herself think about something else, anything: the damp chill of the church, the great rolling chords of the organ as the congregation rose to sing one of Blanche's favourite hymns, 'Guide Me, O Thou Great Redeemer'.

Chapter Fourteen

February 1966

Charley found Nate in a bar in a Holborn hotel. It was a glitzy place, with orange plush armchairs and pea-green and peach curtains. Nate was standing by a window. He was singing a song in Spanish, loudly, and with expansive gestures.

The woman sitting beside him – black hair in a chignon, smart black frock – addressed Charley as she joined them. 'Thank God,' she said disgustedly. 'Take him home. You're welcome to him.' She picked up her handbag and walked out.

The phone had rung half an hour earlier, at nine o'clock, while Charley had been in her bedroom, writing. 'I found your number in Nathan's address book,' the voice at the end of the line had told her, after introducing herself to Charley as Jacqueline Watson, a colleague of Nate's. 'He said to call you. He's behaving appallingly and they're threatening to throw him out. You need to come and get him.'

Nate was still singing. 'Shut up, Nate,' said Charley.

He did so, then looked around, blinking. 'Where's Jacqueline?'

'I think she's gone home.'

'Drink?'

'No. And you don't need one either.' She hauled him out

of the bar. People stared at them as he stumbled between the tables.

She didn't feel up to tackling the Underground with him so hailed a taxi to the Sinclairs' house. Inside the cab, she said, 'Nate, you have to stop this.'

'Do I?' The blurred look hardened as he focused on her and became something akin to dislike.

'Yes, you do. I care about you and I don't want you getting hurt.'

'Charlotte Winterton, so good and noble and virtuous. Since when did you become a bore?'

She hated it when he spoke to her like that. She looked out of the window at the flickering sulphurous gleam of the street lamps, biting her lip.

'This isn't making it any better, Nate,' she said quietly.

'My mother's dead. How is anything going to make that better?'

There was a long, taut silence, during which she tried to squeeze back her tears. Then she heard him say, 'Sorry. I'm sorry. Charley, I didn't mean it. Too much to drink. Bad day.'

'Particularly bad or just averagely bad?'

'Oh, I don't know.' He let out a breath. 'They all seem much of a muchness.' He touched her sleeve. 'Thank you for coming.'

'I didn't mind. Is Jacqueline your girlfriend?'

'Not after tonight, I suspect.' He looked across at her. 'It doesn't matter. Not really. Does it?'

Charley wondered whether it had mattered to Jacqueline, but there was a dead look in his eyes, and her heart ached for him. 'No, of course it doesn't,' she said gently.

They were nearing the Sinclairs' house. She said, 'Is your dad at home?'

Nate shook his head.

'Have you had anything to eat?'

He glowered, trying to remember. 'Probably not.'

Charley paid the taxi driver and they went inside the house. In the Sinclairs' kitchen, she cooked a packet of rather old-looking sausages she found at the bottom of the fridge. The kitchen had the look of a room that had once been cared for and was now neglected and inhabited by two very busy and very unhappy men.

She made sausage sandwiches, which they ate in the sitting room, with only the table lamps on and moonlight pouring through the sash windows.

'How's Rory?' she said.

'I don't know, really.' Nate peeled open a sandwich. 'Back at school. I write to him, but his letters don't say much, the poor little bugger.'

'I'm writing to him too.'

'Good of you.'

'How's the job?'

Nate was working in a merchant bank. 'Bearable. How's the play?'

'Coming along.'

He shrugged off his jacket. She wanted to smooth back the black curls that had tumbled over his forehead. She wanted to make him smile again but didn't know how to.

'So at least,' he said, blobbing tomato sauce into his sandwich, 'one of us is making progress with their life.'

Anne, Piers and Eddie all caught colds. The three of them snuffled and coughed, and Eddie's furious wail as his blocked nose prevented him sleeping pierced the flat at irregular intervals through the night.

Anne hated the gloomy winter mornings. Getting up in the dark, breakfasting in the dark, was not something she thought she would ever get used to. As she stumbled into the kitchen to make herself coffee at seven, blobs of sleet swirled in the square of black sky framed by the window.

Piers was standing by the cooker, swallowing a cup of tea. 'Have to go,' he said. 'I'll be late back tonight. Taking a client out to dinner.'

'How late?'

'Eleven . . . maybe twelve-ish.' He swooped to kiss her.

'There's a banana skin in the sink,' she said.

'The bin's full.'

She felt a surge of rage. 'Empty it, then.'

He gave her a surprised look. 'I have to get to work.'

'You could put your toast crusts and banana skins in the dustbin, Piers. You could wash up your cereal bowl. You could even,' she added sarcastically, 'mop the floor. But I don't suppose you know where the mop's kept.'

He hated being criticised. He muttered something. She caught the words 'your job'.

'Eddie's my job.' She studied him, feeling not a scrap of affection for him. 'Eddie, who isn't well and who was awake most of the night. Just clear up your mess, that's all I'm asking.'

'I haven't time.'

'It would take you two minutes!' She heard her voice rise. 'Just two minutes to put your crusts in the bin!'

'Okay, then,' he said furiously, and grabbed the plastic bowl from out of the sink and swept the debris into it. Then he stormed out of the flat, slamming the door behind him.

There was a cry from the nursery. For a moment Anne closed her eyes, leaning her back against the oven, and then she went to fetch Eddie.

The day didn't improve much. They had run out of milk – Piers had had the last of it on his cornflakes – so she wrapped up Eddie in his snowsuit and pushed the buggy to the store. The sleet stung her face and passing cars sent up curls of grey water. At the shops, she bought bread and aspirins and stewing lamb, as well as Farley's Rusks for Eddie. When she returned to the house, Mr Lord, who lived in the ground-floor apartment, came out to complain to her about the crying and door-slamming and the washing-up bowl that Piers had left at the foot of the stairs – because, presumably, he had been unable to face her shrewishness again, or perhaps because he couldn't be bothered taking it back to the kitchen.

'I'm a light sleeper,' Mr Lord added. 'I wish you wouldn't let the child cry.'

Gritting her teeth, Anne apologised, picked up Eddie, the buggy, her shopping bag and the bowl, and staggered upstairs.

In the flat, she sat Eddie on the rug with his toys and put on the Cona. After two cups of coffee and three aspirins, she felt better. Eddie seemed less snuffly today and was happily chewing the arm of his cloth clown. She hoped Piers might ring and apologise for their falling-out, but he did not do so. She wondered why she had thought he might: Piers never apologised. Saying sorry would have meant admitting he was in the wrong, and Piers Winterton was never in the wrong.

She could have called him and made him laugh about Mr Lord and the washing-up bowl and mended their disagreement that way, but decided not to. Her anger might have been disproportionate – she guessed Piers had thought it so – but that wasn't the point. She knew she could go on like this, feeling angrier and angrier inside while always being the one who said sorry, always drawing back to avoid facing up to the real divisions that had opened between them. She remembered the little rumbles of an earthquake in San Francisco before the ground twisted and shifted, sending books flying from the shelves. She was feeling them now.

She spent the day cleaning the flat, putting washing through the twin-tub and making a lamb stew, all the while tiptoeing and hushing Eddie as soon as he cried because of Mr Lord. She couldn't face hauling baby and buggy down the stairs again so did not go out. She mushed up spoonfuls of the lamb stew in the Moulinex for Eddie's tea, then bathed him. After she had given him his bottle, he settled down to sleep without a fuss.

As she tidied up the sitting room, she wondered whether the amount of love contained in a marriage was ever truly equal. Perhaps one person always loved more than the other, or perhaps the balance shifted over time. She had known that she was taking a gamble marrying Piers. He was ambitious, passionate and strong-willed. If she went along with everything he wanted, then the marriage would survive, after a fashion. But would that be enough for her?

She had returned to England to escape the turmoil that had followed her broken engagement to Glenn, but recently she had begun to wonder whether she had got herself into a worse mess, and whether in marrying Piers she had chosen a man who was in some ways Glenn's opposite but every bit as bad for her. What had worked well enough before Eddie had been born didn't work so well now. His birth had shown up the fault lines in their relationship.

Her independence and self-determination were swirling away in a whirlpool of family obligations. Sometimes she could hardly recall the confident girl who had driven on her own from one coast of the US to the other. She didn't like the woman who had taken her place, the straggle-haired creature who screamed at her husband about things that didn't much matter.

She looked at her watch. A quarter to seven. The tiny kitchen seemed to be shrinking, confining her. Piers wouldn't be home for hours; a long evening stretched out ahead of her. She yearned for a drink and a chat with a grown-up person who didn't spend their days worrying about nappy rash and weaning.

She called Louise's number, and Louise, kind Louise, immediately offered to babysit. But where should she go? Katherine was away and Ceridwen had her night class. She thought of Aidan. It was weeks since she had last seen him. She still hadn't told Piers that she visited Aidan, but that didn't matter, because she would be home hours before him.

'Glass of wine?' Aidan said.

Anne was peeling off her coat. Underneath it, she was wearing black trousers and a fluffy jersey of a pale, wintry grey.

'That would be *wonderful*.'

'You look beautiful.'

'Aidan, my nose is peeling and I have bags under my eyes. And I'm whacked and rather fed-up.'

'Still,' he said, handing her a glass, 'you do.'

In the galley kitchen, he flung wide cupboard doors to find something to go with the drinks. He opened a can of olives and put them in a bowl. When he took them into the main room, Anne was looking at a watercolour.

'I like this,' she said. 'It's one of yours, isn't it?'

'It's north Norfolk. There was a storm, and those wonderful stripy cliffs. Freya and I went there.'

359

'How is Freya?'

'Very well. Very excited about the exhibition.' Anne's friend, Katherine Rose, had offered to put on an exhibition of Freya's work. 'Thank you for talking to Katherine about her, Anne.'

'It was a pleasure. Freya's very talented. Are you two dating?'

'Uh-huh.' He shook his head. 'Just friends.' He put the wine glass on the coffee table. 'Sit down. How's your day been?'

She made a face. 'Not my best. What about you?'

'Much the same – not my best. You first.'

She sighed. 'Piers and I had a fight this morning. Before I'd even had my coffee. It was my fault.'

Aidan doubted that. He thought it was probably Piers's fault. 'Was it about anything in particular?'

'Oh . . .' She sat down on the sofa, tucking a foot beneath her. 'I'm sick of clearing up after him, but it wasn't just that.'

He suspected that if he said any more, she might clam up. He felt a sense of satisfaction hearing that things weren't going well between Anne and Piers, but he knew he mustn't let her see that. He rose and searched through his collection for a record to put on.

'Having Eddie has changed me,' she said. 'I feel as if a hurricane's blown through my life. Or a volcano, or an earthquake. But I can tell Piers doesn't feel the same way. Maybe men never do. He doesn't see that everything's different. He won't even change a nappy, Aidan. He'll cuddle Eddie, but he won't change a nappy. I feel I've kind of left him behind and he hasn't even noticed.'

A little thrill of pleasure, hearing her criticism of Piers, along with a feeling of vindication. Piers and Anne – he had known it would never work.

He put on a record of Chopin mazurkas. He said, 'Maybe you're just having a bad day.'

'Maybe. But it's not only Piers, it's me as well. I don't think I'm cut out for domesticity. Housework . . . childcare . . . some women love all that, don't they? Even Eddie – I adore him, but I'm going out of my mind being stuck in the apartment with him.'

When he motioned with the bottle, she held out her glass for him to top it up. 'I've realised that I find it hard to cope with chaos,' she said ruefully. 'And with a baby there's always chaos, because it's all so unpredictable and messy. What's happening to me, Aidan? I had a bohemian upbringing, I shouldn't mind about toast crumbs in the sink.'

'You can't help what bothers you. It's what you are.'

She kicked off her shoes and hunched her knees to her chin. 'It's lonely being at home with a baby. No one tells you that. I can't help thinking we women aren't supposed to live like this, shut in our homes with only a tiny little thing that can't even talk for company. Maybe we should all live together while you men go off and hunt mammoths, or whatever it is that you do.' She gave a little laugh, though there was no amusement in her eyes.

He said, attempting casualness, 'Does Piers know you're here?'

She shook her head. 'He's out late tonight. Louise is babysitting. I'll only stay an hour or so.' She twisted her mouth to one side, something he had noticed she did when she was feeling guilty. Then she asked him about his day.

Winterton's profit-and-loss accounts lay on the coffee table between them. 'Pretty lousy,' he said. 'I had a meeting with our accountants. We're losing money. Not a lot, but profits are going down each month.'

'I'm sorry. Tough times. Piers is finding it tough as well.'

He poured more wine into their glasses. 'We've been losing

361

money ever since Uncle Henry died. As I said, not a huge percentage, but enough to make a difference.'

'What will you do?'

What indeed? 'Miss Rolfe is retiring soon,' he told her, 'so we won't replace her. And maybe one of the shop assistants will have to go.' He hated the thought of that. All their employees had worked for Winterton's for years; they were like family.

'The trouble with a business like ours,' he continued, 'is that you can't cut corners. We have to look expensive and exclusive because that's what we do, it's what we are.' He let out a breath. 'I don't know, Anne. I've been thinking about it all day and haven't managed to find an answer yet. I hate it, having to be the person who makes this sort of decision. I'm afraid I'll get it wrong. I wish Uncle Henry was still here. He always seemed to know what to do.'

'You and Piers should be working this out together.'

He gave her a sharp glance. 'You know that's impossible.'

'Is it?'

'Anne . . .'

'Go and talk to him.'

'The last time I tried that, he slammed the door in my face.'

He thought she would let the subject go, but she didn't. 'Then you should try again,' she said. 'Piers is very proud. He'll never be the one to make the first move.'

'This is all Piers's fault,' Aidan said stiffly. 'If he hadn't flown off the handle in the first place, none of this would have happened. I don't see why I should be expected to beg his forgiveness.'

'I'm not asking you to beg, I'm asking you to find a way of repairing this stupid feud. It's hurting your family and it's hurting the business. Surely you can see that, Aidan. Surely you can see how unhappy your mother and Juliet feel about it. And the reason you have to find a way of healing it is because Piers won't.' She said this without rancour, but without sympathy either.

When he did not respond, she shrugged and said, 'No? Okay. I didn't think you'd agree, but I had to try.'

He said, rather heatedly, 'You must see that it isn't fair that—'

'Not much in life is fair, Aidan,' she interrupted him. 'Haven't you learned that yet?' When she swept back her hair from her face, he saw the pallor of her skin, and her hollow eyes, which held an expression of resignation, or perhaps despair.

'Sorry,' he muttered. 'But I can't do it.'

Chopin swirled in the silence. 'It's like some horrible game you're both playing,' she said, putting down her glass. 'You and Piers. And I'm sick of being caught up in it.'

'Anne.'

He went to sit beside her and put his arm round her. She rested her head against his shoulder.

'My father used to play this,' he said. A bittersweet melody filled the room. 'On the grand, in our house in Maldon. Maybe I should put on something more cheerful. I'll open another bottle of wine.'

'I should go . . .'

'One more glass, then I'll phone you a taxi.'

He put *Rubber Soul* on the gramophone and went into the kitchen. He unearthed a bottle of Chablis from the back of a cupboard and took out the cork.

When he returned to the sitting room, Anne was lying on the sofa, asleep. He spread a travelling rug over her and turned down the music. He poured himself a drink and began to go through the figures. Now and then he looked at her, at the silvery sheen of her hair and the fragile bones of the hand that rested against her face. He thought of waking her, but didn't. He thought of what she had said about Piers. He had never heard her talk that way about Piers before. Here she was, in his flat, telling him that she was fed up with married life. He told himself that at least she was happy here, and that he was protecting her, offering her a refuge, and he disregarded the voice in his head that murmured that he was lying to himself, and that his motivation was not as charitable as he liked to pretend.

Anne woke from a dream in which the lounge in her apartment had expanded hugely, the ceiling stretching high above her head, and the immense walls were hung with pictures. She yawned and opened her eyes. She was in Aidan's sitting room, and Aidan was stretched out on the opposite sofa, his eyes closed, paperwork spread out around him.

She looked at her watch and saw that it was ten minutes past twelve. She shrieked, startling Aidan awake.

'I've got to go,' she said. 'My things . . .'

She grabbed her coat and bag and ran out of the house. Reaching Cheyne Walk, she glimpsed the yellow light of a taxi and waved an arm madly. *Please don't let Piers be home yet. Please let him be late.*

The taxi seemed to crawl and every traffic light was red, but at last she reached home. She paid off the driver, let herself in the front door and ran up the stairs quietly, so as not to annoy Mr Lord. As she unlocked the door to their apartment, she said, 'Louise, I'm so sorry . . .'

'I sent Louise home.' Piers rose from a chair.

She crossed the room and brushed a kiss against his cheek. 'Have you been back long?'

'Hours and hours. My dinner was cancelled.'

'Oh. I'm so sorry, darling – if I'd known . . .'

'Louise told me you were with Aidan.'

She'd had to tell Louise she was visiting Aidan in case of any problems with Eddie. 'I'd meant to be back,' she said, flustered.

'I'm sure you did. Do you often go and see him?'

'Now and then, yes.' She took off her coat. 'Piers, we're friends, we've been friends for years. I told you that ages ago.'

His blue eyes looked blank. 'Now and then . . . how often would that be?'

'Every three or four weeks, something like that.'

'You never mentioned it.'

She felt wrong-footed. 'I'm sorry, I've been so distracted with the baby and everything.' She knew her excuse sounded feeble.

He frowned. 'Louise knew and I didn't.'

'Piers.' She gave a small laugh, trying to lighten the mood. 'You're making it sound like a conspiracy.'

'Louise covers for you while you visit Aidan. It's a nice cosy little arrangement.'

'For heaven's sake,' she snapped. 'Louise babysits for me because she doesn't mind doing it and she's good with Eddie. I go and see Aidan because I like him, he's my friend. I'm sorry I didn't mention it to you, I should have, but do you want to know the truth?'

'I'm still waiting for it,' he said nastily.

'Okay then. I couldn't face telling you. You can't be rational about Aidan, can you? You fly off the handle if anyone so much as mentions his name.'

He gave an unpleasant little smile. 'Looks like I had good cause.'

'What do you mean?'

'It's half past midnight.'

'I know. I'm sorry. I fell asleep. I was tired and we had a drink and I fell asleep.'

She went into the kitchen to run a glass of water. There was a bunch of roses in the sink, hothouse flowers, scentless, their crimson petals almost black in the low light.

She went back into the room. 'Piers, what gorgeous flowers, how sweet of you.'

He shrugged. 'I'd had a good day. Our best day so far, and I thought . . .' Just then he looked bewildered instead of angry.

'Darling, that's wonderful.'

'I thought so too,' he said. There was still that tang of confusion in his tone. 'I thought we'd celebrate. But then I came home and found you were with Aidan.' He frowned. 'You fell asleep . . . Come on, Anne. You're an inventive, creative woman. Can't you think of anything better than that?'

She stared at him. 'What are you suggesting?'

'You spent five hours with Aidan *asleep*? Was that what the two of you were really doing?'

It took a second or two for it to dawn on her that he was accusing her of being Aidan's lover. The thought was so shocking and so preposterous that for a moment she was speechless.

'Piers,' she said. Her voice shook. 'Aidan and I are friends. Just friends.'

'I don't believe you.'

'I'm telling you the truth. I'm sorry if it disappoints you.'

366

'Disappoints?' he said angrily.

Suddenly she was tired of the pair of them. Nurturing their grievances, dragging the rest of the family into their squabble when they could have mended it with a smile and a handshake. She was too weary to fight or to try to mend bridges. If this was what they wanted, if their mutual animosity was so important to them, then so be it, she would leave them to it.

She plumped up a cushion angrily. 'You'd like to have some justification, wouldn't you, for all your bad feelings about Aidan. But I'm afraid I can't provide you with any. I fell asleep on the sofa while Aidan was going through Winterton's accounts. He fell asleep too, and when we woke up it was midnight. That's what happened. That's *all* that happened. Whether you believe it or not is up to you.'

His lip curled. 'You must think I'm an idiot.'

'No.' She gave him a steady look. 'I think you're so obsessed with being better than Aidan and so eaten up with jealousy that you make yourself imagine things.' She picked up her bag and scarf. 'I'll tell you what I really think, Piers. I think you keep your resentment going to save yourself from confronting the truth. You don't want to face up to what sort of man your father was, and you don't want to acknowledge that sometimes you're in the wrong. And do you know what? You're dislikeable when you're like this. You're not the man I thought you were. What happened with your father and Aidan is done and dusted. Get used to it. Don't take it out on me.'

'He took my inheritance and now he's taking my wife.'

Inside, she was tearing apart, but she said, 'My God, can you hear yourself? I'm not listening to any more of this, Piers. I've had enough.'

*   *   *

Charley's play, a courtroom drama called *Knight's Gambit*, ran for three nights in February. The first night was a shambles, pieces of scenery falling over, the actors forgetting their lines. She would never, ever attempt to put on a play again, she decided.

The second night was better. Daniel came to see the performance. Charley had a small role and was helping with props; after the final curtain, she went to meet him in the foyer of the church hall.

'What did you think?'

'Terrific. Loved it. *Three* curtain calls. Well done you.'

She linked her arm through his as they walked a few streets away to a pub that no one else from the drama group would be likely to go to. She felt tired and elated at the same time. Daniel bought beer and crisps and they picked over the performance. That bit where Kevin had left the stage on the wrong side and had to run all the way round the wings. The denouement, where the real villain was unmasked – brilliant, Daniel said, he had been on the edge of his seat.

'When they put on your play in the West End,' he said, 'I promise I'll come and see it.'

'*Daniel*. Yesterday was so awful I nearly chucked it in.'

'You mustn't,' he said seriously. 'Don't you dare give up. I'll never speak to you again if you do. I liked it a lot. Now and then one of your characters said something and I found myself thinking, yes, that's so true, that's *right*.'

'I liked writing Max best.' Max was the villain.

'That touch of regret you put in at the end, when he confesses. The woman next to me had tears in her eyes.'

'I'm good at regret. I've had lots of practice.'

'Not as much as me, maybe.'

He looked weary today, she thought. 'How's Jeannette?'

'Not too good. Simon has mumps. My mother-in-law's staying over.'

'Poor Simon. And poor Jeannette. And poor you.'

'Don't waste your sympathy on me.' He tipped back his head, stretching his arms up. 'I've been looking forward to tonight for weeks.'

'Things must be awfully grim, then.' An automatically flippant Winterton response, and she had spoken without thinking, but she wished, seeing his expression, that she had chosen her words better.

'I thought I wasn't going to make it,' he said. 'Jeannette tried to cook Simon's tea and dropped a box of eggs on the floor. She can't grip properly. She was terribly upset. I had to spend ages calming her down.'

'You're very good, Daniel.'

'No, I'm not.' His eyes were sombre. 'All the time she was crying and telling me how useless she felt, I was having to force myself not to look at the clock. I was thinking, please stop crying so I can get out of the house, please stop crying so I don't end up missing my first night out in a month.' He shrugged. 'Jeannette's a kind person, a decent person. I'm not.'

'That's not true. You're lovely. I'm very fond of you, you know.'

'And I am of you, Charley.'

It gave her a warm feeling when he said that. Then he said quietly, 'I never loved her. Never.'

Shock, and then a flood of sympathy for him. She put her hand over his and he curled his thumb around her fist.

'We were only kids when we got married.' He gave a short, dry laugh. 'Jeannette was my first girlfriend. I wasn't in love with her – we were just having fun. And then we made a stupid mistake and we'll spend the rest of our lives paying for it. I like her and I respect her, but I don't love her. I'd never leave her. She's having such a miserable time and she never complains. If it was me, I'd be moaning all the time about how unfair it was. She's so good with Simon and he adores her, and I love to see them together. But every now and then I stand back and have a look at my life and think, how did this happen? How did I get here?'

'I'm sorry.' It was all she could think of to say.

He gave a lopsided smile. 'No, I'm sorry. This is your special night and I'm spoiling it, being a wet blanket.'

'Daniel, don't be silly.'

He looked at his watch. 'I'm going to have to go, I'm afraid. It's been fun.'

Outside, it was bitterly cold and the air was chill and musty, frost sheening the pavements. Only a few cars made their way along the streets.

Outside the Underground station, Daniel turned to her. 'What I'm trying to say is don't waste your chances. Make the most of your opportunities. I'll be rooting for you all the way.'

She hugged him. And then suddenly they were kissing. He held her close and his mouth explored hers and she wanted to go on kissing him and never stop. It was as if she was joined to him, becoming a part of him. The sounds of the city became inaudible and she was aware only of the taste and feel of him, the scent of his skin and hair and the urgency of his kisses.

When he drew away from her, she felt the loss of him, as if a space had opened up inside her. They parted, she running down the steps to the station, he heading for his bus. Sitting in the carriage, her lips felt bruised and her skin was sore with the rasp of his cheek. Her first kiss: she had passed through the barrier at last and longed to tell someone about it. She would have liked to have shouted it aloud as the train swooped through tunnels and shuddered to a halt at stations.

On the short walk home, she considered what would happen next. Maybe she and Daniel would simply remain friends but would kiss now and then in a sad, regretful way, never speaking of what might have been. Or maybe she would rent her own flat – she imagined somewhere bookish and bohemian near Russell Square – where they would conduct a discreet and passionate affair.

She let herself into the house. Louise and Gabe were in the sitting room. The radio was on; Gabe was eating a box of Black Magic and Louise was knitting.

Louise looked up. 'How did it go?'

Charley had forgotten the play. A quick mental readjustment was required before she said, 'So much better than last night. Such a relief.'

Gabe waved the box of chocolates at her. 'Help yourself.'

Charley chose a toffee. She had the sense of having interrupted something. She looked from Louise to Gabe.

'What? What is it?'

'You haven't heard?'

'Heard what?'

'About Anne.'

Her name always inspired in Charley a pang of guilt. 'What?' she said again. 'What's happened?'

'She's left Piers,' said Gabe. 'Mum told me. Your mum told her.'

Charley's elation vanished, like someone wiping steam from a window pane. 'Left him . . .'

'Yeah . . . awful, isn't it? She's gone to live with some friends of hers in Notting Hill.'

'Live with . . . You mean, for *good*?'

Gabe's blue eyes focused on her. 'I wouldn't know.'

'What about Eddie?'

'She's taken him with her.'

'Oh no. Poor Piers.'

'Piers?' said Gabe scathingly. 'I expect it was his fault.' She put another chocolate in her mouth.

'You don't know that, Gabe,' said Louise.

'No, but it probably was.'

'But they've only been married a year and a half!' Charley felt ill. 'And Eddie's still a baby!'

Anne had asked her whether it was true that Piers had married her to spite Aidan. She had said, I *can't stop thinking about it*. Charley knew that she was to blame, that it was her fault that Piers's marriage was coming apart. Her jealousy and resentment had sowed a seed of distrust in Anne. She must believe that Piers had never loved her. And so she had left him.

Louise and Gabe went to bed soon afterwards. Transfixed with misery and guilt, Charley remained in the sitting room. She had to talk to someone. She thought of Nate. It was late, but Nate never slept before midnight, so Charley phoned the Sinclairs' house.

Nate answered the phone. 'How did the play go?'

'Fine.'

A rustling over the line; she imagined him taking a fag out of a packet. 'Is that it, *fine*? Charley, are you okay?'

'Anne's left Piers.'

'Seriously?' The click of a lighter. 'I mean, properly left him, not just got fed up with him for the annoying bastard he is, but walked out on him sort of left him?'

'Yes. And it's my fault, Nate!'

372

A pause. She imagined him digesting this and recollecting that awful evening at Marsh Court when they had quarrelled on the bank of the estuary, and then thinking what a terrible person she was.

But he said, kindly, 'Charley, it isn't.'

'It is. It's because of what I said to her, I know it.'

'No. Wives don't leave husbands because someone says something tactless. It takes a lot more than that.'

She snuffled, 'It can't have helped, though.'

'I'd imagine Anne's sick of playing second fiddle to Piers's obsession with pulverising Aidan to mincemeat.'

She didn't think he was completely right, and knew that somewhere along the line she had a responsibility, and that she needed to sort it out, but she felt a little better and said, 'How are you, Nate?'

'You'll be pleased to hear that I've stopped behaving like an idiot. I'm clean-living and pure of heart now, an altogether better person.'

'Well that's a relief.'

A pause, then he said, 'I was getting pretty sick of myself, and it occurred to me that other people might be getting sick of me too.'

'I'd never get sick of you, Nate. But I am fed up with the Water Board. I'm thinking of leaving. I've decided to concentrate on my writing.' She sounded pompous, she thought.

But Nate said, 'Good. About time,' and then they said goodbye and rang off.

That night, she lay awake for hours, thoughts stabbing through her head from different directions. The play and the kiss and Anne. She knew that the play hadn't been as good as Daniel had kindly told her it was, that the plot had been derivative, a sort of watered-down Alfred Hitchcock, and the

373

construction saggy. There had been good bits, lines that she was proud of, but they had been scattered through the stodge like currants in a pudding.

She also knew that she and Daniel wouldn't have the discreet, passionate love affair she had imagined. Not only because Daniel wasn't someone who would be able to carry out that sort of deception, but also because she wouldn't let it happen. She knew she would never feel the thrill of his kiss again. If she had played some part in Piers and Anne's break-up, how much more at fault would she be if she had a love affair with a married man?

Daniel would continue looking after Jeannette and Simon because he was a good, loyal person. The thought that he might go on feeling trapped for the rest of his life made Charley feel desperately sad. He had told her that some things could not be repaired; though she still fought against believing that, she was dreadfully afraid he might be right.

However annoying Piers was, and even if Gabe was right and he was to blame, she hated to think of him alone in his horrible flat. She knew she needed to make amends but didn't have the slightest idea how to; in fact, she didn't seem to have the slightest idea about anything much right now. Her own dislike of Anne seemed childish and unreasonable. She had fulfilled her promise to Nate to become a friend to Anne in only the most half-hearted way. Something else she must try harder at.

Part Four

The Causeway

1966

Chapter Fifteen

May–June 1966

When Piers had been a boy, his godfather Gillis Sinclair had taken him out to tea twice a year at Gunter's, a treat that he had looked forward to immoderately because he had been allowed to eat vast amounts of cake and ice cream. Since he had become an adult, the tradition had continued, though tea had metamorphosed into lunch, taken most frequently at Rules.

Gillis had phoned him the previous week and suggested a date. Piers had felt reluctant – the business was starting to pick up and he had masses of work to do, and he had detected a certain flatness in his godfather's voice and so anticipated a difficult two hours during which he would have to keep cheerful conversation going to prevent the old boy veering into sentimental reminiscences about Aunt Blanche.

He accepted, though. His godfather had always been good to him. When Piers had been younger, he had admired Gillis tremendously: the war hero, the man who was equally at ease sailing a yacht, firing a gun and ordering a cocktail. At Blanche's funeral, he had felt sorry for him. Some of the life seemed to have been knocked out of the poor old devil. He wondered whether Gillis was feeling lonely.

His godfather was waiting for him in the restaurant. He had ordered champagne, as he always did: it had become their tradition. Piers didn't particularly like champagne, but it was far too late to tell Gillis that. They talked about politics, business and sailing while polishing off first oysters and then steak and kidney pudding.

Later, over coffee, Gillis said, 'I heard you left your wife.'

Piers shook his head. 'She left me.' The recollection of the day he had come home from work to find Anne and Eddie gone, their belongings packed up and taken away and a letter for him on the coffee table, still made him go cold with fury. What the hell did she think she was doing, walking out on him? They were *married*, for heaven's sake.

'Why? What did you do?'

Piers bristled. 'It wasn't my fault.'

Gillis gave him a thoughtful look. 'Sure about that?'

'Yes,' he said stiffly. 'Of course.' He scowled at his godfather. 'Who told you? Mum?'

Gillis shook his head. 'Not at all, it was your Aunt Jane. Came across her in Claridge's, getting pie-eyed on vodka martinis.' He gave his old, wicked smile. 'I kept her company for a while.' Then his expression altered. He took out his cigarette case and offered it to Piers. 'I spent the whole of my married life getting it wrong. Don't make the same mistake.'

'What do you mean?'

Gillis's sharp blue-grey eyes rested on him. Piers didn't care for the expression in them.

'I didn't realise how much I needed Blanche until she fell ill. Funny thing, in some ways those last few months were the best of our marriage. I'm a person who gets bored easily, who likes to move on to the next thrill. I think you're the same. Career, business, women . . . it didn't matter, I was always chasing after something. What a fool. What I needed was right there in front of me, but I hadn't the sense to see it until it was too late.'

A blink of the eye, as if a curtain had fallen, and Gillis became once more the affable, generous godfather. 'Here.' He shuffled in his pocket and produced an envelope. 'Buy something for your boy.'

After they had finished their drinks and cigarettes, they left the restaurant. They parted with a handshake and then Piers made for Notting Hill, where he was to pick up Eddie from Anne. Anne had phoned him, suggesting he take Eddie for an afternoon a week, which would give him regular time alone with his son and allow her to catch up on chores. Piers had agreed to look after the baby on Wednesday afternoons, half-closing.

He collected Eddie, the pushchair and a ludicrously large bag of nappies, clothing and baby equipment and took them home to the flat. Because money was still tight, he went on the Underground rather than taking a taxi, which he soon discovered was a mistake because of the steps and escalators. The train was busy and he ended up standing in a rattling, swerving carriage with Eddie howling because he didn't like the noise of the train. Or that was what Piers assumed; Eddie was almost a year old and couldn't explain why he was howling. Then the same thing in reverse at South Kensington, where he alighted with the baby tucked under one arm and the pushchair under the other and the bag hooked over his shoulder. People barged in front of him and brushed against him in their hurry to get up the escalator. He wanted to remonstrate with them but didn't, because of Eddie.

Back at the flat, he longed to sit down with a coffee and get his breath back, but a whiff told him that Eddie's nappy needed changing. Unpeeling the square of soiled cloth, he felt nausea rising in his throat but managed to choke it down and clean up his son. Then, like a comedy useless father, he stabbed himself with the nappy pin and yelled and sucked his thumb. Eddie seemed to think it was hilarious, and chortled and then peed over the clean nappy and the towel that Piers was changing him on. The flood soaked his vest and bootees as well, so in the end Piers dunked him in the bath while he searched for a plaster. Swivelling to try to reach Piers's razor on the edge of the bath, Eddie slipped and banged his head on the enamel and, after holding his breath for an alarmingly long moment, let out a tremendous scream. You're an idiot, Piers told himself, as he rescued the sobbing baby and, wrapping him up in a towel, tried to comfort him. An absolute bloody useless idiot.

Things calmed down eventually, and he dressed Eddie and sat with him on the sofa. They must have both dozed off, because when Piers next opened his eyes, the hands of the clock had moved round to half past four. Eddie's warm head was nestled against his shoulder, his knees bunched up against his chest. Piers kissed the fine thatch of white hair that covered Eddie's head. He was stabbed again, but this time with love for his son. He thought his heart might explode with love for him.

Then Eddie woke, crotchety and demanding. 'It's his grizzly time of day,' Anne had warned him. Piers had to make Eddie's tea of a mushed-up boiled egg and soft white soldiers with Eddie perched on his hip, because every time he tried to sit him on the floor with his toys, he whined. Most of the egg went over the floor and he dribbled his milk on his jersey, so Piers had to change him again.

After tea, unable to face the Underground, he took a taxi back to Notting Hill. 'How was he?' Anne asked, as he handed over Eddie and his belongings.

'Fine,' said Piers. And then, pricked by a need for honesty, 'Actually, it was bloody hard work. Exhausting. But fun, in a way.'

He went back to the flat. The bathroom was strewn with wet towels and cotton wool, the kitchen floor with egg. He made tea and toast and ate it in the sitting room with the radio on.

He missed them. The flat seemed empty without the two of them, empty and ugly and rather grubby, because no one was cleaning it these days. Not much of a home. If Anne had been there, she would have been making supper, badly and bad-temperedly because she always cooked badly and bad-temperedly, and Eddie would have been fussing, as he always did, before going off to sleep. Piers wouldn't have thought he would miss such ordinary events, but he did. Though he tried to conjure up some sense of justifiable anger with Anne for lying to him about Aidan, he couldn't quite manage it. He discovered that he didn't feel angry any more, only desperately sad. He wanted her to come home but couldn't see how to make it happen. He didn't even know whether she wanted to come home.

He put on his jacket to walk to the corner shop and buy something to eat, and found the envelope Gillis had given him inside his pocket. He opened it, expecting a cheque for twenty-five quid, his godfather's usual gift.

But he saw, startled, that this time the cheque was for a

381

thousand pounds. He stared at it, wondering whether the old boy had made a mistake – but no, it was all in order, signed and dated. He knew he should feel grateful, and he did, and relieved too because he would be able to pay off some of his debts, but he found that he felt troubled as well.

One Friday night, Gillis sailed *Sea Dancer* out of the Crouch estuary on the evening tide. The stars sketched patterns on the clear sky and the wind was fair. He knew these waters like the back of his hand, knew where the hazards were, the sandbanks and islands and old wrecks, sunk in the mudflats. Once, he had come across a mine, marooned on a sandbank like an oversized rusty iron conker.

Sea Dancer was a sizeable boat to sail single-handed, but he was used to her and knew what she could do. They had known each other for twenty years and were old friends. And he had always loved to sail alone, especially at night. There weren't many other vessels out, and it seemed, by the time he reached the open waters of the North Sea, that he had the whole vast expanse to himself. He turned off the outboard motor and set the sails. A sense of peace as he looked up at the sky and felt the rise and fall of the waves beneath the boat's hull and heard the soft thwack of the wind in the canvas. He was tired and out of sorts, hadn't really been himself for some time now, and was relieved that his beautiful, elegant *Sea Dancer* more or less did the work herself.

Gillis unscrewed his flask and drank a mouthful of whisky. You could have measured out his life in boats, from the little dinghy of his childhood to his father's yacht, sold after his bankruptcy, and then, during the war, the corvettes and destroyers and MTBs he had taken in to the Danish coast secretly at night. And the great flotilla of ships that had made possible the evacuation of the remnants of the British Expeditionary Force in the summer of 1940. Whatever his failings, he had taken part in that, and could feel pride in it.

But Dunkirk made him think of Morgan, and his fleeting calm vanished and was replaced by the jittery anxiety that had dogged him since Juliet had told him that the Welshman had reappeared. Morgan had telephoned him at his office the day after Juliet had spoken to him in London. He had left Gillis no choice but to meet him and pay him off.

Morgan had demanded money in exchange for keeping quiet about Thea. Gillis had given him enough to make him go away and prayed that he would use the cash to drink himself to death. But he hadn't, damn him, and a month later the Welshman had contacted him again. 'I want to buy a house,' he had told Gillis. 'I've found a nice little cottage near Swansea. I need to put down a deposit.'

Gillis had written out a cheque. Blanche had by then been desperately ill, and the thought of David Morgan speaking to a reporter, or worse, to one of the family, had appalled him.

He hadn't seen Morgan again until after Blanche had died. He had come out of the house one day and had glimpsed him on the far side of the square, his nemesis, and had known then that the man would never let him go. What a fool he had been ever to entrust him with his secrets, and what a fool he had been to believe that the bond created during their time in the navy would keep him safe. There wasn't a scrap of loyalty or conscience in Morgan.

He had had a good run for his money but he knew that it had come to an end. He thanked God that Morgan had spoken to Juliet rather than to Blanche, and that Blanche had never known about Frances. The thought of Blanche made tears spring to his eyes. Leaning on the guardrail, he swallowed more whisky and looked down to where the waves smacked against the side of the boat. He wept, remembering her awful end. Six weeks before she had died, the cancer had gone into her spine, paralysing her. She had suffered terribly, poor Blanche, and he had been able to do nothing to help her. The doctors had been equally useless. Staunch Christian that she was, she had begged to be allowed to die. There were a lot of memories he found hard to live with, but that was the worst.

Slap, slap, slap: the water struck the side of the boat with hypnotic, rhythmic force. The wind was getting up. He had first gone into the North Sea in the April of 1940, on a bitterly cold night when the war in western Europe had been kicking off and his ship had been holed by a U-boat. Half a dozen sailors had pulled him out on to a life raft. He had never forgotten the shock of the icy waves. The taste of salt in his mouth and a slow paralysis creeping through his body. Before then, he had always assumed that he would fight death until the last breath was squeezed out of him, but he had learned that night something different about himself. A few minutes longer and he would have given himself up to the cold, would have closed his eyes and spread out his arms and let the tide take him. And he wouldn't have minded all that much.

He felt more clear-headed now than he had for months. The girls were both well set up and would help Nate keep an eye on Rory. After Blanche had died, Gillis had redrafted his will, leaving Nate the London house and setting up a trust fund for Rory. The Wiltshire house he had left jointly to Claudia and Flavia. He assumed they would sell it.

Morgan had become a parasite, a monster. These days, Gillis's heart pounded at every ring of the telephone and every knock at the door. The waiting had worn him down to almost nothing, and the knowledge that Morgan could at any time he chose to destroy his life was not to be borne. The last time he had seen Morgan he had threatened him with the police – blackmail was a crime, after all – but the Welshman had laughed in his face. 'We both know you won't do that,' he had said. 'What I've done wrong would make a paragraph on an inside page. But the wrong you've done would be splashed all over the headlines.'

He and Blanche had spent lavishly throughout their marriage – the two houses, the skiing holidays and fortnights in the south of France, school fees, cars, weddings, and the entertaining and charitable donations that had been so important to Blanche. They had never saved. The two houses and a small portfolio of investments were his capital; what cash he had was fast draining away. If he lived till he was eighty, Morgan would still be there, hounding him, squeezing him dry, the living embodiment of a decision he had made on the spur of the moment twenty years before. A moment of cowardice, a moment of optimism; he could no longer be sure.

It wasn't that he didn't deserve this reckoning, but he had to think of his children, of their futures. His own father's bankruptcy had forced him to start from scratch, without a penny, and his early years, before he had married Blanche, had been marked by struggle. He wouldn't inflict the same difficulties on his own sons. He wouldn't let their lives be tainted by his shame. He might deserve it; they didn't.

He swallowed the remainder of the whisky as he gazed out to sea. It no longer looked serene, but black and menacing.

The thought of losing himself in that vast darkness horrified him. Funny how you clung on to life even when it no longer had any savour. Gillis screwed the top back on the flask and put it in his pocket, and stood for a while watching the rise and fall of the waves.

A last check of the steering equipment. He patted *Sea Dancer*'s mast, as if to thank her. Then he went back to stand at the guardrail. It hadn't been a bad life, really, except for these last sour years. No regrets, though. The places he had been, the things he had done, the women he had loved: he had no regrets. He had never believed in having regrets.

It was the end of May, the Whitsun holidays, and Juliet was staying for a long weekend with her friend Olwen on the Sussex Downs. Olwen, who had once taught French at the Maldon prep school where Juliet taught art, had set up her own school, Merivel Hall, near Lewes. The school took in pupils that other institutions found difficult to deal with – the disruptive, those who struggled with reading and writing, as well as children who found it hard to fit into school life.

That Saturday, the weather was fine, so Juliet offered to accompany half a dozen pupils and one of the teachers, Miss Hewitt, on a hike across the Downs. The girls, whose parents lived too far away for them to come home at half-term, were working towards earning their Guide badges.

The walk successfully completed, they were ushering the tired pupils back along the narrow roads towards the school when they passed a village newsagent. The girls went in to buy ice lollies.

Miss Hewitt and Juliet waited outside. Miss Hewitt talked about her fiancé, who was in the army.

'I'm not sure I'll like Cyprus. Trevor says it's awfully hot.

I get prickly heat and I'm not much of a swimmer. Where are those girls?' Miss Hewitt sounded fretful. 'I hope they're not buying cigarettes. I wouldn't put it past Denise Adams.'

Juliet offered to hurry them up. Inside the shop, the girls were unpeeling the paper from ice lollies and looking at the comics on the counter.

A headline on the evening paper caught Juliet's eye. *MP's Yacht Found Run Aground.* When she glanced at the article beneath, the name of the yacht, *Sea Dancer*, sprang out at her. *Sea Dancer* was Gillis's yacht. Fred Brandon had built her at his yard on Mersea Island. Her heart pounding, she fumbled for change in her purse and bought a paper.

Outside, it seemed colder. She told Miss Hewitt that she wanted to make a phone call from the box on the corner; the teacher and the girls should head on without her. When they were gone, Juliet climbed a stile into a field and sat down on the grass. She needed to be alone while she read the article.

Gillis was missing at sea. They had found his yacht grounded off Shoeburyness. He had taken *Sea Dancer* out late on Friday evening from the marina at Burnham-on-Crouch. No one else had been on board. The article didn't say much more, only that the coastguards and lifeboats were searching for him.

She sat on the grass, trying to absorb the news. Blanche first, and now Gillis; those poor children. It was hard to comprehend. Gillis was an experienced seaman. He wouldn't just fall off a boat into the North Sea. She couldn't help thinking there was some sort of mistake, that she would go back to the school and make a phone call and he would have turned up and everything would be all right. She remembered the dinghy. Something must have gone wrong with the yacht and Gillis would have taken to the dinghy. Sooner or later, the lifeboat would find him.

She walked back to Merivel Hall. Olwen, who was waiting for her in the hall, told her that Charley had been trying to reach her.

Charley was at the Sinclairs' house. 'Mum, it's so awful,' she said. She sounded shaken. 'Poor Nate. Poor Rory.'

Juliet asked her about the dinghy. It had still been attached to the yacht, Charley told her, and Juliet's heart gave a disquieting thud.

'The yacht had drifted on to a sandbank,' Charley said. 'Nate asked whether there was anything wrong with it, but no one's told him anything yet.'

'When did they find it?'

'This morning. Nate said he'd offered to go sailing with Uncle Gillis but Uncle Gillis said he was taking out some men from the yacht club. But he didn't, Mum, he went out on his own.'

'Maybe he changed his mind,' said Juliet. But she found herself thinking of the raw sound of Gillis's weeping at Blanche's funeral.

'I'm coming to London,' she said. 'I'll be with you in a couple of hours.'

She packed, and Olwen drove her to the station at Lewes. At Brighton, she changed trains for the London line. It had been a shock to hear that the dinghy had still been attached to the yacht. She wondered whether Gillis had slipped and fallen overboard. If so, he must already have been in the sea for some considerable time. No one could survive an extended period in the icy North Sea, not even a man as strong and fit as Gillis.

She walked from Victoria station to St James's. It was still light, and the park looked green and mysterious. A few tourists were peering through the gates of Buckingham Palace.

As she rang the doorbell, she tried not to think of the many other occasions when she had come to the Sinclairs' house, the dinners and cocktail parties and family celebrations. She tried not to think of the deception she and Gillis had carried out for so many long years. So much of what had taken place in the past now seemed shabby and futile.

Nate answered the door. They embraced, and she felt the tautness of his frame beneath her arms.

'I'm so sorry, Nate. So dreadful. Have you heard any more?'

He shook his head. Then he said in an undertone, 'Rory still thinks the phone's going to ring and it'll be him. He's such an idiot.'

They went into the kitchen. Charley was standing at the stove, stirring a pot. Gillis's elder daughter Flavia was laying the table. They kissed.

'Toby's away so Claudia can't come till tomorrow because of the children,' Flavia explained.

Rory was poring over a map of the Essex coastline, spread out over one end of the table. 'Perhaps Dad overshot the estuary when he was coming home in the dark,' he said.

'It was a clear night,' said Nate. 'Stars. Moon.'

'Here. It might have been cloudy there.'

'Oh, for God's sake,' muttered Nate.

'Let's fold up the map for now,' coaxed Flavia, 'so we have room to eat.'

Rory made a mess of folding it up so Nate snatched it off him and did it properly. Charley caught Juliet's eye.

'Do you have a bottle of wine, Nate?' asked Juliet. 'I think we could all do with a drink.'

Nate went off and came back with a bottle of burgundy. He opened it and poured out five glasses, including a small one for Rory.

They ate, and Juliet told them about the hike to fill some of the silences. Nate said little, but Rory chattered about his father, lifeboats and sea rescues. When they had almost finished the stew that Charley had made, Nate fetched another bottle of wine.

Rory pushed his glass towards his brother. 'Can I . . .?'

'No.'

'Nate.'

'Shut up.' Nate refilled his own glass and drank it quickly. 'That's not fair—'

'Isn't Tommy Cooper on the telly tonight?' interrupted Flavia. 'Come on, Rory, I adore Tommy Cooper, don't you?'

They went upstairs. 'Christ,' said Nate, gripping his head in his hands. 'Thank God.'

Charley squeezed his shoulder. Nate said angrily, 'Why can't he bloody well understand that he's dead? I told him about the dinghy. Why can't he see it?'

Because he doesn't want to, thought Juliet. Because he can't bear to.

Nate stood up, brushing off Charley's hand. 'Dad was a brilliant sailor. He was in the navy for years, for Christ's sake. He's sailed that coast hundreds of times.'

'But if something unexpected happened . . .'

Juliet backed Charley up. 'Gillis always used to say that the sea was unpredictable.'

'He would have launched the dinghy.' Nate sounded as if he had gone over it in his head countless times already. 'He would have launched the bloody dinghy.'

'Nate, you don't know.' Nate's words echoed all the questions in Juliet's own mind. She wanted to hug him again but he had a tense, don't-touch-me air. 'No one knows,' she said gently.

'He might have been taken ill,' said Charley. 'Didn't you say he was worried about his heart?'

Nate rested his spine against the dresser. Tiredly, he said, 'Perhaps. Yes, perhaps he fell ill.'

The phone rang and Nate went to answer it. Charley said, 'He doesn't mean to be horrid to Rory.'

'I know, darling.'

'It's just that he's so worried.'

'I know.'

Nate came downstairs. 'Someone from the constituency, that's all.'

Charley hugged him. Nate closed his eyes, cradling her against his shoulder.

He said, 'Sorry. I know I'm being foul. I'll go and check on Rory.'

Juliet and Charley finished clearing up the kitchen while the others remained upstairs, watching television. The house had a jangling, expectant air and the phone rang over and over again. After the kitchen had been sorted out, they left, bidding the Sinclairs goodbye. 'If there's anything I can do,' Juliet said, parting from the three of them, but the words, she reflected, had rarely sounded more inadequate.

Juliet phoned Joe from London and told him of Gillis's disappearance; he offered to pick her up from the station at Witham. He was her comfort, her consolation and her joy, and away from him, she yearned for him. She missed his slow smile and the way his eyes lit up when he looked at her. She missed his touch and the cool caress of his mouth on her skin and the pleasure that flowered inside her when they made love.

A few weeks earlier, when they had been walking beside

Mundon Creek, she had sketched him looking out to the estuary, shading his eyes with a hand. A pencil stroke for his long, straight back, a few more for his black hair, ruffled by the wind. Another curve or two to show the solidity of his shoulders and the shape of his lip. She had tried to capture his tautness, the way he always seemed to be on the brink of movement.

Her need for him broke into her thoughts while she was teaching and distracted her with a sudden soaring of the heart while she was sending out reminders for this summer's concert series. The possibility of joy had returned to her life since she had met Joe. Sometimes she had found her mind dancing, picturing futures for them: quiet evenings in that remote house of his, or journeys to London for a concert, or long walks on a shingle beach. Sunday mornings lazing in bed, reading the papers and making love. Or they might travel – to France, to Italy, or even to Egypt, a country about which they often talked.

But sitting in the railway carriage, these fantasies seemed to have thinned, like a length of cloth worn away, and soon her mind returned, shocked and finding no comfortable place to rest, to the events of the day.

He was waiting on the platform as the train pulled into the station. She half ran to him and looped her arms round his neck and kissed him, needing the comfort and warmth of him, careless of who saw. A neighbour was gawping at them. Juliet said a crisp good evening to her as they walked arm-in-arm from the station to the car.

When they were out of earshot, Joe said, 'Who was that?'

'Diana Warburton. Henry and I used to dine with her now and then. It'll be all round the district tomorrow that Henry Winterton's widow and Joe Brandon are seeing each other.'

'Do you mind?'

'Do you?'

'No, I'd prefer our relationship to be more open. It's more than two years since you were widowed, Juliet. That's a decent enough time. I'd like to meet the people you care most about. Your friends . . . your family.'

'I'd like them to meet you too. Joe, you're the best thing that's happened to me in years. It's been so wonderful and I don't want anything to hurt us. I'm afraid of something hurting us.' She gave a thin laugh. 'Sorry, it's silly of me.'

He kissed her again, a soft pressure of his lips against hers. 'You're tired, that's all, you've had a very difficult day. I'm so sorry about your friend.'

'It's awful, Joe. His poor children.'

'What was he like?'

'Clever. Handsome. Ambitious.' And self-seeking, she thought. And one of those people who, when they chose, could brighten up a room.

They got in the car and headed through the dark country lanes. Where the road narrowed, branches beat against the sides of the Rover. Sombre grey smeared the fields and copses. No street lamps out here in the countryside, and tonight not a scrap of moonlight.

She said baldly, 'Joe, I'm afraid it was suicide. I'm afraid Gillis killed himself.'

A quick, frowning glance. 'Darling, are you sure?'

She shook her head. 'No, I can't be sure.' Joe had not, she noticed, tried to buoy her up by telling her that Gillis might still be found alive; he knew the North Sea better than that.

'Do you know of any reason why he might have taken his own life?'

Plenty of reasons: guilt and grief . . . and fear, perhaps.

Morgan must have contacted him. What had passed between the two men, what threats, what promises?

'Gillis's wife died of cancer six months ago,' she said. 'It was utterly ghastly, poor Blanche. And I think he was worried about his own health.'

A vision of those evenings she and Henry and Gillis had spent at Marsh Court, talking late into the night, fluttered into her head. They seemed so long ago. Different times, and perhaps they had been different people then.

'Gillis was Henry's friend long before he was mine,' she said. 'He charmed Henry, and very few people were capable of that.'

'Not you?'

'No, not me. I only had the knack of annoying him. I don't think I was much good at being married. I don't think I had the knack of it.'

'Is there a knack?'

'Yes, I expect there is.'

He took her hand, squeezed it. 'All that's past now. You can start again.'

Could she? Though she ached with tiredness, at his words a wave of relief ran through her, the first grain of comfort in too long a day. Henry was gone, and now poor Gillis too. That chapter of her life, with all its secrets, grief and regrets, was closed and need never trouble her again. Frances Hart and her lost daughter Thea, and her own betrayal of Blanche – all these things she could put behind her.

Joe was right, she told herself. She would grieve for Gillis and then she would start again.

They found Gillis's body three days later, washed up on the coast near Canvey Island. The post-mortem confirmed that he had died of drowning. By then the rumours had started, sly insinuations in newspaper articles that emphasised his naval background and his expertise as a yachtsman. A 'friend' spoke of the setbacks that Gillis had endured in his career, and the recent death of his wife.

Jane confided in Juliet that Gillis had asked Peter's advice in choosing a heart specialist. Through Charley, Juliet learned that Nate had been questioned by the police about his father's mood at the time of the incident. Had he money worries? Did he drink heavily? She thought of David Morgan. *You won't hear anything more of Morgan*, Gillis had said to her. *I promise you, Juliet.* And she hadn't. So Gillis had dealt with his old naval comrade, one way or another. But at what cost?

But the coroner released the body for burial after giving a verdict of accidental death. The following week, mourners gathered on the gravel path in front of the small Wiltshire church before the funeral service. It had rained earlier that morning, and the leaves of holly and yew gleamed. The Winterton family had turned out in force to celebrate the life of Gillis Sinclair, their old friend and Piers's godfather. Charley and Louise were talking to the Sinclair boys. Jane and Claudia were standing beside the porch; Claudia was blowing her nose. Piers was deep in conversation with Flavia; Gabe and the twins, a little late, were hurrying down the gravel path to the church.

In the dark, dripping trees to one side of the graveyard, Juliet glimpsed a shadow, and her heart lurched. As she watched, David Morgan, with his dog, Bryn, prancing beside him, emerged from beneath the trees and moved through the churchyard towards the path.

She was transfixed with horror. Morgan's gaze swivelled to her, and she registered the challenge in his eyes. Murmuring apologies to the politician she had been talking to, she quickly crossed the grass.

'What are you doing here?' she hissed.

The dog, twitchy and excitable, nosed at a gravestone. 'I came to pay my respects,' said Morgan. 'Like you, Mrs Winterton.'

Rage boiled up inside her. 'You drove Gillis to his death! You!'

'Oh, I don't think that's true. I'd say he did it to himself. But let's not quarrel about that. You and I need to have a little chat.'

'I've nothing to say to you.'

When he moved closer to her, she found it hard not to recoil from him. She smelled his breath, and saw the yellow hue to the whites of his eyes and the crazing of purple veins on the sides of his nose. She remembered Gillis telling her that Morgan was a drinker.

'Might want to think about that, Mrs Winterton,' he said softly. 'Gillis may be dead, but I still know your secrets. Told the family, have you, about what the two of you got up to in those hotel rooms?'

She felt a surge of nausea. How did Morgan know that? She remembered what Gillis had told her: *he worked for me after the war.* Perhaps Gillis, hurried and overburdened with his parliamentary work, had given Morgan the task of booking the hotel rooms he had chosen for their assignations . . . and perhaps Morgan had waited outside to see who Gillis was meeting, watching, stowing up information that might be useful to him in the future.

Out of the corner of her eye she glimpsed the mourners moving slowly into the church. Piers was coming across the grass towards her.

'I have to go,' she murmured.

396

A scrap of paper was thrust into her hand. 'Call me,' Morgan said.

Then the dog ran off, barking loudly, racing through the copse to the open fields. 'Damn you,' growled Morgan, and then, shouting, 'Bryn, heel now, sir!' he strode away after him.

Piers called out, 'Mum?' and she turned to him.

'Mum, are you all right?'

'Yes, of course, I'm fine.' But she was trembling; she forced a smile on to her face.

'Who was that man?'

'No one. He'd lost his way, that was all, and was asking for directions.'

They went inside the church. Charley had kept them a space on the pew beside her. The vicar spoke and the congregation rose to sing a hymn. After the hymn ended, the eulogies were given. As a parliamentary friend reminded the mourners of Gillis's efforts before the war to waken the country to the threat posed by Hitler's Germany, Juliet opened her handbag and, using the pretext of searching for a handkerchief, glanced at the piece of paper that Morgan had given her. A telephone number was written on it. She stuffed it into the zipped compartment and closed the bag.

A naval officer was speaking of Gillis's courage fighting in occupied Europe. He quoted Homer – *Like that of leaves is a generation of men* – and the words brought tears to her eyes. Think of the flickering patterns of light reflected through the branches of the trees outside on to the old stone floor, she told herself. Think of the musty church smell, overlaid by a woolly fug of wet coats and umbrellas. Don't think of the night of the storm, and don't think of Morgan saying, *told the family, have you, what the two of you got up to in those hotel rooms?*

397

And yet in spite of the horror of her encounter, the voice of the naval officer was soothing, and an unexpected calm drifted over her. Memories flooded back, memories of the handsome, golden young man she had met for the first time on that long-ago autumn day. Of the lover, passionate and complex, a man of extraordinary talents and qualities that had not always seemed to knit together, and of the flawed hero, perennially disappointed by his failure to fulfil his early promise, who had squandered what faculties he had been blessed with through greed and egotism. Because that had been his failing, poor Gillis, that he had believed he could have everything, and it must have been a bitter lesson that stormy night on the Blackwater to discover he could not.

Someone was missing in the church today. Gillis had fathered three sons and three daughters. His four legitimate children were sitting side by side in the front pew. Edmund Hart had perished in the Blackwater, but somewhere out there, Thea still lived, ignorant of the fact that they were burying her father today. And only Morgan and Juliet herself knew the truth.

Chapter Sixteen

June 1966

Freya had bought a new frock for her private view at the World's End Gallery and was having second thoughts about it. It was short and red; you wouldn't, she thought grimly as she tugged the zip, miss her in a crowd. She should have bought something grey or brown, so she could sink into the background.

In her bedsit in Holborn, pulling on stockings and slipping on heeled shoes, she was convinced she had made an awful mistake. What if no one came to the exhibition? What if, though she had nagged them, her friends didn't turn up? With only an hour before it opened, she found herself imagining the scene: trying to make conversation with the gallery people while they made small talk to cheer her up when not a single person appeared. What if people paused to look at the photograph displayed in the window and then walked away? She should never have agreed to this. She felt exposed, anticipating a painful rebuff. Her work was a part of her, and any rejection of it felt the same as a rejection of her. Some people thought anyone could take a photograph: you just pointed the camera and clicked.

Pull yourself together, Freya, and stop being so feeble. She put on some lipstick and brushed on a little mascara, peering at her reflection in her hand mirror. Then she twisted her hair into a knot and secured it with a tortoiseshell comb, all the while lecturing herself sternly. There was little point creating anything if no one ever saw it. Fear of rejection was a form of vanity. She should be grateful to Aidan, Anne and Katherine, who had made this happen, instead of threatening to fall apart because of a bad attack of nerves.

It had been Anne Winterton who had persuaded Katherine Rose, the gallery's owner, to put on the exhibition. Anne was married to Aidan's cousin Piers, though she was now separated from him. Freya had realised a long time ago that Aidan was in love with Anne. He had not told her that he was, but then she had not needed him to because Aidan was easy to read. It added to Freya's apprehension about the evening, the fact that Aidan was in love with Anne. Because she, Freya, was in love with Aidan.

She hadn't meant it to happen. When you lacked certain things, when you lacked a history, as she did, you had to compensate for it. You had to make yourself become someone. She had always had ambitions and had seen early on how love might get in the way of them – had seen, also, that it was harder for a girl. Freya's school friend Linda, who had intended to train to become a dentist, had been in the Lower Sixth when she had discovered she was pregnant. Married at seventeen, a baby at eighteen, and the little family of three now living in two rooms in a damp house in a ropy part of Oxford. Then there was Tessa, who had worked in the office across the corridor from Freya at the hospital. Tessa had had an affair with a married consultant; after he had broken it off, she had stopped eating and had grown thinner and thinner. The last Freya had heard of her, she had been confined to a mental hospital near her parents' house in Manchester.

So love, Freya had concluded, was best avoided. Though she knew, theoretically, that the path of love might run smoothly – her parents, for instance, had been childhood sweethearts – often as not, it didn't work out that way. Freya had been attracted to Aidan Winterton the first time she had met him, on the causeway to Thorney Island. She had appreciated his tall handsomeness and the warmth of his chestnut-brown eyes and the seriousness with which he had spoken to her about her work. She had asked him for his name and address. What would she have done if she had known about Anne back then? She would have said a breezy goodbye and thanks for reminding me about the tide coming in and made sure never to see him again.

So: there had first been attraction. You could recover from attraction, but friendship had quickly followed, and it was far harder when you liked someone as well, when you knew you could talk to them about anything and they were kind and generous and interested in the same things you were. And when seeing them made your heart beat faster and a warmth flower at the core of you.

Attraction and friendship had made a heady mix that threatened to bubble up into something stronger. She, who was careful about love, had become rash. She had felt herself slipping into something beguiling, something she wanted to last.

And then Anne had left Piers. Freya had seen a flicker of triumph in Aidan's eyes when he had told her. It was obvious to Freya that Anne was still in love with Piers. Freya understood this, but Aidan didn't seem to, yet. Aidan was capable of stubbornness, and saw changing his mind as a weakness.

He didn't want to accept that Anne would always love Piers, yet surely he must, sooner or later?

As she checked that her purse and lipstick were in her handbag, locked the door of her bedsit and ran down the stairs, her confidence returned. Even if only one person came to the show, and that person liked her work, then that would do. She was only twenty-four years old and still had plenty of time to prove herself.

Walking to the Underground station, it occurred to her that she couldn't remember when she had last had the dream. The dream of the causeway had haunted her since childhood. Sometimes it came to her when she was tired or anxious or unsure where her life was going. It was always the same: a dark sky and black, choppy water rushing over a narrow, sweeping path that crossed from one side of a river to the other. There was a strip of shoreline beneath her feet and fields and hedges on the far side of the river. The landscape was brooding rather than frightening. There were no people and nothing ever happened, and the only movement was the running water. It unsettled her simply because of its repetitive nature.

She had started taking photographs of causeways because of the dream. She couldn't tell why it had locked itself in her head. Most of the time she was convinced that it was a dream, though it crossed her mind that it might be a memory. She must have visited more than twenty causeways before coming to Thorney Island. As soon as she crossed the path between the riverbank and the island, she felt a thrill of recognition. There were the fields, there were the marshes, and there was the causeway, transcribing the same arc as the one in her dream. It was a strange thing, to dream of a place she had never been to.

She had wondered whether they had holidayed in the Maldon area when she was a child, but her father had assured her they had not. She could only assume that she had seen a photograph of the causeway, and that for some reason it had captured her imagination. But why that particular image – and why had it lingered so?

'Louise told me that Anne's working at the gallery again,' said Helen.

'Yes, for several weeks now.'

It was Friday, late afternoon, and Helen and Juliet were on the London train to attend the private view of Freya Catherwood's exhibition. Juliet hadn't wanted to come. Another long journey, the second in a week, and Gillis's funeral only three days earlier, and the fear she had felt talking to Morgan in the churchyard, all snarled in a knot beneath her breastbone.

But the event had been long planned and Helen was keen to attend, to support Aidan and Freya. Juliet had weeks ago agreed to come along to keep Helen company so she wouldn't have to travel alone. But she was not looking forward to the evening.

She had not yet phoned Morgan. She could not decide what to do. She knew that if she phoned him, he would ask her for money. She had no idea how much. She didn't have a lot in her bank account, only the monthly income from her small annuity and the modest sum she earned from teaching. She was afraid that if she paid Morgan off once, he would come back again and again and again, a parasite leeching the blood out of her.

And though this was not a family event, family would be there, and these days the mixture felt combustible. The disintegration of the family and Morgan's appearance at Gillis's funeral – her thoughts darted constantly between these seemingly insoluble problems.

Juliet put her raincoat on her lap so that a passenger entering the carriage could sit down. 'She's working part-time,' she told Helen. 'The two girls she's living with look after Eddie when she's at the gallery. They all take turns looking after each other's children, so they can go out to work.'

'You've been to the house, haven't you?'

'Quite a few times.' Juliet wrinkled her nose. 'It's rather dreary, I'm afraid.'

The Notting Hill house in which Anne was staying had, when Juliet had first visited it, appalled her. It smelled of mildew and wet laundry and managed to be steamy and chilly both at the same time. The window frames were rotten, and chunks of plaster were missing from the ceilings. With three very young children living there, the rooms were cluttered with drying nappies, half-eaten biscuits and plastic toys. The sitting room had been, Juliet felt, particularly depressing, the sofa and ill-matched armchairs worn through to the wadding and one wall covered by a crude mural of a rainbow in a blue sky above a hill dotted with white flowers and blotchy green trees.

Anne was a fastidious woman and Juliet wondered how she was able to bear it. But then, looking after a baby could be a lonely business, especially if your husband worked long hours. She assumed that the shared house offered Anne companionship. The three women's equal participation in the care of the children had also meant that she had been able to return to the work she loved.

Juliet continued in a dogged way to try to bring the

404

separate factions of the family together, but without success. She had remonstrated with Piers and pleaded with Anne. Because Piers blamed Aidan for the break-up of the marriage, she largely avoided speaking of the matter to Helen. Helen would naturally side with Aidan, while Juliet herself felt both men to be in the wrong. Though she didn't for a moment believe that Anne had had an affair with Aidan, and had strenuously told Piers so, she felt angry with Aidan for having allowed the situation to develop. There was an innocence about Anne that Juliet suspected Aidan had taken advantage of. And she could not help but feel obliged to defend Piers. He was her son, after all.

It had put up a barrier between her and Helen and it depressed her to feel that they were not as close as they once had been. She was afraid that the rift in the family might never be repaired. She was afraid that Anne might one day decide to return to San Francisco, taking Eddie with her.

She tried to alter the path of the conversation. 'Has Aidan known Freya long?'

'They met on the day of Henry's funeral.'

Juliet dug back into her memory. She recalled Aidan walking away from the bonfire and along the path by the estuary. The swollen sky, the scattering of snow, and Piers lashing petrol from the can to fuel the flames.

'Are they friends or are they dating?'

'Aidan says they're just friends.'

'But you . . .?' she prompted delicately.

Helen unwrapped a bar of Fry's Chocolate Cream from her handbag and offered a piece to Juliet. 'It wouldn't surprise me if something more came of it. They're well suited. They're both artistic, of course, and they love being out in the open air. Freya's stayed with us a couple of times when they've been visiting the bird reserves on the east coast. She's perfectly pleasant, good-mannered and well-spoken. A lively girl. After she's left the house, you feel a fresh wind has blown through it. Pretty, too, such gorgeous colouring: pale skin and the sweetest freckles, and rather wonderful red hair, so divine.'

Juliet, who had known Helen for a long time, sensed reservations. Helen, searching in her handbag for her powder compact, went on, 'Aidan told me that she's adopted. I know it's unfair, but I can't help feeling *doubtful*. One always wonders about adopted children, doesn't one? Family is so important, and one does like to know where a person's come from.' She peered in her compact mirror and dabbed powder on her nose. 'They're staying with me this weekend. The whole brood will be there, Lou's Josh, too.'

'You'll enjoy that, won't you?'

'Oh yes. So quiet when they're in London. The house feels alive again.'

The conversation moved on to other matters and then the train stopped at Manor Park and four more passengers crushed into the carriage, preventing any further possibility of real discussion. Juliet glanced out of the window. They were travelling through rows of houses with narrow back gardens, interspersed between factories and gasworks. White mops of viburnum and the drooping crimson heads of peonies were bright against sooty brickwork. She had not seen Joe since before Gillis's funeral. She supposed this was a busy time of year at the farm – and perhaps he was taken up with the charity, or with that handsome, idle boy, Neville Stone. Honesty shone out of Joe, it was his defining characteristic. She had evaded telling him the truth over and over again, and in doing so had kept a large part of her life from him, a part that had moulded her, and was still moulding her. Without Gillis, and without all that had followed from their love affair, she would be a different person.

Should she tell him about Morgan? If she did, what would he say? Her secret was like a slick of oil on a clear river, seeping into every clean and unsullied place. Should she tell the family the truth? Should she tell Charley and Nate that their parents had had a love affair? Or Piers, who was Henry's son and Gillis's godson, that the one had betrayed the other for a decade? Or let the Sinclair children know that their father had cheated on their mother, over and over again? Would she allow herself to be forced to do these things by this worm of a man who had already destroyed Gillis? No: with every heartbeat, every drop of blood coursing through her veins, she rejected the thought.

And yet the past pressed in on her, so close it seemed about to pierce through the barriers with which she had surrounded herself. She felt it now, squeezing her, jostling at her, producing in her the beginnings of a claustrophobic panic, just as the crowded compartment did.

Aidan caught sight of Freya as he entered the gallery. She was wearing a red dress and had swept her orange marmalade curls into a knot on the top of her head.

She kissed his cheek. 'I hate these things,' she murmured to him. 'I don't know why I do them.'

'So that some day you'll be rich and famous.' He glanced at the display of photographs. 'They look fantastic.'

She smiled and seemed to relax a little. 'Katherine and Anne have done a marvellous job.'

'And so have you.'

Freya was often quick to run herself down. You would have thought, looking at her, that she had boundless confidence, but Aidan knew that her lively, cheerful exterior concealed a great deal of self-doubt. There was an edginess about her tonight that told him she was finding the evening an ordeal.

The World's End Gallery was smart and fashionable and showed artists from all over the world. Maybe Freya felt daunted by its reputation. Her photographs were arranged along one wall of the long, narrow space. At the far end, behind Katherine's desk, was a huge enlargement of one of Aidan's favourite images, taken at Thorney Island. Structural and austere, it dominated the room.

A record of Vivaldi violin concertos was playing. Freya retreated to a corner with a glass of rosé, but as the guests began to arrive, she stepped forward to greet them. Aidan found himself willing people to come through the door. One or two . . . then half a dozen . . . and then suddenly the room was looking respectably full.

Anne went to Freya's side and murmured in her ear, then they made their way through the crowd to where a woman in a fur coat was walking slowly along the perimeter, studying the exhibits and writing in a notebook. Freya was a couple of inches taller than Anne, broader-shouldered and fuller-breasted. Anne was wearing a white blouse and a short black skirt. She had lost weight since she had left Piers and looked slight compared to Freya, washed-out almost. But then every other woman in the room looked pallid next to Freya. In her red dress, she moved like a flame through the gallery until, with Anne at her side, she stopped to talk to the woman with the notebook.

Aidan might have anticipated that he would have felt unmixed delight on hearing that Anne and Piers had separated, but he hadn't. His own role in the break-up troubled him. He had allowed Anne to go on believing that on the night she had come to his flat, he had fallen asleep shortly after she had, but that had not been the case. He could have woken her after half an hour or an hour, but instead he had let her sleep on. He had been motivated by pleasure that she had turned to him when she was feeling unhappy, and triumph in having discovered that she was at his flat without Piers's knowledge. And resentment, too, and a thirst for revenge. Nothing very creditable.

It disturbed him that Eddie no longer lived with his father. He and Louise had lost their father at too early an age for him to feel any satisfaction about that. He hadn't seen much of Anne since the break-up. When, once, he had asked her out for a drink, she had told him she couldn't get a babysitter. When he had suggested she bring Eddie to his flat, obviating the need for a babysitter, she had looked thoughtful and said, 'I don't think I should do that, Aidan. I don't think it would help.' Her colourless tone had told him that she was deeply unhappy. She had separated herself not only from Piers, but from Aidan as well. And if she was fed up with the pair of them, who could blame her? He had been sneaky and underhand. Often, he felt ashamed of himself.

During the past couple of months he had been taken up with trying to modernise Winterton's more antiquated functions. It turned out Piers had been right when he had accused the business of being stuck in the past. Profits were still declining, sales were down and costs up. Aidan knew that a change of direction was needed but hadn't the confidence to impose it. Design was moving on and Winterton's wasn't satisfying the current thirst for the new. He had talked to Esteban, their chief designer, but didn't like to press the point too much. Esteban was touchy, and if he took it into his

409

head that Aidan was implying that his work wasn't good enough, he might just storm off. And that would be disastrous: without Esteban, Winterton's might not survive.

He had had, in the end, little choice but to sack one of the shop assistants, who spent half his time smoking in the room where they made hot drinks and the rest of it, as far as Aidan could make out, at his bookmaker's. He had had his cousin Gabe, who managed the Sloane Street shop, at his side for moral support while he gave the man his notice. It was a miserable business and he had hated it. He recalled with shame that he hadn't been able to find the right words, and that in the end it had been Gabe who had, crisply and without emotion, told the man he was fired.

Since then, a tense atmosphere lingered in the Bond Street shop. Though the staff treated him with civility, they didn't chat to him any more. Uncle Henry used to greet his employees each morning with breezy comments that gave the impression of being in touch. *Beautiful day, Miss Burstein, you'll be able to get out in the garden this evening*, or *How's that boy of yours, Mr Lewis?* Aidan now did the same, receiving nods and smiles in response, as Uncle Henry had. He was turning into Henry Winterton, he thought miserably.

He took another glass of wine from a passing tray. Freya was laughing and talking animatedly. In her red dress and with her wild hair, she looked more like a goddess of the north than ever. The gallery was packed, guests crowding round the pictures and chatting to each other. More people were squeezing through the door and the evening had the buzz of a successful event. Aidan was delighted for Freya.

He caught her eye and she nipped back to his side. 'That was Sylvie Duvallier,' she whispered in his ear. 'You know, Anne's friend who's starting up an arts magazine. She says she's going to commission me to do some regular work for her.' Freya was fizzing with excitement.

Then his mother and Aunt Juliet arrived, along with Louise, Charley and Josh, talking of an incident at Sloane Street station, a madman tearing off his clothes while he ran down the escalator, and he was obliged to pay attention to them.

Juliet worked her way along the row of photographs until she reached the far end of the gallery, where a single enormous black-and-white image had been placed in the centre of the wall. It was captioned 'The Causeway at Thorney Island', but she knew that, had recognised the subject instantly.

There was the stretch of water that Joe had rowed her across when she had become stranded on the island, and there, somewhere, hidden by trees, was the house in which Frances Hart and her children had lived. There was the place where she had seen the two children playing, the little boy and the girl, Thea in her red dress. Four feet square, the photograph made a dramatic and arresting image, the causeway itself slicing across the composition like a knife cut.

'Do you like it, Aunt Juliet?'

She turned to see Aidan standing beside her. 'Very much,' she said.

That wasn't true. The image unsettled her and she disliked being in the same room as it. It was all too easy to imagine a little girl standing on the riverbank, or a boy wading after his toy boat as the river carried it away.

'Freya has a thing about causeways. That one,' Aidan nodded his head towards the picture, 'anyway. She dreams about it.'

'Really?' she said. 'How odd.'

Then she looked away. Her gaze explored the room,

searching through the crowd, until it alighted on Freya Catherwood's knot of bright red hair.

On the way home, in the railway carriage, she thought about what Aidan had told her. *Freya has a thing about causeways. That one, anyway. She dreams about it.* She wanted to ask Helen if she knew what he had meant, but Helen was dozing. Juliet herself had sometimes dreamed about the causeway, so why shouldn't Freya? Artists often became obsessed with certain scenes. Look how often Monet had painted his garden at Giverny. You couldn't account for it, the urge that made you draw something over and over again, as if you were trying to extract a truth from it. She herself must have painted the view from the sea wall dozens of times.

Freya Catherwood was adopted. A great many children were adopted, so there was nothing extraordinary about that. Thea Hart was on her mind because they had buried Gillis three days ago, and because of the threat embodied by Morgan. She was tired and overwrought and worried beyond endurance, and the evening had been difficult, the various members of the family standing apart from each other and failing to gel, and that was why her imagination was taunting her, making connections that didn't exist and telling her that Freya Catherwood might be Gillis's illegitimate daughter. Telling her that Freya Catherwood was really Thea Hart.

She had brought a Graham Greene with her to read on the train; she took it out of her handbag and opened it. But she couldn't concentrate. Freya's photograph imposed itself over the printed words, the slash of black that delineated the causeway tearing across the page. The rhythmic chug of the carriage wheels became the echo of Gillis's footsteps as he ran away from the island, the child concealed beneath his coat.

She put the novel away. She felt hot and unbuttoned her coat. She must be going down with something; yes, that was it, she was unwell, too much strain, and the worm of doubt that had entered her, standing in the gallery, was a symptom of her illness. Suspicion was like a virus, seeping into the bloodstream, spreading and flowering, unstoppable. But it was not *real*. It was a thought, a doubt, nothing more, and when she woke in the morning after a night's sleep, she would be able to brush it away.

Helen stirred; they were nearing Witham. They left the train and picked up the car. Juliet dropped Helen at her home in Maldon and then headed on to Marsh Court. The house felt chilly, and she kept on her coat as she filled the kettle and put it on the hob.

She stood at the window, looking out to the terrace. Beyond, garden, riverbank and estuary were lost in the night. She would prove to herself that she was wrong. She would remember every scrap of information she had ever been told about Thea Hart, and among it she would find a piece of evidence that would put her mind at rest.

If Gillis had still been alive she could have phoned him and talked to him about the girl. But Gillis was dead, drowned in the same waters that were presumed to have taken his daughter. There was, it had occurred to her, a sour justice in that. Gillis had told her that Thea had been four years old when her mother and brother had drowned. That would mean that she would now be about twenty-four years of age. How old was Freya? In her early twenties, Juliet estimated. What else had Gillis told her? That David Morgan had taken the child to an orphanage in Southampton. That Morgan had given the woman who ran it a false name for the child and told her that Thea was a foundling, orphaned during the war.

413

She recalled her own brief glimpse of Thea Hart, playing on the causeway to Thorney Island: the red dress, the slight, elfin figure. Had the girl had red hair, like Freya? She couldn't remember. No matter how hard she tried, she couldn't remember.

She took a sleeping pill and felt better when she woke in the morning, but as the day wore on, her uncertainty returned, pushing aside even her worries about Morgan. Her recollection of the day of Henry's funeral – the chill, opaque sky, the whoosh of petrol on the bonfire, and Aidan walking away to the causeway where he had met Freya – tormented her. Fact and supposition mingled together and she could not dismiss the possibility that Freya was Thea Hart. And if she was, what malign turn of the card had fated that day that Freya and Aidan should be brought together?

In the afternoon, she drove into Maldon, where she shopped at the market. Then she made her way to Helen's house. Aidan opened the door to her. The young people were in the sunroom; she sensed that she had interrupted their chatter, which started up again as soon as greetings had been exchanged. They were just back from a ten-mile walk, Louise told her. She had mud on her jeans, and Freya's hair stood out in a wild cloud around her face. The four of them were invigorated and laughing, joking with each other. Juliet felt that she was standing apart from them, that she no longer had any connection to them. Josh said something and Freya gave a loud howl of amusement. Quiet, a home girl: that was how Gillis had described Thea. She was mistaken, Juliet thought. She had to be mistaken.

Yet when Helen slipped out to the kitchen, Juliet drew Freya aside. She'd adored the exhibition, she said. She was thinking of buying a photograph. Could they talk?

They went out into the garden. A blackbird was singing in the branches of an apple tree, and the walled garden caught and concentrated the spring sunshine. Freya smiled. Had Juliet an image in mind? Which one had she liked best?

'The photo of Thorney Island was rather magnificent.'

'Thank you.'

'I'd like to know why you took it.' Her laugh sounded false to her. 'I paint a little myself, and it's always interesting to understand another artist's inspiration.'

Freya dug her hands into her trouser pockets and screwed up her eyes at the sun. 'It's rather odd.' A sideways glance at Juliet, as if taking the measure of her. 'I've dreamed about that scene for years and years, and then I found it.'

'Found it?' she echoed.

'There, at Thorney Island. It's as if I remember it, but I don't, I can't do, because I've never been there. So weird, the first time I went there, I recognised it. It looked just like my dream. I suppose the photographs were a sort of exorcism. Actually, I wondered whether they might be a way of making the dream stop.'

Raised voices, good-natured, flaring out from the sunroom. The knot of dread beneath Juliet's breastbone tightened, almost choking her.

'I don't understand.'

A shake of the head, red corkscrew curls flailing. 'Nor me, really. If I've been there before, my father says it must have been when I was very little, before I was adopted.'

Helen was standing at the door, calling to them. Juliet turned jerkily, unable to take in what she was saying. Something about coffee. Freya made to go back to the house, but Juliet grabbed her sleeve.

'How old were you when you were adopted?'

415

'Four. I was four years old.'

'How old are you now?'

A slight raise of the eyebrows: surprise at the question. 'I'm twenty-four.'

'May I ask . . .' She squeezed the words out like pips from a lemon. 'Do you know anything about your background? Do you remember anything?'

A shake of the head. 'Nothing at all. My father told me that I'd been placed in an orphanage.'

'Where?' Her voice scratched.

'Southampton.'

The sun blinded her, dizzied her. Gillis had told her that David Morgan had taken Thea Hart to an orphanage in Southampton.

Freya was still talking. 'Before that . . .' She raised her shoulders. 'I don't know anything. My parents came to the orphanage and chose me.' Tenderness in the girl's bluish eyes – were they Gillis's eyes? – and she smiled fondly. 'My father said that as soon as he and Mum saw me, they knew I was going to be theirs. I can't think why, because I was an ugly, scrawny little thing. And I didn't speak a word. The lady at the orphanage thought I wasn't right in the head. Four years old and I didn't say a word. If it had been me, I expect I'd have walked straight past and found a pretty little girl who chattered a lot. It was a miracle, my dad always says. They were waiting for me, and I was their miracle.'

Freya swept back a hank of hair from her face. 'I was trying to make the photo look like my dream. So the onlooker could see my dream.'

Then she spoke of exposures and focal lengths. Juliet didn't listen to her. Not a dream, she thought with horror, but a nightmare.

*　　*　　*

416

She must have drunk coffee with Helen, but had no memory of it; no memory either of the drive back to Marsh Court. At the house, she unpacked her shopping but seemed to have forgotten how to carry out the simple task and found herself staring at her pound of carrots, wondering what to do with it. She sat down at the kitchen table. She watched the small, involuntary tremor of her hands.

On the night of the storm, Gillis had found his little daughter in the house on Thorney Island, hiding in the cupboard on the landing. He had smuggled her off the island to the cottage at Marsh Court, from where, sometime in the night, Morgan had taken her away. He had driven Thea to the orphanage in Southampton, with money and instructions that she was to be put up for adoption. The girl had been speechless, the consequence, presumably, of shock. *She didn't say a word all that time*, Gillis had said when he had finally told Juliet the truth about the events of that night. Freya had used almost exactly the same words when describing her own muteness. That had been the moment when Juliet had felt certain that Freya Catherwood was Gillis's missing daughter.

The Catherwoods had adopted the child and brought her up as their own. Freya – Thea – claimed to have no memory of her life before the adoption, but she was mistaken. Something of her past remained: a recurring dream of the causeway on which she and her twin brother had played when they were small children. The image had haunted Freya because of the forgotten traumas that had occurred there, staying with her into adulthood and driving her to find out whether it actually existed. And so, on the afternoon of Henry's funeral, she had come to the Blackwater, where Aidan had met her.

Lulu was sitting by the kitchen door, panting optimistically.

Juliet fetched her lead and let herself out of the house. Since the afternoon, clouds had covered the sky and the sun, dulling the landscape. Once, in Winterton's, she had tried on a necklace of grey pearls. Henry had taken them out of a cabinet and clasped them round her neck. They hadn't suited her complexion and had soon been put away, but she recalled their hard gleam now. She was surrounded by the same cheerless, unreflective shade, enclosed by river and sky like an insect trapped between paper and glass.

She was walking to the causeway, walking to the place that had taken Frances Hart and her son, and where Gillis had made his fateful decision to conceal the survival of his daughter. To the pathway that had haunted her since the day she had glimpsed Edmund and Thea Hart playing there. It was hard to raise her eyes and look around her. Who might she see? The children, playing in the shallows? Or Morgan, watching her from the riverbank?

Impossible to try to tell herself that it didn't make any difference, that Freya Catherwood was nothing to do with her and Joe or the rest of them. Impossible to try to convince herself that Freya might slip out of the lives of the Winterton family as easily as she had come into it. She knew it wouldn't do. It wouldn't surprise me if something more came of it, Helen had said to her when they had talked about Freya and Aidan on the train. They're well suited. If Freya and Aidan were to become more than friends, how then would Juliet bear it, seeing her and knowing what she did? What new evidence might come to light, what letters from the orphanage or recollections of Freya's adoptive father, that might lead to questions, answers?

Back at the house, she went through the motions of thinking about supper and pouring herself a drink. She had put two and two together; one day, someone else might do the same. Someone might mention the tragedy at Thorney Island to Freya, who, out of curiosity, might read the same newspaper articles she herself had studied in Maldon library after Joe had told her about Gillis and Frances Hart. It might strike Freya that although the boy had been found, the girl's body had never been recovered. And she might wonder.

She opened a can of sardines, sliced bread for toast. She remembered the time in the early years of the war when the estuary had frozen over. Out walking the dog, she had tried to cross the bridge of ice to the island. But the thaw must have set in without her realising it, and under her weight, cracks had flowered through the grey-white sheeny surface and what had seemed solid had begun to shift and break up. This was what was happening now. Nothing was safe or constant any more. Everything she loved and held dear was threatened.

Take the bread out of the toaster, butter it, put the sardines on top. She sat down at the table, staring at the plate and her glass. She took a mouthful of gin, then rose and scraped the sardines into the cat's dish. The toast she tore up and put out for the birds.

The front doorbell rang. She wanted to leave it, to let it ring, to hold on to the precious remnants of happiness a little longer.

She opened the door. It was Joe. She let herself drink in every detail of him – windswept black hair, strong, firm shoulders, and the smile that sprang to his eyes when he saw her.

She showed him into the drawing room. She said, 'Were you away?'

'I was in London.'

'Were you seeing Roy and Paddy?' Her voice sounded light and artificial.

'We had a chat, yes. I saw Neville as well, briefly.'

He looked ill at ease. Had he heard something? Perhaps their conversation about Gillis the other day had prompted him to recall that he had once seen Gillis with Frances Hart. Perhaps he, like her, had remembered the tragedy. Or perhaps – she quelled a shudder – Morgan had gone to Greensea to spread his poison. She hadn't phoned him yet. The scrap of paper he had given her was still tucked away in her writing desk. She seemed to feel its presence in the house. Perhaps Morgan had grown impatient with her. Perhaps he had decided to punish her.

But Joe was taking a small blue box out of his pocket. 'I went to London to choose this for you.' His gaze returned to her, full of warmth and affection. 'I never thought I'd love again, after Molly. I thought I was through with all that. You are my miracle, Juliet. You are kind and loving and generous and beautiful and you've made me remember what happiness was. You've made me live again and I can never thank you enough for that. And I wondered whether you would consent to become my wife.'

Her head jerked up; she stared at him. 'What?' she whispered.

'Marry me, Juliet. Would you? You'd make me the happiest man alive.'

Panic rose in her throat. Had he asked her the same question a month, a week ago . . .

He was putting the box in her hand. 'Open it, my love.'

She did so. Inside it was a diamond ring.

'It was hard, buying a ring for a Winterton,' he said. 'I hope you like it. You must know that it's offered with much love and respect. But if you don't care for it, you must choose something else.'

Square-cut diamonds set in a scrolled gold setting, orna-
mented with seed pearls. It was, she registered, quite lovely,
and she closed her eyes, allowing herself a few moments in
which to imagine a different future, one in which she might
accept Joe Brandon's proposal and marry him. He was the
right man for her, she had understood that some time ago.
She could have been happy with him for the rest of her life.

But she could never marry him, and perhaps she had
known since the day Morgan had walked up the drive to
Marsh Court that this moment would come. Though she
loved Joe, she must part from him. She wouldn't do to him
what Gillis had done to her. From the moment he had decided
to take Thea to the cottage, she had been implicated. Morgan
had believed that she was involved in Gillis's concealment
of the child, and really, when you looked at it rationally, you
could see why. She had been Gillis's lover. Gillis had hidden
Thea in Winterton property. However loudly she might protest
her innocence, she had the appearance of guilt: guilt by
association. She was not, as she had longed to believe, free
of the past. She would never be free of it.

Gillis had not protected her, but she would protect Joe.
She would not infect him with the taint that clung to her. She
was standing in the river and the water was rising up to her
neck, and she could not save herself.

But she could save him, and with terrible clarity she saw
what she must do.

She put the ring back in the box. The snap of it closing
was like a door slamming.

'I can't marry you, Joe,' she said. 'I'm so sorry, but I can't.'

He frowned. 'I understand that you have reservations about
the institution, but I am not Henry Winterton. I would not
treat you as he did.'

'It's not that.'

'You blame yourself for the failure of your marriage, but you're wrong, Juliet. You have nothing to be ashamed of. You did your best. You told me the other day that you thought you weren't any good at marriage, but it's not a question of being good or bad. You make of it what you can. And we would make something good and beautiful, I know it.'

Despair flooded through her. 'Joe, I can't.'

'Not now, then. But in six months, a year. Tell me I can hope.'

It wasn't enough that she refuse to marry him, nor even that she walk away from him and never see him again. No – and her heart fractured – she must ensure today that he never *wanted* to see her again. Only then would she be able to protect him.

'No, Joe, not ever.'

Her words hammer blows; the light went out of his eyes. 'Why?'

Do it, she told herself. Get it done. Once, in Cairo, she had seen a butcher slit the throat of a goat. The quick, clean slice of the knife, the spill of blood from the wound.

'Because I don't want to,' she said calmly.

'I don't understand. Something is wrong.' He had paled. 'Juliet, are you ill?'

She must make him hate her. She must look at him and conceal the despair she felt, and then she must adopt a tone of callousness – no, indifference – and find the words that would make him despise her.

No – her heart cried out against it.

But she must.

'I don't love you, Joe,' she said coldly. 'I thought I did, but I don't, not properly.'

'Never say that!' He took a step towards her. 'You're keeping something from me. Something has happened!'

'I suppose it has. I didn't think you'd noticed.' A light trill of a laugh. 'I've been trying to drop hints that I didn't want to see you any more, but you never seem to get the message.'

He whispered, 'Juliet, why are you saying this?'

And she pasted on a smile and set the blade to his throat.

'How could you possibly think it would work, you and I? Why did you imagine that just because I let you into my bed, I might find you a suitable man to be my husband? Oh Joe, how naïve you are! Did you honestly think I'd leave Marsh Court and go and live with you as a farmer's wife? Can you see me milking cows and feeding pigs? If you can, then you don't know me as well as you think you do. You really, really don't.'

When he had gone, when she had shut the door on him for the last time, she sat down on the lowest tread of the stairs and pressed her palms against her face. She heard the sound of the jeep heading up the drive, and then it faded away to silence. She was alone at Marsh Court, and she would go on being alone for months and years, for time without end. The pain in her heart was an ache now, but she knew how it would expand and burn and consume her.

At last she began to weep, dry, choking sobs that racked her body as she gasped for air. And then the tears fell, soaking her face and hands, and she bent forward, curling up her spine and covering her head with her arms, trying to make herself small, to erase herself, to stop herself existing.

Anne's flatmate Maria was talking. 'It was him,' she said. 'I'm sure it was. It was Michael. He was outside the house. He was in a different car and he drove off when I saw him, but I know it was him.' She gnawed at a hangnail. 'How did he find me? I haven't told anyone where I am, only my mum.'

Charley was at the house in Notting Hill. She babysat Eddie regularly, once a week. It had taken her a while to persuade Anne that she was a responsible person, the sort of person Anne would be happy to leave in charge of her beloved baby son, but she had, eventually.

Anne was supposed to be going out but was instead comforting Maria. Michael was Maria's violent husband, from whom she had run away.

Anne said, 'Do you think he'll try to cause trouble?'

Another piece of nail was efficiently ripped off. Slight frame, brown curls and freckled complexion, Maria was pretty, Charley thought, apart from her shredded hands.

'He said he'd kill me if I left him. He would, you know.'

'Is there anywhere else you could go for a while?'

Maria shook her head. 'I can't go back to Mum's, I wouldn't dare. Anyway, my job. Unless you want me to go.'

'Of course not.'

'You don't know what he's capable of. You don't know him.'

Anne put an arm round Maria's shoulders. 'You're safe here. Even if it was him, he can't come in here. You'll be all right.'

Maria stared at Anne. Then, turning to Charley, she said in a conversational tone, 'Michael hit my head against the kitchen sink. Lots of times, I don't know how many, I was trying to count to take my mind off it but I blacked out.' She clenched her fist and mimed a repeated striking action, as if she was knocking on a door. 'Then he locked me in the house. I couldn't get to the doctor for two days.' She

424

stood up. 'I'll go and check on Nancy. You go out, Anne, have some fun.'

After Maria had left the room, Anne said to Charley, 'I'd better stay with her.'

'What'll you do if he comes here?'

'I'll call the police.' Anne rose and turned the key in the back door. 'We should have a phone. And a spyhole on the door. I'll pay for a phone myself, if necessary. Anyway, it's uncivilised, not having one.' She tidied up coffee cups. 'How's Nate?'

'Oh well, you know. Pretty awful, I think. We talk for hours and hours.'

'He's grieving, it'll take time.'

Once, Anne's earnestness would have irritated her. It didn't any more. The two of them had come to terms. She was making an effort to appreciate Anne's honest and caring nature and Anne was learning not to dissect every flippant remark.

'I'll stay here with Maria,' Anne said. 'You go home.'

At the door, Charley paused. 'Aren't you worried that . . .'

'What?'

'That man, Michael, might come here. Wouldn't you think of . . .'

'Going back to Piers?' said Anne. 'Was that what you were going to say?'

Shut up, big mouth, Charley lectured herself. But then, thinking an instant later, *what the hell*, she said, 'Better to be with Piers than with a man who hits women's heads against sinks.'

'Piers hasn't said he wants me back.'

'He does, though.'

'But he needs to say it.' For a moment Anne looked dreadfully unhappy. 'He needs to say it in the right way.'

Charley left the house. It was almost nine and she thought she might go and see Piers. She kept in regular touch with both Piers and Nate, which was sometimes an effort because both men were in a mess.

Because it was a fine night and not that far, she walked to South Kensington. She thought about Maria and her violent husband. Why would you hurt someone you had promised to love? It troubled her that love could turn so easily to hatred, as if they were two sides of the same coin.

Reaching Piers's flat, she rang the doorbell. When Piers opened the door, she said, 'Just a coffee.'

The sitting room shelves were furred with dust, and a plate bearing the remains of a meal – beans on toast by the look of the dried-up orange streaks – was stranded on the carpet. There had been a time when Piers had seemed perpetually angry, but now he was perpetually sad. His sadness made Charley feel sad as well.

Piers made instant coffee, powdery and tasting of something other than coffee. Charley had to clear papers and a dressing gown from the sofa before sitting down.

'How's the shop?'

'Picking up.'

'I've just seen Anne.'

He looked guarded. 'Have you? How was she?'

'Fine. She misses you.'

His mouth twitched irritably. 'Charley, I know you mean well, but you don't know. If she missed me, she would have come home. There's nothing to stop her coming home.' He swigged some coffee. 'I keep thinking, any moment now, someone'll tell me she's gone off with Aidan.'

Charley was seven years younger than her brother but sometimes felt much, much older. Oh Piers, she thought, how can you get it so wrong? An old memory flipped into her head out of nowhere.

'Do you remember the summer Uncle Jonny died? I was fed up because you were ignoring me and spending all your time with Aidan and Anne.'

He shrugged, made an uninterested face and tipped a cigarette out of a packet of Woodbines. Ignoring this discouragement, Charley ploughed on.

'One day I followed you to Thorney Island. You and Aidan were having a race over the causeway. You won, and you hugged Anne.'

'Charley, this is all very affecting, but—'

She cut through his bored drawl. 'I saw the expression on her face. She was in love with you then. *Nine years ago*, Piers, she was in love with you. And she's still in love with you now.' There was never any point beating about the bush with Piers; you had to spell it out.

He flicked his cigarette lighter; when it failed to ignite, he dropped it on the table with a muttered curse.

'*Piers*,' she said crossly.

'What?' His eyes were like blue stones.

'She needs to *know* you love her, you idiot.' Something occurred to her, and she looked at him closely. 'You do, don't you?'

He gave her a furious look, but then puffed out his cheeks and slowly let out a breath, shaking his head. 'Yes,' he said rather hopelessly. 'I think so.'

'You *think* so?'

'I'm not very good at these things. How do you tell?' He sat forward, his forearms loosely on his knees, staring at the coffee table. 'And anyway, she doesn't seem to need me any more, so what's the point?'

427

One of the things Anne was trying to teach Piers was, Charley suspected, that she was perfectly capable of looking after herself and Eddie, and that love was about something more than paying the bills and fixing the washing machine when it went wrong. But would he ever understand that?

'It would help,' she said patiently, 'if you sorted out this flat and took your shirts to the laundry.' His cuffs were greyish.

He blinked. 'Do you think so?'

'I know so.'

He rubbed his eyes. 'Sometimes I think there's something wrong with me.'

'There isn't,' said Charley kindly. 'You're just a man, and a rather hopeless one at that.' Then she ruffled his hair.

Chapter Seventeen

June–July 1966

The house was smothering her, crushing her. It was all she had left, and she hated it.

Helen rang, but Juliet told her that she was busy with school work. Other friends, from London and Maldon, phoned and wrote, but she put them off. She called the school and said that she was ill. She was too tired to cook, and ate, when she remembered to, out of tins.

One day, Joe came to the house. She heard the rumble of the jeep's engine heading down the drive. He rang the doorbell and she stood in the hallway, eyes closed, hands clenched. Then he hammered on the door. 'Juliet, talk to me, please!'

She didn't move. Several heartbeats passed. She heard him strike the door with his fist. 'Why won't you talk to me?'

It crossed her mind to go out there and tell him the truth. He was a good, kind man and perhaps he would understand.

But she stayed where she was, and after a while she heard his footsteps on the gravel and the sound of the jeep as he drove away. Her eyes ached and her head pounded.

She was losing everything that had once been precious to her. Nothing was any good any more. She had already lost

Joe; as for the family, Freya was like an unexploded bomb planted in the middle of them, liable to tear them to pieces. Not that there was much left to destroy. They were already in splinters.

The dog still needed walking: once a day, she tramped along the estuary, Lulu ferreting in rabbit holes, sniffing at the grass. On the rare occasions when someone else came into view, Juliet started, as if she had forgotten that other people existed. Once, catching sight of a man standing by the salt marsh, she flinched, thinking it was Morgan. But the man lowered his binoculars and she saw that he was only a birdwatcher, a mild-looking man in his sixties, who bobbed his head in acknowledgement of her.

There came an evening when, nearing the island, she thought she saw the little girl again. A flash of red in the willows on Thorney Island's shoreline, like a red dress flaring in the wind. She gave a low cry and reached out to the fence to steady herself. Her heart raced with sickening speed and she thought she might faint. Forcing herself to look again, she saw that a length of cloth had caught in the strands of dried grey-green pondweed that fell in swags from the branches overhanging the river. The scarlet fabric flapped in the breeze.

As she returned to the house, she passed the place where the Winterton family lit their bonfires. Now the circle of ashes seemed a symbol of disintegration rather than celebration. When she closed her eyes, she pictured the people who had once stood with her there, watching the flames leaping into the air. Henry and Jonny and Gillis and Blanche – all gone now, their closeness a thing of the past, turned to shadows that danced raggedly in the twilight.

That night she dreamed that she was drowning. Not in

the Blackwater, but in the turquoise blue of some southern sea recalled from her childhood. At first she was close to the shore. The sand and the palm trees, the row of shops and hotels, seemed familiar to her. But she began to drift out to sea, and soon she was out of her depth and her feet no longer touched solid ground. She was alone; there were no other swimmers, and no matter how hard her arms whirled and her legs kicked, she was unable to make headway to the shore. The waves were swelling up and smacking against her face, the sand and palm trees had slipped out of sight and the sea became dark and cold. A huge wave struck her hard, pushing her below the surface and filling her mouth and nostrils with water. Water poured down her throat into her lungs and she knew she was drowning.

She woke gasping for breath. It was not yet dawn, not a crack of light around the curtains, the darkness solid, pressing down on her. The creaks and rattles of the old house transformed themselves into the footsteps of the people who had once lived there. She should never have stayed here, she thought. She should have left the house long ago. Marsh Court had become the burial chamber of all her hopes.

The morning came. She didn't get up. She couldn't see the point.

Sometime in the afternoon, hunger and the dog forced her out of bed. In the kitchen, she fed Lulu and made tea and toast for herself with the stale end of a loaf. Then she let the dog out of the back door, put on wellingtons and an old raincoat over her pyjamas and went outside.

Silvery gusts of rain blew in from the east, interspersed with flashes of sunshine. She took the keys to the cottage with her; freed from the confines of the house, Lulu bounced around her feet as she made her way along the path. Juliet unlocked the door to the cottage and went inside. The furnishings were dusty, and the books and puzzles provided for the entertainment of Winterton guests now looked old and shabby. She pictured Gillis and Blanche coming into the cottage, Blanche slipping off her heels while Gillis related to her the argument he had just had with Henry. A different image: Gillis crouched in front of the fire, cradling his daughter on his lap and coaxing her to drink warm milk from a teaspoon.

This was a place of treachery, full of lies. The air smelled sour and musty, and it stifled her.

She swept armfuls of jigsaws and paperback books into a cardboard box and walked down to the fire pit, where she upended it, dumping its contents in the centre of the ash circle. Back up the slope to the cottage, where she dragged curtains from their hooks and rolled up dusty rugs. She arranged them carefully so that they would not stifle the flames. Though she felt weak and tired and heartbroken, she was still a Winterton, and she was going to make a bonfire that was a beacon all over the marshes.

Freya had told her that her photographs were a sort of exorcism. Juliet too must immolate the past; only then would she be able to make out a future for herself. She returned to the cottage time and time again. Wooden coat hangers, a wicker chair and a cushion: she built them into a conical heap. Newspaper, this time from the house, along with volumes of The Field magazine that Henry had liked to read. Frocks she no longer wore, battered toys the children hadn't played with for years, a chair with three legs, a broken croquet set.

She stuffed dry twigs into the gaps, then took a can of petrol from the shed and splashed it over the pyre. She put her cigarette lighter to the newspaper, took hold of the dog's collar and stood back. A low crackling at first, and then a roar as the petrol caught and flames rushed out in all directions. Lulu whimpered, and Juliet knelt, rubbing the soft spot behind the dog's ears to reassure her. She was making a pyre of the past, burning away the lies and the faithlessness. She was burning away her history.

Crimson sparks danced in the sky and the flames cast a ruby light on the trees. She pictured their branches catching fire, the grass blackening and turning to powder, the flames rushing up the lawn and swallowing Marsh Court with a roar and a crackle. With Lulu in her arms, she went to stand on the far side of the conflagration, where the thick white smoke formed a screen between her and the house.

Waking early the following morning, she bathed and dressed and teased the tangles out of her hair. Some cold cream, a little lipstick. She felt shaky: she needed to eat. There were some eggs in the fridge; she made herself an omelette, heated up tinned tomatoes and drank black tea because the milk had gone sour. Then she went outside. It was a fine day and the air was cool and fresh. Sunlight refracted colours from the dew as she walked down the garden. The bonfire had diminished to a round, greyish carpet. Embers smouldered in the centre of the circle, fuchsia pink in colour and fringed with white. Wisps of smoke rose from the ashes, and within them she made out the skeletons of old, burned things — a brass hinge, a curtain ring.

She had often regretted her decision to marry Henry Winterton, wondering whether she had sold herself along with a pearl necklace. Today she did not see it like that, and acknowledged instead that it had been a brave choice during a period in her life when she had had few options open to her. In time, her decision had given her great riches – a home, a country and a family.

She needed to find the same courage now. She must put right what could be put right. First she must deal with Morgan, and then she must repair the fissures in the family. And Joe . . . she longed for him, she yearned for the comfort of his arms, and his strength and faith in her. She had sold him short, she thought, and hadn't trusted him enough. Trust was an essential part of love. Something else she needed to put right.

She had allowed her fears to multiply and they had overwhelmed her. Whatever the risks involved, the thought of returning to the depression and anomie of the last week frightened her more. She was, she supposed, secretive by nature – or perhaps the characteristic had been imposed upon her by a childhood spent in countries she had not belonged to and where she had often been the sole prop and confidante of a man who had nursed his own demons. But now she needed to change.

Today she would drive to Maldon, to go to the shops and buy food. But there was something she had to do first. She went into the house and took from her writing desk the piece of paper Morgan had given her on the day of Gillis's funeral. Then she dialled the number.

Morgan answered the phone. He demanded money from her, as she had known he would.

'No,' she said crisply. 'I'll bring you something better.' She told him to meet her at the causeway at eight o'clock on Saturday evening. And then she put down the phone.

The children were in bed and Anne was upstairs, checking her work clothes for the next day, when she heard a noise

434

from below. A loud crash, as if something – someone – had burst through the front door. Then shouting.

Very quietly, she checked that Eddie, Nancy and Owen were asleep, and closed the doors of their bedrooms, which were at the top of the three-storey house. Then she crept halfway down the stairs that led to the first floor.

Pieces of splintered wood were scattered over the lino in the hall and a man was yelling, 'You're coming with me, you bitch, if I have to drag you out of here!'

Maria was crying and Ceridwen was speaking in a calm, reasoning tone. 'Michael, let's talk about it.'

'I'm not here to talk about it. And you, fucking shut up. Stay here where I can see you, but fucking shut up.'

A movement in the hall below her. Anne sank back against the wall. But it was Ceridwen, who, catching Anne's eye, mouthed police, and then disappeared out of sight again.

Michael went on yelling, his words bouncing up the stairs, so Anne knew the three of them were still in the hall. She wouldn't be able to get out of the house that way. She inched down the remainder of the treads to Ceridwen's bedroom on the first floor and opened the door. Then she tiptoed across the floor to the window and heaved up the peeling sash, praying that Maria's husband wouldn't hear the squeaking noises. She wondered whether she was doing the right thing, leaving the children, including Eddie, in a house with a madman, or whether she should go and scoop them all up somehow and take them with her, but she saw that was impossible and instead wormed out of the window on to the flat-roofed kitchen extension below, and ran across the bitumen roof. Then she crouched, and jumped down on to the grass.

A gate led out of the side of the house to the main street.

There was a queue for the phone box, but when she hurried along it, explaining to people that it was an emergency and she must phone the police, they let her through. An older woman in the booth ended her call and beckoned her inside.

Her hands shook as she dialled 999. What if Michael did something awful? What if he killed Maria or set fire to the house? She longed to run back for Eddie and take him to safety.

A voice answered the phone. Quickly, Anne explained what had happened.

'A quarrel between a married couple?' repeated the voice on the other end of the phone. 'We find it best not to intervene in events of a domestic nature, madam.'

Anne thought he hadn't understood her. She tried to make clear the urgency of the situation.

'Her husband's been violent in the past. He's threatened to kill her.'

Was that a sigh she heard? 'Husbands and wives have their own ways of sorting out their differences. These domestic tiffs, the last thing they want is the police turning up on the doorstep.'

'Please—'

'If we have a man free, we'll send him round. My advice to you is to go home, love, and make yourself a cup of tea. Takes two to make a quarrel, that's what I always say.'

The call cut off. Anne stared at the receiver, her heart pounding and her mouth dry. What should she do? She thought of Piers. Could she ask him to help her? Should she?

She didn't have a choice. She dialled Piers's number. 'You're not to come on your own,' she insisted. Suddenly she was terrified for him. 'You need to bring someone with you. Someone really big.'

* * *

436

'You'll need a couple of bolts on that door,' Piers said. 'I'll come round tomorrow evening and sort it.'

It was an hour later, and they were sitting in Anne's bedroom, drinking the very strong coffee she had made. Piers and his friends Jamie and Rob, both rugby players, had turned up, and eventually Michael had left the house. Ceridwen had put Maria to bed with a sleeping pill and Jamie and Rob had gone to the pub along the road.

Anne was cold, but no matter how many sweaters she put on, she couldn't seem to get warm. Because she couldn't bear to let Eddie out of her sight again, she had put him in her own bed and they were talking quietly so as not to wake him up.

'I've got to get a phone,' she said. 'I'll see about it tomorrow.'

'Come home,' said Piers, as she had known he would.

'I can't.'

'Anne, for pity's sake . . .'

She was sitting on the edge of the bed and he was beside her. She had only to reach out and he would take her in his arms. It was hard not to.

'Piers, I can't.'

'I miss you. It's not the same without you.'

She remembered how relieved she had felt when he had arrived at the house, flanked by Jamie and Rob, and how he had calmly and determinedly persuaded Michael to go.

'I know,' she said, shivering. 'It's not the same for me either.'

He said, 'I was wrong about Aidan, I admit that I was.'

He spoke as if this was a great concession, and she said, with as much spirit as she could muster, 'Of course you were wrong. I don't love Aidan, I never have. I've never even found him attractive.'

She felt far too tired to deal with the demands of Piers's pride. She longed to curl up next to Eddie and go to sleep. But they were having the first proper conversation they'd had in an age, so she made an effort to try to get through to him.

'You need to decide what's more important to you,' she said. 'Eddie and me or what you feel about Aidan.'

His eyes flashed. 'They don't infringe on each other.'

'They do, Piers, they always have. It takes up your thoughts, this stupid rivalry. Did you even notice, for instance, how much I minded stopping work at the gallery? Did you even realise that it was as bad for me as losing Winterton's was for you?'

'I knew you enjoyed it . . .'

'But I have my baby. That's what you thought, wasn't it? That's what everyone thinks. I love Eddie more than I can possibly express, and I think I'm making a good job of bringing him up, but it's not enough for me. Plenty of people think it should be, but it just isn't.' Her heart was racing. She put her coffee mug on the bedside table; she shouldn't drink any more. 'I need something else as well, that's what I've realised, something I'm good at. I'm far better than I was at all the domestic stuff, but it's not where my heart is and it won't ever be. I'm good at my work, I know I am. I want to use all that knowledge and experience. It gives me a place in the world.'

A silence, as if he was absorbing this, then he said, 'If you came home, you could still work at the gallery. We could find a nanny or an au pair. The business is doing better now.'

'I'm pleased to hear it, but—'

'Come back with me.'

She shook her head, unable to speak.

'*Please*,' he said. 'Please, Anne.'

It was the first time he had begged her. 'No, Piers,' she said quietly, and kissed his cheek. 'You should go now, but thank you. I don't know what we'd have done without you. You were wonderful. I feel so proud of you.'

Downstairs, she opened the front door and looked out along the street, checking for Michael.

Piers said, 'What if he comes back?'

'He won't, not tonight, I don't think. You've scared him off.' She spoke with more confidence than she felt.

'I'll stay. I'll sleep on the sofa, if that's what you want.'

She shook her head. Then, catching his eye, she said, 'I won't come back to you just because I don't feel like staying here any more. You've got to really want it, Piers. You've got to want us to come home more than anything else in the world.'

Juliet sat at her dressing table, jewellery boxes spread out around her. Cornflower-blue sapphires from Kashmir, a Winterton heirloom, spilled from a velvet case. Emeralds sparkled against white satin. Her fingertips ran first over a gold bangle, then the aquamarine bracelet that Henry had given her for her twentieth birthday, and then a brooch, a spray of flowers encrusted with gems.

But her touch settled on the green leather case containing her pearls. She unclasped the box, noting their symmetry and lustre. She remembered the day of her fifteenth birthday, when her father had given them to her, and how, at that callow and sullen age, she had disliked them. And how she had come to adore their rarity and mystery and the way they echoed the colour of her eyes.

And then her father had died and she had resolved to sell

them, and Henry Winterton had come into her life. Her pearl necklace belonged to her and was a part of her. It seemed to her that her Winterton jewels had only ever been borrowed. But the pearls were hers, and so she would use them to make her bargain. They were her last, desperate attempt to protect her family.

Sometimes she no longer loved them. Sometimes she thought they had cost her too much. She swept them into her palm and left the room.

That evening, the tide was on the turn, water rushing out to sea as Juliet walked to the causeway, carrying with it spars of wood, a trio of swans and an empty wine bottle, bobbing in the current. Shadows pocked the fields and hedgerows, and the evening sky was chalk white. Woodsmoke in the air – someone must have lit a bonfire – and pale, pinkish flowers on the brambles and purple vetch among grass the colour of sand. Ahead of her was the island, a swell of bright green crowned with a fringe of darker green trees.

Her fingers brushed against the necklace in her pocket, and she felt the pearls' cool silkiness. Light glared on the river; she shaded her eyes and saw him, standing on the bank, throwing a stick to the dog. Many men had a piece of darkness inside them. It had been there in Gillis, allowing him to abandon his daughter, and in Henry, who had exerted an iron control over his family. It was closer to the surface in Morgan, and stronger, blacker.

The arc of the stick in the air, and Bryn, a pale dart rushing along the grass to fetch it. Again her hand went to the pearls, as if she was touching a talisman.

As she approached him, he said, 'What have you brought me?'

'This.' She took the necklace out of her pocket, felt it slip through her fingers.

Contempt on his face. 'That bauble . . .'

She shook her head. 'They're worth a lot of money. Saltwater pearls are rare. My husband had them valued and these are of the finest quality.'

He reached out to her. 'Let me see.'

'Not yet.' She clutched the necklace to her breast.

'I said, give them to me.' He lunged at her, and she shrank back from him. A clumsiness to his movements and the smell of alcohol on his breath told her that he had been drinking. Though he wasn't a tall man, he was heavy and muscular and she was aware of his physical strength. What had Gillis said about him? *No pity, no conscience.*

'You have to know something first.' She made herself look into his bloodshot blue eyes. 'I'll never give you anything more, do you understand that? You must never try to see me again, you must go away and never come back here.'

Bryn had trotted to Morgan's feet, stick in mouth, whining, dancing round his master's legs. Behind them the Blackwater, racing out to sea, had begun to narrow, and the start of the causeway was now visible beneath shallow water.

Morgan snarled at the dog. 'I don't think you're in any position to strike bargains, Mrs Winterton.'

'If I ever see you again, I'll call the police. I will, I swear it. Whatever it costs me.'

He held out his hand for the necklace. The pearls slid into his palm.

'No you wouldn't, you silly bitch.' His lip curled. 'You'd whimper and whine like the rest of your sort and then you'd do as you were told.'

Impatiently, the dog nipped at Morgan's ankles. He swore

441

at it, tugged the stick out of its jaws and hurled it over his shoulder. Bryn darted after it, racing into the water that lapped over the start of the causeway. The river caught the dog up and carried it away, bobbing and swirling in the fast-running current.

'Bryn!' Morgan screamed. 'Bryn, come back, damn you!'

He too ran through the shallows, splashing and slipping on the wet stones, and then waded into deeper water, his arm outstretched, trying to reach his dog.

'Bryn! Bryn, here, boy!'

The river swirled up first to Morgan's thighs, and then to his waist. He grabbed at the bull terrier, seeming to touch it before losing his footing. And then the tide seized him, whirling him round like a spinning top before ducking him, so that he was swallowed up by the Blackwater.

Surfacing, he screamed, 'Help me!' He reached up his hands in supplication to Juliet, standing on the bank. 'For pity's sake, I can't swim!'

For a moment she remained motionless, watching the drowning man. Her limbs were made of stone, her heart also. And then, scouring the mud and marsh, she caught sight of a long spar of wood and grabbed it. She ran along the bank and held out the spar to Morgan.

'Catch hold of it,' she called out to him, 'and I'll pull you in!'

He flailed in the current, which was carrying him away from the end of the spar. Juliet waded into the river after him. Her feet sank into the mud and she gasped at the sting of the ice-cold water.

'Take it!' she cried. 'Here – quickly!'

She felt the length of wood jar as Morgan seized it. She stepped deeper into the river, afraid that he would pull it

442

out of her hands as she strained to haul him to shore. He grabbed at her, tugging the hem of her skirt. The spar slipped out of her fingers and then they both tumbled through the churning water, swept away from island and causeway. She was pulled down by the heaviness of her wet clothes, and by Morgan, who clawed at her for purchase, as if she could give him ballast.

She was out of her depth, her feet thrashing as she frantically tried to touch the riverbed. Above her, the sky was dimming. Water was pouring into her mouth and nose and she could not breathe. The cold seemed to freeze her lungs, and she was swirled round by the current, riverbank, island and marsh circling in a mad whirl. Her strength was failing. Morgan, a dead weight, was dragging her down, down into the dark heart of the river. She was drowning.

Then his grasp loosened. His fingers uncurled and let her go, and she fought her way to the surface. The last time she saw him, he was lying face down in the water, drifting downstream, carried away by the tide.

There were countless rivulets and mudflats in the estuary, and islets where flotsam and jetsam might be washed up. The channels made coils and whorls in the vast wilderness of mud and grass as the Blackwater wound through the jigsaw of creek and inlet and island.

She must have lost consciousness for a while, cast up on the mud, because the whisper of the reeds and the rush of the water woke her. She was lying on the slope of a grassy island. She had swum to the shore, her limbs straining against the current to prevent herself being cast out to the mouth of the estuary. Every muscle burned in the aftermath of her exertion. Mud dried on her limbs, crazing as she shivered.

It was dusk, and the Blackwater was narrowing to a coffee-brown conduit. She scanned the river and banks but could not see Morgan.

She could have lain there and slept, but she hauled herself to her feet, slipping and shaking in the mud, using a clump of couch grass for balance as she staggered to higher, firmer ground. Then she stood up and looked over the river again. Night was coming; she could not see the further shore. Of Morgan and his dog there was no sign.

As she walked back along the path that led to Marsh Court, it was at first all she could do to put one foot in front of the other. But thought and wariness reasserted themselves, and she found herself looking cautiously from side to side for birdwatchers and boats. No one must see her walking home like this, her clothes torn and muddy, riverweed in her wet hair. If Morgan was dead — and she shuddered, knowing that he was — there must be nothing that could link her with him. Nothing must give rise to the suspicion that she had met him this night.

But with a fluttering of the heart she remembered the pearls. Had he put them in his pocket, or had he dropped them in his hurry to rescue Bryn? She imagined a body fished from the water, the police going through the pockets of his jacket in search of identification. And finding the pearls, her valuable, recognisable, memorable pearls.

A pink glow showed to the west, where the sun was dying. She reached the causeway. It had emerged from the river, a grey spine linking mainland and island, marginal and evanescent. She stood on the bank, drained and exhausted as the events that had taken place there reeled through her mind. She recalled the relief she had felt, swept along by the river, when his grip had uncurled and he had been borne away. All emotion had been washed from her. She would put these things aside and never think of them again. She would not lay them down in memory. She would forget them.

She saw a gleam amid the stones and weed, lustre trapped among the drab greys and browns, and gasped. She reached into the mud and drew out her pearl necklace. Caked mud fell from it, tiny stones and shells crumbled away. She closed her eyes, swaying in the darkness, clasping it to her. And then she walked back to the house.

It was only when, later that evening, she was soaking in the bath that she saw the myriad of cuts and scratches on her hands and knees from where she had crawled out of the river to safety. She dabbed disinfectant on them and washed the grit and fragments of weed down the plughole. She ran her pearls under the tap until they were clean again.

Then she lay down on the bed and closed her eyes. It was hard to imagine that she would ever be able to move again, and as she trembled, she wondered whether she was starting a fever. She reached out a hand, as if by doing so she would touch Joe, lying beside her, and warm herself against his body. She was tired of being alone, had sickened of it a long time ago, and anyway, Joe was in her veins, he was soaked through her, inseparable from her, a pearl that she would keep for ever in the folds of her heart.

With the money she had saved from her annuity and with Piers acting as guarantor, Charley had bought a house in Roupell Street, in Waterloo.

On Saturday, Nate helped her move in, ferrying her belongings from the Chelsea house to the south bank of the river. 'Josh is more or less living with Louise,' she explained to him as they hauled cardboard boxes, 'and I feel in the way. And Gabe's going to buy a flat of her own.'

Nate had an appointment with the Sinclairs' solicitor, so left at midday. Charley set about unpacking boxes. The house was terraced and built in the 1820s. The estate agent had described it as a 'craftsman's cottage'. There were two bedrooms upstairs and a kitchen and sitting room downstairs. Some of the window frames were rotten and a chunk of plaster was missing in one of the bedroom ceilings, and the lavatory was at the rear of the building in a little house all of its own, necessitating trips across the dank and overgrown garden. Charley loved it. She was going to use the second bedroom, the one with the hole in the ceiling, as a study. She had started work on another play.

The doorbell rang as she was searching for the kettle to make a cup of tea. She went to answer it.

Nate was at the door. He said, 'Rory's run away from school. No one knows where the hell he is. Charley, I don't know what to do.'

While they drove to the Sinclairs' house, Nate filled her in on what he knew.

'They think he left yesterday evening. One of the other boys covered for him. The school didn't realise until after breakfast. They thought he'd gone for a walk or something – he's been a bit funny since Dad died – and when he didn't come back, they phoned Flavia. She phoned me but I was out, of course, so she tried Claudia. She thought he might have gone there. Claudia's husband, Toby, was waiting at the house when I got back.'

'Flavia and Claudia haven't heard from him?'

'No, nothing.' Nate looked sick with worry. 'Not a thing.'

'The boy who covered for him . . . did he know anything?'

'He thought Rory had taken a tent.'

'A tent?'

'From the Scout hut. His headmaster said there was one missing.' Nate gave a quick shake of his head. 'What if he's just . . . taken off? What if he's decided to join the merchant navy or something stupid? I wouldn't put it past him.'

Charley wanted to squeeze his hand, but couldn't, because he was driving. They had reached the Sinclairs' house. Nate parked the car and they went inside.

Toby was reading *The Times* in the front room. He stood up when they came in. 'Anything?'

'No, nothing. You?'

Toby shook his head. 'Claudia phoned. She wondered whether he might have gone somewhere you used to go on holiday, something like that.'

Nathan stared at Toby. 'What?'

'Happy memories and all that.' Toby folded the newspaper with a twitch. 'We used to holiday on a freezing-cold river in Scotland. My father yelled at us all the time because we made too much noise and scared off the salmon. Wouldn't go back there if you paid me. Still, worth a thought.'

'We often went to Antibes,' said Nate. 'Or skiing.'

Toby cleared his throat. 'Maybe you should think of having a word with the police.'

Charley was perched on the arm of a chair. She thought about the tent. 'Did you ever go camping when you were children, Nate?'

He shook his head. 'Never. Dad wouldn't. He preferred sailing.' He let out a breath. Charley knew he was thinking about his father and the yacht, *Sea Dancer*. Then he frowned. 'Though Mum . . .'

447

'Nate?'

'Rory went camping once with Mum. He kept going on about it, so she took him. He was about eleven or twelve. He loved it. Wouldn't stop talking about it.'

'Where did they go?'

He stared at her. 'I can't remember the name of it.'

She rose and went to stand in front of him. There was a wild look in his eyes. She took his hands in hers. 'Nate?'

'You know if you drive east from Marsh Court? A farmer let them pitch the tent in his field. They were near enough to Marsh Court that Mum could go back and have a bath. What's it called? That weird marshy beach that feels like the end of the world. There's a chapel. And I think there was a Roman fort.'

Charley said, 'The Chapel of St Peter-on-the-Wall.'

Nate said, 'It's been so bloody lonely. All that time I was away in South America – well, I missed Mum and Dad now and then, but not all that much, if I'm honest. I suppose I knew they were back here and I'd see them again. But now – I hate that house. I bet Rory hates it too. It's not a home. I don't suppose anywhere feels much like home to him any more.'

They had driven out of London and were heading northeast. Nate's knuckles were white where he clutched the steering wheel. He said, 'I should have made more time for him. I mean, the poor little blighter's only sixteen. Where now?'

Charley looked at the map. 'Turn right. Nate, you mustn't blame yourself. You're doing your best.'

'I don't blame myself.' He turned off the main road. Charley noticed how conscientiously he drove, never breaking the

448

speed limit, judging junctions with care, as if he expected danger to come out of nowhere.

They were travelling along a leafy side road. 'I blame Dad,' said Nate. 'How could he? How could he *choose* to leave us? He planned it.'

'Nate—'

'Think about it. The yacht. Crewing it alone. I'd offered to go.'

'You don't know.'

'That doesn't help.'

'No,' she said sadly. 'I don't suppose it does.'

They drove for a while in silence. The further east they travelled, the narrower the roads became. A house on its own in a field, a village, a woman walking a dog. The branches of the trees spilled overhead so that they travelled between flickering patterns of dark and light.

She said, 'Uncle Gillis was one of the most *alive* people I've ever met. But sometimes he got the blues, Nate, you know that. His black dog, he called it once, like Churchill. But all sorts of things might have happened. And I can see that's hard.'

Again, silence. She thought: I want to make it better for you. I want to hug you and kiss you and show you how much I love you. And then, realising what she had just thought and how powerfully she meant it, and how she had hidden what she felt for Nate not only from him but from herself, for ages and ages, her face flooded with heat and she pretended to look for something in her bag.

She found, among the old bus tickets and stubby lipsticks, a tube of Polos. She picked off the bits of fluff and handed one to him.

'I can't help him,' Nate said suddenly. 'I don't know what

449

to say to him. How can I make him feel safe when nothing feels safe to me any more?'

Charley thought that maybe nothing ever was safe, you only thought it was, for a while. She said, 'Perhaps you have to pretend.'

'I'm not sure I can. Sometimes I think I may as well not be here.'

She looked at him. 'What do you mean?'

'I hate my job. Using money to make more money, it's not for me. Maybe I should go abroad again. I didn't, because of Rory. But if I've failed him, what's the point?' An exhalation of breath. 'Jesus, Charley. What if he's decided to go for a swim and drowned himself? What if he's got sucked up in a quicksand? Or hitched a lift with some maniac? You know what he's like.'

'Don't,' she said. 'Nate, just don't.'

She began to talk to him about her part-time job in a bookshop in Bloomsbury, and the new play she had just begun to write, which had been sparked by her encounter, on that awful evening with Christian, with the old woman and the wheeled basket: a play about how you might manage in London if you had nowhere to live, and how you might end up like that, with your home in a wheeled basket. Anything to distract him. And all the time she thought, what if he isn't at St Peter's Chapel? Nate was right. Rory was accident-prone.

They stopped at Bradwell-on-Sea for Nate to call Toby from a phone box. Coming out, he shook his head.

'Toby hasn't heard anything. If we don't find him, I'm calling the police.'

A winding road through a village; the road became a track, and then, where the track ran out, Nate parked the car.

They walked along the side of the field. She tucked her hand round his arm and tried not to think about anything. Ahead of them, silhouetted by a sun that was sinking through a grey and indigo sky, was the chapel. Reaching it, they walked a little way along and saw, pitched in the rough grass near the shore, a tent, and Rory beside it, feeding a fire with dead leaves and twigs.

Rory had looked up and seen them crossing the grass and had waved, and Charley had been afraid that Nate might yell at him. But he hadn't, had said only, 'Good fire. Mind if we join you?' and Rory had said, ''Course you can. Would you like some cocoa? You'll have to share a cup.'

Rory had spent the night wrapped up in his mother's old sheepskin coat, which he had, without Nate knowing, taken back to school with him. 'It still smells of her,' he had said, which had made tears spring to Charley's eyes.

'I just wanted to think about her,' he had told them. 'And Dad. The thing about school, you can't think, not properly.'

Charley had left the brothers to talk to each other and had gone back to the car to wait for them. Purple shadows tumbled from the willows and across the fields. She found it impossible to pinpoint when she had started loving Nate: it was like writing a play, she thought, there was no fixed single moment of conception. Her love for him was made up of all sorts of things: the crush she had always had on him when she was a girl; his kindness – and crossness – with her after he had come back from South America; and that time in the Sinclairs' kitchen, when he had taken her in his arms and held her as if she had been the only solid thing in a world that was breaking up around him.

And she remembered the night Nate had shown her and

Louise the Geminids. Half an hour passed before she caught sight of two dim figures, Nate and Rory, heading towards her through the dusk. She looked up at the sky and willed herself to see it again: a star, tracing itself across the pitch-black universe.

On Sunday, Joe rose at six and did his usual tour of the farm. If the fine weather held, they would be bringing in the harvest early.

Two problems had taken up his time since the day Juliet had refused to marry him. Gary, the boy she had found in the muddy creek on Winterton land, was the first. He had been caught breaking into an ironmonger's in Battersea, a piece of foolishness that had netted him a night in a police cell and a charge of burglary. Joe had spoken up for him at the trial, had vouched for his good character and the improvement he had made during the fortnight he had spent at Greensea. Gary was easily led; Joe had pointed out that his accomplice had been an older man, an habitual criminal. But the magistrate had ignored his pleas and sentenced the boy to six months in Borstal, and Joe had walked out of the court with a bitter taste in his mouth.

And then his godson, Neville. He had been working as a carpenter in a West End theatre and had been caught with his hand in the till, helping himself to the petty cash. His mother, Virginia, had phoned Joe, desperately worried. Another journey to London: he had accompanied Virginia to the theatre to try to persuade the management not to press charges. When, after a difficult hour, they had consented not to involve the police, he and Virginia had thanked them and left the building. Out in the street, she had wept. Joe had held her in his arms as tourists and theatregoers flooded past. He had never seen Virginia cry before, except on stage.

He had taken Neville back to Greensea with him, where he had given his godson the dressing-down to end all dressing-downs. He had pointed out to Neville that his mother had worked herself to the bone to give him a decent education, and that in spite of having an infinitely better deal in life than the slum lads who came to Greensea, he had almost thrown the lot away. And then he told Neville that his father, had he lived, would have been ashamed of him.

The following day, chastened, Neville had promised Joe that he would do better. During his time at Greensea, he had made an effort, getting up without complaint in the morning and working with Joe from dawn to dusk. Joe thought Neville was improving. He almost had hopes of him.

The bitter irony remained that the lad he had told the truth for he had failed to save, while the one he had lied for had been given a second chance. He had affirmed that Neville was fundamentally honest and decent when he had known that was not always so. He had lied because he loved and cared about Neville.

The ground was as hard as nails after a spell of hot weather, but a fat curl of cloud on the horizon to the east told him that rain should soon be on its way. As he walked through the orchard, the dogs rushed and leaped ahead of him. A year ago, he had walked with Juliet beneath these trees. In low moments, he wondered whether there had been any truth in the vile things she had said to him on the day she had turned down his proposal of marriage. It was hard to imagine elegant, beautiful, refined Juliet Winterton living the life of a farmer's wife. It would be like throwing a ruby into the dust. Their relationship might be one that worked well given periods of distance but crumbled if forced into too close a proximity.

Today, leaving the cool darkness of the orchard for the blinding sun of the open fields, he refused to believe that. His heart rebelled against it: he knew her, knew there was not an ounce of cruelty in her, nor snobbery. Something was wrong: she was keeping something from him, something that had made her decide to reject him. It was not to be borne, this absence, and he resolved to return to Marsh Court and try to speak to her again.

As he walked to the creek, he threw a rubber ball for the dogs, who tore across the meadows, noses pointing. The Jack Russell cut his paw on a broken bottle some fool had thrown on to his land, so Joe tucked him under his arm and headed back to the farm. He rinsed the damaged paw beneath the tap in the yard. 'Just a scratch, old fellow,' he murmured, and the dog limped away. Then he stripped off his shirt and held his head beneath the tap and let the icy water wash away the dust.

He straightened. The heat of the sun was such that it immediately began to burn away the drops of water on his skin.

A flicker of movement on the far side of the yard. A voice said his name. Turning, he saw her.

Church bells chimed over the marshes as Juliet drove to Greensea. The fields had bleached to the colour of sacking, and her head ached and her courage faltered as she approached the farm.

Three days had passed since she had dragged herself out of the Blackwater. During that time, she had lain in bed, feverish and exhausted. But that morning she had woken

454

clear-headed and refreshed, her temperature back to normal, and had risen and bathed and dressed.

She parked the car in the driveway. No one answered the front door, so she walked to the back of the house, then through the kitchen garden. Her thin cotton frock clung to her legs in the humidity.

She saw him in the yard, by the barn, pulling on his shirt. She spoke, and he swung round to her.

'Juliet.'

Hearing her name on his lips, something inside her crumpled and folded in on itself. She must have swayed, because he was at her side, his arm round her waist, supporting her. With his help, she stumbled into the house. He took her to the kitchen, which was blessedly cool.

He pulled out a chair and made her sit down, then ran a glass of water and put it in her hands. 'Drink that. It's hellish hot out there.'

'Joe . . .'

'Don't talk, drink.'

She drank, and the room steadied. When she had emptied the glass, she said, 'I'm so sorry, I've been unwell. Nothing much, but . . .'

'You look ill.' His voice sharp. He sat beside her, frowning.

'I've missed you,' she said softly. She closed her eyes, shutting out the room and Joe, unable to bear it. 'I was so horrible to you!' she whispered. 'Can you ever forgive me?'

He passed her his handkerchief and she blew her nose. He said, 'There's nothing to forgive.'

'There is,' she said soberly. 'You don't know.'

'Then tell me.'

She thought what a sweet smile he had, so full of love and kindness, and again she faltered. 'You'll hate me.'

455

'I won't. I couldn't. Whatever it is, we can share it.' He studied her, then smiled. 'Let me guess. You're married already. A secret liaison with a decadent aristocrat.'

She too smiled. 'No, not that.'

'What then? Juliet, are you going to tell me that you have a past? Which of us doesn't?'

'Mine seems to have caught up with me.' But she knew that the time for secrecy had passed, and she gripped his hand and said, 'Dear Joe. How very dear you are to me. Thank goodness I met you. I haven't loved often, you see, and I haven't always loved wisely . . .'

Then she told him her story. Of Gillis, the man she had once loved beyond reason, and the night of the storm, and the drownings, and her discovery many years later, prompted by Joe himself, that Gillis had been the father of Frances Hart's children. And all that had followed from that: Blanche and Freya and her encounter at the causeway, three days ago, with Morgan.

'I wondered whether you'd heard anything,' she said, when she had finished. 'Whether a body had been found.' She pressed her lips together.

'Nothing.' He took her hands in his. 'There are a thousand little inlets and pools where the tide might sweep a drowned man. If he's dead, it may be some time before they find him.'

'He's dead,' she said. 'I'm sure of it.' She would never forget her last sight of Morgan, lifeless, face down, buffeted by the tides.

He put his arms round her, holding her close to him, and she rested her head against his shoulder. 'You should have told me,' he said. 'I would have dealt with him.'

'I know you would, Joe, but I didn't want you to be a

456

part of it. I didn't want you to get hurt. That's why I said those terrible things. It broke my heart and I wanted to die.'

He stroked her hair. 'We'd do anything to protect those we love. We'd lie and thieve and sell ourselves to prevent them from being thrown to the wolves. You're not the only one, Juliet. But you must promise me that if anything ever troubles you again, you'll come to me.'

She promised. A weight lifted, and she felt lighter than she had for a long, long time. Then she sighed and said, 'I have to talk to Freya. I have to find a way of telling her the truth without implicating Gillis. Because of the Sinclair children, you see, Joe. They've suffered enough. I'm going to go to London. I'll visit Aidan and ask him to tell me Freya's address.' And at the same time, she resolved, she would make him see sense. Piers, too. This wretched feud between the cousins was tearing the family apart. She was going to put an end to it.

'Let me come with you,' he said.

'No, Joe. Thank you, but no. I have to do this on my own. But when I've put things right, then I'll come home – to you, if you'll have me.'

She looked up at him, full of hope. 'After you come home,' he said softly, kissing her, 'I don't intend ever to let you go again. In fact, it might be an idea if we just stayed in the bedroom. Neville could look after the farm, and maybe Christine would bring us something to eat now and then. What do you think?'

'I think,' she said, as his hand ran over the curves of her body: waist, hip, thigh, 'that's a simply marvellous idea.'

Chapter Eighteen

July 1966

Juliet hadn't seen Aidan's flat before. She thought, looking round it, how the clean white walls and varnished boards suited him. He made her coffee and she asked him for Freya's phone number. A large oil painting near the window caught her eye, and she went to look at it while he was fetching a jug of milk. Sunlight spilled from between clouds on to a landscape of marsh, sand and sea. You could almost hear the whisper of the wavelets.

'I don't usually do oils,' he said, coming to stand at her side. 'It's always been watercolours. I like the way the colours drift into each other. But I thought I'd give it a go.'

She turned to look at him. 'You're wasting yourself at Winterton's. You must know you are, Aidan.'

'I need money. Not just for me, for Mum.'

'Of course you do. Everyone needs money. But making a lot of it has never been important to you. You're not like Piers, you've never cared about outward show. And you have a sister who's very successful and has money to spare. And I know Helen, she'd rather live off bread and cheese than have you make yourself unhappy.'

As she kissed his cheek, preparing to leave, she said, 'Are you sure you're staying at Winterton's because of Helen? Or is something else holding you back?'

She had always found it easier to talk to Piers when she was doing something – driving a car or walking in the countryside, anything that avoided face-to-face confrontation – so she armed herself with rubber gloves and Ajax before calling at his flat.

She handed him the Ajax and told him they would start on the kitchen. He grumbled a little but did as he was told. She explained to him how to clean the sink, and thought things might have turned out better if she'd taught him years ago.

She scrubbed the hob, a sticky mat of food fragments and oil splatters.

'I didn't have an easy marriage,' she said. 'We married after a fortnight's acquaintance, your father and I, and we didn't have much in common. If I hadn't had you, I would have left him. I found consolations, you might say, elsewhere, and so did your father.'

'Mum . . .'

'You're a grown-up, Piers, and it's time you knew these things. Your father was a good provider, but he had a sharp tongue, and I'm sorry that you sometimes had the worst of it. I tried to protect you but I didn't always manage it, and perhaps I didn't do it in the right way. That's one of my biggest regrets and I can see how you might feel resentful. But resentment doesn't do you any good. It eats into you – it's eating into you now, I can see it. Your Anne's worth a hundred of Henry. You should remember that.'

'Mum.' Grey water dripped from his raised hands as he swung round to face her. 'I asked her to come home. She said no.'

'Then ask her again. Keep asking her till she forgives you. You're a Winterton, Piers, and you don't give up.'

She rinsed the cloth under the sink so that she could buff up the hob to a nice shine. She said, conversationally, 'How's the business?'

'Coming on.' Then, suddenly, 'It's been a weird day. Freaky. Bridget's brooches flying off the shelves. We sold twenty of them today, Mum. Twenty.'

'It doesn't surprise me. I always knew you'd do well.'

He paused, cloth in hand, looking puzzled. 'There's a photo of Louise wearing one of Bridget's brooches in this month's *Vogue*.'

'Louise always had good taste.'

'But why would she do that? Why would she help me?'

'Because she's your cousin,' she said patiently. 'Because she loves you. Because you're *family*.' She nodded to the sink. 'Good job. Now you need to do the taps.'

Piers sprinkled Ajax. She said, 'There's another thing I want to talk to you about. I think you should sell the house.'

'Which house?'

'Marsh Court. Though you should get rid of this flat as well.'

'I like this flat.'

'No you don't, or you'd have looked after it better. And nor does Anne. She never did.'

'I can't sell Marsh Court.'

'Why not?'

'It's where you live, Mum.'

'It's far too big for me. Anyway, I might like a change.'

'What?' he said, looking shocked. 'What are you thinking of?'

'I'm not sure yet,' she said evasively. She was going to live

460

at Greensea, but she wasn't going to tell Piers about Joe today. One thing at a time.

'Anyway,' she said briskly, 'I thought you could use some of the money you raise to buy a house in London. Eddie needs a garden. And I daresay the business could use more capital, couldn't it?'

The following morning, Anne was supposed to be working at the gallery, but Eddie wasn't well and so she had phoned Katherine and told her she wouldn't be able to come in. She would make up her hours when he was better. In a way, it was a relief to have an excuse to stay at home with her son; because of Michael, because she was afraid he might come back to the house, she felt uneasy about leaving Eddie with Ceridwen or Maria.

She was washing nappies when the doorbell rang. Piers had fitted a bolt and chain to the door; Anne drew the bolt and peered cautiously out and saw Juliet.

She let her into the house. 'Eddie's having a nap,' she explained. 'He has a cold, poor sweetie. Can I make you a coffee?'

They took the mugs out into the garden. In the brighter light, Anne thought Juliet looked thin, and rather pale and tired.

She said gently, 'You should come and stay for a few days. We've a spare bedroom. It's not very smart, but I'd make it comfortable for you. Then you and Eddie could spend a good amount of time together. He'd love it, and so would I. It must get lonely in that big old house.'

'I'd like that,' Juliet said. Her eyes raked round the things in the garden, the sandpit and the tangle of trikes and pull-along trucks.

She cleared her throat. 'I've always tried not to interfere. I never had a mother-in-law but I imagine that if I'd had one, I wouldn't have wanted her overburdening me with advice.'

'You've never done that,' said Anne. 'You've always been kind to me.'

'Well, why wouldn't I be? You're the perfect daughter-in-law.'

Anne smiled. 'Juliet, that's very sweet of you, but it's not true and you know it. Me and Piers, running off to get married – that must have been a dreadful shock for you.'

'Piers has always been headstrong. I'd never have expected him to do the conventional thing.'

'You welcomed me into your family, this American girl with strange manners and different ways. I don't suppose it was easy.'

'Good for us,' said Juliet firmly, 'to be shaken up a little.'

'And then this mess Piers and I are in . . . So if you want to interfere, then go ahead.'

'I saw him last night. I taught him how to clean a sink.'

'Good.'

'I'm not going to tell you how much he misses you and how much he loves you because I'm sure you know that already. But I wanted to say that I can see how good you are for him. He's always needed a calming influence. He needs someone who stands up to him as well, of course, and you've done that. And I wanted you to know that I hope you can find a way of working things out between you.'

Juliet left shortly afterwards. Rinsing the nappies and hanging them on the washing line, Anne thought about what she had said. She remembered Juliet's kindness and accept-ance of her, and the generosity of the Winterton family. She thought about that awful dinner party where Gabe and Claudia had helped her cope with the crying baby and the scorched soufflé. Even Charley had come round and was trying to help with Eddie. She saw that in her anxiety to become part of the family, and aware of her different background and way of doing things, she had perhaps been overly touchy. She had anticipated criticism, which had not occurred. Juliet valued her for what she was; that was what she had come here to tell her.

She glanced at the clock. Eddie had been asleep for more than two hours. She went upstairs to check on him.

He was awake, lying in his cot, his gaze wandering listlessly over his bird mobile. His nose was runny, his eyes watering. Seeing her, he snuffled, and a smile spread over his face.

She picked him up, cradling him against her. His face was red and his body felt warm against hers. 'Poor little boy,' she murmured. 'You're not well at all, are you? Let's get you a nice cold drink and see if that makes you feel better.'

Past six, and Piers was closing up the shop when someone rapped on the window. Raising the blind, he saw Esteban.

He opened the door. 'Hey, Esteban.'

Esteban clapped him on the shoulder. 'Piers, good to see you.' His darting dark eyes took in the shop. 'Nice place you have here. A little bird has told me your pieces are flying off the shelves like hot cakes.'

'Well,' said Piers modestly, enjoying the mixed metaphor. 'Business is picking up.'

The designer offered to buy Piers a drink. He accepted; as he locked the front door, the phone rang, but he disregarded it. They walked to the Lord Nelson.

Esteban put a pint of bitter in front of him. 'To your business,' he said. 'To Piers Carlisle.'

Their glasses chinked. What if she never came back? He should have felt elated as the success he had striven so hard for began to happen at last, but his triumph tasted of ashes. He felt himself acting out pleasure rather than feeling it.

'And to Winterton's,' he said generously.

Esteban pulled his mouth to one side. 'Your cousin is a good fellow but he hasn't your father's ability. You need to know what sells not just now, but in one, two, five years' time.'

'And Aidan doesn't?'

'No. He . . .' Esteban flapped a hand. 'He waits till something happens, something bad, not enough profit or a line not selling, and then he does something.'

'He reacts,' said Piers.

'Yes, that's what I'm saying. You have to see into the future. You have to' – another waggling of the fingers – 'be a fortune-teller.'

'Be clairvoyant, yes.' Piers drank some beer. 'It's been a tough couple of years. I thought I'd got it wrong. Nearly went under.'

'But you didn't.' Esteban pushed a packet of Gitanes and his lighter across the table. 'You're like your father. You have the gift.' He waited until Piers had lit a cigarette before saying, 'I think maybe it's time I leave Winterton's.'

Piers almost choked. 'Leave Winterton's? Esteban, you've been there—'

'Too long,' the Maltese finished for him. 'I am stale, like an old piece of bread.'

Piers laughed. 'Rot. I've never known you run out of ideas.'

'Maybe if I was working somewhere else, I would find inspiration again.'

Piers felt a rush of excitement as he understood why the designer had come to see him. Carefully he balanced his cigarette on the side of the ashtray, then looked up at Esteban. 'Go on.'

'You have a young business. I'd like to be in at the start of it. We'd be great together, I know it. Say I came to work for you, Piers. I'd want to be your chief designer, naturally. The woman . . .' Esteban clicked finger and thumb.

'Bridget.'

'She would have to work for me. And I would want a share of the profits – twenty-five per cent, say. And artistic control. A pay rise, that goes without saying.'

The word 'okay', sealing the bargain, almost came out, then didn't. Piers found himself saying instead, 'Let me think about it, Esteban. Thank you for coming to see me; it's very flattering, and I appreciate it. I'll get back to you by the end of the week.'

The two men parted shortly afterwards. It was a fine night, so Piers decided to walk home. He thought about Esteban's unexpected offer. Esteban was jumping ship because he thought Piers Carlisle was a better bet than Winterton's. What greater confirmation of his success and ability could there be than Winterton's chief designer offering to work for him?

It was everything he had ever wanted. Winterton's wouldn't survive without Esteban. *Aidan* wouldn't survive. He would have failed.

And yet Piers had hesitated. It didn't make sense. Threading between the crowds that thronged the dusty London streets, he tried to understand what had happened. He was tired, a bit burned out. It seemed years since he had had a proper holiday, and he found it hard, these days, to think about anything other than Anne and Eddie.

He let himself into the house. He heard the phone ringing from his flat and bounded upstairs three at a time.

He picked up the receiver. He thought it might be Esteban, having second thoughts, withdrawing his extraordinary offer.

'Hello?'

'Piers.' Anne's voice, shaky and frightened. 'I'm at the Westminster Children's Hospital. Eddie's very sick. He had a fit. It was awful. He's on an isolation ward. At first the doctors wouldn't tell me what they think is wrong with him, but I made them. It might be measles, or it might be, it might be . . .'

Her voice disintegrated. He could hear her sobbing. 'Anne,' he said as gently as he could, clamping down his own terror. 'Darling.'

'Or it might be meningitis. That's a disease of the brain, Piers. Oh God, you have to come, I need you to come here now.'

Juliet was sitting at a table at the Lyons in Coventry Street, a coffee in front of her. Looking up, she saw Freya. They kissed and sat down. Juliet ordered coffee for Freya and a plate of cakes.

She said, 'I wanted to talk to you about your photograph of the causeway at Thorney Island.'

'Have you made up your mind about it?'

She wondered whether Freya and her mother, Frances, had shared the same colouring. If they had, she understood why Gillis might have fallen in love with that rose-gold prettiness. 'Yes,' she said. 'I've made up my mind.'

Then, taking her time so that Freya was able to absorb what she told her, Juliet related the story of the tragedy that had taken place in 1946, the death by drowning of Frances

Hart and her son, Edmund. Not the whole story, though, not the part played by faithless, reckless Gillis, because that would only have done harm.

Instead, she spoke of the little family who had lived on Thorney Island and the events of the night of the storm. And of the twin sister, Thea, presumed drowned also, whose body had never been found.

Freya's eyes widened. She put down her coffee cup. 'A twin . . .' she said.

'I wondered whether you might possibly be Thea Hart. Whether you might be Frances Hart's lost daughter. It would explain why you remembered the causeway. You're the right age, Freya, and you were adopted as an infant.'

She fished out of her bag the notes she had made. 'I went to Maldon library and looked out the newspaper reports in old copies of the *Essex Gazette*. There was only one photograph of Frances Hart and it wasn't very good, but I thought there was a likeness. I'm afraid I did something very bad – I took the page from the newspaper when the librarian was looking the other way and smuggled it out in my handbag.'

Freya unfolded the sheet of newsprint and stared at the small photograph. 'You think this woman might be my mother . . .'

'I think it's possible. I wondered whether the child might have been swept further up the estuary and somehow reached the shore.' This was the least credible part of her version of the story, with rather a lot of holes, so she glossed over it quickly. 'And maybe whoever found her didn't realise who she was. Perhaps they hadn't seen the newspapers, perhaps they didn't listen to the radio. Life was different then, people were much more cut off, and the east of the county was an isolated place. And maybe whoever found her took her to an orphanage.'

'But,' said Freya, 'my orphanage was in *Southampton*.'

'I know. It's a long way away. But at that time, children were moved around a lot, I believe.'

'I'd been in a different orphanage before. My father told me.'

'Do you know where?'

'London, I think. I could check with him.'

Juliet recalled Gillis saying that Morgan had told Mrs Farmer at the Southampton orphanage that Thea was a foundling who had been discovered in the street during the London Blitz.

The risks in telling the truth were not only to Juliet and the family, but to Freya too. She had gone pale beneath her freckles.

Juliet reached out a hand to her. 'I don't know whether I've done you a disservice in telling you this. I hope not. I might be wrong. Or you might rather not have known. It's taken me a long time to make up my mind what to do. But I remember that night so well. I've never forgotten it. I saw those children once, playing on the causeway, and I thought that if I was that girl, and if my family had left me nothing but a memory, then I'd want to know.'

She slid a sheet of notepaper across the table. 'The *Essex Gazette* said that Frances's family came from Broad Chalke in Wiltshire. Her parents are probably dead by now, but her sister may still be alive. If you wanted to, you could try to find her. But you must do as you think best.'

It was two in the morning and Piers and Anne were in the hospital canteen. The counter was closed up and the metal chairs were stacked on tabletops, but Piers had taken Anne there so that she could cry in private.

Tears of relief. Eddie was sick with measles, not meningitis. The doctors had reduced his temperature with medication and a nurse had sponged him down, and he was sleeping soundly in a cot on an isolation ward.

Piers lifted down two chairs. 'I don't know why I'm crying,' Anne said. 'He's going to get better.' Then she looked at him. 'Oh Piers, don't. Don't, my darling, please.'

But he couldn't stop. Tears sprang from his eyes as he wept. He felt a fool; men weren't supposed to cry.

She hugged him. 'It's going to be all right, my darling. He's going to be all right.'

'I thought we were going to lose him.'

'We're not, sweetie.'

'I've lost *you*.'

'No you haven't. I love you.'

He pressed her head against his chest, afraid to let her go. 'I love you both so much.'

They sat down. He blew his nose, rubbed his face on his sleeve, rummaged in his pocket for his cigarettes and then put them back again. Anne looked in her bag and found some chocolate peanuts. She split open the packet.

'When did you last eat?'

'Cheese sandwich at lunchtime. A beer at six.' Impossible to believe that he had talked to Esteban only eight hours before. It seemed like a week.

She said, 'I should have taken him to the doctor earlier.'

'You didn't know.'

'I *should* have known, I'm his *mother*. I thought it was a cold. And then when he fitted . . . Piers, I thought he was going to die.'

'Thank God you'd got the phone,' he said. 'Thank God you were able to call an ambulance.'

'I don't know what I've been doing.' Her voice sank to a whisper. 'I've been thinking of me, not of Eddie, I've been thinking about what I need. That damp house . . . He probably caught it from one of the other children. And leaving him there when that madman came round . . . I'm such a useless mother.'

He had been a useless husband, but he knew that now was not the time to say it. It had, Piers thought, been the worst evening of his entire life. He knew that the memory of Eddie, small, unresponsive and fragile, tubes coming out of him, would haunt him for a very long time. His fear and his sense of precariousness remained; he had been given a warning of what might happen if you weren't careful, if you were stupid enough to fail to identify what was most dear to you.

'You're a terrific mother,' he said. 'Eddie's a terrific little boy. It's me who needs to change, and I will, Anne, I promise you that. I'm so sorry about everything. I've been such a fool.'

Overcome again, he looked away. He heard her say, 'I think you need more peanuts,' and she uncurled his hand and poured them on to his palm.

'Chocolate peanuts, the cure for everything,' he said savagely. 'Do you think they'll cure idiocy and selfishness and jealousy?'

'I wouldn't have married you if you hadn't had your better points.'

'Do you regret it?'

'No, not at all.' She wrinkled her brow. 'Sometimes I have. When I thought you didn't love me.'

He brushed back her pale fringe from her forehead, then took her hands in his. 'I love you. I love you so much. I'll make it up to you. I'll give up the business, if that's what you want. I'll sell it.'

470

'You don't have to do that.'

'I'm just saying, whatever it takes.'

She shook her head. 'I love your fire, Piers, your energy. We have to get the balance right, that's all.'

He was going to do better, he thought. He wouldn't make the same mistakes with Eddie that his father had made with him. He would praise his son when he did well and he would tell him he loved him.

'Come home with me, Anne,' he said. 'Please come home.'

On the train back from Salisbury, Freya was relieved to find an empty compartment and a seat by the window. Sitting down, she leaned her head against the glass pane. On the station platform, people rushed about, buying magazines, hurrying for trains. She wondered whether her mother had once stood on the same platform, impatiently tapping the toe of her shoe, flame-coloured curls escaping from beneath a chic little thirties hat. Or wearing the uniform of the WAAF on a cold winter's night, snow in the air, her train overdue.

When Marion Thomas, Frances Hart's younger sister, had opened the door to Freya, she had put her hand to her mouth and said softly, 'Oh.' Then she had turned away, dabbing at her eyes with a folded handkerchief.

'I'm sorry,' Freya said. 'I didn't mean to shock you.'

Marion tucked the handkerchief back up her sleeve. 'You look so like her. The spitting image. Except for your eyes. Fran had brown eyes. I wasn't expecting it, that's all, I thought there must be some mistake.'

Marion Thomas was in her mid-forties. She had curly brown hair with a few strands of grey in it, and lively blue eyes, and she rushed about making coffee, putting biscuits on a plate and finding Freya a comfortable seat. Marion was

471

Freya's aunt. She had an Uncle Eric, too, and three cousins, Mark, Lorna and Sam. Sam – thirteen, a chatterbox, bouncy – was home from school with a cold. He hurtled through the room, barely pausing to say hello when Marion introduced them.

'Back to school tomorrow,' said Marion drily.

Cousins: it was a lot to take in.

Marion had lived in the same house all her life. Both she and Frances had been born and brought up in the Wiltshire village of Broad Chalke, among the rolling hills and watercress beds. The Dairy House was built of stone and brick; part of the roof was thatched, and there was a well in the cobbled courtyard. It looked, Freya felt, like something out of a fairy tale. Her compact camera was in her handbag; her fingers itched to record it, to make sense of it.

In a sitting room crammed with well-stuffed floral sofas and a dark wood dresser crowded with blue and white china, Marion took a handful of photographs from an envelope and spread them out on the coffee table. Their father, she said to Freya, tapping a snapshot an inch square – her and Frances's father – had run the dairy, but the business had closed down in the early fifties.

'Dad died in 1952,' Marion said. 'After the twins were born – after you and Edmund were born – we weren't allowed even to mention Fran's name. Because she wasn't married, you see. She came here once with you and your brother and he wouldn't let her through the door. He never forgave her. He blamed her for my mother's death, said she'd broken Mum's heart, but that was nonsense, of course. Mum died of cancer, and she was ill long before Fran met him.'

Freya said, 'Met who?'

Marion pushed another snapshot across the tabletop. 'Look.

472

She must have been about your age then. The spitting image. She was sweet-natured, Fran, but scatty. Always losing her bus fare and her homework when we were girls.' She paused to pour tea. Her hands were shaking. 'I don't know who your father was. Fran never told me. Her lover. When she spoke of him, that's what she called him, her lover. He must have been married, of course, I wasn't so naïve I couldn't work that one out. She met him in 1940 and I didn't see much of her after that. She was in the WAAF and I was rushed off my feet with Mum being so sick and helping Dad in the dairy. And then I married and had Mark.' Marion passed Freya a cup and saucer. 'Fran distanced herself from me. She didn't want me to know about him. He was her secret. I wondered whether he was someone famous, someone you'd see in the papers, but she'd never tell. We'd been close when we were girls, even though there was five years between us. But we were so different. Fran was pretty and I wasn't, Fran had ambitions and I never wanted anything else than to stay here, at home, with Mum and Dad.'

'What sort of ambitions?'

Marion sighed. 'Oh, the usual ones young girls have. To see the world. To have babies. To fall in love with Prince Charming and be whisked away to a castle and live happily ever after. Well, she found her Prince Charming, but I'm not sure he made her happy. I think for a while he did, but then it went wrong, as these things do. Not that Fran would ever have admitted it. She adored him, I could tell she did. She didn't write often, but when she did, it was all about how exciting her life was, and how pretty and clever you and Edmund were, and how you'd soon be living in a nice house and I must come and stay with her. It was all cloud cuckoo land, of course, but that was Fran.'

Freya felt as if she was holding her breath. 'What was Edmund like?'

'He was a dear little thing, though he ran rings round poor Fran. I remember he had beautiful golden hair. Fran said it was wasted on a boy. He was a handsome little chap. I've a picture.'

She handed Freya a small print. Posed, a studio photograph of a style twenty years out of date, the little boy in shorts, a white shirt and miniature bow tie, hair parted to one side and plastered down. The girl – and it took her breath away as she recognised her much younger self – in a cotton dress, a ribbon in her hair. Did she remember that frock, with its cheerful pattern of stripes and roses? Perhaps, somewhere in the deep well of her memory, she did.

'She gave it to me the last time I saw her,' said Marion. 'I told her she looked tired – and she did, worn through to the bone – but she wasn't having any of that. Frances always saw the world how she wanted to see it, and you had to go along with it, she'd take offence if you didn't.' She offered the plate of biscuits to Freya. 'But she did admit that she was lonely sometimes. That she didn't see him, her lover, as often as she'd like. She was sick of waiting for him, she told me, waiting for the letters and phone calls. I was in the same boat then, with Eric in the Far East, and we had a good chat about bringing our kids up on our own. When I left, she hugged me and said I must come more often, but I never saw her again. We hadn't the time or the money for travelling, and I was so busy with the kids and Dad. And then she went to live on that island.' Marion pressed her lips together and shook her head slowly. 'She hated it there. She said it felt like a prison. I should have made the effort. I thought I had all the time in the world. You do, don't you?'

474

The train heaved itself out of the station. The back gardens of terraced houses gave way to green fields, copses and chalk streams. This was an ancient part of England, soaked through with history, from standing stones to medieval cathedrals. Freya thought that one day she should get to know it.

Marion had offered to take her to see her mother's grave. They had walked through the village to a pretty flint church with a square tower and crenellations. In the churchyard, near a hawthorn, a headstone marked the last resting place of Frances and Edmund Hart.

Freya's heart felt as if it had been put through a wringer, squeezed by the rubber rollers until she no longer knew what shape it was in. Would she, as Juliet Winterton had wondered, have rather not known?

No. This was a gift, an unexpected and painful one, but a gift for all that. She had always been missing a part of her: her birth certificate, shorter than most people's, gave the names of her adoptive parents only, as if she had been born at four years old.

'Do you remember them?' Marion had said, as they stood in the churchyard, and Freya had shaken her head.

But she did, she thought, in her way. This she had always lived with: an absence, as if a wind had dropped. A voice just out of earshot. A shadow locked on to her feet wherever she walked, and an ungraspable presence so vivid that sometimes she found herself turning to look for it.

She knew what it was now. Her twin, Edmund.

After nine days, once his rash had faded, they took Eddie home from hospital. Though there was a huge sense of relief in having him back in the flat again, a milestone passed, Anne did not, as she had thought she might, relax. For the first few nights she slept on a camp bed in the nursery. She would never forget her terror when her baby had had his febrile seizure, the sudden possibility that her world might be torn in two, and would never again take her son's good health for granted. She knew that they had narrowly avoided disaster.

She felt the same about her marriage. She and Piers were careful with each other. There were rough paths on which they might stumble and rivers into which they might slip, having lost their footing. They loved each other, though, she felt sure of that at last, and perhaps that would be enough for them to find a way through.

One evening, he spoke to her of his father. A part of me hated him, he said, but I admired him too. I wanted to be like him, strong and fierce and not caring what other people thought of him. I loved him, I suppose, and all I wanted was for him to love me too. Maybe he did, in his way, but he didn't show it. His generation − well, Dad had a pretty stiff upper lip. If you ever hear me talk to Eddie like he talked to me, if you ever hear me telling him to toughen up and be a man, then for God's sake shut me up. I think it made me feel that love was risky. That you might give a lot and get nothing much back.

Anne was sitting on Piers's knee. She rested her head against his and he stroked her hair. The nursery door was open so they could hear Eddie if he cried. They planned to hire a part-time nanny so that Anne could go back to the gallery when she was sure Eddie was well enough. In the autumn, they would put the flat on the market and look for a house. Not yet, though. They needed to take it slowly, one step at a time.

*　　*　　*

476

For the time being, Rory was coming home from school at weekends. Nate had taken him camping on the first weekend; just now, both Sinclair boys were helping to sort out the spare bedroom in Charley's new house, where more chunks of ceiling had come down in the night, burying her typewriter under powdery white snow.

Nate had wrapped a scarf round his face and was perched on a stepladder, prising off loose lumps of plaster, while Rory carried the debris out to the back garden. Charley shook the dust out of her typewriter.

Rory was out of the room when Nate said to Charley, 'You're usually expelled if you run away, but Claudia went to see his headmaster. You can't argue with Claudia, no one can. You do know you're going to have to take this ceiling down, don't you? You'll be buried alive.'

'I'll be fine.'

'Seriously. I'll take it down but you'll need to find a plasterer.'

'You do like my house, don't you, Nate?'

'It's got character,' he said. 'Like you.'

Rory came back. 'You could make a rockery with all those chunks of plaster. Just put some soil on top of it and plant some flowers. Mum and I made one once. I'll do it if you like.'

Charley thanked him. Then Nate told them to stand back, so she and Rory went on to the landing while a huge section of plaster fell in a great whump to the floor.

'Cool,' said Rory.

'I'll give you a hand with that.'

'I can do it.' He went downstairs, staggering under the weight of it.

'Do you really want a rockery?' Nate asked her.

'I'll want one that Rory makes. I'm buying a carpet for the sitting room. Just think,' she said lightly, 'me with a carpet and a rockery.' Sometimes, in the evening, the house seemed very quiet. She was living on her own for the first time in her life. She missed the chatter and turmoil of other people.

He said, 'One of Mum's charities is going to hold a dance, a fund-raiser, as a memorial for her.'

'Nate, how lovely. You'll go, won't you?'

'All four of us will.'

'Will you take one of your girlfriends?'

'Preferably not.' He leaned forward, ruffling his hair with his fingers to get the plaster dust out.

'Aren't you in love with them any more?' she teased him.

'Good God, no.' He climbed down off the stepladder. 'Never was. But I am in love with someone else.'

A falling-away, a shrinking, as if someone had turned a tap and all her happiness and optimism was draining out of her. She needed to say the right things to encourage Nate, who deserved to be happy again.

'Will you ask her, then?'

'I don't know if she's interested in me.'

'You have to ask her,' she said firmly. 'It's the only way to find out.'

He gave a croak of laughter. 'God, Charley.'

'What? What have I said?'

'Can't you see? That it's you. It's always been you. Never anyone else but you.'

She stared at him. 'Me?'

'Yes.' He came to stand in front of her. His fingers threaded through hers. 'I'm in love with you. Have been since I came back from South America. There's never been anyone else.'

'Me?' she whispered. She put a hand to her heart. 'Nate . . .'

'Oh, don't howl, it's not that bad, is it?'

Unable to speak, she touched his lips with her own. His were warm and dry and tasted of plaster.

Then, footsteps on the stairs, and Rory, seeing them, said, 'Oh Lord, yuck, honestly, Nate,' and they drew apart. But she knew, standing among the ruins of the room, that they were at the beginning of something that was going to be quite perfect.

Louise had told Aidan that Eddie had recovered and that he and Anne were back at home. The next morning, Aidan went to see Piers at the shop in the King's Road.

Piers's secretary, a small, dark girl, showed Aidan through to his office. Seeing him, his cousin stood up so suddenly he knocked over his chair.

Aidan said quickly, 'Hear me out. That's all I'm asking, just hear me out.'

Surprising Aidan, Piers called out to his secretary, 'Tricia, can you get us a couple of coffees?' and yanked a chair to the other side of his desk.

'Sit down.'

Aidan did so. He said, 'I want you to have Winterton's.'

Piers put his own chair upright. 'Aidan—'

'The business. Have it. You should have had it ages ago.'

The girl, Tricia, came in with two mugs of coffee. Piers said, 'Why?'

'Because I don't want it. I never did. And because I'm no good at it and you will be.'

'It's instant,' Piers said as Aidan picked up his mug. 'I like instant, don't you? I can't tell Anne, she's almost religious about coffee, so I only have it at work.' Then, frowning, he said, 'I don't need Winterton's, I've got this place. I'm doing all right now.'

'I thought you might like to have both of them.' And Aidan, scratching his head, tried to convey the conclusion he had come to after Juliet had visited him.

'I should have gone to art college,' he said. 'I should have insisted, should have told the family years ago that I had no interest in the business. I've been telling myself I'm doing it out of duty to the family and because I need to support my mother, but the truth is I was afraid. It's hard to become a successful painter and I was afraid I might fail, make a fool of myself and foul up.' He looked up at Piers. 'The trouble with our family, we have this golden touch, don't we? We can't fail because Wintertons don't fail. So it was easier not to try, easier to do what was expected of me. But I dread going into work. Every morning, I dread it. Uncle Henry would never have felt like that, and he'd never have felt sick because he had to sack a member of staff. And I don't suppose you would either, Piers. You're like your father, you relish a conflict. I'm not like that. You can't run a business thinking like I do. If I stay there, I'll destroy it.'

Piers hadn't touched his coffee. He was staring at it, glowering. He looked up. 'You'd do that? You'd just give it to me?'

'Yes.'

'After everything that's happened?'

'Yes. Gladly.'

'Even Anne?'

'Even Anne.' This was harder to be generous about. 'I loved her,' he said. 'But I don't any more, and I haven't for quite a while. I went on telling myself I was in love with her through habit, I think. Or obstinacy. And anyway, she never thought of me as anything other than a friend.'

'I know,' said Piers. There was a silence, rather tense, and then he said, 'What about money?'

'I've got the flat. It's good for painting, a nice light. And I don't need much.'

Piers tapped a pencil on his desk. 'Creative director.'

'What?'

'We've never had a creative director and we should do. If I were to put the two businesses together – it would make sense to keep Piers Carlisle a younger, less expensive brand within Winterton's – we'd need someone to keep an eye on the designers. You know what Esteban's like, he likes to throw his weight around. And Bridget's good, really good, and I wouldn't want to lose her.' When Aidan did not respond, he went on, 'Part-time. You wouldn't have to have an office there if you didn't want one. Consulting creative director, if that's what you'd prefer. You know the place, you know Esteban and the others, and you've always liked that side of it. You'd be perfect.'

Slowly, Aidan nodded. People said it took ten years to get a career in the arts off the ground. A small income wouldn't go amiss during that time.

Then he stood up. 'You should keep Gabe in charge at Sloane Street,' he said. 'Actually, you should think about making her manager of both shops. She's good. She loves it, and she's frighteningly competent and utterly ruthless. She reminds me of Uncle Henry.'

'Keep it in the family,' said Piers.

'Yeah.' Aidan held out his hand. 'Deal?'

'Deal.'

They shook hands. Piers said, 'Come and see us. I'd like you to meet Eddie. I'm sorry I was such an ass that time.'

'I will.'

Leaving the shop, Aidan felt lighter, as if he had cast off a burden. He walked along the King's Road with a spring in his step. Freya, he thought, he was going to tell Freya about the decision he'd made. He'd tell his mother and Louise and all the rest of his clamorous, importunate family in good time, but just now what he wanted most in the world was to tell Freya.

In the sitting room of the red-brick house in Woodstock Road, Oxford, in which Freya had grown up, she sat down with her father and said, 'I think I've found my birth mother.'

She told him about the Harts, and how the dates tied in with what she knew of her own history. She showed him the picture of the twins, her and her brother, that Marion Thomas had given her, and a photograph of Frances.

Her father looked old suddenly, old and sad and tired. He'd always thought there was something fishy about the adoption, he admitted. No paperwork. The woman who ran the orphanage, a Mrs Farmer, had been fluttery and over-anxious to get the child off her hands. She had told him some lightly sketched-in tale about Freya being found abandoned in the street in the Blitz and consigned to a London institution which had since closed.

'I should have asked more questions,' he said. 'I didn't dare. Your mother had her heart set on it.'

His was the hand that had held hers when she had first come to this house twenty years before. His was the hand that had gripped hers when he had walked her to school on her first day, and when he had taken her home from the hospital after she had had her tonsils out.

She took his hand now. 'I wouldn't have had it any other way.'

482

'And your father?'

She shook her head. 'Nothing.'

'Do you mind not knowing?'

She thought for a while. 'No, I don't think so. It didn't sound as if he was around all that much. He's not important, is he?' She rested her head on his shoulder. 'You're the best father I could ever have had. And Mummy was the best mother.'

But afterwards, when she returned to London, a restlessness remained, a sense of events shifting, creaking with a rasp and a scrape into a different position. Sylvie Duvallier, the proprietor of Image, had written to her, commissioning her to take a series of landscape photographs, to be featured in the magazine. A whole year's work. Freya felt herself to be on the verge of something wonderful. She was catching a first glimpse of a new world.

This is the beginning, she thought. It's what I've always wanted and could hardly believe would ever happen, and this is the start of it.

Through the open window she heard the rumble of traffic and car horns. As a drunk wove across the road, he bawled curses at a van and thumped its bonnet. The horizon was a tangle of roofs and television aerials, the vegetation sooty privets and sticky lime trees, and the sky clotted, like rice pudding. London was fine, but she was through with it. It had given her a start but it wasn't where she belonged. She wondered whether her mother had felt the same, whether she had itched to escape that pretty, over-furnished house in Wiltshire.

She wanted more than her mother had had, and besides, times had changed. She wouldn't wait around for the man she loved, as Frances had waited for her lover. Freya saw things precisely, with a photographer's eye, and she thought that Aidan had feelings for her. But he would have to discover that himself. She had things to do.

She pulled her rucksack down from the top of the wardrobe and flung things inside it.

With Piers's agreement, Juliet had put Marsh Court up for sale. A young couple – how could they possibly afford it? she wondered – looked round and commented critically on the old-fashioned kitchen and the lack of central heating. 'We'd have to pull all this out,' the wife said, wrinkling up her nose at the bathroom. Juliet wanted to point out to them that she'd lived there for twenty-eight years, that she loved the house and her babies had been born there. But she managed to remain silent and endured the remainder of the unenthusiastic tour before seeing the couple out. Flattened, she returned to her old-fashioned kitchen, put on the kettle and made a pot of tea.

She phoned Anne to check that Eddie was still improving and then settled down with her programmes, lists and a pen. There would be no more concerts at Marsh Court after this summer's, so she meant to make the final series the best ever. Essex friends were coming, London friends too.

Though she had done her best to repair what could be repaired, the bridges she had built seemed fragile. Piers and Anne were trying to make a fresh start, but she could not tell what lay ahead for them. Could not know, either, the repercussions of her decision to tell Freya of her link to the Hart family. As for Charley and Nate, they were very young, and who knew how long their love affair might last? Though she thought it would. There had always been a bond between those two.

She would introduce Joe to the family as soon as the dust had settled from the latest upheavals. When Marsh Court was sold, she would move into Greensea, that remote old house that seemed a part of the countryside that surrounded it. She and Joe would breathe the same air and would share their hopes and fears. And she would learn to be a farmer's wife.

A letter from Freya was waiting for Aidan when he came home from work. He peeled off his jacket as he ran upstairs; inside the flat, he slit open the envelope and read it.

Freya wrote that she had given up her job at the hospital to pursue a full-time career as a professional photographer. And that she had decided to go back to Orkney.

Orkney. Aidan sat down on the sofa, floored. He read the letter again. Freya had already left London. She didn't say how long she'd be staying on the islands. She might, he thought, rereading it for a third time, have gone to live there permanently. He wouldn't put it past her.

Freya and I are just friends, he had said to Anne, not so long ago. What a fool he had been. He respected and liked Freya, and he enjoyed her company immensely. They liked the same things and never ran out of stuff to talk about. But he was also hugely attracted to her. Why had it taken him so long to realise that he was in love with her? Because, he thought savagely, he had made a habit of failing to realise what it was he most wanted until it was too late. A habit of failing to see – mortifying in someone who liked to think of himself as an artist.

Well, no more. He picked up the phone and called Piers's number. Would Piers consider taking over the business sooner than planned? he asked him. Such as, for instance, tomorrow.

485

'Christ, yes,' said Piers. And then, perhaps aware that he had been over-eager, 'Is everything all right?'

Aidan assured him that it was and ended the call. Next he phoned Gabe, firing off orders so Winterton's would continue to run smoothly without him. 'Piers will be taking over from me,' he told her. He imagined her, blue eyes like saucers, bursting with curiosity.

'*Piers?*' she repeated.

'Yes, Piers,' he said unhelpfully. 'Any problems, talk to him.'

He put down the phone, got out his rucksack, walking boots, a cagoule. Binoculars, tent, sleeping bag, a sketchbook, the small knapsack in which he kept his painting stuff.

How the hell did you even get to Orkney? The phone rang, Winterton's chief accountant moaning to him about taxes, as Aidan flicked through a railway timetable.

The Inverness train left Euston station shortly after eight o'clock. The journey took more than eight hours, during which time the landscape Aidan saw through the window changed from city to hill to meadow and back again many times.

Somewhere beyond Pitlochry, he dozed, and woke at Aviemore. Yellow gorse flared on the slopes, and blue-grey mountains, topped with snow at midsummer, rose on the horizon. Blankets of emerald moss spread themselves beneath copses of birch and pine. He watched, awed, and then wandered to the buffet car, where he bought coffee and a mutton pie. He ate and drank, transfixed by the view.

He stayed for a night in a bed and breakfast in Inverness. It was raining, and the streets and buildings were grey and chill, but now and then sunlight showed between the clouds and flashed on the wet roads. In the morning he returned to the station to catch the Thurso train. A couple of hours later, leaving Thurso station, he hauled his rucksack on to his back and walked to Scrabster harbour, glad of the chance to stretch his legs after his long journey. Clouds billowed up in a white and grey sky, the sea was the colour of granite and a fine rain dimpled the puddles at the roadside. Solitary grey houses, small-windowed and low-roofed, faced out to the wild weather of the Pentland Firth.

He took his place in the queue; the ferry docked, and after a while the passengers went on board. Aidan found a seat on deck, pulled the hood of his cagoule over his head and watched the port grow smaller as they set out to sea.

The rain eased and he took out his sketchbook, and then put it aside as the tall red cliffs of Hoy came into view. He went to stand with half a dozen other passengers at the guardrail. The wind battered his face and the clouds cleared and the sun poured through like molten gold. His neighbour pointed out to him the Old Man of Hoy, and he peered through his binoculars at the rock stack poised like a red-brown giant, guarding the island.

Two hours after leaving Scrabster, the ferry put in at Stromness, on the largest of the Orkney Islands, Mainland. It was an orderly, attractive little town of cobbled alleyways wedged between grey houses, dominated by the harbour. He wandered the length of the town and then along the quayside. His fingers itched to paint the contrasting materials, the yellow-grey paving slabs, the tin shacks, the clumps of lime-green seaweed that sprouted from the sea wall.

He bought a cup of tea and asked directions to Kirkwall, Orkney's capital It seemed as good a place to start as any. A bus arrived and he was taken through a grassy, watery landscape. No trees, and nothing you could have called a mountain; instead, rolling hills and glimpses, often, of a lake or the sea. The land shaved away to a narrow isthmus between planes of water.

The heavens opened as the bus came into Kirkwall. He had no idea where Freya was, or where she was staying. He asked around a bit, rain peeling from his cagoule, in shops and pubs. Had anyone seen a tall, red-haired English girl? Plenty of redheads here, he noticed.

He took a room in a guest house, got something to eat. A rainbow shimmered, strands of coloured silk in the sky above the harbour. He walked round the back of the town to Scapa beach. The white sand was scattered with shells, peaceful now, but twenty-seven years ago, out at Scapa Flow, the *Royal Oak* had been torpedoed by a German U-boat and more than eight hundred men and boys had drowned. Oystercatchers chipped their orange beaks at the mud, and a soft wind blew across the sea. Waves whispered over the sand and stones, telling stories. Aidan felt something inside him soften and disentangle, something that had been knotted for a very long time. He thought of his father, wished they could have come here together for some birdwatching, a bit of walking. Rain washed across the bay in a silvery gust; he headed back to the town.

When he woke in the morning, the sky was a blisteringly clear blue. Aidan breakfasted, then went out. Not far from the great red sandstone bulk of St Magnus Cathedral, he found a bookshop. He bought a guidebook and leafed through it while drinking coffee in a café. Inside the volume he found photographs of standing stones and stone chambers. Some of the menhirs were tall and slim and pointed; others seemed to have been sliced off at an angle. And always around them the shallow hills and the water.

She wasn't in Kirkwall; this he was certain of by the end of the day. It was a small place and he would have seen her. The next day, he checked out of the guest house. He bought bread, apples and cheese, and then took a bus inland. He was travelling through a landscape in which the distant past, Neolithic and Pictish, revealed itself often, as if it was only just out of sight. His pencil flickered over paper.

The bus dropped him near the Ring of Brodgar. Freya wasn't there, and he spent the day sketching the salt sea and the freshwater lake and the standing stones that crowned the hilltop. The stones formed a perfect circle at the centre of a vast bowl formed by the rising landscape. Lady's smock flowered in the wet grass, and the intense yellow flowers of the marsh marigolds seemed to distil the sunlight. He trudged uphill, boots dipping into the soggy earth, to the circle of stones. Earth, air and water: all three combined to work their magic here. His fingers were loosening up, his pencil was starting to do what he wanted it to. He was learning to see again.

He spent the night camping in a farmer's field. When he woke in the morning, a chill dew sparkled in the grass. The farmer's wife invited him to share their breakfast. In the farmhouse kitchen, as she poured out tea, he asked her whether she had seen a red-haired girl – tall, slim, about his age. English.

'She was up at the stones two days ago. She camped out here, like you.'

'Did she say where she was heading on to?'

'Skara Brae.' Thick black tea streamed into a mug. 'My son Donald gave her a lift.'

Skara Brae was on the west coast of the island. Aidan hitched and walked, but Freya had moved on by the time

489

he arrived there. He wondered whether he was fated always to be a day behind her, as if in some fairy-tale quest. He lost track of time, wandering round the Neolithic dwelling places by the shore that had been buried beneath the sand dunes until a great storm had uncovered them a hundred years ago. A cliffside studded with tiny blue and white flowers, skuas diving over the headland, and the waves churning below. And always the sound of the sea. He sat on the grass and took out his watercolours and painted the land that was spread out around him: the swoop of green grass, the perfect beach with its strip of white sand, and the distant islands riding the blue-grey sea like porpoises. Better, he thought when he had finished the sketch. Not dead-looking any more.

He camped in a field, but the weather turned foul in the night, threatening to whip the tent away. He ran round in the dark wearing only his jeans, bashing in tent pegs with a stone. Rain blew through the flap and soaked his sleeping bag, and he shivered throughout the remainder of the night. A grey dawn, and his clothes were damp when he woke, and he wondered whether he might already be too late. Freya might have travelled on. She might have sailed to another island, or headed still further north, to Shetland or the Faroes.

He ate his last apple and a heel of bread, packed up his belongings and made for the Brough of Birsay, high up on the north-west corner of the island. The wind was strong, whipping up a white foam on the sea, but the sun dried his clothes as he walked to the causeway. The island – the Brough – was a high slab of green-topped rock at the far end of it. A shallow ebbing tide washed over the stony path.

He was tired and hungry and a little dazed, but he saw her, standing on the rocks, looking out over the channel. Her hair and the hood of her khaki cagoule flared in the stiff wind.

490

He clambered over the boulders. When she caught sight of him, she straightened and scooped her hair from her face.

He walked towards her. 'Aidan,' she said. 'Oh my God, Aidan.'

'Hello, Freya.'

'But . . .' She stared at him and then laughed. 'What are you doing here? And what about, well, *everything* – Winterton's . . . your work?'

'Winterton's can go to hell. And I came to find you, of course.'

'Did you?' Her eyes danced and she laughed again.

'Of course I did. Did you think I wouldn't?' Gently he stroked the side of her face, marvelling at the translucency and softness of her skin, loving each of the tiny freckles that dusted her nose.

'I wasn't sure,' she murmured.

'I wanted to see the place that you loved,' he said. 'I wanted to be with you. But if you'd rather be alone, if you're thinking what a damn nuisance, then I'll get the train back home. After I've tried to persuade you otherwise, of course.'

She shook her head. 'Aidan, I don't want you to go back home. I really, really don't.'

They kissed for a long time. When at last they drew apart, he looked about, scanning the vista before turning back to her.

'All this beauty. It's almost too much.'

'Isn't it?'

'I've been burning boats. A whole fleet of them, actually.'

'Good,' she said seriously. 'I'm glad.'

When the sea fell back, they crossed the causeway hand in hand. Arriving on the island, they kissed. As they climbed up the stones, they stopped now and then to kiss some more.

Chapter Nineteen

December 1966

S omeone tapped a spoon on the side of a glass, and then, when the level of conversation remained at a roar, Gabe bawled, 'Let's have some quiet for Piers and Aidan!' and the noise tailed off and the guests looked round to where the two cousins were standing side by side at the counter. Helen gave a little raise of the eyebrows that Juliet instantly understood to convey relief and thankfulness and an acknowledgement of the fact that there had been times when neither of them had ever thought this day would come. A waitress moved through the crowd, offering glasses of champagne.

Piers began to speak, welcoming the Wintertons and their friends, colleagues and clients to the opening of the new premises of Piers Carlisle, a young and contemporary brand within the parent Winterton company. There was a ripple of laughter as he hit his stride, amusing his audience with an anecdote about his great-great-great-grandfather, Hayden Winterton, the company's founder. Smiling, Juliet leaned back against Joe and his hand settled lightly on her hip.

They had married two months earlier at the church in Maldon, the quiet ceremony witnessed by those closest to them, those they loved most. Joe had been so easily absorbed into the family, she wondered why she had put it off so long. There had been enough Boule de Neige roses still in flower that autumn to decorate the church; she cut them before breakfast while their creamy-white petals were beaded with dew, and Helen swept them away to the church. An ivory silk shantung dress and coat, a rosebud pinned to her collar. No jewels except her engagement ring.

They had fixed the date of the wedding as soon as the house was sold. Marsh Court had meant so much to her, she had not liked to leave it empty. There had been times when she had despaired of finding a buyer, but then, out of the blue, Louise and Josh had offered to purchase the house. 'I'm planning to retire from modelling in a year or two, you see, Aunt Juliet,' Louise told her. 'Marsh Court will make a wonderful hotel. I've been thinking for a while that I'd like to run my own hotel. And there'd be plenty of space for the donkey sanctuary in the grounds.'

Piers was still speaking, serious now. 'Winterton's success has been a consequence of keeping to its principles, the use of the finest-quality gems, in particular, diamonds, sapphires and pearls set in designs of elegance and originality.'

Juliet had not worn her pearls since she had plucked them from the mud of the causeway. She did not know whether she would ever wear them again. The best jewels had a magic, they carried their story with them. A dark narrative lay at the heart of her pearls.

They had found Morgan's body three weeks after she had met him by the Blackwater. It had never been formally identified, but she had no doubt that it was Morgan. After its long immersion in the tidal estuary, there had been little to distinguish the drowned man apart from a couple of small tattoos. A description had been circulated in the local news-papers – a male in his fifties or early sixties, heavily built, approximately five foot eight in height, a naval man most likely because of the swallow and anchor tattoos on his wrists. The dead man found in the mud of Bradwell Creek had occupied the headlines of the local newspapers for a week, and then, finding no resolution, the mystery had been relegated to the inner pages and, after a while, dropped.

But it had taken a long time for her heart not to pound at every chime of the doorbell and unexpected ring of the tele-phone. She had dreamed of Morgan, dripping wet and caked with mud and salt, rising up out of the river to stand looking down at Marsh Court, on the bank that bordered the field.

The nightmares had left her when she had gone to live at Greensea. She felt safe there, walled off from the outside world by yew and holly and salt marsh. She had given up her teaching job at the end of the summer term. She was learning to be a farmer's wife. She was learning to share a kitchen with Christine Brandon, and to coax Neville out of his occasional bouts of surliness. And she was learning how love could transform, and the deep, quiet pleasure of making and returning it. She was learning to be happy again.

A burst of applause as Piers's speech came to an end. Anne said to Freya, 'I love the photos. We'll be purchasing some so they'll have a permanent place here.'

Huge prints of Freya's photographs of Orkney decorated one charcoal-grey wall of the shop. 'You don't need to buy them,' said Freya. 'I'll give them to you, Anne.'

'We'll buy them,' said Anne firmly.

'Then thank you. And thank you so much for doing this for me.'

'Actually, Piers thought of it. I had the idea of making this an event, a happening, not just another dull old cocktail reception, and he suggested we show your new work.'

'It looks marvellous,' said Freya, her gaze scanning the crowded space. 'You're both so clever.'

The right premises had come up in the King's Road, and Piers had snapped it up. The showroom was four times the size of the tiny shop in which, two years earlier, he had started up his business. He and Anne had worked together on the interior. They were learning to share. Piers looked after Eddie on Wednesday afternoons, half-closing, while Anne was at Katherine's gallery, and on Sunday mornings too, so that she could catch up with things.

The sale of Marsh Court had allowed them to buy a house in Loudoun Road, on the west side of St John's Wood. Anne loved it. The rooms were quiet, spacious and graceful. There were five bedrooms, a rear garden and no front steps, so that it was easy to push the pram into the house.

'We're moving in two weeks' time,' Anne said when Freya enquired after the progress of the sale. 'There'll be a lot to do, but Piers feels the same, we can't wait.'

She was itching to get her hands on the new house, had amassed wallpaper and paint samples and swatches of fabric. She loved looking round drapers and furniture shops and had decided to pursue a career as an interior designer. She knew that the job would absorb her, and that if she was based at home it would be easier to fit her work round Eddie. She had confided this ambition to Louise, who had asked her to take on the redesigning of the bedrooms and reception rooms of Marsh Court, in preparation for its metamorphosis as a hotel. A huge project, a baptism of fire: she was both terrified and excited.

As Piers handed over to Aidan, Anne asked Freya about the cottage she and Aidan had bought on South Ronaldsay, in Orkney.

'The roof leaks when it rains,' Freya said, 'which it does rather often. We're hoping to fix that next week. And then we'll put in electric lights. The romance of candles palls after a bit.' She blushed. 'It needs to be snug and finished by early summer.'

Anne said, 'Freya?'

'We're expecting a baby in May.'

'Oh Freya,' said Anne. 'How simply wonderful!' She hugged her.

'We're going to get married,' said Freya. Reaching behind her, she looped up her red curls in a messy knot. 'I suppose we should have got round to it before, but there've been so many other things to do. We told Helen last night. A quick wedding, no fuss. When the baby arrives, we'll go on doing what we're doing now, travelling to London for a week each month. You can fit a carrycot into a compartment of the sleeper train. My dad's so excited about becoming a grand-father, he can't wait.' A round of applause for Aidan, as he began to speak. Freya clapped her hands vigorously.

He was honoured to be carrying on the great tradition of Winterton design, Aidan told them all, and delighted to be working with two designers of immense talent. Esteban punched a fist in the air and Bridget smiled modestly. Charley, standing with Nate at the centre of the semicircle of guests that surrounded the cousins, applauded along with the rest of them.

'They're like cat and dog,' Aidan had confided to her earlier that evening. 'Bridget thinks Esteban is an unbearable bighead

496

and Esteban pats her on the bottom and calls her "little girl". I bet you we'll lose both of them before the year's out.'

Then he had said, 'I'll stay at Winterton's until I make it as a painter' – adding quickly, superstitiously, 'If I make it as a painter.'

For three weeks each month Aidan painted in Orkney; the fourth week he travelled to London by sleeper train to stay in the flat and carry out his role as the firm's part-time creative director. Charley and Nate had gone to stay with Aidan and Freya on South Ronaldsay the previous month, after Nate had given up his job at the merchant bank. There, on the island, Aidan had showed Charley some of his paintings, impressions of the seas and landscapes of Orkney, and Charley had thought that if there was any justice in the world, Aidan would make it as an artist.

Justice wasn't always to be found: this she had learned. She was writing a play about domestic violence entitled *Takes Two*, inspired by Anne's friend Maria, the woman whose husband had battered her head against a sink. You made a bad choice and it marked the rest of your life: this she had also learned. A couple of days earlier, while leafing through the shelves in Foyle's, she had bumped into Daniel. They had had a coffee together; she had asked him his news.

'I'm not sure I have much.' He said this without self-pity, something she had always admired in him. 'Still working for the Water Board, though Fielding's moving on to higher things, thank God. Jeannette's been through another bad patch but seems to be over the worst, and Simon's great, learning to read and we got him a little bike with stabilisers. What about you?'

'Well,' she said, and was about to launch into a narrative of all the things that had happened to her recently: her play, the one about the old woman with the wheeled basket, which had been successfully put on in a room over a pub in Ealing, and, of course, Nate, whom she was to marry in the spring. They were selling their London houses and moving to a lovely old place in the Hampshire countryside, so they could be near enough to Rory's school that he would not have to board. And then, simultaneously, she realised the impossibility of recounting all these wonderful things to poor Daniel, and saw how patronising that realisation was.

'Well,' she said, 'I'm still writing, and I've met someone.'

'Good for you.' He gave his tip-tilted smile and asked all the right questions. Then he said, 'I do have some news, actually. Jeanette and me, we're doing our A levels at evening classes. It'll probably take us years, but we've promised each other to keep going till we get there. And then, who knows? We won't have any more children – Jeannette isn't strong enough – and Simon is at school now, so that means we have more time. And maybe, I hope, if I do well, I'll eventually be able to take my degree. I don't know how, but I'm not giving up, Charley.'

They parted, a kiss on the cheek and promises to keep in touch, which she knew would never be fulfilled.

I've met someone. It didn't begin to tell the truth about her relationship with Nate. She had never *met* Nate; he had always been there. She had loved him and fought with him from the beginning, and she loved and fought with him still, and would, she supposed, until the day she died.

Toasts had been made to the new shop; Juliet, Helen and Jane gathered in a corner, talking.

'A year chock full of weddings,' Helen said, rather dazed,

after confiding to her sisters-in-law about Aidan and Freya. 'Do you think it's possible to get tired of weddings?'

'Can't we do them all at once?' Jane lit a cigarette. 'Stack 'em up in the aisle. Louise and Josh, Nate and Charley, Aidan and Freya.'

'It would be efficient,' agreed Juliet. 'Just one enormous cake with three little statuettes of the bride and groom on top of it.'

They giggled. Helen said to Jane, 'And Gabe and Adam . . . do you think . . .?'

Jane pursed her mouth, shook her head. 'She's enjoying herself far too much, managing the three shops, bossing everyone around. Poor Adam hardly gets a look-in these days.'

'I'm afraid Aidan's insisting,' said Helen, 'on the entire family travelling hundreds of miles north to that freezing cold windy little island for the wedding. I can just see myself, mother of the bride, in my raincoat, hair all over the place.'

Jane said, 'Why is there never enough to drink at these things?' and vanished into the crowd in search of a glass of wine.

Juliet said to Helen, 'But you love her, don't you?'

'Oh yes, I do. She's a dear girl.' Helen smiled. 'And think of the gorgeous red-haired grandchildren I shall have. I just had to get used to it. That's the point, isn't it? You have to get used to things.'

Aidan said, 'Thank God that's over,' and Freya said, 'You were magnificent. I was so proud of you.'

They were standing in a corner of the room beneath Freya's print of the Brough of Birsay. The sea funnelled between the island and the mainland, crashing over rocks. Gulls wheeled against a dense, stormy sky.

Aidan said, 'I can't wait to get home, though, can you?'

A smile of complicity. Their house stood on a wind-lashed bay that wheeled with seabirds. It needed a great deal of work, and was, Freya accepted, not a practical buy, but they had known, she and Aidan, the first time they saw it that they would live there.

'Longing for it,' she said.

'How's the sprog?'

'Good. Yes, good.'

Her palm rested against her stomach. She was making roots. She was creating for herself a history. If the baby was a girl, they were going to call her Ingrid Frances – Ingrid because it was an Orkney name, and Frances after the mother of whom she had no memory. And if it was a boy, he would be Edmund, Edmund Aidan Winterton. And perhaps one day he would join the family firm. Or he would be a painter. Or something of his own invention – who knows?

Guests had begun to drift away from the reception. The young people had gone on to a restaurant. Charley had tried to persuade Juliet and Joe to come with them, but Juliet had felt a sudden stab of longing for the remoteness and serenity of Greensea. She had thanked her daughter but refused, using the excuse of Joe's work on the farm.

The crowd had thinned; Joe was on the far side of the room, talking to Jane and Peter and Helen.

Juliet moved through the shop. Her gaze was caught by the jewels in the vitrines. The Wintertons were joining together new pieces, she thought, refashioning the links and clasps that held them together. Shining gems were being added to the strands of gold and silver that threaded through their lives, bright rubies and topaz and the muted shades of garnet and citrine. A silver christening spoon, a wedding ring of yellow gold. An antique pendant and a brand-new silver bracelet studded with black granite pebbles.

Joe looked up and smiled. Then he crossed the room to her, taking her hand in his. 'Shall we go?' he said.

'Yes, I'd like that. I'd like to go home.'

They walked out into the starlit winter streets.